I0691954

Dances
of the Heart

by

Andrea Downing

This is a work of fiction. Names, characters, places, and incidents are either the product of the author's imagination or are used fictitiously, and any resemblance to actual persons living or dead, business establishments, events, or locales, is entirely coincidental.

Dances of the Heart

COPYRIGHT © 2014 by Andrea Downing

All rights reserved. No part of this book may be used or reproduced in any manner whatsoever without written permission of the author or The Wild Rose Press, Inc. except in the case of brief quotations embodied in critical articles or reviews.
Contact Information: info@thewildrosepress.com

Cover Art by *Tina Lynn Stout*

The Wild Rose Press, Inc.
PO Box 708
Adams Basin, NY 14410-0708
Visit us at www.thewildrosepress.com

Publishing History
First Yellow Rose Edition, 2014
Print ISBN 978-1-62830-634-7
Digital ISBN 978-1-62830-635-4

Published in the United States of America

"Just follow me," he said as his right hand went to her back. A cover of a Vince Gill ballad started, the mournful tune setting a moderate tempo. "Perfect." He held her right hand high and applied slight pressure to move her backwards. "Fast fast slow slow, fast fast slow slow."

Carrie felt a light bulb go on. She got it. It was good. It was fun. And she relaxed in his embrace. He was an excellent teacher, a fabulous leader on the dance floor. Would wonders never cease?

"You're doing well. You're doing fine," he assured her. "We're gonna try a little promenade now, and then a twirl, so get ready."

Carrie couldn't stop herself from smiling, anticipation bubbling for just a second. And then out of the corner of her eye she caught Ty watching them, beer half-raised in salute and a smirk plastered on his face. A moment's hesitation and she missed the step.

"What happened there?" asked Ray, oblivious to the effect the onlooker had on her.

Other couples were finally joining them on the dance floor, but despite the company, Carrie's discomfort increased. "That boy, that Ty," she told him. "He was watching us. It made me feel…uneasy."

Ray scanned the sidelines, but Ty had gone, nowhere to be seen. "Oh, don't pay him any mind. He's harmless enough."

Praise for Andrea Downing

"*LOVELAND* is a fantastical frontier epic! The author does such an incredible job of immersing the reader in the old west, that they can nearly feel the grit of the dust on their face. The characters come alive and the conflict calls for page-turning impatience. Downing also creates a strong female character that doesn't make the mistake of overshadowing her man...Why I reckon this un's a keeper!"

~Sandy Ponton, InD'Tale Magazine
~*~

"[*LOVELAND* is] serious, emotional, and historically fascinating. Author Andrea Downing spins a romantic tale of separation and reunion, of cultural differences and emotional discovery...Great storytelling! Even though the happy ending is a given, the journey was much more satisfying because of the snappy dialogue, the pivotal plotting, and the realistic progression of Alex and Jesse's emotional connection. I'm happy to give this book Five Stars!"

~Lynda Coker, Between the Pages
~*~

"What a darling short story! Ms. Downing deftly spins an engaging story about love and justice...*LAWLESS LOVE* features a bold heroine tenaciously handling what life has dealt her family. This lovely romance also provides an earnest hero with a steady moral compass who quietly yearns for the seemingly out-of-reach goal of wife and family...Andrea Downing cleverly weaves a unique and fulfilling romance that will have readers seeking more of her talented work!"

~Anna Fitzgerald, InD'Tale Magazine

The act of extreme heroism credited to the character Robbie in this book was actually carried out by Marines LCpl Jordan C. Haerter and Cpl Jonathan T. Yale, KIA 22 April, 2008, in Ramadi, Iraq.

Both men were posthumously awarded the second highest decoration from the United States government for valor in combat, the Navy Cross for Extraordinary Heroism.

No other similarities between these men and the character exist.

~*~

It is to warriors like these that we owe our liberty.

Acknowledgements

Some time ago I put out a call on the Women Writing the West listserv and asked for a critique partner specifically from Texas. My idea was that only a Texan could properly check the language of my Texan characters, along with the veracity of scenes that take place in that state. Little did I know that this request would lead to a friendship I now treasure. And so, my deepest thanks to fellow author and tiny Texan, Karen Casey Fitzjerrell. I'm still tryin' to keep it between the ditches, darlin'.

Karen, in turn, put me in touch with Mark Moseley, Certified Professional in Rangeland Management, from Helotes, Texas. Mark was a huge help with various technical aspects of the manuscript, and then some non-technical aspects, too. My sincere thanks to him.

Any mistakes, on any of these features, are mine alone and my responsibility.

While the creation of a story and characters is the author's trade, it never ceases to amaze me how the repositioning of a clause, the addition or deletion of a phrase or word—not to forget correct punctuation—greatly improves the story. For these enhancements I am greatly indebted to my editor, Stacy D. Holmes.

And finally, where would I be without my best traveling partner—or perhaps I should say, 'pardner'—my daughter, Cristal? Not only did she accompany me on a trip to Hill Country, Texas, but she did all the driving to Luckenbach, Bandera, and Fredericksburg. Sweetheart, you're the Lone Star in my life.

Chapter One

The last of a heavy rain hit the windscreen as thunder crackled overhead. It was a good match for Carrie Bennett's mood; the descending drops on the glass reminded her pointedly of the tears her daughter had shed over the past few months. Paige had driven in sullen silence from the airport, causing Carrie to wonder if this trip together would be the success for which she had longed.

As an accident up ahead slowed traffic to a standstill right before their exit ramp, her daughter turned her head, glancing in the same direction as Carrie.

A soldier stood on the local road, among the weeds and trash strewn on the verge, his bag at his feet. Oblivious to being observed, he lifted a bright red kerchief from a pocket, blew his nose and wiped the rain from his face. His clothes must have been sodden, yet he thrust out his thumb casually, as if averse to doing so, while passing cars raced by him. The dirty water from the puddles splashed up as each car sped by, forcing the soldier into a kind of dance, stepping back and away and then coming forward once again. Carrie's heart went out to him.

The parting clouds let a reluctant afternoon sun leak color onto the far horizon as Texas spread its grandeur around them.

As her daughter started the car down the exit ramp, Carrie tapped her fingers decisively on the dashboard. "Let's pick him up." Her voice hardly rose above the radio. "He must be going home."

"Are you kidding me?" Paige snarled back. "Just because he's in army camouflage with a duffle bag doesn't mean he's really a soldier. They buy that stuff, you know, to look innocent."

"Paige, he's a soldier. I cannot in all conscience leave him standing there getting soaked by every damn car that passes. Really. Stop."

"He probably has a gun on him and—"

"I strongly doubt it. In any case, we'll just have to take a chance." Carrie drew in a sharp breath as if she'd just run into a wall. "He *is* a soldier. Poor thing is soaked to his skin. Stop."

The car came to a standstill on the shoulder of the road. As Carrie rolled down her window, the soldier picked up his bag and walked briskly to the car. He bent and stared inside, a blur of surprise fleeting across his features, his gaze registering Paige.

"Where are you going?" Carrie took in the bright blue eyes, the small dimple in his square jaw. Even the lousy army haircut didn't diminish the chiseled face. *Oh, to be young again.*

"Luckenbach." The Texas drawl was apparent in the single word.

"Have you got a gun?" She gave him a smile to betray her humor.

"Ma'am?"

"Never mind. Throw your bag in the trunk and hop in." She sensed him hesitate before going to leave his gear. "It's all right," she called. "We won't steal your things."

The trunk popped open. She noted her daughter's annoyed yet curious glance in the rearview mirror as the soldier sprang around the back, slung his bag in the trunk, and opened the rear passenger door. He tried to scrape some mud off his boots before ducking his large frame inside and hauling the door closed after him. Carrie swiveled around and gave him a smile.

He lifted his wet shirt away from his body as his gaze skipped from one woman to the other. "Name's Jake Ryder. I hope this isn't gonna be out of your way."

"Not at all, Mr. Ryder."

"Jake."

"Jake." A moment's hesitation, then she said, "I'm Carrie Bennett and this is my daughter, Paige."

She eyed her daughter briefly, wondering if she would be pleasant to the new passenger, or as mocking and derisive as she had been to everyone over the past months. But Paige remained involved with watching traffic for her chance to pull out. Carrie faced Jake.

"You got quite a bit of luggage back there. You here on vacation, ma'am?"

His gaze slid again from one to the other, a crease of question in his brow. If he was pondering why two well-heeled women would pick up a hitchhiker, even a soldier, he didn't voice it. His attention settled on Paige, but she didn't speak.

"Yes, vacation." Carrie turned back to the front. Silence filled the car like damp air on a hot day. "Have you been…abroad?" she finally proffered.

"Iraq."

The silence thickened.

"Going home?" Paige asked brightly. Her voice

startled Carrie and, no doubt, their passenger—a light coming on without warning as if an interrogation might begin. Her luminosity suddenly filled the car, but Carrie could hear the sarcasm behind it, the snide note, knew too well where Paige's questions could lead.

"Yeah." He leaned forward slightly.

Carrie snapped down the vanity mirror to refresh her lipstick as Jake scanned her daughter—the swanlike neck with wisps of dark hair misbehaving at the back, the smooth, unblemished skin. She would give anything to be that age again, to be that unscarred, so flawless and unscathed, the hair still its natural color, the body perfect and desirable.

The soldier's long legs bumped the back of Carrie's seat. "Either of you got a phone I might borrow? To call my dad to pick me up?"

She shuffled into the large handbag at her feet, came up with her cell phone and reached back to hand it to him. "Be my guest."

"Thanks."

The dialing beeps punctuated Kenny Chesney singing about the "Boys of Fall." Paige reached out to turn the radio off, then apparently thought better of it and stopped. The song didn't quite give the young man privacy, but his conversation was brief.

"About twenty minutes," was all he said before he handed the phone back with another thank you.

"Are you on leave?" Paige asked.

"No. I'm out. For good. Had a four year enlistment and it's over." Jake leaned back again, staring at the rear of Paige's head.

The conversation was going nowhere. After all, you couldn't really ask a returning solider what it was

4

like. What could he say? *F-ing awful, an unmitigated disaster, the worst experience of my life?* The answer certainly wouldn't be, *Great fun.* Or, *Gee, I really had a fabulous time.*

"I guess it's good to be home," Carrie said as if the thought had escaped her mouth.

"I guess." The scenery filed by, scattered trees dotting the undulating landscape, billboards loud with color and pronouncements. "So, where are you vacationing, if you don't mind my asking? Hill Country?"

"Yep." Paige's voice had a false note of gaiety in it. "That's where we're headed," she expanded. Their eyes met for a brief rendezvous in the rearview mirror. "The Lone Star Dude Ranch. Ever hear of it?"

The tone she was using irked Carrie, as it was no doubt meant to. "My daughter is not overly excited about my idea," she explained. "It's not really a vacation—I'm doing some research for a book."

"Research? At the Lone Star?"

She twisted back to see the young man's questioning gaze slide again from one to the other; for a brief moment, he looked as if he was watching a tennis match.

"My mother is a writer. A romance writer. Isn't that interesting?" Paige's tone said otherwise.

"Yeah." There was a note of uncertainty in his reply. "Is that like—"

Carrie didn't let him finish. "It's not sex, and it's not a synonym for pornography. They're love stories. And they've given you, young lady," she went on, whipping around toward her daughter again, "the fancy education and all the luxuries you enjoy." Discomfort

5

for their passenger hit her—poor guy gets into a car with two women and they start arguing. "You didn't have to come," she added quietly to Paige.

"I did have to come. You asked me to come. You know you don't like traveling on your own. And I'm not complaining."

Carrie didn't feel assured by her daughter's small attempt at conciliation. "No. It was the way you said it. I know you don't think much of my—"

"I never said a thing. I simply—"

"Go left," Jake put in suddenly, stopping them. "You have to go left. It's a better road, a short cut. Go left."

Paige pulled over and stopped the car. She reached around, looked the soldier full in the face for the first time, and grabbed the map from the back seat.

"He's right," she said when she finished considering it. Setting the map down, she drove on, turning left where he'd indicated.

Carrie could hear the sound of Jake rubbing his chin, his stubble grating, harsh like sandpaper. It used to annoy her, that sound, in theaters particularly when a man nearby would start. For some reason, she now found it rather pleasing.

He was probably around the same age as Paige, twenty-six, and there was a slight nervousness about him, and an air of anticipation, which she found endearing. Then she wondered if it was the stony silence making him nervous so she said, "I guess your folks will be glad you're home safe and sound."

"I guess," was his only quiet reply as he continued to stare out the window, lost in his own thoughts. "Romance, huh?" he said at last. "That's probably good escapism for some."

Though the soldier had aimed the remark at Carrie, it was her daughter who replied. "Yes! Happy endings all over the place. Always happy endings."

"Paige…" she appealed to her daughter.

"Well, they are, aren't they? Your books always have happy endings, Mother. Always. That's the formula. A romance must have a happy ending: boy meets girl, boy overcomes obstacles for getting girl, boy marries girl. Boy never gives up, never ever has some dreaded disease like leukemia, never dies."

"Paige…"

"There's my dad's pickup," Jake broke in.

The car came to a halt a bit before the man's mud-splattered truck. Jake started to open the door, then brought it back a bit. "You want directions for the ranch?" he asked.

"No. We'll be fine," Paige answered. "My trusty map."

"Okay. Don't count on that GPS, though. Lone Star is down a ranch road and a GPS doesn't work well with them." He waited for a response, and Carrie nodded. "I'll get my bag then," he said. "And thanks."

"Our pleasure," she responded, then added, "Good luck for the future."

The trunk release clicked as the soldier got out and went around the back to get his duffle. Carrie wondered what her daughter was thinking about him, about anything, as Paige spun back, grabbed the map off the seat, and studied it again.

Jake walked without any hurry to the truck. She didn't expect him to run into his father's arms, but the hesitancy was not what she'd anticipated.

Out the window was the faltering light of the late afternoon, Texas reaching toward the horizon like an infinite meadow, the ramshackle outpost that was Luckenbach. She faced her daughter, who grimaced and threw the map back on the rear seat.

"Got it." Paige pulled the shift back into drive and began to pull out.

Carrie sighed and watched Jake reach his father. The two men hugged briefly. The father, Stetson tilted back, well-worn boots poking out of his dusty jeans, leaned casually back on his pickup to hear what his son was saying before turning his head toward their car as it passed. And for one split second, his gaze locked with Carrie's, took her in and held her, before Paige drove on.

****

"Things haven't changed any I see. Looks good." Jake shoved the ancient pickup truck's door closed, then reached into the bed to retrieve his bag.

His father was waiting, playing with the keys in his hand, before he bounded up the steps to the porch and yanked the screen open. He held the door for Jake to pass into the house before following him inside.

"No change here either I can see," Jake mumbled. "Where are the dogs?"

"Dogs are in the office at the moment. Larry had them down there for some hunter education class he was running. Why would you expect change? I look after things, it doesn't need changing."

Ray Ryder spoke in the flat, straightforward way Jake remembered so well. The keys were thrown on a counter in the kitchen, before his dad came back in.

"Well, let me have a look at you then," he went on,

briefly gripping Jake in welcome. "You all right?" his father asked.

Jake set down his bag. "Yeah. Sure."

"Can I get you something? Coffee? A beer?" There was an awkward nervousness to him, the same restlessness of which Jake had long been aware.

"Coffee'd be fine."

His father headed into the kitchen. Slouching into his favorite leather armchair, Jake dangled one long leg over another, throwing his head back. His clothes had more or less dried now and he settled into a comfortable unwillingness to go change. Unsure as to whether he was really happy to be home, he kept what he knew within him like a package waiting to be unwrapped.

At the snap of a metal pull-tab on a can of what was no doubt beer, Jake shook his head. Then there was the clatter of a mug being filled from the coffeemaker.

"You not having coffee?" he called through to the kitchen.

"Naw, I'm swimming in it already. Thought I'd get myself a—"

"Thought you'd given up, Dad," Jake confronted his father who came back into the living room and handed him his coffee. "Thought you'd stopped drinking?"

"Yeah, well." His father lowered himself into another armchair. "You know how it is. Gave up Jack for a while but, what with worryin' 'bout you being out there and all, and dealing with Leigh Anne…" He slugged his beer.

"How is Mom then?"

"Well, I don't have much to do with her, Jake. You know that. Lawyers see to everything. I don't want her

9

hanging 'round my neck for the rest of my life so I'm tryin' to…" His voice trailed off before he took another gulp of beer. "You fixin' to see her?"

"I guess." Jake peered into his mug, his black liquid reflection as wavering as his response.

He got up to go over the photos scattered around the room. A rustic wood mantel above the fireplace held most of them, but they also sat on side tables and the top of a row of bookshelves. Picking them up one by one and carefully replacing them, he was conscious of his father's gaze following him as the man sat there finishing his beer.

"Got a new gun vault out in the office there." His dad nodded toward the door to his right leading to a small room. "Dang thing works with both a key and a combination. I can't remember the combination—have it on a piece of paper in my bedside table. Key's in the office drawer when you need it." There came the sound of the beer can being crushed in his hand.

"I guess there is one other change here, though," Jake challenged his father who had risen to face him. "You've removed all the photos with Mom in them."

His dad walked into the kitchen and opened the fridge to reach in for another beer. There was a moment's hesitation before he snapped the tab, took a swig, then sauntered back to face Jake. "No point dwellin' on the past. What's done is done, marriage is finished." He set the beer down on a side table. "Truth be told, it was finished a long time ago, even before…"

A kind of sorrow wormed its way through Jake, surprising him. A bitterness took hold. "You didn't remove Robbie's photos," he grumbled. "Robbie is still here, every last one of his photos." He let a scowl wash over his face.

"Robbie's dead, Jake, that's different. He didn't go sleeping around like some tomcat in an alleyway. He didn't go using my house—*this* house that's been in my fam'ly for well over a century—like some dang brothel."

Jake's fist came up before he realized what he was about to do—and to whom he was about to do it. His father, however, was just as strong and quick. His hand gripped Jake's wrist and held it there for a moment before he let go. Jake stood back, glaring into his father's eyes yet, even as he did so, he was wondering how he could have considered hitting his father, this man he idolized, who'd brought him up, taught him everything.

The anger within him receded, ebbed like a river rolling out to sea.

"That's my mother you're talking about." He made his voice intentionally low. "And you drove her to it. You took to drink, and she took to men. It's as simple as that."

"And you, Jake, what did you take to? You took to the goddamn army, didn't you? Wanted to get yourself killed as good as your brother, didn't you?" His father picked up his beer and glanced at it a moment. "We all deal with things in our own way. So. There you have it. Whatever it was, best to get on and move on with life, put it behind us. That's what I say and that's what I'm doing." He eased himself back down into his chair. "You want photos of Leigh Anne, keep them in your room. I don't have to look at her."

Jake paced a bit. The living room had the smell of home, the cedar cladding, the stone fireplace which, although empty now for the spring, still carried the aroma of wood smoke, the sharp scent of the leather and coffee, which always permeated this room, mixed with the fresh perfume of the Texas spring grasses and juniper stands.

Nothing like Iraq. Nothing like the stink of burning cars, or rotting bodies lying under the blister of desert sun. The stink of fear.

He ran a hand through his cropped hair then slumped back down into his chair. "How's the Rocking R going? Miss Mabel still come in?"

"'Course Mabel still comes in. As ornery as ever. In fact, she comes in more often since your mama left. Never did get on, those two. Mabel thinks this house is her responsibility now. Cleans it like one of them whirling dervishes, does my laundry once a week and ironing, and leaves me enough cooked suppers to feed the whole of Gillespie County, then gets in that beat-up Ford of hers and collects the grandkids from school. Laila run off again last Thanksgiving—I think I emailed you—and left her with the brood. What with George passed and living out there on her own, I don't know how she manages an' all, but she does. Heart as big as all outdoors and a temper to match it."

Jake gave a small laugh and rested his head on the back of the armchair, the comfort of home slowly washing through him. He reached down and picked up the mug of cooled coffee by his feet.

"Let me get you some hot?"

"No, don't bother." He sensed an easier silence between them now, each lost in thought until he said, "Still can't figure them women."

"Which women?" his father snorted. "I can't figure

any dang woman. Which ones are we talking about?"

"The ones who gave me a lift. Damn truck driver dropped me in the pouring rain at the exit on I-10, and then those two come roaring down and picked me up. Down here from someplace up northeast is my guess. Some city or other. I couldn't believe my eyes when they stopped. I thought women never gave rides to hitchhikers. Though, she did ask me if I had a gun." A grin lit his face as he remembered the encounter.

His dad chuckled as he finished off his beer and crushed the can again. "What did she expect you to say? 'Yes, ma'am, and I plan to rob and shoot the both of you?'"

"I think she was joking. I think…I think the other one, the daughter, didn't want to stop. She was sort of bitchy-like, angry. One helluva looker, though. Don't usually like short hair on women but, my lord, she had eyes like saucers and a real little pixie face." He smiled. "Damn cute little thing. Staying over at the Lone Star."

"The Lone Star? What the heck are they doing there?"

"The mom's a writer—Carrie Bennett—writes romance or something."

His father's forehead wrinkled. "Oh, heck. I know who she is. Leigh Anne used to read her stuff. Well, you can always take a ride over to visit Doris there. I'm sure she'd be glad to see you back."

"Ah, no. I got enough people to see."

"Want to go have a ride 'round the ranch? I can saddle up Devil and Brady and we can go out, get some fresh air."

"Maybe. A bit later maybe. How're we doing anyway? How's the hunting side goin'?"

"Goin' well, real well, both the horses and the hunting. Got a lot of corporate contracts this year from firms up in Dallas wanting to give their execs some fun. Mark Shandler's taken over managing the horses for me, and I still got Larry Gruhl in the office doing the hunting. Got several good guides, a decent cook for the guests and made some improvements to the lodge over yonder." There was a pause. "You think about what you want to do now? Though it's early days yet. I don't want to rush you into anything. You might want to go back to finish school."

Jake sighed, though he appreciated his father's interest. "What I want to do, Dad? What I want to do is go find Grant and Toby and the rest of my friends, go on over to Luckenbach or maybe up to the Cowboy Bar or Arky's at Bandera and get as fried as one of Mabel's hushpuppies. A regular Friday night, only it's Thursday. Then maybe, just maybe, I'll think about the ranch or school or any other dang thing." He got up and stretched, stifling a yawn before bending to pick up his bag. "The mother wasn't bad lookin', either. Maybe *you* should go on over and say 'howdy' to Doris?"

His father chuckled a bit and picked a loose thread from the seam of his jeans before Jake moved to go down the hall.

"Welcome home, son," he said quietly. "Welcome home."

****

Paige shoved the cabin door open with her shoulder, clutching a box of groceries to her chest and hauling a suitcase. She let the screen door swing closed behind her, not really on purpose but with little consideration as to it hitting her mother, who followed with a laptop and her own case. Her mom's foot went out just in time to stop the door. Paige didn't help as her mother turned her back to push it open once more, dropping the handle of her case.

"Was that absolutely necessary?"

"Was what necessary?" She frowned and dumped the groceries on a small countertop.

A lengthy sigh signified indulgence while the older features softened into acceptance. "Never mind."

Paige could get away with virtually anything these days.

She started to investigate the cabin: a small living area with a kitchenette, a bedroom with two queen beds, a wardrobe and dresser, a bathroom off the bedroom.

"Early Salvation Army, your grandmother would have called this."

"Isn't this what you expected?" She made an effort to keep impatience out of her voice; after all, her mother had chosen the place. She must have known what she was getting into, and could have chosen some fancy hotel instead.

"Pretty much. It's homey, I guess you could say. Rustic. Actually, it's sort of similar to the ranches we used to go to up in Colorado and Wyoming when you were small—patchwork quilts and well-worn furniture."

"'Well-loved,' I think is the expression." Paige busied herself finding places for the groceries as unpacking commenced in the bedroom. "But the air is different. It's not that mountain air. It hasn't got a chill in it."

"No." There was a hesitation in her mother's voice

as she held a pair of jeans in mid-air. "I'm glad you came. I like it when you come on my research trips. It gives me a different perspective on things, another view."

"But that wasn't the reason you invited me," Paige retorted, shoving her own case aside as she went into the bathroom and slammed the door. Alone for three minutes. She needed this.

"Are you all right? Paige?"

Her mother would be standing there, listening. It was obvious she worried, would not leave her be. It annoyed her, irritated her beyond reason. "Oh, for goodness sake. Can't I even take a pee without you watching me?"

"Sorry." The word was mumbled, barely audibly. "I'm worried about you," came through in a louder voice. "Can't a mother worry?"

"Yes, but you make a profession out of it." Paige flushed the toilet and let the sound of the water precede her entrance into the room by several seconds. "I came because I know you hate traveling alone, hate driving around on your own—*not* to be molly-coddled, and worried over every five seconds."

"I'm sorry," came the quiet reply. "I'll try…to let go a bit. It's just…I wish you would talk about it. Talk about Steven a bit mo—"

"I don't *want* to talk about it," she yelled. "I don't want to talk about him or anything to do with him. I'm not having that conversation. Not with you, not with anyone!"

And that, she decided, was it. She traveled here because her mother needed her, wanted her here. *Not* because 'getting away' was good for her, a change of scenery to take her mind off her loss, make her forget. This certainly wouldn't get her 'out of herself.' She was not going to enjoy this in the least; it was not going to 'perk her up' as various friends and relatives had suggested. This was for her mother only. This was not the end of her depression or a new beginning.

Her mother let out a long breath. Paige matched it with her own, letting the tide of tension ebb. No doubt her mom's heart ached with her inability to ease her pain, compensate for her loss. She must accept that, accept that it wasn't her mother's fault, that it had been no one's fault, and that friends and family were trying to help her.

Finished with unpacking, her mother started toward the kitchen area. A sudden spurt of children's laughter wafted in an open window like the murmur of a breeze as a line of youngsters on ponies went by, led by a tall wrangler. Paige rolled her eyes, aware it hadn't been all that long since she had been that carefree.

"I'll make dinner," she pronounced.

"All right then. I have to check my emails and get back to some people." Her mother set her laptop on the small coffee table and opened it out.

"Why don't they offer dinner here? Seems strange to do breakfast and lunch but not dinner."

Her mother's initial reply was a shrug. "They say people like to eat out. It doesn't matter, does it? I need to visit the local nighttime haunts anyway."

Paige opened the fridge and started to lift out and arrange what she needed on the counter. "What's the book about?"

"Oh, it centers on two older people who meet again after many years—they'd had a college romance and broke up because their parents didn't approve for reasons which now seem so remote. But I wanted to set it out west again, and Texas seemed like a good idea. Anyway, you never read my books, so what difference does it make?" There was humor rather than pique in her voice.

"I do read your books. I read *A Light in the Window* and *Little Black Dress*. I can't read them all—I was in law school you know. When do you think I had time to fit in romance novels, for goodness sake? Ah yes, 'Torts and Romance Novels'—I forgot to take that course. Sorry." She shook her head at her mother's inability to conceive her workload.

"Paige, I've been writing since you were four years old."

"Well, did you want me reading romance then?" She tried to put a light note in her voice to amuse her mother. It took a great deal of effort.

There was another deep breath as her mom settled once more at the coffee table in the living room before reading aloud, "'*Burial Insurance?*' Do you insure against being buried? '*Maximize Gentleman for a bigger penis size.*' I'll take any penis I can get at this stage."

Paige laughed. Her mother had a routine of clicking on her spam file first to make sure nothing of importance had gotten into the wrong folder, and the dry humor never ceased to amaze her.

"'*Congratulations, you have been chosen!*' I bet I have. '*Date Singles Over Fifty.*' How the hell do they know how old I am?"

Paige started to chop vegetables.

Her mother abruptly stood. "Don't cut your

fingers," she warned.

"Mother!"

"Sorry. Let me help."

"No. You're working. Get on with it."

Her mother remained standing. A shout outside the window caught her attention. Paige glanced through the pane as the woman who had checked them in walked by; she had been friendly enough, almost nosey, inquisitive. They probably didn't appear the usual dude ranch types despite their jeans and boots. Or maybe it was her imagination and the woman—was her name Doris?—had just been trying to get to know her guests. She hated that interrogation, that attempt to be friendly with people you wouldn't know in four days.

Paige considered once more the waste of time at being here. She wasn't her mother's muse, nor was the trip going to lift her depression or help her come to a conclusion about returning to law school. In fact, it was nothing more than making her mom feel slightly better about the daughter who had lost a fiancé, the child whose world had changed suddenly, almost in the flash of a moment, unexpectedly and unpredictably in a nano second she hadn't had time to see coming. That was her life now. That was what she had to deal with. And in her own way, she would deal with it.

Her mother faced her with a weary look. "I wonder if I'll be writing the same crap when I'm seventy, eighty," she said almost under her breath. "Getting old sucks."

Paige put down the knife, a fan of zucchini circles lying on the chopping board. "What brought this on? You love writing. It's what you do, who you are."

Resignation and exasperation crossed the features

of the older face, but they left almost as quickly as she had noticed them.

"I may make fun of your books," Paige acknowledged, "but you know I'm proud of you. You're probably just tired. Why don't you give it a rest for tonight; we did only just fly in, after all. Tomorrow everything will seem different."

"Will it?" The tone was somewhat arch, stringent.

"Yes. Of course it will." Oh, what a lie. Nothing would be different tomorrow. Steven would still be gone, and she'd still hate being here, still hate the thought of going on without him.

****

In the dense blackness of the Texas night, headlights of a pickup scanned the dark living room of the Rocking R ranch house before the truck came to a stop. Laughter and voices met Ray's consciousness before the motor groaned back to life and retreated, followed by footfalls up the porch steps, the whine of the screen door and shock of lights coming on. He put a hand over his eyes and waited, but his son just stood there. The crickets' chorus was punctuated by the belch of a frog and, somewhere, an owl hooted its one note in answer to a solitary nicker from a horse. Hot night air blanketed him as he tried to squint into the brightness.

His son stood for a moment as Ray waited for the reprimand that would surely come, but the only rebuke was the march of Jake's feet toward his bedroom. Then, suddenly, the boy was back and filled the hall doorway, and Ray let his hand finally fall from his face.

"He's dead, Dad. Robbie's dead. It's goin' on five years now. And no amount of drinking or feeling guilty or sorry for yourself is ever gonna bring him back.

Ever. You talk to me about movin' forward and getting on with your life? What a load of bull. You're in the same damned place you were five years ago, sitting there in the dark with an empty bottle of Jack and a shitload of guilt and self-pity."

Chapter Two

Friday had been spent with Paige driving while
Carrie scribbled notes on scenery, people and the
idiosyncrasies of the Hill Country lifestyle. She had
listened to locals in shops, on the street and at the
ranch, got a feel for their voices and their gestures, the
way they dressed and moved, while Paige had
witnessed it all with her usual cynicism. A couple of
hours back at the ranch and a quick supper reheated
from yesterday's leftovers, and they had headed out
once more.

Now, oncoming lights glared and then fell again
across the bug-speckled windshield as she gripped the
wheel and grimaced into the dark. In the early May
night, the windows were open and, as successive cars
passed them, bursts of music or laughter came and
went, momentary images in a moving peepshow. The
warm breath of night tampered with her short hair.

"Why did you want to go to this joint outside of
Bandera? I thought Luckenbach was the place to be."

Paige's voice competed with the radio, and Carrie
reached out and turned it down. "Yes, but Bandera is
the supposed 'cowboy capital of the world.' We can go
to Luckenbach tomorrow perhaps, although that Doris
woman said there is a dance at the ranch we should
attend. Let's see what happens tomorrow."

The GPS suddenly advised them to make a left-hand turn in 200 yards. "Do you think that's right?" Paige asked. "That Jake guy said a GPS didn't work out here."

"No, he said it didn't work on ranch roads," corrected Carrie as she executed the left. "See, there it is. I guess. My gosh, look at this lot."

An oversized barn stood alone on the roadside, strings of lights scalloping the roof and windows, enhanced only by flashing beer advertisement signs. Cars, pickups and motorbikes surrounded the building, parked everywhere and every which way without any sense of order: down the road, on the grass, facing front, facing back, sideways on. Stetsons bobbed and nodded to some imaginary tune while small groups gathered on car hoods or tailgates, or stood holding drinks. Cigarettes produced low clouds of hazy smoke while staccato shots of laughter punctuated conversations drifting out into a hum of night music.

Carrie slowed the car down for fear of hitting someone while searching for a sensible place to park, but she was well past the dancehall before she steered off the road and brought the car to a halt. She let out a breath as if exerted from difficult exercise, then snapped down her vanity mirror to check her face.

"I don't know why you didn't let me drive. You hate driving when you don't know the route."

"It's fine. Here," she said, holding the keys out to her daughter, "you can drive back."

Paige gave the keys a dirty look. "I thought you were going to drive back so I could drink."

"It's fine then—"

Her daughter grabbed the keys out of her hand and threw open the door before stepping out with an unmistakable air of annoyance.

"Paige—I'll drive back. Give me back the keys." Carrie got out on her side, glancing around while adjusting her shirt and smoothing her jeans. She reached back into the car for a small bag and hefted it over her shoulder before shutting the door and peering over the car roof to her daughter. "Paige? I said I'd drive back."

"Never mind. We'll see later. I'll keep the keys."

The car beeped to announce it was locked.

Carrie picked her way down the road behind her daughter, a Hansel and Gretel line of cigarette butts marking the path. She was all too aware of the brief halts in conversations as revelers scrutinized them, studied them, then returned to focus on someone else.

A strong sense of not belonging hit her, of being out of place, but Paige was bolder than she. She followed closely as her daughter broke through the groups on the porch and swung into the noise of the dancehall. Guitar and fiddle had feet tapping and bodies moving in time to the tune. Paige led the way along the edge of the floor, trying to avoid the contact that a collision might bring. Carrie could see men scan them over, probably finding them an odd pair to be out together. And she could figure most of the cowboys were in their twenties or thirties, for which she was grateful; it would mean no one would ask her to dance. A couple of drinks at the bar for the purposes of research, then home to the ranch suited her fine.

Paige elbowed into the bar crowd which shimmied over to make room, one cowboy nodding to her before Carrie pushed forward. He tipped his hat with another nod and moved away to let her stand next to her daughter, bent across the bar trying to get the bartender's attention.

"My gawd," breathed Carrie, fanning herself with her hand. "It certainly is hot in here."

****

When his father asked Jake if he would like to join him for a few drinks over at Mulligan's, his favorite bar, he had been faced with a conundrum. An evening at Mulligan's would end with his dad's usual binge whether he was with him or not. And if Jake left his father on his own, he would probably return to the same scene encountered last night. The Stagecoach dance hall was more like a compromise; while he couldn't babysit his father or force him into sobriety, perhaps more of a social life would get his mind off the past, the divorce and Robbie, and his drinking would reduce. Maybe, with a bit of mixing with people, getting out and about, his father would drink less.

His dad had agreed to go, in order, he'd pronounced, to spend some time with Jake.

But his scheme wasn't proceeding well. His dad had made a head start on drinking and loaded some more beers into the pickup. Nothing Jake could say or do at that point was going to change his father's attitude. This resulted in his dad pressed into a back corner of the dancehall taking a pull on his beer while Jake leaned against the wall surveying the crowd.

"Glad you came?" he ventured, studying his father's face for a moment before turning back to the scene.

"Was that a question or a statement?" his father probed, his mouth slightly puckered. "I guess it's good to get out some, though I'm a mite long in the tooth for this lot, Jake."

"Why don't you ask someone to dance?"

"What? A twenty year old? No thanks. I like women, real women, not a babe in arms."

Jake let a smudge of impatience cross his face before he straightened, stretching a bit to see through the dancers. Exasperated, he came to the realization his idea had gone awry and been a bit optimistic. He knew now he should have stopped his father from loading the extra six-pack into the pickup and more staunchly denied there'd be any problem in getting a drink at the bar. And to make matters worse, to his own reluctance, he had proved his father wrong by getting two bottles straight away, and then noticed the hip flask tucked in his father's back pocket. There seemed to be no answer to stopping his father's drinking.

A two-step played and, as dancers circled around, the crowd at the bar came in and out of view, a curtain opening and shutting. Jake wiped the sweat from his beer bottle on to his jeans as he took in the scene.

"Good lord, that's them," he said to no one in particular.

"That's who?" His father's hand tapped around his back pocket, probably checking his flask.

"Those women—the ones who gave me a ride. The mother and daughter." He studied Paige for a second, her animated features making her seem more approachable than she had been in the car. "Come on, I'll introduce you."

"Oh, no." His father shook his head. "You go ahead, son. I think I'll get me some fresh air and—"

"You're going to get another drink." His aggravation took a moment to settle. "Look, join us.

Come on, they won't bite."

His father bent his head slightly. "No, you go on. I'll be outside. I'm not fighting this crowd tonight. You go. But don't drink too much—you're driving."

Reluctantly, Jake moved off, weaving in and out of dancers to get up to the bar. For a moment, he glanced back, just in time to see his father slip out the front door. He turned again and made his way forward toward Carrie and Paige.

"Hey," he nudged the mother a bit as he prodded another man aside to stand next to her. "How you doin'?"

Carrie faced him with a blank expression before realization dawned. "Oh! Jake, isn't it? I didn't recognize you for a moment without your army fatigues. How are you?"

Paige leaned across the older woman as he tried to catch her eye. Her brow crinkled before she straightened.

"Look, Paige. Look who it is." She jabbed her daughter with her elbow before turning back to him. "You seem so different with the Stetson on and all, not to mention the five o'clock shadow."

"More like nine o'clock," he corrected, rubbing his hand over his bristles. "How you both enjoying Texas then? How's the ranch?"

Carrie moved slightly so Jake was better able to see Paige.

"Ranch is fine. Texas is great—what we've seen of it." She took a sip of her wine. "Are you settling in again? It must be strange to be back home."

"No, not strange. Well," he added, "not too strange." He tried to gauge her daughter's reaction, but

27

she'd hidden herself once more behind Carrie. "You enjoying yourself, Paige?" He stretched to address her, hoping she might pay him some attention.

"Yes. It's all right." She looked askance at him for a moment, then back at her glass. "It's fine," she mumbled.

"Do you come here…" Carrie's voice trailed off as she suddenly reached into her bag to jerk out her phone. She held it out to see the number. "Oh dear, I better take this. It's my agent. Sorry."

Jake watched her clamp the phone to her ear and make her way out through the crowd to the door.

****

Ray grabbed three cans of beer from the cooler in the back of his truck, refilled his now empty hip flask and took a swig from a bottle of Jack for good measure. He sauntered back to the hall porch, finding a place off on the side where he could settle. His long legs dangled into some bushes, but when the couple who sat next to him got up to go back inside, he shimmied himself over to the wall of the building and leaned back, beer cans in his lap. The door was constantly whining open and shut, emitting disjointed shots of country music.

For a moment, he considered jamming the door open when a tall woman came out, phone plastered to ear. She stood by the pillar at the end of the porch. Native American turquoise jewelry decked her wrist and neck, while a crisp, white blouse was tied at her waist over some sort of tee or camisole. Jeans, a bit too clean, were finished off with an expensive-looking pair of what were no doubt Lucchese or Tony Roma boots, and a small, expensive-looking bag hung over her shoulder. The face was older, probably near his age but well cared for, little make up, good skin, cropped blond hair.

Ray took it all in and decided she was what he might call 'well turned out' in a sort of fake western way. For a while, he considered the familiarity of her, then it dawned on him—she was the mother, the writer, Carrie Bennett. The one who'd been sitting in the car when Jake got out. Well, if there was a word for a fake Texan—like 'buckle bunny,' no, 'wannabe,' that's it, a cowgirl wannabe—she was it.

As the woman leaned back against the pillar, her gaze caught Ray's scrutinizing glance. She whirled back around and stepped down off the porch, taking a few steps into the dark.

"Oh, hell, I'm losing you, Jason, hang on." Forced to move back to the porch, she stood just below the pillar with an unsuccessful effort not to shout to make herself heard. "Did you say Diane Keaton and Tommy Lee Jones? Wow, that's amazing. What a cast! Gosh, thanks so much for calling…and on a Friday night." There was a break while the voice on the other end replied before she said, "Okay, great. I'll speak to you on Tuesday then, and we can tie things up. I'll be in your office at eleven." The phone bleeped off. She drew in a deep breath of satisfaction before hoisting herself back onto the side of the porch, stumbling slightly.

"Whoa there, cowgirl." Ray reached a hand forward to steady her.

"Thanks." She stared down at him for a moment and blinked, a flash of recognition crossing her face.

"Sounds like a good cast. One of my favorite actors, Tommy Lee Jones. I'll see just about anything with him in it."

Carrie bristled, an air of indignation setting her shoulders straight. "Do you always listen to other people's conversations?"

Ray laughed and snapped open another beer. He started to bring it to his lips before thinking better of it and extending his hand to offer the can to her. She answered with a shake of her neat little head and an abrupt, "No thanks," before starting inside.

"I don't think I could avoid hearing your conversation when you come to think of it. You were shoutin' like the Baptists on a Sunday, and I'm sitting right here."

She stopped in her tracks and looked back at him, a brief gurgle of laughter escaping her. "'Shouting like Baptists on a Sunday,' huh? That's one I haven't heard." There was a moment's hesitation before she plunged, "You're Jake's father, aren't you?"

"Ray Ryder." There was a groan of stretching to give her his hand as she told him her name. He then fell back against the wall and patted the space next to him. "Have a seat, Carrie Bennett."

"No, I really—"

"Jake is with your baby, isn't he? He'll be takin' real good care of her. I should leave 'em be for a while." *Eyes like saucers*, Jake had said about the daughter. Well, there was no doubt where the girl got them. "Let 'em have a few dances at least. They'll be fine. I promise." He patted the floor next to him once more. When she didn't move, he said, "Oh. I guess you don't want to dirty those jeans, huh?"

"No, that isn't it."

Pique slid into outright annoyance as she got shoved toward him and almost tripped thanks to a rowdy bunch of youngsters surging into the dancehall.

"Look." Ray ran his thumb around the rim of the can before dropping it down by his side and sliding his legs around. "Sit here on the edge with your legs hanging off, have a beer and relax. Enjoy yourself."

He extended his hand again, and this time Carrie clasped it, gingerly squatting next to him before letting her rear hit the deck and scrunching over so her legs could hang off the side.

"Have a beer," he repeated. "Or should I go get you a white wine. My guess is that's what you drink."

"You have me all figured out, huh?" She flicked some hair behind one ear. "Well, you're right—I don't drink beer, but I'm not drinking anything more tonight, thanks. I'm the designated driver, so I had better stay sober."

"'The designated driver?' Wow." He couldn't keep humor out of his voice. "That must be some responsibility. *The designated driver.*" He mulled this over a bit, toying with the idea of winding her up. He brought out the flask and had a long pull, and spied her glance at her hands as if she were considering a manicure. "That sounds sorta like being one of the good Lord's chosen people." He swallowed his laughter as he tucked the flask back in his pocket. "I tell you, that must be some big East Coast thing, you know. 'The designated driver,'" he repeated again, enjoying her annoyance.

"Okay. Look. I'm sure you find it very funny, but it's not so funny if one of us loses our license—or, indeed, our life. I need to be able to drive."

"I'm sure you do, sweetheart, but how many drinks did you actually have? One?" He shoved his hat back and nodded to the clusters of people hanging around outside the hall. "They'll all be at least slightly over the legal limit and likely not a one of them will be stopped unless they're really far gone. And I promise you, all of them will make it home safe and sound."

"You're very sure of yourself. Tell all that to the Mothers Against Drunk Driving who have lost children thanks to folks with your attitude, Mr. Ryder."

"Ray. No, I'm just stating a fact of life. Sheriff might come by and give someone a warnin' every so often, but he knows the folks. They've all grown up together, and 'less someone's really off the deep end, he knows it isn't worth his time pulling 'em in. Won't do to embarrass your friends' families. Anyway, none of them will be going far and, mostly like myself, down ranch roads."

Carrie listened but wasn't converted. "Well. It just takes a moment's loss of concentration to go across the lane and hit another car. Anyway, I'm from out of state, so my guess is he can meet his tally by giving me a ticket, and I don't want that."

Ray took a gulp of beer and wiped his mouth with the back of his hand. He figured anything more said on the subject would annoy her into leaving, and he rather enjoyed the sparring. In fact, she was pretty damn good looking if you came right down to it. "My wife used to read your books. You are the writer, aren't you? Jake said…"

"Yes, I am a writer."

"Yeah, my wife was a real fan. Used to keep me awake with 'just one more chapter.'"

"*Was* a fan?" Carrie hedged.

"We're…divorced. I guess the marriage just didn't

32

live up to all that romance she was reading."

"I'm sorry." There was an uncomfortable silence before she said, "Divorce is very unpleasant. Is it recent?"

"Oh." Ray pondered a moment. "Yeah," he finally said. Changing the subject, he went on asking, "Living in New York?"

"Yes. Most of the time. I have to travel a fair bit for either promotion or research. It's research I'm doing here in Texas."

"Research, huh? How does that work? I mean, are you researching me and everyone here, researching Texas dance halls, what?"

"Sort of. I'm trying to get a feel for the area, a sense of it so I can describe it realistically."

Ray considered this. "A Texas romance, huh?" He took another swallow of beer. "Sounds good." There was a somewhat sardonic note he couldn't keep from his voice.

"Well, I'm struggling. But then I always do." She sat with him, watching the fireflies for a moment before musing, "I thought these places served beer in a Mason jar?"

Ray tilted his head back to get the last out of his beer. "Ha! A country music fan?" He crushed the can, contemplating this fact. "Well, nowadays it's mostly Shiner and Lone Star beer served as they come. But if you wanna go country, I can dig out a Mason jar for you if you like."

Carrie threw her head back and laughed, like wind chimes ringing in the warm night.

"No, I'm fine, thank you." She smiled at no one in particular, smoothing her hair at the back before asking,

"I guess you're really glad to have Jake home, huh?"

About to open another beer, Ray's hand stopped in mid-air and he put the drink down again. He held her in his sight while considering his answer. "'Course I am. You send a child off to war, you can be sure you thank the good Lord if and when he comes home safe. You thank Him with every damn bone in your body. And then you get down on your knees and thank Him again."

****

If she heard the words, 'Welcome home, Jake' or 'Good to see you' one more time, Paige would stomp on their Texas Swing feet and walk out. Everyone knew everyone else and, while he made brave attempts to keep introducing her, the curious glances she received did nothing to make her feel welcome.

"Sorry 'bout that," he offered after another brief reunion. "I was out last night and thought I'd more or less seen most of my friends."

"Well, you obviously have more friends than you know." She stood, uncomfortable under the gaze of his ozone blue eyes, and shifted around to look through the crowd. "I guess I'm something of a curiosity, a novelty, huh?"

"Well…"

"Do they expect to see you with someone else? Did you leave a girlfriend behind?"

"Nope. No girlfriend."

Jake put his elbows back on the bar before he took a swig of his drink. Her gaze ran over his lean, muscular body and found it difficult to believe one of the local belles hadn't scooped him up. 'Lanky' was a word made for this Texan, and when the black hair grew in, he'd be downright irresistible.

But not to her; he wasn't Steven, and a sudden yearning flowed through her veins like poison from a snakebite.

"You all right?" he asked suddenly.

She put her glass down on the bar. "Of course I'm all right," she murmured. "Of course."

The first strains of a slow dance brought couples out onto the floor. Jake extended his hand to her, questioning, palm open, and when she saw it, she stared a moment as if the hand were some foreign object, then caught the look of concern on his face.

Feeling as if she were in a slow motion movie, she held the proffered hand and let herself be led out onto the dance floor where he gently brought her in close and started to guide her to the tempo of the music. The warmth of his touch to her back dissipated the venom of loss that ran through her, and she let herself succumb closer to the heat of a man's body. Solid, rock hard strength met her hand, and she would have liked to run her fingers down the arm, know the muscle and sinew underneath. Jake appeared to study her, consider her, let her be lost in her own thoughts, and for that she was grateful.

"You're crying."

His voice came like a whisper through a dream, bewilderment disorienting her. Suddenly aware of the damp streaking her face, she blinked up at him.

Jake stopped dancing for a moment, his hands still holding her. "Do you want to leave?"

"No," replied Paige quietly. "I want to be held."

****

Carrie had let a silence settle between them, a

welcome quiet in which she enjoyed the warm Texas night.

Suddenly, Ray said, "Excuse me while I lean upon a hedge."

He jumped down into the bushes off the side of the porch and disappeared into the shrubbery. A few minutes later, he returned with another three beers, thrashing his way through the plants like an explorer through jungle before stopping a moment and unsteadily arranging himself back into position on the edge of the porch. Disapproval played with the corners of her mouth.

"Not as young as I used to be," he offered as an explanation.

"Nor as sober, I believe." She waited to see what his reply would be but, when none was forthcoming, changed track. "A cowboy who quotes Shakespeare. That's a first."

"Lean upon a hedge? Oh, we're full of surprises out here, the first one being we're not all cowboys."

"Sorry. I didn't mean... It wasn't used as a pejorative term. I only meant—"

"It's okay, forget it. But I prefer being called a rancher, 'specially as cows are not my business."

"Well, how can you ranch if not with cows?"

"I run a horse and hunting ranch. Breed Arabs—the horse that is." His humor shone through. "And run a hunting lodge operation."

Carrie wondered how the gun side of this venture went with the alcohol.

"I never drink until after work," he added, apparently reading her mind.

"Arabs? Wow." Her head tilted in contemplation of

this fact.

"You ride?"

"Yes. We had a couple of horses when Paige was growing up. Then she got more interested in boys than in horses."

A laugh like a bass drum being tested came from Ray along with another of his smiles only showing in his eyes. "And did you get more interested in boys, too?"

Carrie's back straightened, and she faced away.

"Sorry, that was rude of me," he apologized. "I didn't...I only meant, you didn't have to give up horses as well."

"I didn't. I just didn't have the time to care for them, and time for actual riding was at a premium."

He acknowledged this with a small nod, reaching again for his flask. "So, is there a Mr. Bennett at present?"

"There *was* a Mr. Bennett. He's moved on to greener pastures."

"Sorry. As you said, divorce and all, not pleasant."

His speech was beginning to slur, and a shade of what she took to be embarrassment colored his face.

"Well, it was a long time ago, Mr. Ryder," she said more brightly, "and I am long over it." She used the "Mr." to put distance between them, then regretted it, thinking he probably found her stuffy.

He nodded in acknowledgement, swaying slightly as his fingers whitened with his grip on the porch. "Ray. Please call me Ray." He was obviously having difficulty controlling his voice; its timbre had dropped to a sigh.

"How did you settle on Arabs, then? Over, say,

Morgans or whatever." Her gaze met his, and she was surprised to find a pain, a hurt evident where the humor had once been.

"It was my son's decision, my son's idea." His voice had gone flat.

"Jake?"

"No." There was an abrupt note in his voice as he forced the matter to rest, puckering his mouth somewhat as if his lips had been glued to form an O, or perhaps he might whistle. "Say, I think it's about time this hombre headed on home." He reached out to lay his hand flat against the wall and give himself some leverage to get up. "Jake'll get a ride with friends." He swayed to his feet, stumbled, then steadied himself.

"Look, I really don't think you're in any condition to drive, Ray. Let me go find Jake for you. Please." Carrie stood and tapped him gently on the shoulder, surprised at the bulk of muscle she found as he turned to face her.

"Sweetheart, you won't be able to find Jake in this lot. I promise you. Jake and your baby girl—what's her name?"

"Paige."

"Jake and Paige are havin' themselves a good time. Let 'em be. As I told you earlier, I'm quite capable of driving, and I promise no harm will come."

He lifted his keys out of his pocket and swung them for a moment, a moment too long as Carrie grabbed them out of his hand. The surprise that crossed his face almost brought out a laugh in her, but she found the situation too serious.

She propelled him back against the wall and passed into the hall to search for Jake. "Stay there!" she ordered, poking back out a second later. "Don't move."

The scene greeting her was a heaving mass of bodies, but all she could see was the conviction of youth, their confidence in themselves, in one another, the beauty of their certainty in life. A small gasp escaped her and she whispered, "They're so young."

"Yep. They sure are."

Ray stood beside her, and his hand went tentatively to her shoulder as if to comfort her, but he was only steadying himself again. The grainy odor of beer on his breath made her take a step away.

"Best give me back them keys, if you don't mind, and I'll be on my way. I'm sure Jake and your baby will eventually turn up, if you don't mind waiting a while."

"I will *not* give you back the keys. I'll drive you myself," she sputtered out, suddenly decisive. "I'll text Paige where I am. She has the keys to our car, so she can come with Jake and collect me when she reads it. Assuming one of them can still drive…"

Her gaze locked with Ray's in a battle of wills, seeing him for the first time. Dark eyes, strong chin, Stetson way down. He had that unshaven look, neither beard nor shadow, but something in-between. Her heart lurched for a moment, and an uncontrolled heat warmed her cheeks as well as her insides.

Whipping out her phone and starting to text, she avoided the penetrating stare that tried to read her back.

"Sure is difficult always tryin' to do the right thing." He paused in an uncomfortable silence. "All right then, come on Miz Designated Driver. Pickup's down the road a bit."

****

Jake gently released Paige's hand as she relaxed

back against the building and sighed, her eyes blinking shut for a moment before widening to stare at him. He had led her out a side door where there were fewer people, a scattering of couples kissing or talking quietly, away from the throng. Now, he wished Paige had meant what she had said, that she wanted to be held, because holding her was exactly what he wanted to do at this moment. Yet, she appeared so distant, so alien in her attitude and demeanor, he hesitated to approach her in any intimate manner. Her distance was a wall, a barrier which was almost impenetrable, as if she had once held the key and thrown it away.

"You all right?" he asked quietly.

"Yes. Maybe I just needed some air." She tilted her head, a sigh escaping like the suspiration of the wind.

"Paige..."

She shook her head in response as the glare of overhead lights reflected in her sad eyes. "Jake, I..." Her voice trailed off and she was saved from continuing by the telegraphic beeps of her phone. "Oh, a text." Paige straightened, pulled out her cell phone and scrolled down the words. "Jeez," she murmured. "My mother is driving your father home. That's funny—they must have met outside. She says we should come and collect her when we're ready." She peered up at him. "Maybe we should go? Or I can go alone and collect her if you give me the address."

The abruptness of the situation puzzled Jake. He grunted. "You wouldn't find it in a month of Sundays. Not with GPS or anything." He let out a breath of exasperation. "Come on, I'll go with you." With this opportunity past, the drive would serve as time alone with her.

Paige studied him, and for one heady moment, there was the sense she might lean in and kiss him. She appeared to melt like ice in a warm bath. His desire for her was palpable, but if she was aware of it, she ignored the fact and shook her head as if ridding herself of cobwebs.

"One more drink," she said, gaining her self-control again. "We'll have one more drink then go."

****

Ray pointed to his pickup, smirking slightly with the knowledge of what her reaction would probably be.

"You must be joking."

He could hardly hear the mumbled comment, but it was exactly what he'd been expecting.

She glowered, a brow definitively arched in query. "What year is this thing?"

He attempted to wipe the amusement away from his face with a hand that rubbed his stubble in a satisfying scrape. "Sorry, I left the Cadillac at home this time." A raised brow questioned if she took him seriously. "It's an '89, and still runs as smooth as the day I got it."

"Which was, what? Last year?"

Ray shook his head and proceeded to the passenger door. "You have the key, sweetheart," he said, patiently standing and waiting.

"Listen!" Carrie put her hands out as if to stop any further conversation. "First off, I am not your sweetheart. And second, if by any chance you think you just may have gotten lucky tonight—"

"Whoa, whoa now." Ray was truly mystified at the turn events were taking. "Not that I wouldn't be honored and damn well pleased, but I sure as heck wasn't thinkin' along those lines...and truth be told, you know, I'm hardly up to it." He considered this for a second, a fog clearing for a moment's view of the road. "And I don't mean I need Viagra either." He noted her staring at the key as if it might turn into something else. "No, it doesn't open automatically," he informed her at last.

She shoved the key into the handle and got the door open, climbed up into the cab and reached across to unlock the door for him. Her gaze ran over the dashboard, uncertainty scrunching her face like a bitter fruit.

Ray folded himself into the passenger seat and slouched back, tipping his hat over his eyes. "Just let me know when you give up. I'll be right here, darl..." *Yeah, better not.* He could almost feel her indignation, listening as she squirmed around and adjusted the seat.

"It'll be a cold day in hell, mister, before I give up!" The key turned and the truck sputtered to life, then died again.

"You ever drive manual before?" he mumbled from under his Stetson, and sensed Carrie eyeing him. "That's what I thought," he answered to her lack of response. "Put your foot on the clutch, move her into first, release the brake, and get goin', slowly releasing the clutch."

"Who the hell drives stick shift anymore?" she muttered as she followed his terse instructions. The truck lurched forward as she spun it off the grass toward the road.

"Right," Ray directed, feeling suddenly nauseous with the pitch of the car. Bile rising, he opened the door and spat before yanking it shut again. "Can you get the damn thing into second? Foot on the clutch, move the shift and let's go if we're going."

"Fine! You don't have to yell at me."

Ray sat up, shoved his hat back from his eyes and glared at her, reining in his frustration and anger. "I was not yelling at you, but you know dang well we'd be far safer with me drivin'. As it is, I'm gonna need a new transmission."

The truck staggered again. "I know no such thing." She bent forward to swipe at the windscreen to clear it. "We haven't got seatbelts on," she murmured.

"We're not going fast enough to need them."

Carrie ignored his last remark and appeared to concentrate on keeping the truck moving. It sputtered again, and Ray let out a sigh of resignation just as flashing blue lights appeared in the side mirror. She pulled over, and the motor unceremoniously died.

"Damn!" she cursed, reaching down for her bag at Ray's feet. "Let me get my license."

"You won't need it." When the patrol car's door slammed, he repeated, "Believe me, you won't need it."

"How can I not need it?" Carrie started to struggle with winding down the window. "Give me the—"

"Evenin'." An almost perfectly square face topped by a sheriff's hat peered in the window; porcine, virtually lashless eyes, which had caterpillars crawling above them, moved from Ray to her and back again. "Ray?" the officer drawled, "I thought I was at last gonna have to take you in, the way this old rattle trap was swerving. What's up?" The piggy eyes darted between the two of them again.

"Hey, Dex. I got me a 'designated driver' tonight. How d'ya like that?" He brushed his hand across his mouth to hide a smile.

"Well, I'd say you got a driver tonight, but y'all're gonna have to get yourself a new truck tomorrow." He let out a belly laugh at his own joke while Carrie sat as if inanimate, an object the two men were discussing.

Ray patted her tentatively on the knee. "Ah, she's doing real well, Dex. First time driving manual."

"Well, listen," the sheriff continued, "I know y'all're only a short distance from your turn-off, but next time, maybe you ought to keep the lesson to your ranch road." He smacked the side of the truck and stood back, then leaned forward into the window. "I hear Jake is returned from Iraq? Wish him well and welcome home for me, will ya?"

"Will do."

"And lady? Keep it between the ditches, will ya darlin'?"

Ray sat with her in silence as Dex made his way to the patrol car and drove past them with a wave.

A gurgle escaped from the driver's side. Ray leaned forward to try to assess the damage to her pride. "You're not crying, are you?" Concern etched his voice. "I mean, it wasn't that bad."

Her reply was a burst of laughter so unaffected and self-effacing, it caught Ray completely off guard.

"No, I'm not crying." She appeared a bit sheepish, the laughter still evident around her mouth. "I suppose you find me incredibly stuffy and arrogant."

"Well, see, I didn't know you could laugh. Isn't that something?"

"Oh, I can laugh. At myself mostly." The key twisted in the ignition. "So, where to—where we headed next?"

****

By the time the pickup grunted to a standstill outside the Rocking R ranch house, whatever tension had existed between the rancher and Carrie had dissolved. Dogs barked and yapped in anticipation of seeing their master, and she could hear the scratching at the door of the house. She glanced across at her companion, a sense of his loneliness and isolation dissipating any last remnants of her own aloofness. She sensed a connection, an empathy she could not quite understand, yet it was there, nonetheless.

When Ray didn't move to get out, she said, "I can wait outside if you want to go in to sleep."

"No, no." He jerked the door open and swung his legs out. "You come on in. I think I may have gone a bit overboard tonight, truth be told. I'll get us some coffee."

"I can't drink coffee this late, but water will be fine."

She followed Ray as he stumbled up the steps and clutched the screen door before yanking it open. He found the light switch and the room came to life, dogs jumping and begging for his attention before taking note of their new visitor. Carrie stood uncertainly while they milled about her, sniffing, then she doled out pats to the entreating canines.

Released at last, she offered, "Your keys, before I forget." She held them out to him as he faced her, regarding her a moment before taking them, nodding, and heading into the kitchen, the dogs at his heels.

"They're Labs, aren't they?" she called as she took in the masculine air of the room.

A living room or front parlor, she didn't know

what it would be called out here, it displayed no sign of feminine life, no mark of a woman's hand ever having been there. A regulation Elk head—or was it Moose?—with antlers gave her a glassy-eyed look of superiority from above the fireplace, while a mounted bass on another wall pompously assessed her, countered only by the noncommittal glance of a deer. Braided rugs on the floor lent some fading color to an otherwise brown room. But two things surprised her: a stack of newspapers by the sofa included the pink of the Financial Times, and a virtual parade of photographs went around the room.

She started a tour of them, carefully lifting each photo, replacing it, studying the next.

Ray re-entered from the kitchen and handed her a glass of water, the dogs milling around him.

"You have another son," she stated, remembering his comment about the choice of Arab horses to breed. "Does he live here, too?"

He shifted away from her, almost tripping on one of the Labs who let out a squeak of protest. "I better close them in." He bent to grab one by the scruff of its neck and herded them into the kitchen, shutting the door behind him before he faced her.

Carrie held out a picture of two boys, the elder in army fatigues with a younger Jake smiling widely.

Ray reached out and gently took the photo from her. "Had another son," he said quietly as he put the snapshot back on the shelf. "Had."

She turned to him and knew, saw him standing there shaking slightly in his pain and anguish. As if by some form of osmosis, some unleashed intuition, she understood his story, grasped Ray, comprehended who he was. Yet, "I'm sorry," was all she could say as she moved to let him have his private grief, tears already swimming in the lagoon-dark eyes.

Carrie let the screen door close quietly behind her and sat on the steps, the cool glass still in her hands. Peering up at the canopy of heaven, she suddenly experienced a sense of being so small, infinitesimal; it was as if the world loomed over her, spreading out from the one axis of her being. Rather than celestial entities in the infinity of space above her, to Carrie, the stars were holes in the fabric, entries to the endless expanse beyond, gateways to other worlds of which she would never be a part. The lights inside switched off and, for a moment, it appeared as if Ray had gone to bed.

"I'm sorry." His voice came through the screen. The words were hoarse with drink and pain. "I... Can I join you?"

"Of course."

He came out and carefully lowered himself onto the step, the coffee in his hand slopping slightly over the side.

"Don't burn yourself."

He set the mug down and stretched his legs forward, hands coming to rest on his thighs. "Robbie died in Afghanistan," he started. "He was my eldest. It was five years ago, you know, and the pain is as fresh now as it was then. You never expect...you never think your kids are gonna go before you and all. And then Jake went off to Iraq, well, see..." He hesitated. "I told them, I said you take, but you give back. That's what we do, we give back to our country, we serve. Robbie, well, Robbie just wanted to breed his horses—those damn Arabs meant everything to him, but I told him he had the…" There was a gulp of tears fighting to come out, the assault on a man's pride he tried to cover. "I told him he had the rest of his life to breed those horses. I said every man in this family has served his country, and he wasn't going to shame me, he wasn't going to be the exception."

"You served in Viet Nam, didn't you?" Carrie lowered her voice to the whisper of a secret.

"Yeah. Right at the very end. I was lucky, I guess. Got over there just about in time to get out." Ray tapped his hat back, then must have thought better of it and took it off, laying it carefully on the step beside him. Strands of damp hair lay plastered down the side of his face, but he made no attempt to push them back.

"Do you know how… I mean…"

"He was on guard duty, him and another kid. Some truck driven by them suicide bombers came at them laden with bombs, trying to get into the compound where all his buddies were. 'Course the two of them could've run away, could've stepped out of the way, but that's not what you do, is it? They blasted the truck to stop it, blew it up outside to save the lives of the men inside that compound. Now, his mama has his Distinguished Service Cross and the flag that draped his coffin, as if that would make amends." Ray cleared his throat, a sob mixing with his speech and anger. "But you know," he went on, covering his mouth as if it would stop the tears, "you know it was my damn fault. I mean, what the hell difference would it have made if Robbie hadn't gone, hadn't of served? And what the hell are we doing there anyway? I mean, Viet Nam, Afghanistan, Iraq, what the hell are we fighting in those countries for? It's meaningless, it's just dang foolishness is what it is, kids dying for nothing...nothing at all."

"Ray, you don't believe that. Of course it made a difference, his serving. It made a big difference. You don't believe that it was meaningless for one second."

"Well. Tell you the truth, I don't know what the hell I believe anymore. I criticized you for wanting to do the right thing, that business 'bout the designated driver an' all, but, well, I guess it's me. I just always tried, you know, I tried to do the right thing, but it never seemed to come out straight."

"Of course it has," Carrie assured him. "If Robbie hadn't gone you would—"

"Oh, I know. I would've been angry with him for the rest of my life, been thinking what son of mine could do that, stay back. I'd've been shamed." He sighed and glanced over as if noticing for the first time she was there. "I married Leigh Anne 'cause she was pregnant—that's what you did, the right thing. You get a girl in the family way, you damn well married her. I'd been a kid when I went to Nam, and when I got back, I was quite a hell-raiser. Went all over the place, doing the rodeos, workin' ranches. Then I got back here, and I was just taking over the ranch. Hardly had a dime to my name in those days, but you did the right thing. Well..." He ran a finger along the line of a crack in one of the steps. A hint of his earlier humor flashed on his face. "Is this when you New York folks say, 'Thanks for sharing?'" he quipped.

Carrie let herself laugh. "Oh, dear." She played with some loose hair, thinking of how she had misjudged him earlier, feeling the depth of his character and his sadness. She fixed the curl behind her ear and sat with him, watching lights now moving on the horizon.

"That might be them." Ray pointed out as a pair of headlights moved down the ranch road. Then they stopped, disappeared. "Well, I'll be…"

"What? Have they stopped?"

"Seems like…" He hesitated, then said, "I hope Jake is not up to anything with your daughter. He certainly seemed to have an interest in her, shall I say?"

"Paige." Carrie sighed. "Paige just lost someone, Ray. I don't think she's ready for another relationship just yet. Her fiancé died last year from a very aggressive form of leukemia. She quit law school and all."

"Oh, I'm so sorry. Well…he's not the sort of boy to force himself. Boy?" He shook his head in admonishment of himself. "Twenty-seven years, I guess he's a man. Anyway, he's a real gentle soul is Jake. Except with me, of course. Paige'll be all right."

****

"Watch out for the cattle guard."

Jake's warning reached Paige through the darkness as the car bumped and screeched before she brought it to a stop.

"What're you doin'? I thought your mother was waiting?"

She didn't know what she was doing. The memory of his gentleness at the dancehall, his comprehension of her, ran through her mind. And then there was the feel of his body beneath her hand, the heat that had reached her, the strength.

Paige sat a moment longer, still gripping the wheel, before facing Jake. She stared at him for several seconds before reaching across and running her finger down the outline of his chin, a solitary tear finding its way down her cheek. He wasn't Steven, no, but Steven wasn't here, Steven wasn't anywhere; Steven would never hold her, or kiss her cheek or make love to her again.

Jake extended his own hand, and with his thumb, wiped the trace away, then he leaned across and kissed her, gently at first, but more pressing, deeper as it went on. She clasped him tightly, need overtaking her as his hand slipped up under her blouse to undo her bra, his tongue tasting the sweetness of her mouth...

Just as suddenly as she had yielded to him, she thrust him back. "I can't. I can't! Stop, stop it, Jake." She shoved him away, protecting herself by turning her face to the window.

"What? You...I thought..."

"I know what you thought. I'm sorry."

"What? Are you some sort of tease or something?" Confusion brought his voice to a higher pitch. "I thought...you stopped the car and all." He collapsed back against the window, anger and disappointment coloring his voice.

"Yes, yes I know. I'm sorry. I just can't."

She reached backward to re-hook her bra, then leaned back against the cool of the window to stare at him. Jake held his head, frustration forcing his breaths in ragged beats.

"I'm sorry. I'm sorry," she repeated. "I never should have..." She waited to contain herself, to try to explain. "I had a fiancé. He died. He died last year and...I thought..." She spoke in faltering bursts, finding the words from somewhere deep inside her, as

51

if speaking a foreign language she would never quite master. More quietly, hardly a whisper, she said, "I thought if you made love to me, if we made love, perhaps...I don't know, it would wipe out the pain for a bit. It would make me feel...better. But I can't. I'm not ready. I'm sorry."

Jake ran his fingers through the turf of his scalp. In the confines of the car, there was tension in the air like a thunderstorm receding.

"How did he die?" he asked gently.

She shuddered, tears streaming now, anguish engulfing her. "Leukemia."

"Jeez," was all he said. He cleared the mist from his side window and looked up toward the house. "I lost my brother five year ago. I guess it's not the same but, then again, you lose someone you love, it messes you up. Sure as hell messed up my parents."

"Did they divorce because of it?"

"Well, sort of. Dad took to drink and my mother...I guess you could say she started running around. Lord, parents, huh?"

Paige grimaced. "Yeah. My mother found my bottle of sleeping pills next to my bed and immediately presumed the worst. I'd quit law school to be with Steven, and then moved back home. The doctor had given them to me, but she immediately assumed I planned to kill myself."

"And did you?"

Jake's expression was questioning, with curiosity, but she also saw fear there of what the answer might be.

The query hung in the air between them like a bad odor before she replied, "I guess I sort of considered it. But it's not what Steven would have wanted. He would have wanted me to continue, to stay at school."

"Will you? Go back to school I mean."

"Maybe. I don't know if I'm ready yet, ready to see my friends, ready to concentrate on classes and write papers."

Jake glanced again toward the ranch house. "My dad blames himself for Robbie's death. He doesn't know…" He stopped, his gaze traveling from Paige back up to the house. "The lights are off. That's strange." He gave her a rather mischievous wink. "You don't suppose they're…you know…"

"Oh, lord, no. Not my mother." She snorted in denial. "She's, like, afraid of men."

"I don't suppose my dad could get it up anyway, what with the drink and all." He waited a moment as if assuring himself she was better now, then leaned across and kissed her softly. "We better go."

Paige started up the car once more, the headlights spotlighting the road ahead. "What is it he doesn't know?" she asked as she drove away.

"Who doesn't know?"

"You said your father doesn't know. What is it he doesn't know?"

"That it wasn't his fault," Jake replied slowly, like a guilty prisoner under cross-examination. "Robbie's death—it wasn't my dad's fault. It was mine."

Chapter Three

"Oh, my word, is that you, Ray Ryder? What in heaven's name brings you out to the Lone Star?" Doris McKay extended her meaty arm across the front desk to give him her paw. "And are those for me? Goodness, this must be my lucky day."

Ray had been carrying his bunch of flowers out in front of him like a bride going down the aisle. He quickly pointed them south and extended his own hand to the smiling ranch manager, shaking her hand being something akin to squeezing a small pillow.

"Hey there, Doris. How're you doin'?" He purposefully ignored her remark about the flowers. "Long time and all that."

"Long time? Long time? Heck, I haven't seen you since...I don't know when. When was it? You recall?"

He scratched his head in a pantomime of thinking. "Mighta been when you and Hank come over to see a couple of my Arabs for sale. That'd be it."

"Yeah, well..." She eyed the flowers again, waiting for an explanation.

"Say, you got a lady and her daughter from back east name of Bennett staying with you, haven't you?"

Doris leaned across the expanse of desk in a confidential manner. "Famous author," she whispered, her hand covering her mouth. "Puttin' us all in her next book."

"That so?" He attempted to act as if he believed her. "Thing is, lady sort of did me a small favor last night, and I'd like to thank her, so I come on over to give her these. You think she's around at the moment?"

The hefty manager straightened into a professional manner and eyed him sternly. "Really shouldn't be giving out any information on my guests, Ray. But seeing as how it's you," she went on with a softer tone, "and you promise to stay on for our Saturday evening dance starting in just a short while, well, they're over in Cabin Three. Now, you make sure you knock and don't go peeking in any windows."

Ray nodded his thanks and was gone before she could continue.

****

Carrie stood peering through the screen door, just swallowing a last mouthful of chicken when two things went through her mind. The first, which made her giggle, was that Ray, standing and holding a bouquet of flowers out in front of him, resembled a young suitor come to take a girl to the prom. The second was how really pleased she was to see him.

"Come in, come in," she said, trying to clear any residue of sauce from her mouth. "What a surprise."

"Yeah, well..." He stepped inside the cabin and glanced briefly around.

A minor wave of embarrassment hit her as she became aware of the various small items of clothing hanging on chair backs and off wardrobe doors, while a brief glimpse into the bedroom revealed one neat bed and one with a mess of makeup and cosmetics strewn over it.

Paige was at the small dining table reading and

eating; she glanced up at Ray inquisitively.

"Hey, Paige," he greeted, removing his hat.

Carrie sensed the sudden nervousness, as if he wished he hadn't come after all, so she offered, "It's good to see you. Can I get you some coffee?"

"Oh, I don't want to be any trouble, Carrie. I just came over to make a peace offering and apologize for my idiocy last night. I guess I sort of did go over the deep end with the drink and all." He held out the flowers, the cellophane crinkling in his hand.

"I...you don't have to apologize. It was fine. You went out and celebrated your son's return home. But thank you, they're lovely." She took the flowers and walked briskly to the sink to search for a receptacle to make do as a vase.

"I think there's a jug in the top cupboard, Mom," muttered Paige, briefly glancing up from her book. "Why don't you sit down, Ray? Take a load off and all that."

He sat on the sofa, turning his hat in his hands as Carrie clattered about the tiny kitchen, dirty dishes covering the small countertop. She measured out coffee into the filter paper and set the machine to work, not quite accustomed to using the coffeemaker.

"Doris was reluctant to tell me where you were," Ray went on, a somewhat hesitant note in his voice. "I hope you won't be mad at her."

Carrie cut the ends off the blooms and dumped them into the jug of water. "Oh, no, it's fine." She reached up for a couple of mugs and smiled back at him.

"You're not seeking her autograph, are you?" Paige put in without looking up. "You don't want a book signed?"

"No, not this time. Though Doris does seem to think she's going to have a leading role in your next one."

Her daughter let out a single laugh, which startled her.

"I don't think you've got that desperate for heroines yet, have you, Mother?"

"Paige..."

"Yeah," Ray joined in. A smile stole across his features. "She's not exactly—well, I don't want to be unkind. She has a good heart, Doris has."

"No doubt a large one," added Paige rather dryly.

"Paige..." Carrie's shoulders slumped as she tried to catch her daughter's eye.

"Paige, Paige," she mimicked.

"Jake says hello," Ray put in quickly. "Said he might give you a call later, Paige, and see if you wanted a dance partner for the night. I left him with some customers who're considering one of our stallions. He's real good with people, Jake is."

Carrie breathed a sigh of relief that he seemed to have defused the situation with her daughter for the moment. She waited to see what reaction the mention of Jake might bring.

Paige slipped Ray a glance then slammed shut her book. "Well," she said, her chair screeching back, "maybe I better go change for the evening's entertainment."

The door to the bedroom closed. Carrie made a face, part apology for her daughter, part 'you know how kids are.'

"How do you take your coffee?"

"Oh, black—as it comes is fine." A look of amusement momentarily stretched his face into a wide smile before his gaze slid away again.

Carrie was conscious of the sudden awkwardness between them. She had the sensation he watched her back as she added the sugar and milk to her own mug, aware of the sound of the fridge door opening and closing, breaking the wave of silence between them. For a moment, a surge went through her, an expectancy of what might happen, but she struggled to suppress it, to pull away. It was as if she were drawing back into herself, containing some portion of her being that might be trying to escape.

"Here you go," she said softly as she handed him the mug and switched Paige's vacated chair to face the sofa. "I hope it's all right."

Ray held his mug between his two hands as if they needed warming. "You know, maybe I shouldn't have come. I guess I could've just sent over a note or left a message or something rather than comin' on over here and bothering you both."

"I'm glad you came. Really, I..." She slipped out of herself, like mercury from a thermometer, one bit and then another of her feelings were attracting and attaching like magnets until the liquid silver of her center would be gone.

"It's just, well, I felt I laid an awful lot of my problems on you last night, and I wondered if you went away feeling, you know, upset or something. Damn, Carrie, I'm not real good with words. Help me out here, will ya?" He reached across and slammed the mug down on the table.

"You don't need help, Ray. You were drunk. We

all do or say things we don't mean when we've had too much to drink." She took a careful sip from her coffee and gazed at him over the top of her mug.

"Yeah, well. There wasn't anything I said, as I recall, I didn't mean. It's just...maybe I shouldn't have said it all." He stood suddenly and grabbed his hat. "I don't suppose you ever get drunk, do you?"

Her gaze met his, startled at his sudden antipathy. The resulting silence made the sounds of Paige's preparations seem louder, like warning bells.

"You think me an awful prig really, don't you?"

Ray's piercing gaze caught her again, the lens of a camera catching the moment.

"No," he said, sitting back down. "No, not at all. I just feel you're very much in control of yourself, is all. You wouldn't let yourself go, like I did last night."

He reached for his coffee as the bedroom door swung open.

Carrie turned to see her daughter glaring at the two of them. She tensed at the look of impatience on Paige's face before turning back to Ray.

He took a sip of the coffee, his face contorting with the taste. "Jeez, that is about the worst dang coffee I ever tasted."

****

Paige had been the one to convince Ray to stay for the dance. She told him if Jake showed up to be her partner, her mother would be left alone to go back to the room and work on a Saturday night, and he couldn't allow that. Her mom had busied herself at the sink clearing the dinner dishes, tossing out the rejected coffee before she excused herself to 'freshen up.'

When the bell sounded outside the main ranch

59

building, the three strolled down at a leisurely pace, Paige slightly behind the older pair, watching their body language. How every time Ray leaned toward her mother, her body would shift slightly away with the next step. How every time her mother said something, Ray would bend his head in much closer.

Hopeless, just hopeless.

And then Ray's hand came out suddenly to stop her mother. "Well, I'll be," he murmured. "What the heck?"

Paige stopped behind them and peered ahead. The cowboy—a wrangler she guessed he was called—the one who had taken them out riding earlier in the day, was sauntering toward the dining hall. Slightly older than Jake, she figured, she had found him tense and wary, uncommunicative. She never did manage to ask him about the scar running down his left cheek.

"Ty Sheldon," Ray's voice called out. "What're you doin' here?"

The wrangler stopped, hesitated, then came part way to meet the trio. "Mr. Ryder? Hey, how you doin', sir? Long time—"

Ray didn't let him finish. "You working here now, Ty? I thought, uh…" He stopped himself, glancing at Paige and her mother, and obviously conscious of them listening.

"Mr. McKay gave me a job. I been clean for a couple of years now. Out…you know…"

Her mother shifted uncomfortably, then said, "We'll see you inside."

Ray shook his head. "No, it's fine," he assured her quietly. "This is one of my son Robbie's old friends from school."

"We met earlier today." She nodded to the cowboy. "Ty took us out on a lovely, long ride."

"Did he now?" Ray stood and crossed his arms.

"Dad, Paige."

Jake's voice drew her attention from the unfolding scene as he approached from the parking lot, then stopped in his tracks.

Recognition spread across his face as the wrangler took a wary step back. Yet Jake continued to stand there without acknowledging Robbie's old friend.

Paige stayed where she was and waited for some reaction.

"I better be getting inside, Mr. Ryder." Ty touched the brim of his hat with a small nod at her mother and headed off as Jake came forward toward his father. If Ray thought it odd his son and the old family friend didn't exchange greetings, he didn't show it. To Paige, it was just that—odd.

"What the hell is that bastard doing here?" Jake asked.

"He's clean, son, he says. Whatever else he was, he was Robbie's good friend." Ray nodded to her mother. "You think a leopard can change its spots?"

Paige waited for her dance partner's response, taking in the way the two men dealt with each other. And then something else caught her attention. After apologizing to her mother for his drunken behavior last night, the rancher now seemed to be ready for a repeat performance.

"Why have you got a hipflask in your back pocket?" The question was suddenly sharp, intrusive.

Ray's hand darted to the flask. He eyed Paige for a moment and then his son. "I guess I just feel I need to carry an emergency supply. Sort of like one of them St. Bernard dogs." He glanced toward her mom to catch her reaction. "Force of habit, I guess."

Paige could see the wheels of her mother's mind turning and working, yet no words came out. And then she caught a grimace on Jake's face that faded away as she faced him.

"Jake," she went on brightly, extending her hand, "are we going to dance?"

****

Tables had been moved to the sides of the wide room and a country band played from a platform set up at one end. Paper lanterns were strung along the wall to give a slightly festive air, while the bar was doing a brisk business. But it was nothing like the Bandera dancehall of the previous night. Ranch guests appeared to be shy about trying the local dances, and only a few couples were out on the floor.

Carrie fidgeted with her bracelet, twisting it on her wrist, unsure whether to offer to buy Ray a drink, unsure of what she was doing there aside from spending more time with this man, a man about whom she really knew very little.

"We're going to go for a drive," her daughter broke in suddenly after a quiet consultation with Jake. "Don't wait up." And with a wave, she was off.

Jake nodded his good-bye as he went to hold the door open for Paige, his gaze scanning the skimpy camisole she wore with her jeans.

Ray grimaced. "They'll be fine," he assured her. "Drink?" he asked, nodding toward the bar. "I believe I'm allowed two before the need for a 'designated driver' is reached."

Carrie laughed. Her body relaxed, let go, as if she might enjoy herself. "You're not going to let me forget that, are you? All right," she said, following him. "I've found they do a mean Margarita, salt and all please."

"So, you're a tequila girl, then, huh? Okay. One margarita, one Jack on the rocks."

He led her to a space at the bar. Carrie briefly acknowledged one of her fellow guests while Ray gave a busy Doris a nod as she passed.

"How long you been divorced, Carrie?" he asked bluntly as he shook a hand at the barman.

"Paige was three. Nearly twenty-four years." She made it sound like a natural fact of life, but his reaction was immense surprise.

"Twenty-four years! And you never re-married? How the hell did you manage that?"

She squinted at him a moment, trying to decide exactly what he meant by his remark. "I managed it by working hard, very hard, since the day he walked out."

"He walked out? Oh, that's right, you said yesterday he'd moved on to greener pastures. Must've been a damn fool, then."

"I thought so."

"And all this time you never re-married? I just find that so hard to believe."

"I didn't re-marry, Ray. I didn't say I hadn't had any relationships." She waited as he grew impatient for the barman. "I was very young when we married, and learned my lesson. End of story. How long have *you* been divorced?"

"Me? I, uh…" He broke off to give their order. "Now, let me guess, these other relationships, my bet is you broke them off, not the men?"

Carrie leaned an elbow on the bar and stared at him. Where was he going with this? And was it any of his business? Her fingers strummed for a moment. "Are you a psychologist in your spare time as well as a rancher?"

"No, no." He handed the barman some cash before picking up the drinks and handing her one. "Salud!"

"Salud," she responded, as he guided her to a space by the window. "But you think you have me figured out," she went on.

"I think…I'm not sure what I think. But I do know it's mighty strange for a good-looking, talented, kind-hearted lady like yourself to still be single after twenty-four years. You must be hiding yourself away, woman."

"Or maybe I just never met the right man," she retorted. "Or maybe I just like it that way."

"Maybe."

She waited a moment, taking a careful sip of the drink and watching the dancers on the floor. Was it worth going on? But she saw a genuine interest—or was it concern?—in this man's face.

"When he left—David, his name was…*is* David—I decided I didn't want anything from him except the apartment and some maintenance for Paige so no matter what happened she had a roof over her head and could attend decent schools. He was going off to Hong Kong anyway, and I figured it would be almost impossible to start legal proceedings to get alimony. I just let him be. He was out of my life, and I figured we were going to have minimal contact with him anyway." She sipped again at her drink, the memory of that awful time bringing back the pain, the humiliation. It wasn't the drink that chilled her now.

"Does Paige see him? Was he part of her life growing up?"

"Not really. She went out to visit him a couple of times when she was older and, of course, when he is in New York, he comes to see her. But David's input was very little. I could choose the schools, basically do whatever I wanted regarding her upbringing." She gave a small shake, trying to rid herself of those memories once and for all.

Ray took notice of his fast-disappearing drink; Carrie wondered if he normally drank whiskey as if it were water.

"So, when did you start writing?"

"The day he walked out the door." She took a sip of her margarita. "It was good therapy."

His dark, piercing eyes penetrated her in a way that made her feel violated. Then, gently, he reached forward, took her drink to put on the windowsill along with his own and extended his hand.

"What? What are you doing?"

"You know how to Texas Two-Step?" he asked.

"No," she said, laughter just below the surface.

"Well, sweetheart, you have come to the right place. Or at least got yourself the right man. By the time I finish with you, you'll be the best dang stepper on the floor."

Carrie looked around. "There isn't anyone else *on* the floor at the moment, Ray."

"Well, heck, I know that. That's perfect for learning."

As soon as his hand closed around hers, the leather of his palm a strange glove over her own fingers, a sudden frisson of connection ran through her she hadn't known in a very long while. He moved her to face him squarely on, a small smile tipping the edges of his mouth, the dark, impenetrable eyes shining with his captured prize.

"Just follow me," he said as his right hand went to her back. A cover of a Vince Gill ballad started, the mournful tune setting a moderate tempo. "Perfect." He held her right hand high and applied slight pressure to move her backwards. "Fast fast slow slow, fast fast slow slow."

Carrie felt a light bulb go on. She got it. It was good. It was fun. And she relaxed in his embrace. He was an excellent teacher, a fabulous leader on the dance floor. Would wonders never cease?

"You're doing well. You're doing fine," he assured her. "We're gonna try a little promenade now, and then a twirl, so get ready."

Carrie couldn't stop herself from smiling, anticipation bubbling for just a second. And then out of the corner of her eye she caught Ty watching them, beer half-raised in salute and a smirk plastered on his face. A moment's hesitation and she missed the step.

"What happened there?" asked Ray, oblivious to the effect the onlooker had on her.

Other couples were finally joining them on the dance floor, but despite the company, Carrie's discomfort increased. "That boy, that Ty," she told him. "He was watching us. It made me feel…uneasy."

Ray scanned the sidelines, but Ty had gone, nowhere to be seen. "Oh, don't pay him any mind. He's harmless enough."

****

"So, this is the man cave," Paige said. She picked

up a photo, glancing briefly at it before putting it back down. "Goodness."

"Yeah, I suppose it is now. Guess you didn't really see it last night." Jake handed her a margarita and then motioned to the sofa, plopping down as she ignored the invitation.

Instead, she wandered the room as if she were looking for some clue, her drink almost forgotten in her hand. She gave occasional glances to Jake, considering him, sizing him up, comparing him to Steven. He would certainly not be like Steven, nothing like her lost man, no one would. Yet suddenly, she needed him, wanted him. There was something about him, something that told her he cared, he was giving, she could trust him to love her for the night and make no judgment, no demand.

Could she trust him?

The sudden rush of desire hit her hard, the need for another warm body.

She slugged back the cocktail. "Is this your brother?" she asked to give herself time to think. "He was in the army, too?"

"Yes." Jake sipped at the dark liquid in his glass.

She could sense his reluctance to answer so she pushed, enjoying the power she felt she had. Jake wanted her, she knew he did. And she wanted…what? A man's body, a release?

"Did you enjoy the army, Jake? Did you like it, the manliness of it all, the camaraderie, the adventure…the danger?" She dragged out the last word, her eyes widening at him like a lioness.

He didn't take the bait. "No. I didn't like it. Not one bit."

She plunked herself down next to him. "So, why did you go?"

"To please my father. I thought it would, but by then he didn't give a damn. Not really anyway. In fact, he tried to talk me out of it. He thought he would lose me the way he'd lost Robbie. I thought, somewhere inside of him, he still wanted me to serve."

"Goodness." She considered this. "If I did things to please my mother, I'd never get anything done for myself."

"You were in law school, didn't that please her?"

"Oh, hell, yes. She came from a family of lawyers—father, brothers, husband, just about every man she's gone out with. But I don't mean that. I mean, the small things. I think I stopped thinking about doing things to please her the day she shipped me off to boarding school. She was no longer my conscience. I stopped hearing her voice in my head. Took up smoking behind the bicycle shed and had sex with just about anyone with a penis. I didn't stop loving her, which is probably what she thinks, but I started to be…independent. You should try it some time."

"Jeez…" Jake rested his head against the back of the sofa. "You think I'm not independent. Interesting. You sure are quick to judge, Paige. You've known me all of, what, forty-eight hours? And already you have this idea in your head—"

"Don't you have an idea of me? Don't you think you know who I am?"

"I guess." He clinked the ice in his glass, then slugged back another gulp. "So, am I another prick on your journey to full independence?"

Paige put down her drink on the side table and

straddled Jake, pushing him back against the sofa. "Not at all," she whispered. "You're an interesting diversion…a *very* interesting diversion."

She sat for a moment, studying him, thinking how beautiful he was, actually beautiful, with eyes like spring hyacinths. She bent in to kiss him. His hand on her back pushed her deeper, then clasped her, held her, wanted her.

She jerked back. "You know…I need you to know…this is not going to go anywhere. I am never going to be some cowboy's girlfriend in Texas. It's not who I am. I need you to know this is, if anything, a one night stand, a distraction for me. Nothing more. It's not that you're…prick of the month. It's just…" What was it? A one night stand to relieve her tensions? An interlude?

Loneliness swept through her and she sat back, shimmied over to sit next to him again, looking straight ahead. "I need a living, breathing body. I need to feel alive."

Jake leaned toward her, his hand reaching then holding her face toward his. He stared at her for a moment. "No, Paige, it's not that you need to feel alive. It's that you need to *know* you *are* alive."

She peered at him, considered asking to go home, resisted—not him, but her own growing need. It flowed through her, heating her body, filling her as if desire were a breath. The need for fulfillment jagged at her memory.

Paige reached her hand out and brought him in closer, let his mouth capture hers. He pulled her back to straddle him once more as his hands slipped under her camisole and lifted it over her head before unclipping her bra. Her need was overcoming her now, her mouth unwilling to stop his assault as Jake's tongue found its way and discovered her sensibilities. And then his arms enclosed her, and he stood, her legs wrapping themselves around him as he carried her into his bedroom.

She could not remember later the minutiae of how their clothes came off or how he had maneuvered her to the bed, but she would always recall Jake's tenderness. Whether or not he was sorely aware he was meant to be a diversion from the ache of her loss, she didn't know, but he loved her as a first lover might, with gentleness, a lightness of touch as his fingers roamed her body, embracing the soft curves of her breasts. His lips made their way down to the enflamed center of her being. And when he entered her, Paige let herself go, melt with each movement of Jake within her.

Another atom of her loss was left behind.

****

Carrie had let herself go, no doubt surprising Ray with bursts of laughter in response to his jokes, and not nagging him further about the extra drink he'd had. Now, she stood awkwardly, leaning back against the cabin door, feeling like a young girl on a first date with parents no doubt waiting—and listening—inside. A breeze carried with it the sounds of the night, the cicada choir and horses whinnying in a distant field. She remembered the feel of being in his arms, the revelation of strength in abeyance, the solidness of his body against her hand, and the black eyes that had their own life.

Ray stood back, those eyes catching the light that hung over the cabin steps. "I guess you're going back tomorrow, or is it Monday?" he asked.

"Monday." She waited, then continued, "I thought maybe—"

"Maybe the two of you might like to come on over for a barbecue," he said at the same time. "I mean, I know you're supposedly...no doubt *are*...doing work, but—"

"We'd love to," Carrie broke in. She straightened, her gaze still on this Texan, this rancher, who had somehow broken down her defenses. "What time?"

"Oh. Any time you're ready. We can go for a ride, if you like."

"And will I be riding Widowmaker or Butt Buster?" she jested, remembering the old jokes from the dude ranch cowboys.

He laughed. "No, they're for amateurs. We'll be givin' you Diablo." He stood awkwardly for a moment. "You think you can find your way again? It was dark when you took me home."

"I'll find it. And if I get lost, I'll give you a call."

"Okay, well then." He hesitated before turning back to the path with a wave. "See you tomorrow then."

"See you tomorrow."

In the privacy of the bedroom, curtains drawn against the intruding night and her daughter still not back, Carrie stood naked in front of the full-length mirror on the back of the closet. Still slender, or at least reasonably so, she tried to envisage herself as a man might now see her. It had been four years since her last intimate relationship, and time had not stood still. No, indeed not—it had advanced like an avenging army.

Her skin, once firm, had a certain flabbiness to it around her stomach, the loss of elasticity giving even her slender frame a different outline than before. The nipples of her small breasts pointed toward the floor accusingly, skin in the bend of her elbow and the crux of her armpit had begun to look like elephant hide, and her neck, while still reasonably firm, bore sinuous markings. Turning sideways to further assess herself, Carrie noted her legs were beginning to look like a road map, an ordinance survey, only instead of mountains and rivers, it was veins, bruises and spider nevus. A smattering of skin tags and light age spots completed the unwholesome picture.

Taking a deep breath to quell the self-pity, she lifted a nightdress to slither over her head and promptly burst into tears just as she heard the front door bang open.

"Oh, for heaven's sake," moaned Paige. "What the hell is the matter with you?" She stood in the bedroom doorway for a moment before bouncing down on the bed beside Carrie and drooping her head onto her mother's shoulder. "Have a fight with Ray?"

"No, no." She shuddered with her misery, sniffed and then threw a tentative arm around her daughter. "No fights, no arguments. Danced all night, and he behaved like a perfect gentleman."

"Ah."

"What is that supposed to mean? 'Ah?'"

"Well. Maybe you were hoping for something else?"

"Hardly. How was Jake?"

Paige gathered herself and stood. "Not the perfect gentleman...*definitely* not the perfect gentleman."

Carrie took in the slightly smudged eye make-up, the disheveled hair, the pinpoints of black in her daughter's gray eyes, and decided not to comment. If she had made a connection with Jake, had enjoyed herself, so much the better. Paige was her own person now, not a child, and she needed this encounter.

Carrie eased herself back on the bed and glided between the turned down sheets. Paige gave her a satisfied grin and headed into the bathroom, then came back out, throwing her camisole off over her head.

"So, what were you bawling about?"

"Oh, I don't know. Aging I guess. I had a good, hard, long look in the mirror and didn't like what I saw."

"You're an idiot," stated Paige, heading back to the bathroom, before facing her once again. "That was what you were crying about? Aging? Mother, for goodness sake, think of the alternative for once. Not only that, but you're the best-preserved woman I know. Look at Diana Shawcross, botoxed into a positive rictus of plastic expression."

Carrie sighed. "It's not vanity. I just can't...face someone. I can't start all over and show myself like that, have someone look at me. And then, of course, I'd be wondering what they were thinking, wondering if they were disgusted."

"Well, then, you should definitely have gone to bed with Ray and seen how it all worked out, because Lord only knows you won't be seeing him again anyway." She made her way back into the bathroom.

"He's invited us over for a barbecue tomorrow," Carrie called after her. "And I've accepted."

Paige stuck her head back out the door. "Whatever possessed you to do that?"

****

Driving back to the ranch after dropping off Paige, nothing but the green lights of the dashboard and country music to accompany him, Jake's mind dwelt on the girl, how unpredictable and detached she was, a chameleon, but never a snake shedding its skin.

A snake? Hardly.

She wore her beauty uneasily, as if it weren't there, as if it were trivial. Yet that was part of her charisma, her detachment from everything and everybody, even herself. That and the sense he had of her vulnerability. Had she always been like that, or was it a consequence of her fiancé's death?

Turning down the ranch road, the pervasive blackness was not broken by lights on the horizon. Momentary panic set in. If his father were back, he would surely have left on the outside light for Jake. But as he pulled up to the parking space in front of the house, there was the old pickup, no lights, no motor on. The dogs had started yowling at his approach, but a shout of "shut up" got them to stop with a solitary whine.

Slamming his car door behind him, Jake started toward the house before catching sight of his father sitting in the dark of the cab, the presumably empty flask being twirled between his hands like a giant worry bead. Moonlight glinted through the windows on the silver of the container and threw a spark of reference, silhouetting his father against the darkness. Jake tapped on the glass then opened the cab door.

"Hey, pardner," his dad said. "You have a good night? You go dancing?"

He ignored the questions. "Come on, Dad, what are you doin' out here? Why aren't you inside?" He watched as his father swung his body around with a grunt and forced himself out. "You're drunk again, aren't you?"

"No-o-o, I am not." There was the denial of the accusation. "I just had a flask full, hardly enough Jack to get a man drunk, Jake." He started to the house, stumbling on the steps for a moment.

"Hardly?" Jake caught his father by the elbow and yanked open the screen door. "You mean to tell me you didn't have any drinks at the Lone Star?"

"Two."

But he was lying.

"I was on my best behavior with Carrie watching me like a damned hawk."

He flicked the light switch and the room came to life; the three dogs suddenly rose as one with small whines from their quiet wait. "And you didn't, maybe, stop over at Mulligan's on the way home…or any other bar?"

His father took a deep breath and faced him. "Listen. I've done fine these four years without you here to tell me what I can and cannot do, you got that? So, let's just leave things be, son. I managed before you got home, and before Miz Carrie Bennett arrived in Texas."

"Well, you sure were all fired up to go on over and apologize to her. Then I go over to see Paige and I find you're about to dance the night away. What happened? She step on your toes?"

"No, she didn't step on my toes—in any sense of the word." His father started to gather the dogs toward him and lead them out, Jake at his heels. "Fact is, I invited the two of them over for a barbecue tomorrow."

He stopped as if he were changing his mind, and headed to the kitchen instead.

Jake stood, hands on hips, as his father reached into the fridge and came out with a beer. He extended it to him, but Jake shook his head and waited as his dad snapped the pull-tab.

"You invited them over," he said at last. "That should be interesting."

"Well, you seemed pretty keen on Paige. The two of you ran off together like a herd of wild horses was at your heels. You gone off her already?" His dad patted one of the dogs who panted and wagged his tail expectantly.

"No, I haven't gone off—look, there's nothing between me and Paige, and there's not going to be anything between me and Paige. You just have to look at her to see that." Jake headed back toward the living room, his father and the dogs following.

"What the heck is that supposed to mean now?"

"It means Paige will go on back to her big city life, and I'll be but a vague memory of something she didn't care about in Texas. She as much as told me so."

His father stood as if he were trying to think this through, as if it were a calculation he were making in his head. "Well," he said at last. "Then a barbecue will be part of that vague memory as well." He headed the dogs down the hall.

Jake stood a moment before turning off the living room lights, listening to his father's faint mumbles as he steered the dogs out to the kennel and came back in through the porch. A few minutes later, he stopped for a second outside his father's door and listened to the predictable sounds of a nighttime routine. But there was no point in pursuing the matter, not the matter of drink, not Carrie, and certainly not Paige.

Paige.

He opened the door to his own room, greeted by the rumpled, unmade bed and the smell of sex.

It was going to be difficult to sleep tonight.

****

Carrie lay in the darkness, Paige's even breathing interspersed with the occasional sigh letting her know her daughter was sound asleep. No such respite enveloped Carrie; her mind was an open reel replaying the day, rethinking events. First Ray, then Paige, then Ray again. At some point, it struck her that her inability to relax with Ray and her incapacity to help Paige overcome Steven's death were related, the two were the same vital flaw in her own character. Her sense of failure increased the more she tried to reach out to Paige, to help her, to break through the barrier her daughter had cocooned around herself. And the more that a connection, an empathy, grew for Ray, the more she stood back. Or...

No, there was no use going over any of this. Barbecue tomorrow, good-bye, farewell, and New York on Monday.

Then at least one of her problems would be solved.

Chapter Four

"Miz Bennett? Paige? You all are not comin' riding today?"

Carrie stood by the car, Paige already on the driver side, when Ty Sheldon approached them. Dressed in his wrangler gear, complete with chaps and spurs, he made the perfect picture of the western cowboy. Only the scar running down his cheek left the portrait less than ideal. That and the way his eyes narrowed accusingly at her.

The beep of the car door sounded as her daughter slid in. "No, I'm afraid not, not today. We've been invited over to the Rocking R."

"Oh, well, I'm sorry to hear that." Ty studied his boots, as if considering whether to go on. "On two counts."

Her hand reached out for the door, but she stopped. "I beg your pardon?"

"I mean," he hesitated. "I'm sorry you're associating with the Ryders. You know, they're not the best people to be hanging around with."

"I..." Carrie stared at the young man, a deep dislike mixing with her discomfort. "I don't really think it's any of your business, Ty, whom I choose to mix with." She opened the door and started to get in.

"It's only, you know, Mr. Ryder has a real bad drink problem, and Jake, well, Jake uses drugs and all. You may not want your daughter mixing with that sort."

"Well, thanks for the warning, Ty, but I think we're both big girls and can handle ourselves for one more day." She heaved the door after her as the engine started up.

In the side mirror, she watched the wrangler as he sauntered off toward the stables. Aggravation deepened her breathing, along with a trace of uncertainty that he might be right.

Paige tugged down her seatbelt. "What did he want? What did he say?"

"He wanted to warn us Jake was a druggie."

Her daughter threw back her head and laughed. "Jake is a druggie? Oh, yeah, and I'm Cleopatra. Jake is no more a druggie than you are, Mother."

"Well, I don't know how you can be so very sure. It's well known a lot of soldiers use drugs to help them get through it all."

"That was Viet Nam. Things are different now. Anyway, he's not the type. I would know. Jake Ryder is as straight as the day is long."

Carrie caught Paige's annoyance with a quick scan. "Okay, I believe you," she conceded as the car reached the highway. "But he also said Ray was a drinker, and that we *do* know to be true."

"Fine. So he drinks. He's not an ax murderer. We're going to a frigging barbecue, and then we'll never see them again, so I don't think there is a problem. If you're concerned, I'll turn the car around, and you can phone him and cancel. You're the one who accepted."

"I'm not concerned. You asked me what Ty said, not what I thought." Carrie snapped on the radio, then smacked it off again. "What concerns me, if anything, is Ty butting into our business. He makes me nervous."

"Life makes you nervous, Mother. That's why you live through your books."

Her daughter kept her gaze on the road, avoiding her sideways glance. For a moment, Carrie turned to survey the scenery. Texas was in a constant state of drought, but the verdant field, colored with wildflowers, belied that. The clear, bright day should have made anyone happy, but Paige remained restive. Days like this were meant for sharing, yet it wasn't her, or even Jake, with whom Paige wanted to share this day.

"That's not true, Paige, and you know it." Her adamant voice brought her daughter back.

"Oh, yes it is. Why did you break up with what's his name, Charles, when he wanted to marry you? Because becoming a broker's wife wasn't the sort of romantic ending you envisaged for yourself. You went out with him for three years, and then decided married life in Greenwich wasn't the happy ending you imagined."

"I broke up with him because he expected me to do all the compromising and move to Greenwich, and I also realized all he wanted was me hanging on his arm to show off. 'Oh, this is Carrie, well known author.' Goodness, he was awful. Not to mention the fact he had a roving eye for younger women."

"It took you *three years* to realize this? Please! He loved you because you were successful, not to show you off. And if he looked at younger women, he probably felt lucky to have you instead." Paige groped with one hand in the driver's caddy before popping a mint in her mouth. "You think one of your perfect, toned, muscular heroes is going to come and throw you over his shoulder and take you away for mad, passionate love."

"Now you're just being ridiculous."

"Am I?"

Carrie took in a deep breath and sighed.

"Maybe a cowboy would do after all—he could throw you over his horse and gallop away with you—though I don't think rural Texas is quite your speed, Mother."

She flicked the radio back on. There was no point in continuing the discussion; Paige was made for the law, her arguments, so solid in her own eyes, were buoyed by her arrogance. The only thing for an opponent to do in the face of such an impermeable wall was to keep her mouth shut. Their relationship extended, at times, like an elastic band stretched to snapping point, then released again into a slack coalition of friendship and filial love. Yet, as it ran through Carrie's mind, there was some truth in her daughter's words. She could have worked in Greenwich as easily as anywhere else; that hadn't been the problem. The problem had been Charles. He was just too staid, too steady, too balanced—too damn unexciting. Everything had been so right, so perfect, so...as expected. No surprises, no spontaneity. Not that she had much time for the spontaneous these days.

"Here's the first turn."

Her daughter's voice wrenched Carrie back to the matter at hand. "Are you sure? I thought it was farther down."

"Positive. I remember that tree."

A giggle escaped her as Paige made the turn.

"What's so funny?" her daughter demanded.

Carrie suppressed a laugh. Farm-to-market roads, ranch roads; it certainly was a different world down here.

Paige acquiesced. "Yeah, I suppose it is sort of funny, finding a route by a tree. New York it ain't."

****

"Ohhh...OHHH!" men's voices cried out in unison just as Carrie put her hand on the doorbell.

"What in heaven's name was that?"

Jake appeared through the screen as Paige said, "Sport, no doubt."

The young man laughed. "Yeah, sorry, we're turning it off. Come on in."

It occurred to Carrie she had not seen the house in daylight. Now, looking around, it had a different aura, a friendlier demeanor than her last, nighttime visit. As she took notice of all this, she was suddenly aware of Ray standing in the hall entryway.

"Well, welcome back to the Rocking R," he said. "I see you found us all right."

"Paige recognized a tree. Then, of course, you're well signposted after that."

"Well done, Paige." There was an awkward moment before he continued. "Well, come on in. I've got the dogs kenneled outside so you won't get attacked. Can I get you something? Or are we going for that ride?"

"I was hoping to meet this Diablo you told me about." Carrie then questioned her daughter with a raised brow.

"Don't look at me, I'm ready." She spread her hands, displaying her western attire.

Next to her, the younger man nodded his approval and grabbed his hat off a hook by the door, handing another to his father. "This should be interesting," he mumbled half under his breath.

"Excuse me?" asked Paige.

"Oh, I'm just…"

"Come on down the back to the corral," Ray put in, saving his son. "Jake and I will saddle up."

Carrie and Paige followed the men down a hallway that had two rooms on either side before it reached another living area, a large, screened-in sunroom with both sitting and dining spaces, looking out onto pasture with the corrals and barns off to the right. The vista was breathtaking: blue-green rolling hills patched with stands of oak and carpets of wildflowers, colors that would no doubt change with the seasons. It took Carrie's breath away.

"It's so beautiful," she gasped. "I didn't know…" She sought Ray for an answer. "It's so lush…"

"We front on the Pedernales River so are pretty good for water. But we still have a drought problem most years. Gets too damn hot. It's only late April. You want to be here July or August when we can only ride early morning or late afternoon." There was a rancher's concern mixed with pride in his voice.

"Fancy waking up and seeing that every morning. You're so lucky."

"As if you don't have great views from your windows," Paige pointed out.

"I do have great views, but it's not the same." Carrie turned to Ray. "So, do deer come right up to the house?"

"Right up. They eat everything in sight. But they're

not the ones we hunt, unfortunately. The hunting operation is way at the other end of the property so it doesn't bother the horses."

Carrie continued to take in the view, memorizing the landscape.

"Come on, then. No use just looking at it from here when we can ride through it."

****

Astride his horse, Ray soon led the way at a lope with Carrie and the two others following. He had a sense of Jake's young blood coming to a simmer every time he looked at Paige, of an uneasiness his son had when he was near the girl. As the two had saddled up, he sensed Jake's restlessness, like a pot of water about to come to the boil. He was fairly sure his son had bedded the gal, a random act of sexual desire consummated after drought years in the army. Maybe that's all it was; maybe that's what it was for him as well, as far as Carrie was concerned. After all, what did either he or his son really know about the two women? Yet, every time he looked at Carrie, a sense of her vulnerability, mixed with a feeling something was beyond the wall she had built, drew him in like raw bait.

At a fork in the bridle path, he put his hand out and came to a stop. "Creek or pond?" he called back to Jake.

"Paige and I would like to take a run down to the lake, actually, Dad. You and Carrie can go—"

"We would?" Paige shifted in her saddle to look across at Jake, then grinned at her mother, mischief in her eyes. "Yeah, why don't you two go on and we'll meet up later. If that's all right with you, Ray?"

"That's fine." What were those two up to? "Ribs are marinating—the longer the better." He paused and glanced at Carrie. "If it's okay with your mom, of course."

Carrie shrugged. "She's a grown woman, Ray. She makes her own decisions. I don't mind."

"Great. We'll see you back around six, if that's okay?" Jake had a telling smile on his face, which almost made Ray laugh.

"We have an early plane—" She stopped short and sighed. The younger couple had taken off down the other trail at a gallop. "I hope…" She exchanged a look with Ray. "I don't want him to be hurt."

"Hey, you know what kids are like today. He can take care of himself."

Carrie rode her horse up alongside his to walk them toward the pond. "Paige knew Steven for five years before he died. They were very close. Well, they would be, getting ready to get married, as I think I told you. She hasn't been the same since his death. This disdain, the sarcasm, the mockery of everything wasn't there so much before. I mean, she was always self-satisfied and independent, self-assured, but never like this, deprecating everything, critical—derisive. It's as if she lost a part of herself with his death. Sometimes I just don't know how to reach her. Sometimes, I just feel as if I've lost her for good, that she'll never get over this."

"When were they going to be married?"

"Oh, not until after law school graduation. I'm hoping…possibly without reason of course…by then she'll be fine, the date won't matter. But who knows? They'd met in the second year at Yale and decided to go traveling for a year together before going on to Penn

Law, and *that* despite the fact Steven was accepted to Harvard. He wanted to be with her. Then this happened, the leukemia. Paige went berserk. They both took off from school, he because of the illness, she to look after him. She moved into his parents' home and helped nurse him." Carrie drew in a breath and shook her head with the memory. "At times, they thought he would pull through, he would go back, but it was too pernicious. It was all over in eight months. Beginning to end, diagnosis to death. Eight months."

Ray cleared his throat. "Makes you wonder...makes you wonder just what the good Lord has in mind sometimes."

"Makes you wonder if there is a good Lord after all."

Silence stretched between them. Ray waited patiently for her to continue, wishing to get her back to the here and now.

"I'd hate to think Jake expected more of this acquaintance," she finally said. "Paige is really not ready, not for him, not for anyone. I'm hoping she'll go back to school in the fall, throw herself into her studies—law school is so hard, so difficult. Maybe sometime, in the future, when she's ready, she'll meet someone whom she'll be able to love—not to make her forget Steven, but just someone with whom she can find happiness again. You know, you see her now and she's this prickly, smart-assed girl, but, as I said, she wasn't always like that. Well, not quite like that, anyway," she went on with a small frown. "She's just so unhappy."

Something inside Ray went cold at the thought of Paige's loss. Having lost Robbie, he knew exactly what she felt—the pain, the anger, the unwillingness to go on. He shook his head to try to remove that anguish as the horses splashed through a creek. Birdsong competed with Carrie's voice as a rise appeared on the other side. Ray could feel his horse pulling to go faster as they climbed the ridge. Then there was a splash behind them, a fish jumping for a fly. Ahead, a meadow opened up at the top, wild flowers spreading in jewel colors like an abstract carpet.

"Can you gallop?" he asked.

"Of course I can gallop."

"Well, then..."

He raced her through the pasture, the rhythmic hoof beats and heavy breathing of the horses pounding out a one-note drumming until another crest was reached and the descent lay ahead. It was release, his way of letting go, and almost as good as the drink at doing so.

Down below was a small body of water, like an emerald set in tarnished green copper, unexpected, almost mystical. As they pulled up the horses, he glanced at Carrie and, suddenly, he felt that the smile that now lit her face was better than the ride and a drink combined.

"How lovely! I thought it was the kids who were going to a lake?"

"This is a pond, actually. It has plant life which gives it that vibrant green color."

"How wonderful. Is this all yours?"

"All mine. I guess. It's still part of the ranch, if that's what you're asking. Come on."

The horses picked their way down the next hill and followed a trail to the edge of the pond. Ray dismounted and tied his horse, then went to hold the other horse's bridle as Carrie dismounted, but she was down before he got there.

Turning to face him, she stopped, leaning back against the mare, breathing in the perfumed air.

It had been a long time since he'd seen anyone so lovely, someone who looked so right in this setting and, for a moment, he felt at peace. He leaned in to kiss her, his face hovering just inches away, before he stood back again. "You know," he said, "I sort of feel like I need permission to do this."

She was silent for the longest time.

He met her steady gaze, raising a brow in query once more.

"I'm sorry," she said at last. "I mean, you shouldn't feel that way."

"Good."

He leaned in again, his lips hesitating, brushing her mouth before he met her. He held back his yearning and remained gentle, tender, before he let his hands come up to hold her, before his tongue searched her mouth, and he ended by grasping her to him, holding her close before he felt her yield. He stepped back to study her, the late afternoon sun lighting her, reflecting in her eyes like flames on the pond water.

"I'm going back tomorrow, Ray. This is…useless. Really. I must go."

He took a few steps away, leading her horse to a tree where he tied it. "You know when I first decided I liked you, really liked you?" he asked, turning back to her. "When you refused to let me drive the damned pickup, even when you found out it was manual. Even though you knew you were going to make a pig's dinner of it, even though you knew it was more than you could handle and you didn't have the faintest idea what you were doing, you just insisted on driving that dang thing. And then you laughed so much at yourself after Dexter stopped us. I thought then, what the hell kinda woman is this? What the hell kinda person just insists on making a damned fool of herself, doesn't give a hoot, just to make a point, just for the principle of it? Somewhere inside of you, Carrie, is a heckuva lot of courage, a heckuva brave gal. I just wish you could find her."

"What has bravery, or courage, got to do with this, Ray? I must go back—I have a life. I have responsibilities. Just like you. It may surprise you to know that women—"

"Oh, now. It doesn't surprise me. That's not what we're talking about and you well know it. I'm talkin' about the fact you won't let yourself go. It's almost as if you're afraid of life."

Carrie took a breath, started to say something, then stopped and started once more. "Do you know Ty Sheldon warned me about you and Jake today? He said you had a very bad drinking problem and Jake had a drug problem."

Ray stopped cold. He tried to think of Ty and Robbie, all those years ago. Why would the boy tell such a lie? He shook his head as if pieces of a puzzle would fall into place. "Did he? Why ever would he say a thing like that?" A breeze blew up, releasing the scent of the flowers. Ray paced a few steps before adjusting his hat and turning back to Carrie. "Okay. I admit I like my drink. But you have to know it's under control—I told you, I never drink hard until after work. Fine, that's me. But Jake with a drug problem? Never. Why would he say such a thing?"

Carrie took in the view of the pond. "I don't know. But I thought you should know."

"Okay. So, now I know. And what…what does that have to do with Miz Carrie Bennett, with us?"

"Ray, there is no 'us.' I have to go back," she repeated. "I *have* to go back. I have a life—in New York. And you have a life here. You've known me for all of three days."

"Can I ask you then why you just let me kiss you?"

Her hand went instinctively to her face as her gaze met his. "I have no idea. But…I would like to know, sometime, you're well, you and Jake are doing fine, but that's it."

He took this in, digested it like a rotten meal, and like a bad meal wanted to spit it back.

"Okay," he said at last. "I'm sorry. I'm sorry for you and I'm sorry for me. I thought, what with you all going back home tomorrow and all, I should speak…I couldn't let the moment pass, you know? I ought to lay my cards on the table so to speak. But I see there wasn't any point in it, now was there? So, you just go on back to New York, to your city view, and your fine friends and all and—"

"Why is it me who's the villain here? Why, Ray? Why me?" Carrie went to grab the reins of her horse. "You damn well come to New York then!" She got a leg in the stirrup, and after a hop, got back up in the saddle. Her teeth gritted as she gazed down at him. "I was looking forward to this barbecue. Why…why did you have to say all that? Why did you have to ruin it?"

****

Jake ran a finger from between Paige's breasts

90

down to her stomach. "Your skin is like satin. It's so smooth."

"Oh, please. Think of a better line. That's so cheesy." She rolled onto her side, her gaze meeting his, and reached out to jerk up some grass.

He stretched out on the blanket he'd brought rolled behind his saddle, their clothes scattered now in the brush. He stared at the lithe figure beside him and reached out to touch her, gently cupping the curve of her breast.

Paige grabbed his hand for a moment and held it, winding her fingers through his as she thoughtfully studied it as if it were some precious artwork. Suddenly she ventured, "You remember how you told me that first night that Robbie's death wasn't your father's fault but yours?"

Jake took his hand away and sat up. Suspicious of where this was going, he let out a tentative, "Yeah?"

"Why do you think that?"

He plucked some grass then stared at her, trying to permeate her mind, figure what she wanted to know exactly. "Because I told him to go, I insisted. He was getting himself into trouble, and I saw it as a way out. So, I told him to go."

"What sort of trouble?"

"It was…" He took in a deep breath. "Trouble, just trouble, Paige."

Her brow creased. "Why don't you tell your father then? If for no other reason than to stop him from drinking so much."

Jake huffed. "Because he'll ask me for an explanation. He'll dig until he gets one. He has this picture of Robbie as the perfect son, the gentle boy who could just about talk to horses, the hero who died defending his country and saving the lives of his buddies. But that's not who Robbie was—or at least not all of it. He had his faults like anyone."

"But he's dead. He's gone, Jake," she pushed. "Don't you think it's better for Ray to know the truth now rather than go on blaming himself forever?"

"How do you want to remember Steven? Would you want to remember the arguments, his final illness, whatever bad times y'all had? Or do you want to remember the good? You don't want someone coming along now and maybe saying nasty things about him, stuff you don't ever want to know, don't ever want to hear like maybe he fooled around with someone else, or whatever. I'm not saying he did, so don't go getting that sour look on your face, Paige. But you wouldn't want to know it now, would you?"

He could see he had touched a raw nerve in her as her face crumpled with a shot of pain.

She turned away and curled up, hugging her knees like a child.

Jake leaned over and brought her to face him, then brushed her lips with a light kiss.

"You're not in love with me, are you? You had so better not be in love with me, Jake."

He jerked his hand back, stung into the realization she would never be his.

Standing suddenly, he grabbed his jeans and shimmied into them, yanking up his fly. "Who would want to be in love with you, Paige? I can't imagine."

She sat up and stared at him. "Bastard! You bastard!"

"Sorry. Sorry," he returned, remembering her loss.

He sat back down and plucked the grass for a moment as she stood and struggled into her clothes. "I didn't mean it…You're just—"

"It doesn't matter. Never mind. This was sex. We both had a good time, that's it. You're not in love with me."

"You're telling me what I feel?" He let a handful of grass fly off on the wind before leaning to grab hold of her leg. "Sit down. Sit down, for heaven's sake." He waited for her to find her spot on the blanket, watching as she crossed her legs and leaned back on hands spread like webs, anger still creasing her face. Then quietly, calmly, he said, "Tell me what Steven was like."

Suspicion crossed her face, as if by telling she might be giving away some dark secret of her innermost soul. Jake suspected she hadn't talked about her fiancé for a long time, not in any evocative way, and it would be difficult, but his desire to know the ghost against whom he was competing was stronger than his fear of hurting her.

"Please. Tell me." He ran his hand down her arm as if he were calming a nervous pony as he let her find her moment.

"He was bright, highly intelligent…but not showy with it. And he was funny. He just somehow managed to see humor in even the most awful, desperate situations, even when he knew he was dying. And…he would make fun of me when I got too serious about something. Nothing fazed him, even the illness. He took it as just another hurdle to be got over." She stopped, tears beginning to bloom, which she swatted away with the back of her hand. "He liked to read, and to travel, and to play tennis and swim. He liked classical music and hip hop and just about everything in between. He could talk to just about anyone, mix with any kind of crowd and be right at home..." The sobs started then, racking her small frame as she bent over clutching herself, swaying with the pain. "And he loved me, just the way I am, knowing all my faults. Loved me unquestioningly."

Jake reached across and gathered her to him once more, held her against his chest and let the anger and the hurt work themselves out as he stroked her head and her back, rocking her gently in his arms. He wanted her more then, wanted to ease her pain and her grief, wanted to be the one she sought in her dark hours. Yet he would never have her, not the way Steven had.

For a moment, he wondered if she had ever cried before, ever let herself go like this, or whether she had put on a brave face like the soldiers he'd witnessed. Had she sat quietly at the funeral? Stood stolidly at the gravesite while others roared out their grief?

Just how long had all this been cooped up inside her? How long had she waited to let this come out?

Chapter Five

Carrie stared absently as the earth fell away—people, buildings, cars and roads became smaller as the plane left behind the patchwork of greens and browns that were the surrounds of Austin. She let out a long breath, thinking through that argument with Ray at the lake, a small ache niggling her, eating at her.

Inside the aircraft, hermetically sealed into a private world, she felt the plane tip and glide and straighten again, gaining height after take-off. The chemical air poured in through vents while cabin staff made various announcements, announcements little heeded if the laughter coming from two rows behind was anything to go by.

She studied Paige for a moment, now settled into her first class seat, her eyes closed against the mephitic air, a magazine lying unread in her lap. Had the trip done her any good? What was her relationship with Jake?

Her daughter opened her eyes briefly to the clink of ice against glass coming from the galley, then closed them again until a flight attendant offered a dish of nuts and a drink.

"Well, thank you for coming with me." Carrie studied her daughter as the plane lifted through clouds and the Texas landscape disappeared.

Paige's head was back against her seat, eyes now

wide open in contemplation. "Sure, any time." She was watching the flight attendants at the front, gabbing and laughing. "You haven't said anything about dinner last night, the barbecue. You and Ray had soured a bit. And then he seemed to be hitting the booze like a man trying to forget."

"Well." Carrie struggled with her seatbelt to be able to bend over and reach her bag. "I hope he does forget. Forget me that is. He sort of…how shall I say?...*declared* himself. I had to make it clear I was going back to New York, and I don't think he was pleased." She drew out a book to mark the end of the conversation and opened it on her lap.

"Well, that's an interesting turn of events." Her daughter gave her a hard stare before reaching across and yanking the book out of her hands. "As I said, I don't think rural Texas is quite your style, Mother. On the other hand, I don't really know what your style is. You know, I don't think you really want a partner, do you?"

"I haven't time, Paige. I have a screenplay to work on and another book to write. Relationships need time, nurturing. They don't just happen unless you can spend the time together." She reflected on this for a moment. "And I certainly wasn't going to stick around for a man I hardly know, had just met. If that was what he wanted, which I think it was."

"And, of course, you can't possibly write just anywhere. I mean, Texas would be an absolute bummer, wouldn't it? All that scenery to distract you."

"Now you're being sarcastic."

"No, no, really," Paige went on. "I mean, the crickets and frogs might keep you up at night and, of course, out there in the country there is always the chance of some stray bullet taking you down."

Carrie snorted with a guffaw. "So, does that mean you and Jake have a thing going?"

"The only thing we have going, Mom, is nude swimming in the lake and some great sex. He's a sweet boy, and that's about all I can say about Jake Ryder." She handed back the snatched book and sat watching, apparently waiting for the snack trolley to return.

Carrie sat with the book opened in her lap, a realization growing like a seed with water—she and her daughter were both lying, lying to themselves and to each other. Paige had feelings for Jake, but was suppressing them, perhaps out of guilt for her love of Steven; she wouldn't let herself go, fall in love again so soon after Steven's death. As for herself, if there had been more time, if she had lived closer to the Texan, if she had had less work, she and Ray might have made a go of it, might have embarked on something meaningful. But it was too complicated, more effort was required than she could offer.

Or was that a lie, too?

Was she just too damn scared, scared of exposing herself both emotionally and physically, scared of eventual rejection? Perhaps her daughter had been right, after all: life was so much better, so much easier in her books.

"I did find out something interesting about those two, however," Paige went on suddenly. "Ray drinks because he blames himself for his son Robbie's death."

"I know. He more or less told me so himself."

"Yes, but so does Jake—blame himself for Robbie's death that is. Apparently, they both insisted

Robbie join the army, but for different reasons."

"Well, what were Jake's reasons? Do you know?"

"Something about getting Robbie away from some trouble he was in. I don't know anything more, couldn't get it out of Jake. But it must have been serious, don't you think, if he had to join the damned army to get away."

"I wonder…"

"I know. Ty. The evil Ty. I'm wondering if he has something to do with it, too."

****

Jake slammed his Suburban's door behind him and took the porch steps two at a time up to the office at the Lone Star.

Doris was busy checking out a guest and gave Jake a tentative glance before going back to the bill in front of her.

"Hey, Doris," he called, leaning on the counter to regain her attention. "Can you just tell me which cabin the Bennett ladies are in?"

"No cabin. Gone. Checked out late last night and took off for the airport early morning before the office opened." She went back to her guests.

Jake tapped the counter in frustration. "Jeez," he said under his breath. "Dammit!" He took a few steps back toward the door before turning back to her. "I don't suppose they left any messages, any note or nothing?"

"Miz Bennett left me an autographed copy of *Sunshine Tomorrow,* and I am not parting with that." She gave Jake a smile. "Sorry."

The only response was the door wheezing shut.

Jake stood on the steps for a second, defeat causing

inertia. What had he been thinking? Why did he bother? Seeing Paige one last time was not going to accomplish anything, was not going to achieve one damn thing. She had left him her cell number, but it seemed meaningless now. He was nothing more to her than some casual sex, some vacation romance—if it could even be called that.

"Well, well," said a familiar voice. "Look who's here."

"Ty." He scowled and made a start to his car.

"Guess that Bennett girl didn't heed my warning, huh?"

Jake stopped, hands on hips, disgust at the wrangler curling his lip. "What the hell do you mean?"

"Just what I said. I saw it as my...hmmm, civic duty...to warn her about your drug problem, Jake. Didn't want no fine lady associating with an addict, now did we?"

"Why, you bastard!" His fist slammed Ty backwards into the car to slide down to the dirt where Jake jumped him.

"Hey, hey, hey," yelled Doris, her hands gathering his collar and hauling him back. "What in tarnation is going on here, for Pete's sake?"

Jake struggled to his feet, ragged breaths coming as he shook himself free of Doris' vice-like grip and squinted down at Ty. "I would have thought better of you, Doris, than to employ vermin around your guests. Maybe you ought to reconsider your wrangler."

"Now, Jake, don't you go telling me who to employ and who not to. I got no complaints against Ty, whatever his past may be."

Sheldon finally heaved himself up by the car door handle and shook himself into a semblance of arrangement.

"I think, Jake, you best be on your way now, son."

"Well, I just got a little bit of business with him, Doris, before he goes." Ty's voice was an offensive mix of courtesy toward his employer and threats to Jake. "If y'all don't mind."

Doris gulped a deep breath and sighed heavily. "Well. All right, but don't you boys start fighting again. I won't have that, you hear? And you, Jake, you get going as soon as this 'discussion' is through." She moved off, giving them a last glimpse before she disappeared back into her office.

"What is it you want, Sheldon?" Jake stood, his fists ready at his side.

"See, I need a little pick up done..."

"You can forget it." Jake reached for the door of his car.

"Not so fast. Unless, of course, you want your daddy finding out about Robbie's interests other than Arab horses." A wide smile spread across Ty's face as he noted Jake's hand release the door handle.

"Why don't you get a mule, Ty? I thought you guys got Mexicans to do the running for you nowadays."

"I did. That's what I been using these past few years. But they keep getting caught, and that costs me. Robbie never got caught. And you in that bright and shiny new army uniform of yours—well, what could be better?"

"Forget it!" Jake clenched his fists.

"I will...but I don't think your daddy will be able to forget once he knows the truth about Robbie. It would just break his heart, wouldn't it, to know his son was running drugs up from Mexico for me. His perfect son. Just like you, Jake. Just like you."

****

Jake peered at his mother through the screen door. A long stream of smoke came from between her lips before she stuck the cigarette back into a corner of her mouth, and gazed at him through the mesh of the screen as she might a monkey in a cage, with curiosity and some contempt.

"Took you long enough, Jake," she said, pushing the door open. "Come in." There was a note of reluctance in her voice, a disinclination to actually admit him, but she led the way into her apartment living room and motioned to a sofa. "Have a seat."

"Who the hell is it, Leigh Anne?" a voice crackled from the back room.

"Go on back to sleep, Cody," she yelled.

Jake settled himself into a worn armchair as the acrid smell of cigarettes and cold cooking grease hit him.

"I wondered when you might show up. Thought it might be a bit sooner than this, Jake."

For a long time, he studied his mother. Her long blonde hair, once natural and well kept, hung in uncombed strands down her back, while her face showed the remains of last night's make up. He remembered the photos of her taken when she was younger, photos of her winning barrel racing, of being Rodeo Queen, of a young girl who looked like she could take on the world. A couple of rolls in the hay in the back of a horse trailer had it all ended, forced her to settle before she was ready, take on responsibilities she didn't care to have. And while his father, to Jake's knowledge, had grown and matured and faced up to his side of the bargain, his mother had been forever looking backward, dreaming of escape, harking back to her glory days and wearing everyone down with complaints and unhappiness. Her life had been built on 'coulda beens' and resentment for what she saw as lost chances, lost dreams, while his dad had thought ahead to what could be, to building a future. The surprise, to Jake, was it had taken so long, had taken Robbie's death, to finally drive them apart.

"I had…a friend I was seeing while she was here," he white-lied. "And I was settling in. It's not easy coming home, Ma."

"Oh, no. And of course your 'friend' takes priority over your own mother." She plunked into a seat and lit another cigarette from the end of her burning one before stubbing the remains out in an overflowing ashtray by her side. "So, how are you, anyway? Alive at least, I see."

Jake ran his hand over his stubble before cracking his knuckles. He studied the dirty furnishings, crumbs and garbage on a dining table, piles of old magazines, laundry draped over a chair. "You ever think about cleaning?" he asked.

"I haven't got Mabel, now have I? And your father refuses to give me any money for living expenses so…"

"That's not true, Ma, and you know it. Dad said he offered you a large lump sum so you can go your own way and do your own thing, so you won't be tied to him forever. What the hell do you want alimony for anyway? You wanted out, so take it."

"Well. He didn't offer me quite enough."

"Lawyers'll get the most of it if you let it go on too

long. In addition to which, if you take the damned alimony and you want to remarry, you'll lose it, won't you? Take the money, for heaven's sake. Make a clean break."

His mother stood suddenly. "Is this why you've come? As your father's representative, his—what's the word?—his *envoy*? To appeal on his behalf?"

"Of course not! Sit down," Jake ordered. "I came to see you. I'm just trying to talk some sense into you." He waited until she sat again, smoke rings bouncing into the air like soap bubbles from a child's blower. "How have you been, anyway?"

"Fine, just fine. I got the horses stabled over at Dawson's in return for giving lessons out there on a Sunday, and I'm doing a bit of bar tending at the Rodeo Club here in Austin. Sure beats living out there in the middle of nowhere, never seeing anyone, never going out."

"What are you talking about? You went out. Dad took you out every Saturday. He spent his life trying to please you." Disgust riddled him while an ache at feeling that way cut through his heart.

"Trying to please me? Ha! That's a good one. Ray Ryder never pleased anyone but himself and that's a fact. Trying to please me..." She stubbed out the cigarette.

Jake sat forward, his restlessness growing. The conversation with Ty had made him feel like a pressure cooker about to explode. "I saw Ty Sheldon—"

"Oh, what's he up to these days?"

"Working at the Lone Star. As a wrangler. Ma, he's...he's not the good friend you think he is."

Jake weighed it up. If he could tell his mother, if he

could get it out, maybe he could go on to tell his father. He would *have* to tell his father or she certainly would. Yet somehow, the words wouldn't come. Whatever their relationship, he hadn't the capacity to sit there and tell his mother her older son had not been the person she had thought, the person she had known. He sensed his mother waiting for something more, some explanation, but the words were lost. "Sorry," he said, making a move to leave. "I have to go. I just wanted to see you and know you're okay."

His mother sat staring up at him before grabbing her pack of cigarettes and tapping out another one. She took her time lighting it, inhaling deep and watching the smoke rise like a genie from a bottle. "Why is it you really came, Jake? You didn't want to see me. Was it to get me to sign Ray's papers? Or to tell me something else? 'Cause it sure as hell wasn't concern for my health."

Jake stood towering over her, the mother without maternal instincts, the woman he hardly knew. He tried to feel some connection, some semblance of love or admiration or pride as he felt so often about his father, but there was nothing.

"No, Ma. None of that," he said at last. "I guess I just wanted you to know I'm all right."

He bent to peck her on the forehead and let himself out.

****

Sunset was draining color from the day like an old fading photograph. Ray sat in his armchair in the front room, so clear headed it almost hurt. He contemplated the mess he had made of the barbecue because of his argument with Carrie, and pondered even harder how he found himself so drawn to the dang woman. She was highly attractive, yes, even if it was in a manicured sort of way, but there was something else. He loved the way she didn't really take herself seriously, loved sparring with her, and the way she so easily fit in.

Well, she was back in New York by now, so that was the end of that.

On the other hand, if he could just get over this hurdle, stop drinking...

Outside, the hum of the Chevy's engine came to a halt and, realizing the blue hour of twilight was closing in, he reached to turn on a light. The dogs got up as one, listening to Jake's approaching footsteps crunching on the gravel, then settled back at Ray's feet, somnolent in the late April heat.

"Mabel left you some meatloaf and potatoes," he called out to his son as the door opened. "I had mine." He went on looking up at Jake. "Good. As usual." His hand absently stroked one of the dog's heads; the Lab let out a low moan of pleasure.

Jake's gaze darted to the table, no doubt looking for the beer or the bottle of Jack, but nothing was there. His brow wrinkled in doubt as he glared down. "You sober?" he asked in disbelief.

"As a judge." Ray took a deep breath as if coming to some conclusion after a prolonged altercation. "May not be for long, though. The jury is still out."

He waited for some reply from Jake, but his son only marched past him into the kitchen. He listened as the fridge opened and a plate clinked as it was stuffed into the microwave.

"I'm trying to see how long I can make it," Ray called though the door. "Maybe the way to do it is a little longer each night."

"I don't think so, Dad. Starting later just means starting later, going to sleep later, getting up later probably as well. You have to stop cold turkey. Maybe I should clear the stuff out. How about that?"

"If you clear the stuff out, I can just buy more. Plus, I want to know I can face temptation." He gave his hand to the dog who licked it and barked, delighted at the salt.

"Did you feed them?" Jake stood in the doorway.

"'Course I fed them." He bent to rub the other dog's stomach, and the canine rolled in ecstasy. "You see your mama?"

"Yeah. She…"

"She's living with someone. You don't have to worry, I already knew it." A second passed. "So what? I wish them well. Let her marry the bastard and solve all my problems."

"Don't think there's much hope, Dad." The microwave bell chimed and Jake sauntered back to the kitchen.

Ray got to his feet and clapped his hands for the dogs to get up. "Gonna take them out to the kennel. You fix yourself out in the sunroom and I'll join you in a minute."

He sauntered down the hallway, dogs at his heels, reluctantly following—like the condemned headed to the gallows. He flicked on the outside floodlight and, as he knocked open the screen, they paraded out toward their second home. Spotting a rubber ball, he decided to tire them out good. He threw the toy; Crockett beat all contenders to come roaring back, suddenly awake and proud as punch, strings of saliva dangling either side of his mouth. Ray knelt and pet him, taking the ball, shaking it free of the wet before throwing it again.

The last remnants of sunset burned through the trees, streaks of deep cerise and amethyst coloring the sky. It was a beautiful view; his forefathers had chosen well and his awareness of time, of generations that had lived and died here filled him with a sense of history, of the agelessness of the land upon which he stood. Carrie would fit in here; the way she had stood in the sunroom gaping at it all, taking it all in, she belonged here.

Crockett stood waiting, winner once again, and Ray gently took the ball from his mouth and put it down on the stoop before leading the way to the kennel. He recalled how Leigh Anne had insisted the dogs sleep outside the house. *"I don't want some slobbery wet thing licking me in the morning,"* she had grumbled, and he had relented to please her, done anything to please, to keep her quiet, for almost thirty years.

He closed the door to the kennel and saw Jake settling himself at the sunroom table when the craving for alcohol hit him. "Think I'll have that drink now," he said as he came in and stomped some dirt off his boots. "Think it's time for that beer."

"No, it isn't, Dad. Sit with me while I eat. Look, there's Carrie's business card. Did you think about emailing her?"

"It's too early yet. They just left." Ray lugged out a chair and sat. He took the card in his hand and glanced at it before flicking it between his fingers. "No phone number. Just an email address. I guess—" He stopped suddenly and got up.

Jake stopped eating.

Ray caught the look of concern on his son's face

before he headed back down the hallway.

"You're not going to get drunk, are you?" His son's words followed him like one of the dogs.

Ray strolled back to stand in the doorway, cell phone in hand. He looked at the screen. "You say it was her phone you used to call me? Not Paige's?"

"No, it was hers. Why, you clever old dog. Son of a gun—if you're not smarter than you look!"

Ray laughed. "Well. There's only one non-Texas area code on this, and I should think that has to be it, 'specially seein' as how it's got Thursday as the call date. Not blocked. Well, I'll be... Maybe I don't need that drink after all."

****

Jake sat in his room with the phone in his hand, then put it back on his desk. His door was open and he could hear the snap of the newspaper pages turning, envisaging his father sitting there under the lamp, reading glasses perched on his nose, quietly content on the outside but a turmoil within. He could almost see the internal struggle. What could he do? Make it worse, tell him everything now, shatter his picture of his dead son? Send him right back to the bottle? No. If his father was trying so hard to get his head straight, there was no way he was going to give him this bit of news.

He picked up the phone again just as the scribbles of Paige's contact information caught his eye. The phone went back into its cradle as he lifted the sheet of paper and stared at it, as if by some form of subliminal osmosis he could make contact with the girl. Oh, lord. She had taken a bite out of him, that was certain. Jake tossed the paper back on his desk. Not ringing her was going to take almost more strength than the call he was about to make.

Turmoil bordering on nausea caused his stomach to lurch. He sat trying to think it through once more, the possibilities, the outcomes, and the alternatives. It was just like Iraq. He had learned you had to kill or be killed. And once you had done the deed, it became easier; there was even an excitement to it, an excitement now lacking in his normal life. But was that a reason to acquiesce to Ty's demands?

His father called, "Good-night," and his footsteps rang down the hall to his room. His dad was going to bed sober for the first time in more years than Jake could figure.

He lifted the phone once more and tapped in the number. A somewhat indistinct "hello?" was an answer, to which he just said, "Okay, Ty. You win."

****

As far as Paige was concerned, the Bennett New York apartment demonstrated success without being ostentatious. Snagging a large swath of a corner on Central Park West, the rooms either overlooked the park or the nearby Museum of Natural History. Most people would consider it beautifully decorated, well-appointed and, in real-estate-broker-speak, 'a gem.' But to her mother, this 'gem' was nothing more than a place to live. Paige knew now that her mother enjoyed her success only in so far as it provided well for the two of them, and proved her mother was self-sufficient, independent and in no need of anyone else in her life. Principally, it 'got back' at Paige's father. Her mom had the apartment, the beach house, the cars and all the other accouterments he might have provided had their married life together continued—and she had got it all on her own.

Paige never really worried about those things. She'd taken this life for granted: the good schools, the summers in the Hamptons, the expensive vacations, the designer clothes, all of it was nothing more or less than what her friends had. A child while her mother had still struggled, she had never been aware of the gradual changes in their finances, her mother's increasing popularity as an author, or even her mother's newfound poise and confidence. What this had all meant as far as Paige was concerned was she *could* be anything she wanted to be, and she *should* be totally dependent on herself alone. To this end, her mother had sent her off to boarding school at age thirteen. With five years there, plus four years at Yale, followed after a gap year by the first two years and beginning of the third at UPenn Law, it had been a long time since she had lived at home.

And she was *not* enjoying it. However much freedom she had to come and go as she pleased, however much independence she had, she was *not* enjoying it.

Looking down the hallway at her mother's figure slightly hunched over her computer, the intense concentration on her writing, Paige had a vision of herself as being useless—and bored. Friends were busy with internships at firms or travel abroad and would head back to school or jobs. She had to come to a decision about her own future.

"Are we moving to the beach soon?" She slouched in the doorway of her mother's study.

"Oh. Memorial Day weekend I should think. Unless you want to go sooner?" Her mom reviewed her computer screen momentarily to finish some writing. "*Do* you want to go sooner?"

"Not sure. But then, I'm not sure of anything these days. Anyway, it's only two weeks away. Maybe we should go this weekend?"

"If you like. What do you want to do for dinner?"

"Eat." She met her mother's exasperated gaze with a smirk. "Seems I can no longer make decisions. I think my brain died with Steven."

Her mother let the comment pass without acknowledging it. "Shall I send out?"

"Sure. Send out. How about some Tex-Mex?" She saw her mother quickly glance back at the screen. "Do you think about him? Ever? I mean…"

"I hardly knew the man, Paige. I assume it's Ray you're talking about." Her gaze ran down the text on her computer, avoiding Paige's scrutiny. "Do you think about Jake?"

She carefully mulled over this. Not such a simple soul, not just a good ol' country boy, Jake was more complex. An enigma of sorts. A puzzle. She had exchanged numbers with him and promises to keep in touch, yet she wasn't sure she wanted…oh, yeah. *Why lie to yourself?* She was curious about him. If nothing else.

"Yes," she said at last, more truthful than her mother. "Yes, I do. But not romantically, not how you think. Just…he was sort of mixed up, or worried or confused about his father and stuff. Maybe I just felt sorry for him."

She waited for some response, some agreement, but her mother still faced the screen, a hand across her mouth. Her face had folded, closed off its expression in

111

a way Paige did not recognize, with a look that reflected pain.

"Are you all right?" she asked.

"Yeah, yeah, of course I am. Let's order in." Her mother's hand still covered her mouth as if it would stop her from saying something wrong. "I'm not in the mood for eating out or cooking. And let's move out to the beach. Tomorrow."

****

Jake stood by his car at the service entrance to the Lone Star, a soft rain laving him as Ty's pickup came bumping down the road. He slouched against his Chevy as the other man climbed out of his cab, a snarling grin on his face.

"Sort of thought you might call. Being such a good son and all. Too bad I couldn't meet you sooner. Had some business I needed to clear up."

"Why the hell don't you run your own drugs, Ty? Why don't you just leave us alone?"

"Us? Your brother made good money out of this, and so can—"

"I don't want your goddamn money. I want you to do your own dirty work." Jake didn't hold out much hope for this, but he said it anyway.

"Can't, I'm afraid. Border guards and police all have me on a list. Won't work."

"All right, let's get on with this then. Just give me the address and instructions, or directions or whatever and let's get this over with. And I want your word this is the last time, otherwise, I'm not going."

Ty laughed. "Oh, you're going to take my word for it an' all?"

"Well, fine. Thanks for pointing out how

112

untrustworthy you are. So, I'm *telling* you, you bastard—this *is* the last time. I do the run once, and that's it. You expecting anything more from me, you can forget it." A chill similar to those he'd experienced in Iraq went through him. It was just like going on patrol. He leaned back against the car.

Ty stared at Jake with disgust. He dragged a sheet from the back pocket of his jeans and handed it to him. "Memorize the name and address then destroy it. You go down to the Eagle Pass Bridge—"

"I know how the hell to get there."

"Good. There's been a change of plans, so you don't need to go down now 'til the end of June, but listen to me, don't change your mind, Jake. You change your mind or go to the police and you'll regret it to your dying day. I swear. I mean it, don't change your mind."

****

As Carrie gathered together the few summer things she kept at the apartment, she considered the missed opportunities of her life. There hadn't been many missed chances, she had to give herself that. As far as work was concerned, she had grabbed every option that came her way. Okay, so there had been a few readings she'd refused to do, a few book signings she had neglected, but for the most part, her career had been a steady stream of successes, a carefully planned progression of steps vigilantly taken.

Her private life was quite another matter.

It wasn't her refusal to marry Charles that had been a missed possibility; a marriage to him would have proved a huge mistake. But earlier. When she was young and just divorced and rejected man after man, maybe those dates could have led to something lasting, of value, if she had just let them.

She threw another summer blouse in her suitcase when her cellphone rang. "Paige, I think that's on the kitchen table. Can you get it for me, please?"

She heard her daughter's greeting and then, "Oh! What a surprise! No, it's her phone. Just a moment, I'll get her."

Paige entered the bedroom, cellphone held aloft. Carrie gave her daughter a questioning glance, but got only a smile in return. *Who is it?* she mouthed, but Paige just handed her the phone and walked away. A quick peep at the screen displayed a number Carrie didn't recognize.

"Hello?" she said rather tentatively.

"Well, that's about the most dang suspicious 'hello' I ever received. I'm not stalking you or whatever the word for unwanted phone calls is, so if you want me to hang up, best say so now and I'll be gone. Won't darken your door, or light up your phone, again."

Carrie sat on the edge of her bed, phone to ear. Amazed, and rather glad to hear from Ray, she shoved the suitcase aside and lay back. "How did you get this number?"

"Well, if I could put on a German accent, I'd say, 'Ve have our Vays.' Seeing as how that's a bit much for a Texas good ol' boy, I'll just say it was on my cell phone from when Jake borrowed *your* phone to call me."

"Ah-ha." Still lost for words, and strangely happy, Carrie waited for him to continue.

"Lookit, if you really don't want to hear from me, say so now, all right, and I really won't call again or bother you or whatnot. You know I'm not much for beating about the bush. I think that much you know about me. So...I just thought...maybe we could start with a few phone calls and see where things took us."

She gave a small gasp but didn't reply.

"You still there?"

Carrie brushed away snail trails mysteriously making their way down her cheek. Thankful she wasn't on Skype, she managed to get out, "I'm here. Yes."

"Is that 'yes, I'm here,' or 'yes, we can start with a few phone calls?'"

She struggled to find her voice. It came squeaking out. "Yes. We can start..."

"Good. So, the first bit of news from this end is I haven't had a drink in over a week. In fact, I would've called sooner, but I felt I wanted to be able to tell you 'a week' rather than something like, 'Oh, I didn't have a drink yesterday.' Somehow sounds better—a week. Doesn't it?"

Carrie sat up, the tears running freely now. She sniffed and gulped out, "It sounds...fantastic."

There was a brief silence before he said, "Shit, are you crying?"

"Yes, but don't drink because of it!" she managed to blurt out.

Ray laughed. "Ah, no. No, I won't do that." He waited another moment. "Say, you don't happen to have a Skype account, do you? Used to talk to Jake in Iraq that way. It's real great if you don't get dropped."

Carrie cleared her throat a bit, swatting away the last of her tears and getting hold of herself. "C-B-Books is my screen name."

"Fantastic," said Ray. "We can have phone sex!"

Chapter Six

Jake took it slow. The last thing he needed was a speeding ticket on I-35, or any contact with the police, even without the drugs on board. He had flicked on the air conditioning and had the music blaring, and all he wanted was to get there and get back in one piece and be done with it. Cars sped by him, the scenery changing little on the highway until the turn-off for Route 57.

At times, he asked himself why he had decided to do this. Protecting his father from knowledge about Robbie was one thing, but getting caught running drugs, well, that was quite another. If he was caught, it would only lead to more heartache for his father. Yet, every time he tried to tell his dad, tried to get the words out, something stopped him, something just wouldn't let him go on.

Over the past month since his father had first called Carrie, the older man had gone around whistling as if the world were his oyster, like a child who had just discovered wishes do come true. He had even told his lawyers to increase the offer to Leigh Anne in the hope of getting the divorce over and done with, once and for all.

So, Jake just went on, letting his father bask in his sudden, newfound happiness. Happiness? It had made him happy, too—happy his father wasn't drinking any more, happy he didn't have to worry about coming home and finding his dad out cold, happy he didn't have to think of ways to take his dad's mind off the next drink. Happy.

Eagle Pass was an uninviting little town, originally growing up around a fort built to protect the border with Mexico during the Mexican-American war, and going on to protect its citizens against Apaches. Trailer parks littered the outskirts and, whatever historic center might have been preserved, there was little to invite the tourist to this outpost on the Rio Grande. Jake had a sudden flash of Iraq, of isolation, the same exclusion from the world he considered normal. Dust blew in a dry heat, specters of the hopelessness for fresh starts, new beginnings. And there was the fear—the fear of the murderous drug cartels, the fear the river wouldn't be enough to separate this side from the other, this world from theirs, the fear the invasion wasn't a thing of past history but an on-going virus, a worm eating the flesh of America. It would take a bigger bite, always wanting more.

Jake shivered, as if someone had stepped on his grave, and then he surveyed the border scene.

As he expected, there was a line of cars waiting to get into Piedras Negras across the International Bridge, but the North Americans would be more or less waved through on this side. Vehicle occupants rubber-necked as choppers flew overhead and a team of Department of Public Safety guys hung around the riverbanks, preparing to snatch ditched cars out of the Rio Grande. It was getting back into the States that would be the problem.

He sat in the car sweating now, fear running through him as his stomach lurched.

As he crossed the river, hills of tin and cardboard shanties glinted with a false welcome, rising out of the dust devils that marked the forsaken sprawl that was a settlement.

It had been easy enough to sort the car papers to get into Mexico. Now, driving through the least desirable section of the Mexican town's filthy streets, a haze rose like released souls from hell, kicked up by barefoot boys knocking around a ball. A pack of wild dogs chased after them. Jake bent his head to try to read street signs, most of which were either torn, hanging off or so dirty they were unreadable. He pulled over to study a map he had printed off the internet, glanced again at the street sign above and decided he had a few more roads to go.

The turning was not promising. Shabby houses, crammed together, lined either side with forlorn old women sitting on doorsteps getting fresh air, more dirty children playing in the street, and an air of hopelessness difficult to ignore. He parked in front of thirty-one; a stench like rotten cabbage mixed with the sickly sweet smell of sour vinegar greeted him as he grabbed his bag and got out of the car. Looking around, he beckoned over one of the boys to negotiate with him to guard the vehicle while he found his contact. Then he knocked on the door.

A hot sun crusted the street as he stood listening to voices within before the door croaked open an inch. The man who eventually stood before him was about half his size and in a shirt so filthy and sweat-stained, Jake doubted it had ever been washed.

The man's black, greasy hair hung down over dark, unfocused eyes appraising Jake, raking him over from head to toe, before he shook his head in acknowledgement and put out a hand to motion him to wait.

"No no, *tengo que entrar para cambiar mi ropa.*" Jake held up his bag.

The contact's eyes darted around the street nervously. "*Ábrela!*" he ordered. *Open!*

Jake slowly bent down and opened the satchel.

The man's hand darted in like a snake attacking to bite, no doubt feeling for a gun, but only the cotton of Jake's army uniform greeted him. Then he found the wad of notes and lifted it to the brim of the bag, letting it drop back in before anyone on the street saw. He waved his hand at Jake and led the way into the dark of the house.

His eyes took time to adjust. A row of three small children sat on a stained, torn sofa in front of an old television set, virtually the only light source in the room.

"*Donde puedo cambiar…?*"

The man shook his head. "*Aqui, aqui,*" he insisted. Then, no doubt recognizing his frustration, he snapped off the television and shepherded the children into a back room.

Jake sat on the edge of the sofa. He yanked off his boots and struggled into his army trousers as quickly as possible before completing the change. He stuffed his clothes back into the satchel before calling out, "*Señor?*" and scrambled to get his army boots tied on.

The contact came out, a large brown paper parcel tied with string held out in front of him. The exchange was made.

"Go," he said in English. "*Salgate ya!* Go."

Jake took the parcel, stuffed it under his two cowboy boots and placed them at the bottom of the bag with his clothes covering. For a moment, he wondered if he should insist on opening the parcel to check its contents, but decided it wasn't his problem; if Ty was scammed by his dealer, that was his worry, not Jake's. His brother's old buddy was just a small-time dealer, a nothing, and what would it matter in the end? But then it struck him, Ty would blame him for switching packages. He glanced back at the man, one of the children by his side. No, it would be all right; if the man wanted more business, he couldn't swindle Ty.

Jake opened the door, nodded once, and got to his car. He had a dollar in the outside pocket of the satchel and handed it to his small guard, got in and headed back to Texas.

The line back into the USA was a sludgy, muddy river of traffic, long and slow moving. Leaving Mexico was easy once the car papers were re-checked, but entering the US was quite another matter.

Guards with sniffer dogs patrolled the vehicles and Jake drew his bag close to him on the passenger seat. Sweat started to color his shirt with dark Rorschach patches of wet and run down his face as his hands rested tensely on the steering wheel. He abruptly yanked down the sun shade and shunted the air conditioning higher, then flicked the shade back to watch the dogs and guard circle and inspect a truck several vehicles in front of him, beasts closing in for a possible kill.

A tap on the glass made him jump, and Jake rolled down the window.

"Open the trunk, sir, if you don't mind."

Jake thrust down the lever, hoping the man didn't notice nerves making his hand shake uncontrollably. His face twitched as he watched in his rear view mirror the door to the trunk go up, then slam shut again after a few moments.

The guard walked slowly around the vehicle before he came back to Jake's window.

"Passport or military I.D., please."

The officer kept a careful watch as Jake reached into his glove compartment and hauled out his passport before handing it through.

"You still serving, soldier?"

"Yeah," Jake lied, just about finding his voice. "Came home for a funeral."

The guard nodded. "Next time you enter Mexico, sir, don't leave your passport in your glove compartment. It's an invitation to have it stolen."

"I'll remember that." Though reaching into the bag wouldn't have been too wise either.

"Okay. You can pull your vehicle over to that lane and go on through. Welcome home...and thanks for serving."

****

Carrie looked forward to Ray's calls, anticipated his calls, wanted them. She didn't bother to question how she had gotten to this point, how her desire to hear from this man had grown from pure curiosity about his well-being to actual heart-lifting happiness every time the phone or Skype rang and it was him.

She appreciated that Ray never once asked why she didn't phone him, why she was never the one to call. To her, it was not that it was his job to keep the relationship going, but it was the mechanics of their lives—he could find the time at the end of the day, *had* a time at which work stopped; she was too far engrossed in her work to stop and think about calling unless the phone actually rang. It was as if Ray expected to take the lead, to do the chasing, and she expected to be the quarry, to be chased.

She saw time on the phone with Ray as her work break, but when she told him, as she had on occasion, that she needed to get on, that she was in the middle of something and couldn't stop, to please ring again later, Ray never complained; he let her set the pace.

And she loved to laugh with him. Discussing the minutiae of their day, Ray would find humor in just about anything, from something one of his dogs did to what one of his hunting guests didn't do. He put a whole different perspective on her life so, eventually, she was able to see the funny side of her dealings with her co-screenwriters, her agent, her daughter and her workaholic life. When she flew to California for meetings, when she had to tramp back into the city for doctor's appointments, when she went to search locations with the director and location manager, Ray's call was the highlight of her day. Using Skype, she worried somewhat as to how she appeared, hardly realizing she actually wanted to look good for him. For him alone.

Yet, she didn't feel she could consider anything more than the phone call, when she might see him again. And Ray never asked, never put pressure on her, never mentioned a meeting or wanting anything more. It was an undercurrent, the eight hundred pound gorilla in the room never declared. And while the calls increased slowly from one the first week through every few days to every couple of days to daily by the end of June, she never spoke with him about taking the next step, about seeing him again.

When next the phone rang, Carrie beat her maid, Carmen, to the cell and picked it up on the third ring.

"Hey," said Ray, "Where are you?"

"What do you mean? I'm at the beach. I have a beach house. I told you that."

"Oh, yeah, you did. I forgot. Sort of." There was a small pause during which she heard him take a deep breath and let out a sigh. "See…I'm in New York."

"What? Sorry? You're where?" Carrie let a longer pause follow this bit of information while she tried to absorb it and process it. She motioned to Carmen to get on with offering her poolside guests some refreshments. "Ray, where did you say you were?"

"See, I just suddenly thought it might be nice to spend the Fourth of July weekend together, so I got the early plane and, well, I'm in New York like I said. I haven't got your address though. It was sort of spur of the moment. Had to grab the plane—the seat they offered—and there wasn't much time really. No time to phone."

Ray is in New York?

Phone plastered to her ear, Carrie surveyed the activity of preparations for her party. It was just past ten o'clock in the morning, and the festivities were due to start at eight p.m. She tried to remember if she had made any mention of all this to Ray in a previous phone call, but it didn't matter.

"Okay," she said, finally coming to her senses. Ray was in New York, she was in East Hampton, and she had to somehow magically get him here in time for the soiree. "Listen to me carefully. I'm two to three hours away—"

"You're joking," he grumped. "I just traveled nearly four hours from Austin. Add to that traveling time to the airport, check-in, security, the whole damn thing, and now you're telling me I got two to three hours more. Carrie?"

"I…I can't help it. I would come into the city for you, but I have a party here tonight. And—look—you didn't tell me, did you? Listen…" She tried to quiet the erratic way her heart was beating. "It's really quite simple. You can get a train or a bus. Well, actually, I think we better aim for the train as that doesn't require a reservation and the buses will be filled this weekend, plus of course there'll be so much traffic," she rushed on. She waited for a reply. "Ray? Are you still there?"

"Of course I'm here. Where else would I be?"

Carrie took a deep breath. "Okay. Listen. You need to get to Penn Station and get the Long Island Railroad to East Hampton…"

"I'm listening. Long Island Railroad to East Hampton…"

"And I'll pick you up at the station…"

"Can I sleep on the train?"

She glanced around for a tissue to blot the wet that seemed to be running down her face. She didn't understand what set her off, whether it was some sort of happiness as he spoke, or nerves about his being there, but, despite not being a lachrymose person, wet streaked her face. "I hope so. We have a party here tonight, so I truly hope so, Ray." There was momentary silence before she said, "Gosh, this is amazing."

"Amazing good, or amazing bad?" he asked with a

hint of humor in his voice.

She threw a hand out in question as Paige strolled into the kitchen to check something on her tablet. "Amazing good, of course… Look, you can get a plane or helicopter. I'll pay for it of course…"

"No! No, no no… Nothing doing, lady." Ray shuffled a bit into a quieter corner, suddenly wondering if this had been the right choice. "I'll sleep on the train. I'll take a nap when I get there. Being a kept man is…not my thing."

Outside, the passers-by beyond the glass doors of the terminal were moving quickly, getting where they wanted to be.

He shoved his bag between his feet for a moment and squinted into the dazzling sunlight outside the building's miasma. "How do I get to Penn Station? Taxi?"

"Let me try to arrange a plane or chopper. It would be so much quicker."

He inhaled another deep breath and sighed once more. He wasn't giving in. "I know you're absolutely dying to see me, sweetheart, but you'll just have to wait another few hours."

Carrie started to say something, but Paige's voice interrupted. "Mom, he can get the train from Jamaica. He doesn't have to go all the way back into the city. I checked and there's a train from Jamaica at 11.30."

"Ray? Paige just told me you can get a train from near the airport. You can be out here by around two p.m."

He heard the excitement in her voice, the joy. He laughed. "All right, I heard all that. Tell me what to do."

****

Carrie's eyes widened at her daughter as she jabbed at the phone to end the call. Paige's Missoni bikini highlighted the sun-gold color she had worked on all month and displayed her beautiful figure to its full advantage. A small shot of jealousy ran through Carrie, and her body slumped with a sigh.

"What's the matter now?" asked her daughter. "Lord, I thought you'd be delighted."

"I am delighted. Only…where the hell am I going to put him, Paige? Your friends are on the television sofa-bed, the Statlers are in the pool house, Diana and Tom have their usual guest suite, as do the Burlinghams, and Jo-Jo and Pete will be arriving shortly for the garage apartment."

"Mother, I don't need a manifest of your guests. Anyway, you're being ridiculous—Ray's going to stay with you, of course. He hasn't traveled half a country to see you in order to be stuffed on a sofa bed or left on his own above the garage."

"I can't!" She threw her hands up to mark the end of that idea.

There was disbelief in her daughter's eyes. Paige held her in her sights like a deer she was about to take down. "You are kidding me, aren't you?" Her voice was slow and crisp.

Carrie nodded back toward Carmen who was re-entering the kitchen with an empty platter. "I can't discuss this here, now."

She started to move toward the sliding doors to the pool area.

"Oh, yes you can. And you will."

Carrie felt the tight grip of Paige's hand on her

shoulder.

"I have watched and seen how you absolutely light up every time that man calls you. Lord only knows why, because I sure as hell can't figure it, but it happens. And you can't go insulting him now, letting him come all this way and then acting as if you don't want him. You don't do that!"

"He'll understand. Ray will—" She knew she was fighting a losing battle, but she continued to struggle.

"Listen! He may be a great guy. For all I know, he may be the best damn man on God's green earth. But he is still a *man*. And there isn't a man—not a straight one anyway—who comes two thousand miles to see a woman and not expect to get laid!"

"Oh, for heaven's sake, Paige—do you have to be so crude?"

Her daughter gulped a deep breath and let it out in frustration. "You better get used to the idea, Mother. You are getting laid tonight. And by my reckoning, there won't only be fireworks out on the beach."

"Oh! Who's getting laid tonight? How exciting!" Diana Shawcross slid her mint-thin body through the screen door.

Tall and elegant, Diana was the epitome of the 'lady who lunches.' At times, Carrie appraised her and wondered how they had become friends, but their friendship went back to college days, and Diana could be uproariously funny and a breath of fresh air.

"In this house?" her friend continued. "Do we all get to listen? Tom never makes love to me when we're guests in other people's homes. In hotels, yes. He sees that as a ticket to ride. But homes, no. Thin walls."

Carrie pinched her lips together and raised a brow

at Paige.

"You're in your own separate wing on one side of the house and no one is going to hear you. I promise. Did you ever hear me when Steven and I were at it?"

"No-o-o." She might as well give up now.

"Well, then."

"Don't tell me the Virgin Carrie is having a male guest to stay? Darling, I never knew you had it in you these days."

"A cowboy lover-to-be," enlightened Paige.

"He is not a cowboy—he's a rancher. There's a difference." Carrie crossed her arms with a little nod.

"Oh, my gosh! Why didn't you tell me all this before? I'm going to camp at the bottom of your wing and listen. Does he ride well? Does he wear those chaps that absolutely pinpoint just how big his package is?"

"Diana!" Carrie started marching out, then stopped in her tracks, eyes wide at Paige. "What should I wear?"

****

Jake sat with his hand poised over the phone for a long time. His disgust with himself for having handed over the marijuana to Ty was so intense, he'd driven around aimlessly afterwards, unable to go home. Waves of revulsion periodically hit him after what he had done, certainly not more frightening than being in Iraq, but against every principle he held. It wasn't drug use to which he was so vehemently opposed—plenty of his friends smoked the occasional joint—but helping a slime ball like Ty Sheldon sell the stuff, make money from others on it, was quite another matter.

On the other hand, there was a thrill, a buzz, the excitement that had been missing since his return. He had been dragging himself from day to day, except when Paige had been around, and the trip down to Mexico had livened things up, given him an exploit. Yet, the two sides of this didn't quite reconcile in his mind, he couldn't explain his own feelings, and behind it all was the fact he had let down his father.

He looked again at the note his dad had left him, an apology that he had suddenly decided to up and visit Carrie in New York, and that he was sure Jake would understand and would be able to celebrate July Fourth with friends or join the ranch party with the hunting guests, and he would be back late Monday.

Jake held the note in his hand for a long time, partially relieved he had a break from the guilt he felt every time he faced his father, somewhat upset his own father wasn't making a fuss of his first Fourth of July at home after several years, and moderately amazed his father had done something so serendipitous, impulsive and spontaneous.

But it did give him a good excuse to finally phone Paige. There was no one he could talk to here, no one else who would listen without caring, give straightforward, objective advice and keep their mouth shut.

Or would she?

If she saw fit to tell his father what he had done, Paige darn well would. No, it was too risky.

And then he examined again the scrap of paper on which she had scribbled her number, and picked up the phone.

"Well, this is a surprise," came her voice without greeting.

"How did you know it was me?" He sat back in his

armchair, wondering whether he had made the right decision.

"I recognize the number from when I pick up my mother's phone when Ray calls, and since Ray is now waiting at East Hampton station for my mother to collect him, and doesn't, to my knowledge, have my cell phone number, it wasn't too difficult to figure. How are you, Jake? Are you sorry you're missing the party?" Her voice was prickly, a small note of sarcasm in it.

"You having a Fourth of July party?"

"Of course!"

"On the mean streets of New York?" A wave of jealousy hit him, that his father was there with Carrie, that he had been left behind.

"We're not in New York. East Hampton, I just said."

There was a moment's silence. "Isn't that…isn't that some way from New York?"

"Two to three hours if you drive."

"Jeez," he let out a long breath. "My dad must've loved that bit of news."

"Listen, I don't want to be rude, and it's lovely to hear you drawling and drooling down the phone at me, but I have a house load of visitors here I'm supposed to be taking care of while our parents have it off with each other."

Jake sniggered. "You think they're at it in a car somewhere?"

"Okay, so they're not at it this very moment. My mother has to mentally prepare herself for it. She's like an athlete in training, getting psyched up for the big moment. However, my take on the whole thing is she'll see Ray at the station and drop her knickers straight away."

Jake guffawed.

"Why did you phone anyway? Was it just feeling left out or to hear my dulcet tones once again?"

"It was…" He started, but couldn't go on. It wasn't the right moment; she wasn't the right person. "Yeah, I just wanted to say hello and know Dad had arrived okay. You tell him I called, will you? Tell him…tell him, it's all right. I'll be okay." He was trying to keep his tone level, to keep the unsaid out of his voice.

"*Are* you all right, Jake?"

"Yeah. Sure. Look, I better go and let you get back to your shenanigans." He hesitated again. "I'm sorry I'm not there, too." And he was. Sorry not to see Paige once more.

"I…It was good to hear from you, Jake. Call again, will you? I mean that."

He let the silence stretch before he asked, "Paige, did you decide about going—" But she'd hung up the phone.

****

Carrie shot down Race Lane and made a turn to find a mess of cars on both sides of the street in front of the station. She pounded the steering wheel of her BMW in anger, blaming herself for being so late, then spotted a car just pulling out in front of Riverhead Building Supplies. Perfect. She parked and gave a cursory glance across the street to try to spot Ray.

Stepping out of the car, she smoothed down her white sundress, patted her hair into place and waited for traffic to pass. And then she stopped.

There, leaning back against a corner of the small

station building, was Ray, his Stetson tilted slightly forward as he chatted happily away with a young man who was shaking his head in agreement. As he spoke, Ray carefully rolled up the sleeves of his check shirt before crossing his arms, displaying a good bit of muscle. And then, as the young man nodded good-bye, Ray lifted his head.

For a moment, she stood there transfixed despite the gap in traffic. And then, starting to cross the road, her gaze locked with his. A smile spread across her face, and her whole being lit as if a match had been struck.

"You've never met a stranger, have you?" she asked, coming up to him and nodding in the direction the young man had gone.

"Nope." He didn't take his gaze from her. "I've seen loons with smaller smiles than what you have, Carrie. If I'da known my being here was gonna make you this happy—"

"Oh, shut up," she said leaning into him, still smiling as she tenderly kissed his lips.

She stood back, drinking him in. *Oh, shit. I'm in love.*

Chapter Seven

Carrie concentrated on making a U-turn, then stopped at the lights by the railroad crossing. She stole a peek at Ray, hardly believing he was there in the seat beside her, and suppressed a smile as the lights changed to green. "I'm sorry there are going to be so many people here this weekend…"

"It's fine. I should've called ahead, I guess, but I thought the surprise—"

"The surprise is wonderful. Wonderful, Ray. I can't tell you—"

"Yes, you can."

He was smiling, and a hasty glance told her it was so. Her heart bounced in her chest. "Everyone is going to love you. But they will be curious. I mean, a Texan rancher—"

"Who they'll no doubt call a cowboy…"

"Whom they'll no doubt call a cowboy, as I did—"

"As you did."

"Anyway, I'm sorry." She gripped the steering wheel as if it would fall from her hands. "And I'm sorry about the extra journey, too. You hadn't counted on that."

"I'm sure it'll be worth it."

Carrie caught the widening smile that curved his lips before he turned away. Her heart lurched, and a small worm of nervousness began to eat its way through her body. "Though, we won't have an awful lot of time alone," she finally informed him.

"We'll have enough," he countered.

She ignored his implications, keeping her eyes on the road ahead. "It'll be a very long day for you."

"Carrie."

He reached across and patted her knee, his mere touch making her want more.

"Stop apologizing. This isn't your fault. I should've called before leaving. And any time we have together is worth the trip. Really. Time with you is worth it."

She loved him for that, loved him for who he was, how he was. And suddenly, the other guests didn't matter, what all those people thought didn't matter a fig.

He was here. Ray was here.

And everything was going to be fine.

****

Carrie's summer home fronted on a bit of beach that lay expensively between Main Beach and Georgica Pond in East Hampton. Ray learned she had bought it, even before upgrading her New York apartment, because her former husband had once pointed it out as the most beautiful house right on the ocean. It was obvious to him that she believed it to be just that. When it had come up for sale, as she told Ray, there had been no doubt in her mind she would do anything to have it.

He got out of the car and grabbed his bag, noting with some amusement the only vehicles in the drive were from the high end of the luxury car market. Surveying the house, a shingled, post-modern dwelling surrounded by lush plantings, he braced himself for what he would find, and the kind of people he would meet. He followed Carrie inside to a hall that spread almost the size of his entire house, then stepped down to a sunken living room that flowed out seamlessly through glass and screen doors to a pool area worthy of a Miami hotel. Two smaller hallways led either side to separate wings, and somewhere—Ray hadn't a clue—the clatter of kitchen preparations indicated a center of operations for the evening's celebration.

He left his hat on top of his bag and followed Carrie out to the pool area.

"Hi, everyone," she announced with what, he couldn't help noticing, was a slight touch of nervousness in her voice. "This is Ray."

The response, practically in unison, was a "Hello, Ray," which immediately reminded him of an Alcoholics Anonymous meeting.

He smiled, gave a non-committal wave, said, "Hey, Paige!" for which he received a crooked, knowing smile in return, and followed Carrie back into the house.

She stopped, almost causing him to trip over her.

"Oh, lord, what am I doing? That was ridiculous, awful. Shall I take you back out and introduce you properly? Do you want something to drink? Something to eat? Are you tired? Do you want to rest?"

Ray put his hands on her shoulders. "What I would like more than anything right now...well, more than *almost* anything right now...is for you to stop frettin' so. Carrie, you been apologizing and worrying 'bout every dang thing since I arrived. Calm down, for Pete's sake."

"It's just—"

"I know what it's 'just.' You want me to fit in and you're worried your friends aren't going to like me or I'm not going to like them. Look sweetheart, it's just not worth frettin' so. Everything will be fine. I'm a big boy. I can take care of myself, and we're not quite so socially backward in Texas as you seem to think."

"But—"

"No 'buts!' I get a lot of real wealthy people comin' on down to hunt on my place, and I deal with them all the time. This sort of thing doesn't faze me. Really." He saw Carrie beginning to open her mouth again. "Eh, eh, eh," he said, wagging an admonishing finger in front of her. "An ice cold drink, maybe a small bite to tide me over 'til supper and someplace to lie down for a spell would be fine just now. Then you'll see—I'll be the life of the party."

Carrie appeared as if she were trying to imagine him as the life of her party. Her eyes were big with apprehension, her mouth puckered with trepidation. "All right," she said at last. "I'll take you…upstairs, settle you in and get you a cold drink and something to eat."

He grabbed his bag, plopped his Stetson on his head and followed her down one of the smaller hallways. They proceeded up a flight of steps to a furnished landing that apparently served as a study overlooking the gardens to one side of the house. A large oak desk topped with a Mac, bookcases stuffed with Carrie's books and various dictionaries and a large inviting sofa all announced this was her hide-out.

"So, this is where you work while out here, huh?" he asked.

"No, not really. This is."

She flung open a door to a bedroom in a rhapsody of creams and blues, dominated by one of the grandest beds Ray had ever seen. And beyond, out through another set of sliding doors, lay a balconied terrace jutting out over the beach. One could almost jump from it straight into the ocean. Feeling as if he had just sauntered into the pages of a glossy magazine, Ray whistled.

"I work out there most of the time. There's an awning that comes down in case of rain so I can stay out, unless it's really dreadful and blowy. Which, of course, being oceanfront it can be. But for the most part..." Her voice trailed off.

Ray stood, hands on hips, taking in the view. "Nah, think I prefer Texas. Gets a bit monotonous—all that water just coming in and going out. I'll take my changing colors and all." He glanced at her to see if she knew he was joking and caught the merest hint of a smile.

"Well, make yourself comfortable and you can rest here for now and—" She stopped as his hands went back to his hips. Embarrassed, she continued, "I'll just pop down and get you something to eat. There's actually a little fridge in the cloakroom on the landing, so just help yourself to a cold drink."

She was barely out of the room before he called after her, "You're not one of these women who gets all coy and doesn't like to presume the man wants to sleep with you, are you?"

Carrie stopped and stared back at him, hesitated as if she were considering a reply, then proceeded downstairs.

"'Course you are," he said to himself.

Carrie took a few minutes to collect herself as well as the food. Plate in hand, she entered her bedroom without thinking, without knocking, and gasped, stopping in her tracks as she beheld Ray there in his boxer shorts. She stifled a small laugh while her eyes no doubt deceived her. "Sorry," she murmured, "I didn't…"

"It's your bedroom." He didn't display the slightest bit of embarrassment as he threw the jeans he was holding over a chair.

Carrie had a sense of being trapped, of being caught between her own desire for a relationship with this startling man and her wish not to be forced into baring herself, her need for privacy and being left to get on with her work and her world. And now, this struck her as ridiculous: a man in his boxers in her bedroom, highly unappealing with his shirt hanging down, half-shaven, his Stetson still on his head.

"I made you a sandwich, or at least Carmen did. Are you going to nap?" she rushed on brightly, leaving the plate on a table. She went to turn down the bed for him, fluff the pillows.

"Either that or make love to you," he responded simply. He raised a brow, a half-smile on his face. Yet, he didn't make a move.

"That's not very romantic," she considered out loud. "You don't just announce your intentions like that."

Ray sighed. "Carrie, I just come two thousand odd miles to surprise and see you. If that don't beat romantic, I don't know what the hell does."

She ran a hand through her hair. He was right; it was the most romantic damn thing to happen to her in however many years. "So, is that why you came?"

"Carrie...for goodness sake." He let out a deep breath and then bent to remove his socks, finally tossing his hat onto a chair. "If all I wanted was to get laid, sweetheart, I coulda saved myself a helluva lot of trouble. But you are some damn woman and...you know...you know how I feel about you. Do I have to spell it out?"

Ray waited for a reply, but the only answer she gave him was her continued stare, wishing and waiting for the ceiling to cave in.

"Hell, I can take a nap and you can think about it," he went on. "But I haveta tell you, making love to you is pretty high on my list."

Panic rose. It started in the soles of her feet and heated her body, made her tremble inside, put ice on her spine and no doubt a flush on her face.

She had known this was coming, but hoped it would be later. Tonight. After a few drinks at the party. No, *a lot* of drinks. Or maybe it wouldn't happen. Too far gone? And then she remembered Ray was on the wagon so...perhaps he wouldn't touch her if *she* had too much to drink. Perhaps. No. These were excuses running through her head. Or wishful thinking. Paige told her this was going to happen, and now it was. She was sharing her bedroom with him, and it was going to happen.

"So, which list is that?" she finally spurted out with a hint of confusion in her voice mixed with playfulness. "Is that the to-do list, or the wish-list or the bucket list?"

"Nope," he said, coming over to her, gently placing his hands on her arms. "It's the 'what I want most of all in this world at this moment' list."

Carrie stood unmoving in his embrace, suddenly wanting him and not wanting to go on, all at the same time. Yet, deep inside, it was what she, too, wanted most of all at this moment. And yet, she stood anchored to her spot, hungering for his touch to continue, yearning to get that first intimate act over with after so many years alone, yet dreading that uncovering of herself, that baring of what she saw as her inadequacies.

"I have guests," she said very quietly, finding an excuse, trying to postpone what was inevitable.

"Seemed to me," he said equally quietly, "those guests were pretty good at looking after themselves for a while. Plus, of course, Paige is there. I doubt you'll be sorely missed for a couple of hours."

"A couple of hours," she repeated.

Ray's hand sought the zipper at the back of her dress, and he leaned in to kiss her neck.

Carrie pulled away ever so slightly. She had a sense he was waiting for her to stop him.

He drew back, his hands again resting lightly on her arms, his gaze most likely assessing the situation written on her face. "You know," he continued hardly above a whisper, "if I didn't know better, I coulda swore you were a virgin. But I think I do know better 'cause we got the proof downstairs, don't we? Is there any chance of you relaxing, or do you just want me to stop?"

Carrie could feel tears just below the surface, and she angled her head so that she didn't look him in the eye. "It's just… It's…"

The Texan released her and let out another long sigh. "Well, I'm not gonna force myself on you, Carrie.

I can sleep out there on the sofa tonight, and no one will ever know."

"No!" There was sudden vehemence in her voice.

Ray smiled, but it was more a bemused smile than a happy one.

"I…I'm embarrassed about my body," she finally blurted out.

His mouth puckered in bafflement. At last, he countered, "Are you going to be in a bathing suit later or tomorrow?"

"Ye-e-es" she let out, knowing exactly where he was going with this. "But…"

His hands went back to her zipper as he leaned in once again to brush his lips along her neck, planting kisses under her ear and working slowly down until he had reached her décolleté and got the zipper down. "I promise you," he whispered as she let her body yield to him at last, "I won't look."

****

Carrie listened to the quiet snores of Ray's post-coital sleep and glanced at the bedside clock.

Oh, shit. 6.15 p.m.

She dragged herself away from the comfort of his body and into her bathroom to shower and get ready, surprised no one had made any attempt to see where she was. Of course not; they would all know, wouldn't they?

They would know the fact of it, of course, that she and Ray had made love, hadn't just been catching up with news the last two hours. But no one would ever know the feel of it, the reality of it, or what it had cost her.

As his hands gently ran over her arms, slipped off

her dress and then reached to unfasten her bra, she had practically screamed for him to stop. Yet somehow, she became aware he wasn't looking after all—not assessing her, not judging her—and Ray was giving himself to her as tenderly as he was taking what she could give to him.

Her plain black, silk sheath dress hung in the closet, and it suddenly struck her she had no idea what Ray had to wear. Should she care? She wanted him to be accepted among her friends, to make a good impression, yet, did it really matter? She wanted him; she wanted Ray like she had wanted no other man before him. And whether Diana and Tom Shawcross or the Burlinghams or the Statlers, or any of her other guests liked him, she wanted a future, some sort of damn future with this man who made her laugh, knew her faults, accepted her for what she was. Neuroses and all.

As she fixed a final diamond stud in her ear and gave herself a once-over in the closet mirrors, she was aware of Ray opening his eyes and quietly making his own appraisal from the bed, his head resting back on his hands.

"I never seen a finer looking woman than you, Carrie Bennett. Come here and give me a kiss, sweetheart."

She fixed on the earring stud and turned with a huge smile for the man in her bed. "I'm going to be late for my own party," she told him, bending to give him the kiss. "What are you wearing?"

"Well, therein lies the rub, as I think Shakespeare might say." Ray shimmied up to a sitting position. "I was counting on New York *City* so the beach wear is a mite thin on the ground. I brought one Armani suit I happened to have, courtesy of business meetings in Dallas—"

"Wow! Armani. That's pretty classy," Carrie broke in, unable to hide the hint of sarcasm and surprise in her tone.

"Yup. But no beachwear. No Vilebrequin turtles crawling over me like I see in the Sunday glossies, no classy Lauren polo shirts pretending to be riding wear, nada. Couple of shirts, a black tee for daytime, pair of jeans, and the Armani suit. Whatcha think?"

"Dig out the black tee, wear it with the Armani suit. Shower and come on down." Carrie bent and kissed Ray on the lips as his hand brought her in closer, deeper. She sat for a moment on the edge of the bed, staring into his midnight eyes as she tenderly rubbed off a smudge of lipstick left at the corner of his mouth. "You're pretty wonderful, you know that, don't you?" she said, gazing at him.

"We can do this," he responded, suddenly very serious. "We can do this, Carrie. Part-time here, part-time there. Jake'll eventually take over the ranch, you know. I can—"

Carrie got up suddenly. "I have to go downstairs. We can discuss it…tomorrow. Or sometime before you leave. But not tonight. Not tonight. Okay?"

"Yeah." He lay there watching her as she slipped into a pair of very high heels, spritzed some perfume around her neck and arms, and proceeded to the door.

"Actually," she said, sticking her head back in, "Jeans'll do. Wear your jeans and the black tee. That'll be fine."

"You sure?" he asked.

"Absolutely," she said. "You'll look great." She stopped a moment. "Don't rush. You have plenty of time."

"You want me fashionably late?"

Carrie laughed. "I want you...period."

****

Ray stood at the upstairs window with a good view of the garden and observed the long stream of cars in the distant driveway spewing out occupants as the vehicles were whisked away by valets. Beyond, he caught a glimpse of the blue-flashing lights of police cars giving a festive air to the proceedings as one or two officers directed traffic.

Dear Lord, what have I got myself into?

Coming down to the landing, he stopped for a second as the hum of cocktail conversation greeted him along with a few inquisitive stares. He could have killed for a drink, and a flash of need hit him so strong, for a moment he started to weaken. But then, he wouldn't embarrass Carrie—if that was what might happen—so, as a waiter passed with a tray, he grabbed a glass of sparkling water. He spotted her mingling with her guests across the expanse of pool mosaic. The need for alcohol passed; like sand running through a timer, it slipped away. And then it wasn't long before a tall, elegant blonde came up to him, cocktail in hand, husband in tow.

"Diana Shawcross," she said. "And this is my husband, Tom."

He extended his hand. "Ray Ryder."

"I'm Carrie's long time best friend," she explained, shoving a crystal-encrusted clutch under one armpit in order to shake Ray's hand. "Or at least I *was* her best friend until you came along. I think."

"Why don't you just say, 'her best *girl*friend,' and we can leave it at that?" he suggested.

Diana flashed a luminously white smile. "How proprietary of you."

"Well," he mused, studying a proffered tray of hors d'oeuvres and selecting one, "I like to think I'm her best male friend. You don't happen to know of another one, do you? Well, one that is, shall I say, *romantically* proprietary?"

"What do you do for a living, Ray? If you don't mind my asking," Tom interjected before the conversation went into deep water.

"I've got a small spread in Texas and run a hunting operation along with Arab horse-breeding." He popped the canapé into his mouth.

"And by small you mean, what? Ten thousand acres?"

Ray's face puckered for a moment as he stopped chewing and bit his lip. "You know, Tom, back down in Texas, you ask a man how many acres he's got, it's sorta like asking the balance of his bank account."

"I love Arabs," Diana put in. "Best horses. You and Carrie will have to come up to our farm in the Berkshires some time."

"Well, I'd like that, I'm sure." Ray caught Carrie's eye. "If you'll excuse me; I think I'm being summoned."

He moved through the crowd, but got stuck with another couple, and then another, and then lost Carrie altogether somewhere in the melee.

A buffet spread was laid out in the side garden, and by ten p.m. most guests were heading that way. Ray spotted Paige looking particularly beautiful in a backless red dress, but only got a nod of acknowledgment as she continued a conversation, drink in hand.

He put down his empty water glass just as the chill of an icy tumbler hit his neck.

"Are you all right?" Carrie asked.

Ray turned to face her. "Well, I could use a little nourishment. Of both the emotional and nutritional variety."

"I think I can help you with that." She leaned in to give him a quick kiss and then looped her arm through his to lead him to the buffet.

"You sure you want to kiss me in front of all these people?"

"I just have, and I don't see the world coming to an end." She stood with him in the buffet line.

The constant introductions and repetitive need for small talk were beginning to wear him down. Happy to have Carrie at last by his side, he took her hand and caressed it. "We gettin' fireworks tonight?"

"Only in the bedroom. Piping plovers nesting nearby."

"Is that a tongue-twister?" He gave her a lopsided smile.

Carmen suddenly appeared by her side. "One of the servers just spilt a cranberry spritzer on Mrs. Bateman's dress. I think you better come, Ms. Carrie."

"Go on," Ray told her. "I'll be fine." *And I'll see you around three in the morning I guess.*

Carrie leaned in once more and kissed his cheek. "Later," she repeated, lifting her brows.

"Oh, what have I unleashed?" And grinning, he

wiggled his own right back at her.

****

Music drifted out into the night air with a counterpoint of the waves drumming the shore. Brave couples had started dancing on a small floor set up beyond the pool. Carrie stood contentedly watching her guests before starting to do another round, contemplating her good fortune a damp mist had not rolled in from the sea and the air was calm.

"He looks like that cowboy in the Viagra ad on TV," her best friend was saying to a small group.

"I can guarantee, Diana," assured Carrie coming up to them, "Ray in no way needs Viagra."

Her elegant friend gave her a starchy smile. "Darling, you really did take a rather long time dressing this afternoon."

There were knowing smiles in the little group and the jangle of ice in glasses and jewelry on wrists.

With a sudden sense of empowerment by what she saw as a strong relationship with Ray, Carrie threw back, "Wrong again, Di. I wasn't *dressing*." It felt good; it satisfied her. After all, why shouldn't she have an adult relationship? She nodded to the group and moved on.

Ray was in a discussion with the Statlers and she headed toward them. Ben Statler was getting a bit anxious about something and her body tensed in response.

"Well," Ray was saying as she approached and stood just behind him, "it's our sons and now daughters who go off to serve while the eastern Ivy League always finds a way out. You're about the same age as me, Ben. Did you serve in Viet Nam?"

The New Yorker stared awkwardly into his drink, then up at Carrie. "I was in university and then law school while the draft was on, Ray. I admit, I got out of it. I don't think you can blame anyone for not wanting their sons to go off to war."

"Well, see, that's where you're wrong, Ben," Ray went on. "Some of us like to think we can, in some way, give back to our country."

Paige suddenly appeared. She held a drink in one hand and her shoes in the other. "Do you not think there are other ways to give back to your country, Ray? I mean, do you have to go someplace where you're likely to be killed just to prove a point? Can you not represent your country, volunteer, do Peace Corps?" She stood, waiting for an answer.

Carrie put a soothing hand on his shoulder. She could feel him breathing heavily, feel his frustration and anger. She also realized this could drive him to start drinking, understood that he wanted to respond, but wouldn't embarrass her. Then she sensed his body relax as he got hold of himself.

"Well, there are two sides to every story, and I think you're *all* right," she finished the conversation, while Ray calmed down. "Are you going to dance with me, mister? I have been waiting all night."

"All night, huh?" He put up a peace sign at Ben, then clasped Carrie by the hand. "Well, at least I found out I have one thing in common with your friends," he noted as she led him away.

"Oh, really." She tightened her hand in his. "What's that?"

"We're all Republicans."

Carrie had to stop where she stood for a little

giggle. Before she was able to move on near the dance floor, the head of catering approached her with a request to try the Irish coffee shots the staff were about to circulate with petit fours.

Exasperated, she tilted her head at Ray. "We *will* get to dance tonight. I promise. I'll be back as soon as possible."

He just laughed. "It's fine. I'm just gonna go help myself to the last of that fruit pudding before someone else steals it. I'll meet y'all later."

"Y'all," she drawled in return, pecking him on the cheek. "Y'all," she mimicked again as she went off smirking with a little bounce in her step.

****

Paige watched her mother and Ray from a distance. She sat by the edge of the pool and dangled her feet in the water, the color of which transformed through a rainbow from alternating, below-surface lighting. She chatted briefly with one of her friends who now excused himself and left her to finish the champagne in her hand. She put it down beside her and rested back on spread fingers, kicking up a shower of bright water and watching clouds race across the moon like an old-fashioned moving picture show. Ornamental torch lights, strategically placed around the grounds, were beginning to send curls of black into the air like smoke signals that the party might be winding down, nearing its conclusion, but Paige figured it had at least a couple of hours to run. No one would complain about the band playing on past local ordinance times because all the immediate neighbors were here enjoying themselves.

Thoughts tumbled through her intoxicated brain like papers on the wind she might try to grasp. First there was Jake and his telephone call. As if she had swallowed the worm at the bottom of a bottle of Mezcal, it gnawed at her. She surprised herself, admitting she had been happy to hear from him, hadn't completely written him off. She rationalized he wasn't erased from her memory due to Ray's numerous telephone calls to her mother. The other basis for being happy to receive his call was...well, was there another reason? He'd fulfilled a need, a temporary need. But then, that need might arise again.

And then there was her mother who had somehow morphed into another person since Ray had come on the scene. Paige tried to debate with herself, think logically. Was she jealous? Did she resent Ray because now her mother wasn't fawning over her every five minutes, making sure she was all right? Or did it just seem unfair for her mother to be so damn happy while she was unable to move on with her own life?

Which led her to think of school. It was July now, and she hadn't confirmed with Penn her intentions to return in September. Admissions wouldn't like that. What was she doing, living at home, moping? What did she really want to do with her life?

She watched as Ray, plate in hand, stopped to chat again with Diana and then nodded to Paige through the crowd. He gave her a wave, and Paige started to reach for her shoes with the idea she might like to take a walk on the beach when he was suddenly standing over her.

"Don't go, Paige. Mind if I join you?" he got out between mouthfuls.

"Of course not. Anyway, I meant to tell you Jake called while you were still traveling. He said for you not to worry."

He accepted this bit of information, then groaned into a sitting position next to her. He put the plate down on the stone deck and removed his own boots and socks, before rolling up his jeans to dangle his feet in the water beside her.

"You really don't give a hoot what people think of you, do you, Ray?"

He helped himself to another bite of the pudding. She watched as his gaze obviously scanned the show of wealth, of what money, serious money, could buy. "Well. Let me think. The only person whose opinion I really value here—aside from yours of course," he put in with a smile, "is your mama's. And I don't think she would mind me wetting my feet one bit. Fact is, I think she'd just laugh if she saw me. What do you think, Paige?"

"I think you're probably right." She sat with him in silence for a moment, taking no notice of the people moving behind them. "She doesn't really care about any of this, you know," she continued. "It was all just to get back at my father, to show him she didn't need him or his money. Then, of course, she was so successful it just went on. But I don't think she really cares. Though she does love this house. She'll come out in the dead of winter sometimes, and I think she really likes it best then, without the people."

Ray nodded in agreement. "Well. I think you're right."

He sat for a moment, watching the moon suddenly make a full appearance from behind clouds and cast a wavering reflection out on the ocean. With the fluctuations in the water, the silver disc changed shapes like an amoeba. Paige understood Ray's fascination with this, but she admitted to herself that was about all she understood about him. Her mother and him. A rancher. A Texan. She made a move once more for her shoes.

Ray finished the pudding before pushing the plate aside. "You know, I sorta get the feeling, Paige, you don't like me much, and I have to wonder why? Can you tell me, do you think?"

She was suddenly alert, assessing her opponent as if in court, then leaned back and grimaced. "I don't like anyone these days, Ray. It's not just you. I'm afraid I'm not what you'd call a people-person."

"Yeah. I guess I understand. It's not easy at your age, losing someone you love. Fact is, it's damn early for that. But I'm afraid that's what life is, just one long series of losses along the way, but with a whole lot more gains I'm glad to tell you."

Paige breathed in deeply, ready to make some sardonic comment about cowboy philosophy, but found she couldn't. He was studying her, ready for the riposte, waiting, but she suddenly found she couldn't hurt him, or even try.

"How…how did you get over Robbie?" she asked quietly.

"I didn't. You never get over the loss of a child. And you'll never get over the loss of your loved one. But time, while it doesn't heal everything like they say, it does make the pain less. A little less—a miniscule less—each day, until one day you realize it's nothing more than a niggle, the creak in your back when you first get up in the morning. You expect it, you know it's there, but you've learned to live with it, deal with it to an extent. You come to realize you know they're gone and they're not coming back. You stop wondering what he'll say when you tell him such and such, and then finally you stop expecting to tell him anything at all."

She took a sip of her champagne, thinking this through, wanting the pain to go away, just go away. "But you drank. You were drinking, when we met you. Only a short time ago. You weren't over Robbie. It wasn't just a niggle."

Ray flexed his toe into the water and tiny rings eddied out. "Well. I think the drinking had become a habit, an addiction, Paige. It no longer needed an excuse. I was in the habit of coming in after work and starting up. You know, Jake left for the army just a year after Robbie passed, my wife and I were arguing non-stop, there was no longer any glue to hold us together. My whole world seemed to be falling apart. I suppose loving your mama has helped." He turned to her and smiled. "I promise you, your fiancé would want you to go on with your life, and it'll soon be clear to you what you're meant to do."

"I don't know…I don't know if it will. We had such plans. We planned our lives *together*…"

"I know you did. But he would want you to go on, Paige, you know that. He would want you to meet someone else you can love, want you to go back to school and become that unbeatable lawyer you're meant to be, do all those things y'all planned. He wouldn't want you to be mourning him forever."

The pain shot through her, but now it was mixed with something else. A resolve. She sipped again at her glass as music started after a lull. Paige sat listening for a moment, then said, "You know, I think you're probably the best thing that's ever happened to my mother?"

"No, Paige, I'm not. *You* are, sweetheart. Believe me, you are."

"Soooo," said her mom, towering over them, heels cast aside. "My two favorite people…"

"Mother, I think you're somewhat tipsy!" She sent a conspiratorial glance toward Ray. "How much champagne have you had?"

"Not enough, not nearly enough." She lowered herself carefully behind Ray and hugged him, letting her head rest against his shoulder.

He reached around and gently ran his hand down her jaw, awkwardly trying to see her face.

A shot of jealousy suddenly flamed through that new resolve in Paige, flaring up anger for her loss. The unfairness of it, the loneliness as she studied her mother as the one now part of a couple. The course her life had taken enraged her now and, without knowing why, she directed her spleen at the man who had helped her gain her new resolution. "What was your wife like?" she asked, almost spitting out the question.

The two stared at her. There was tension on her mother's face, but Ray obviously tried to make light of it. "Well, she was very different from your mama, I'll tell you that. But then, I was a whole lot younger when I met and married her. And it actually was a shotgun wedding."

"Are you making excuses?" the lawyer in Paige cross-examined.

"No, of course not. I'm explaining. We change as we grow older. We mature, our tastes change, the way we see the world. Some people grow together, others not."

"Well," she said as she swung her legs one at a time out of the pool and shook them to get rid of water. "You're quite the philosopher, aren't you, Ray?"

"Paige…" her mother protested.

Paige put a hand on Ray's shoulder as she slipped on her shoes before bending over to do the straps. As she straightened, her gaze met her mother's and slight remorse began to replace the anger.

Carrie nodded slightly in acknowledgement of that change before she rubbed her cheek against his back and he reached again to pat her face.

"I wish I'd met you thirty years ago," her mother sighed.

"If you had, you wouldn't be the woman I love, the woman you are today. You wouldn't have Paige." He glanced up at Paige once more with a smile that said, 'no hard feelings.' "I wouldn't have Jake. You can't look back, Carrie—we have a future. The past just doesn't matter anymore."

Paige watched for a moment and finished her glass. She knew she had been rude, knew it was unreasonable to be jealous of her mother, wrong to deny her mother any happiness now. She returned Ray's smile, aware he had been right. Nothing was going to bring back Steven, and Steven wouldn't want her squandering her time. She needed to get on with her life and let her mother get on with hers.

Ray patted her mom's shoulder once more. "We gonna dance or what? I've been waiting all night, Miz Bennett."

He got his socks and boots back on and the couple went off holding hands. Her mother smiled and waved as she went by guests and Ray led her to the dance floor. As if the band knew what was required, they started playing a George Strait ballad.

Diana sidled up to Paige, watching the couple for a moment with her. "What the hell is that they're dancing? It's like something out of the nineteenth century. Or, no, a bad western—that's it. Your mother and her country music, for heaven's sake. They're the only couple on the floor. What is it?"

The anger in Paige completely receded, replaced by humor at the scene her mother presented. She laughed, then swiped another champagne off a passing tray. "It's the Texas Two Step, Diana. And it'll be sweeping the Hamptons before long!"

Chapter Eight

"I tried calling you yesterday, but you didn't pick up. I guess you were still traveling." Jake's voice had a slightly worried tone to it.

Ray pressed his cell phone to his ear and shuffled to sit up in bed. If his son could see him, still in bed at 10 a.m., he'd have a good laugh. Especially if he saw him in this bed.

He put his head back against one of the millions of pillows and peered up into the intricately pleated fabric of the bed crown, suddenly realizing Carrie wasn't there. "Yeah," he croaked out, "I had a bit more traveling than I bargained for."

There was a slight pause before Jake said, "Did I wake you, Dad? You sound sort of groggy. You haven't been drinking again, have you?"

"No, no, not at all. We had a real late night here last night. A party. And after all that traveling and what have you…" His voice trailed off while the desire for coffee hit him.

"Yeah. Did Paige give you my message? That I called?"

"Yeah." Ray waited a moment, then said, "Look, I'm real sorry, I feel real guilty about leaving you for July Fourth just when you're back, but—" He played with the sheets, rumpling them in his palm as he thought again about leaving Jake behind. It hadn't been fair to do that to his son.

"It doesn't matter, Dad. Really. I went on over to Toby's place. His family had a barbecue. But I'm sorry I didn't go along to see Paige—in a way. How is she?"

Ray tried to spy around the edge of the curtains to see if Carrie was there, but couldn't see anything. "Oh, she's fine. She and I had a good chat last night. She's fine, Jake. Maybe you ought to give her a call."

"I did. Well, yeah, maybe I'll phone her again, but I don't think that's goin' anywhere, Dad." There was a pause before he asked, "Did she say she was goin' back to school? To law school?"

"No, we didn't discuss that." His head was clearing, and he kept thinking there was something in his son's voice not quite right. "Are you okay?" he asked at last.

"Sure. Listen, I think I need to get the vet out for Snowflake. She's off her feed. Is that all right with you?"

"Yeah, of course. If you think so. Jake, is everything else okay? Have *you* thought about going back to college?"

"Dad! Maybe next semester. Not September. Not now, it's too soon. I have to think whether it's the right move, you know. I'm twenty-seven now. Those college kids are so much younger and all. And can I really learn anything more about taking over the ranch, do you think? We'll discuss it when you get home. Okay?"

Ray drew in a deep breath. "Yeah. Okay. Listen, I better go. Haven't had breakfast and don't want to miss my chow. You know me."

"Haven't had breakfast? At—what time is it there?—like ten or something? What kind of a life do those people lead?" His son would have a smirk on his face.

"Well, it was July Fourth..."

Jake grunted at the excuse, then waited a minute. "Dad?"

"Yeah, son?"

"You have a good time there, ya hear? Don't hurry home on my account. Okay?"

There was a moment before he guffawed. "I'll be home late Sunday, Jake. It's fine."

Ten minutes later, Ray emerged from the bathroom, having put on his boxers, and slid open the door to the balcony. He leaned against the doorframe.

Carrie sat at her computer, either oblivious to his presence or ignoring it altogether.

"Well, this is quite a view," he began when she said nothing.

There was no response for several moments filled with the tapping of her fingers on the computer keyboard. "Yes," she finally got out. "I like the ocean." And then, as an afterthought, she added, "And good morning to you, too."

He smiled. "Oh, it wasn't the ocean I was admiring. You sittin' there an' all, it does a man's heart good." As the tapping continued, he asked, "How long you been there, Carrie?"

"No idea. I'm afraid my brain can't stop working." Her fingers, however, stopped and she met his gaze. "Sometimes, I'm afraid, I just get up in the night with an idea. One night, I remember, I got up seven times. It's part of the job, Ray, the unsleeping brain." She tapped a few more sentences into the computer. "How about you? Did you sleep all right?"

"Like a baby." She sat typing there for a moment before he said, "So, you lead a literary littoral life, huh?"

"Literal life?" Carrie's nose scrunched in misunderstanding.

He laughed. "L-i-t-t-o-r-a-l."

"Ah!" Her face brightened with a big smile. "You're very clever. Or at least very alliterative."

"Or even…" Ray searched for a word.

Carrie raised her eyebrows at him, her face expectant.

The lack of food and the desire for something more no doubt affected his brain and he gave up. "Never mind. I can't keep that going. So, what's on the agenda for today? Anything special?"

Her gaze went back for several moments to scan what she had written before she glanced back. "I think getting you swim trunks is pretty high on the agenda. What do you think, handsome?" She clicked once with her mouse and then closed the cover of her laptop.

"I think you can decide on anything you like for your toy boy, sweetheart."

"My 'toy boy?'" Carrie queried.

"Yeah. I did a search on you on line before I came out and discovered you are a year older than I am. So, that makes me your toy boy, doesn't it?" He wondered if she saw the twinkle in his eyes, but Carrie paled at this bit of news.

"I'm older than you?" she gasped.

"Oh, Carrie," Ray shook his head in dismay at what might be considered his faux pas. "We're not going to fret over this, are we? One year?"

She put a hand across her mouth, studying him for

a long, hard minute. "I don't know. I don't think you should have told me." Her eyes went wide as she considered this.

He bit his lip, her sensitivity to her age both tantalizing and maddening. He decided the best way to deal with it was to ignore it.

"I'm hungry as hell and wantin' to make love to the prettiest gal in all of the Hamptons," he told her at last.

"Jeez, you're not going to have a go at my daughter now, are you?" she countered.

"Carrie Bennett, you have some strange ideas. Have you ever showered with a Texan, lady?"

Her hand came away and she smiled. "I bet that is about the best damn shower anyone can imagine."

He let his smile widen at his success in distracting her as he extended his hand. "There's a bit of Texas Two-step in it, a bit of spa massage, and a bit of Fourth of July fireworks."

She got up slowly from her chair and locked gazes with him. "And a bit of Playboy Porn?" she offered.

That was a turn-up for the books. Ray smiled to himself at the new woman he had helped create. "Well, I don't like to mention that." But he certainly looked forward to it.

"But surely," she said as she scraped her chair back from the balcony table, "That's the very best bit of all?"

****

Jake loved Mulligan's. Especially on a Saturday night. It was the sort of roadside bar that appeared in small towns all over the West—a wooden shack with a gas station out front. To one side of a large room it had a small shop where items for the passing trade could be bought—water, soft drinks, candy on the counter and an ice cream chest—and to the other side there was a long wooden bar for the locals. The lighting was negligible, service was, at times, on an honor system to which the regulars adhered, and the bar stocked what its patrons wanted, namely Jack Daniels, Jim Beam, beer and tequila, with a few bottles of cheap local wine for the ladies. When the gas station closed down at 7pm in the evening, the forecourt became a parking lot for pickup trucks. Music, always country of course, blared out from an old juke box in the corner, which had a habit of breaking down and leaving the customers to sing—usually out of tune or off-key—to finish the song. Neither the bar nor the gas station took credit cards, which meant, with no one at the pumps, the client had to come inside to pay. Only once did Mulligan's lose money because of this, and the license plate had been out of state. In other words, Mulligan's was a congenial place for the locals to have a few drinks and catch up in a friendly atmosphere.

Jake navigated his way up to the bar and elbowed in between two other regulars who nodded to him before turning back to their conversations.

"Hey, how ya doin'?" called Mike Mulligan, extending his hand for a welcome shake. "Long time and all that."

"Yeah, Mike. Last few times I was in, you weren't here. How've you been?" He leaned on the bar as the cares of the day were left behind.

"Fine, good." The owner signaled to someone at the other end, who was shouting his name, and pointed to the bottles, watching for a moment as the man went round the back of the bar and helped himself. "So, what's your poison tonight? Jim or Jack?"

"The usual, Jack and Coke—"

"Make that two," said a recognizable voice behind him.

Jake tensed and twisted back slowly to look into the snake-like grin of Ty Sheldon. "What the hell are you doing here? Why don't you crawl back under whatever rock you came from?"

"Oh-hhh," Ty drew out the single sound. "Now, is that any way to be speakin' to your brother's very best friend?"

"Get lost."

The drinks came, and he steadfastly kept his back to Ty.

"I think we need to have a little conference there, Jake. You know, you did so well doing me that little favor last time I just—"

"Forget it!" His voice came so loud, several people halted their conversations to see what was happening, surprised at the sudden intrusion into their quiet drinking.

Ty leaned in, reaching past him for his drink from the bar, but staying in close so Jake could hear him clearly.

"You better listen, Jake, I mean it. Unless you want your father's glowing picture of Robbie the hero destroyed forever. You know what—"

"I know I'm gonna bust your face if you don't move away, Ty. I'm sorting things with my dad. I'm going to tell him 'bout Robbie, so you can just push off." Would he believe that? Would he let go?

"You gonna tell him 'bout Lucinda, too?"

Jake's back stiffened. He had his hand out for his

glass, but it hovered there, unable to grasp the drink. "What about Lucinda?"

"You know Lucinda's married? Finally got hitched early this year. No kids as yet of course…You think her husband knows?"

Jake's fist came flying into Ty's face with a suddenness and strength that sent the wrangler flying. Crashing into some other patrons who were standing nearby, he landed on his butt as drinks got splattered and glasses shattered before the bystanders could back out of the picture.

Ty dabbed at his nose and came away with blood as Mike called out, "Hey, hey, hey! Take it outside, the two of you! Out!"

Jake reached back for his glass and downed his drink. Slamming it on the bar, he headed to the door past his prone opponent as some others helped Ty to his feet and checked him over. As he glanced back for a last look, Sheldon shook them off and reeled to the door, almost tripping out after him.

"You better hang on, soldier boy," he called. "I don't think your dad is gonna like it none too well if I press charges now. I got lots of witnesses in there."

"No one's gonna pay any attention to you, you damn crook." He swiped at some drops of rain that had begun to fall, feeding his anger like water to a thirsty man.

Coming up to him, Ty wiped away blood with a bandana he had stuffed in his pocket. "One last time, Jakie," he sneered. "Come on now, you did so well with that army uniform and all. It's a cinch. And I leave you and your daddy alone. Plus, of course, the added bonus Lucinda's new found family don't hear anything about her none-too glorious past. By the way, does your dad know about Robbie's part in that? I wonder..." The tone was a seductive mockery, like a wild cat circling in for the kill, beautiful to watch but deadly.

Jake stood like a snared animal. At some stage, he may be able to tell his dad, but what about Lucinda? If her husband didn't know the truth... And what would this extra bit of information about Robbie and Lucinda do to his dad?

The first run *had* been relatively easy, if nerve-wracking.

No, it wasn't that it was nerve-wracking. He would capitulate because it was exciting. Like Iraq. It energized him, made him feel alive; it was a cat and mouse game that got his pulse going. Like making love to Paige, because he could never really have her. But then again, doing the run was bound to get easier if the border guards didn't recognize him, get suspicious, and do a search of the car. Not the second time, they wouldn't. Surely, not the second time.

"When?" Jake snarled at last.

Ty dabbed at his face again. "Well, that's more like it," he approved in a voice like molasses dripping in the heat. "Next week, if you wouldn't mind, Jakie. Same address, so it'll be real easy. Only one bit of advice."

"What's that?"

"Change the border crossing. Go down to Laredo or over to Del Rio. You used Eagle Pass last time. Switch out. They get to know you."

Jake stood still and studied the wrangler. "What difference does it make, Ty, if this is the last time?"

He snorted. "It *will* be the last time. I've got someone else lined up, but they're not here yet. Just this time. I promise you. But don't take chances. Change the damn crossing. You got maps, don't you? You'll find your way. And one more thing, Jakie…"

"What's that, you bastard?"

"Don't change your mind. I swear, you change your mind…you're gonna be one very sorry boy. *Very* sorry."

****

The Sunday sunshine sparkled on the pool as Paige scrolled down the numbers of recent calls on her phone and found the Texas area code. Her finger poised above the send button before she drew it back to study a chip in the polish on her nail. She grimaced and lay back again in the sun lounger, relieved all the guests had gone, all that is except for Ray who was no doubt upstairs making love to her mother. He certainly wasn't taking this long to pack.

She craned her head around to try to see her mother's balcony jutting out from the far corner of the house, but only caught a glimpse of a curtain billowing like some fat person trying to get out of the room. Nope. Mom and Ray were definitely having a last tumble before he left. Paige glanced at the phone once again and jabbed 'call.'

"Hello?"

Jake's voice came across unusually disinterested in the fact it was she who was calling, and this irritated her for no particular reason. "Well, if I'm disturbing you, I can call another time," she started. "What are you doing?"

There was the split second of his coming to realize who had called. It made Paige smile to herself.

"I'm lying in bed as it happens, stroking one of the

dogs."

"As long as you're not stroking anything else." She imagined his expression at that. "Are you naked?"

"And if I am? Did you phone for a trip down memory lane or is this some sort of courtesy call?"

There was the sound of sheets rustling. Paige had forgotten the time difference but, even allowing for that, it was late for Jake to be in bed, even on a Sunday.

"You're in a mood," she said. "I can tell. Tell Mama Paige what the matter is."

His sigh crackled down the phone. "You remember..." he started, but trailed off. "Never mind. How are you? How was the party? Has my dad left yet?"

"Fine, fine and no, in that order. The party was our usual uproarious success and your father is now upstairs humping my mother before he leaves."

Jake snorted. "I think that's more information than I need, Paige. Or maybe not," he added with some amusement. There was a moment's hesitation. "So...to what do I owe this honor? I'm sure you didn't call to simply hear a Texas drawl one more time."

"I—there's something I don't understand. You're twenty-seven, right?"

"Right."

"And you were in the army for four years, right?"

"Right."

"Which takes you back to twenty-three or maybe twenty-two depending on your birth month."

"And?"

"And so, why hadn't you finished college by then? I don't understand it." Curiosity had got the better of her. Or was it just a damn good excuse to talk to him, talk to someone who was detached from the whole Hamptons scene she was dealing with, someone who seemed to care and who wasn't her mother.

"Because, like you, when Steven died, I quit my last year when Robbie died. I never graduated, never did my finals. Robbie and I were very close. I... Why do you want to know all this? What does this have to do with anything? What made you suddenly think of all this anyway?"

There was rising anger in his voice, or maybe it was something other than anger—hate. Hate at being dragged back to that point in his life? He had told her it was his fault Robbie had enlisted; he had told Robbie to go in order to avoid trouble.

"I..." She stuttered, searched around for some words to try to give herself time to think. "I just wanted to know. I was curious. I think I'm going back to law school and it all struck me." But no, she had made it an excuse to phone him. Angry with herself, angry at being so weak she needed some sort of male companionship, some male attention, she sat up suddenly, tears just below the surface. "Sorry. I shouldn't have called."

"Don't go!"

There was an urgency in his voice, and Paige sat back again, thoughts trying to fall into place like the pieces of a puzzle.

"I'm glad you called," he said in a steadier tone.

She took a deep breath and stared out at the vacated pool area. Tapping the chipped nail several times on the chaise armrest, she finally continued. "Your father...he talked some good sense to me at the party actually. I think I need to get on with my life, get back to work. There's no point hanging about here feeling sorry for myself. Maybe... Why didn't he talk you into going back, Jake?"

"Because he doesn't see the point any more than I do, really. Anyway, he's leaving me to decide. Dad won't push. He never went to college and he's done fine. I don't need a dang piece of paper to say I studied for four years. I'm going to take over the ranch. It's my life, Paige. It's what I know, what I enjoy."

"But maybe, sometime, you'll need a business course or something like that."

"Paige..."

She could almost hear the cogs of his brain turning.

"I already studied what I need to know, and I've lived here all my life. It's not like studying law. Anyway. Is that what you want? To go back to law school? Really want?"

She hesitated only a moment. "Yes. It's what I want."

****

"Ah, hell, Carrie, when you said you had called for a car to take me back to the airport, I didn't realize it was gonna be a dang limo. Call me a taxi, for heaven's sake. I can't ride in that." Ray took in the long, black limo and its uniformed driver with some distaste.

Eye to eye, Carrie put her hands on his shoulders. "You can. And you will. Please. It's on my account. Anyway, you've missed the train, and the only jitneys are all going to be full. Listen," she continued, leaning her face toward him so their noses touched, "We had two extra hours together, which you must admit were pretty *worthy* of your time." She stood back a second to flutter her lashes at him. "And it was a compromise between the train and a chopper. That's fair, isn't it?"

"I don't know about 'fair.' But the extra time was sure worth it."

The driver came around and picked up his bag to put in the trunk before holding open the door.

Ray regarded him with an intense aversion. "Just give me an extra minute, will you? I think I can manage to get in by myself." He received a smile from the chauffeur and waited until the man was back in the driver's seat. "Listen," he said, taking hold of Carrie's hands. "We never had that chat, did we?"

"You can call me on your cell phone and we can speak as you go to the airport. Which, by the way, would not have been very convenient in a crowded train."

Ray had a sense Carrie was trying to be stalwart at his leaving and that tears were not far from the surface. She was definitely trying to avoid a face-to-face discussion about where their relationship was going. Her hands fluttered like butterflies searching for a place to land.

"Okay. I want you to think about what I have to do to get you to come out to Texas for a spell. You make your list of requirements and then give me a call. I'll be sitting in that damn thing, waiting, in air conditioned splendor."

She nodded her head in acknowledgement, a hand clapped across her mouth as tears surfaced.

"Oh, come on now," he said, taking her into his arms. "We had three wonderful days, which is three more than we would have had if I hadn'ta got this brilliant idea." He stood for a moment before kissing the top of her head and holding her away from him.

"Oh, lord," moaned Paige, suddenly coming down the front steps. "Is this the big good-bye? Am I missing it all? Is she bawling already?" She gave her mother a disgusted look and hauled a crumpled tissue from her robe pocket to hand to Carrie. "Do you want him to remember you with a red nose?" she mocked, then pecked him good-bye on both cheeks. "Give Jake a big sloppy one for me, will you, and tell him to go find Miss Texas or the Rodeo Queen. He deserves the best."

Ray gave a laugh in answer before turning back to Carrie and kissing her good-bye. He studied her one last time before he ducked into the car.

An empty space opened within him, like a black hole into which his heart was falling.

****

Her daughter's arm came around Carrie as they headed back up the steps to the house, now empty of its visitors and accompanying tumult. The pool beyond resembled some David Hockney painting waiting to be finished, and the quiet was almost unbearable after the hubbub of the last few days.

Bereft, she ached for Ray, a soreness like an open wound in her chest. The hand-holding walks in town and on the beach, the games of volley ball in the pool, the jokes with the others at meals, how he had fit in so easily. Even Ben Statler, with whom Ray had had the altercation at the party, said he liked him. There had been laughter, and there had been loving.

Lots of loving.

In all its forms.

"So, what will you do?" Paige demanded at last. "He's got a business in Texas and you...you're all over the place. Can you make it work?"

"I thought you didn't like him. You made all those comments about him not being right, about Texas..."

"Oh, Mother, haven't you learned? I make comments all the frigging time. Do what's right for you, for heaven's sake. Don't pay any attention to what I, or anyone else for that matter, say."

Carrie collapsed into a chair and stared out with the vacant mind that comes of loss. After a long sigh, she said, "I've got a book tour coming up, the new book to try to finish, and commitments all over the place. L.A. wants help with the screenplay of *The Divide*... I don't know."

"But he is right, Mother. You can work in Texas. That's one thing. At least part of the time."

She considered this for a moment, a sudden quandary striking her. "What about you, Paige? I can't just leave you—"

"Oh, for pity sake. Really. I'm a big girl now, and I have my own friends. And anyway," she said, dropping down into a chair, "I'm going back to law school in the fall."

"You're what? When did this happen? Are you sure? Is that what you want? Are you ready?"

"They told me I would have to re-take the second year as I messed it up when Steven started running to doctors. So, that's what I'm going to do, if that's all right with you."

"Of course, it's all right. But are you sure?" she asked again.

"Yup. I'm going back to Penn."

****

Jake tapped in Paige's number, but it went straight to voice mail. He could phone Grant or Toby to discuss his predicament but, since returning, a gap had been evident between them that hadn't closed as yet. They viewed him differently. He'd been abroad; he'd served, and, in a way, he was out of touch with their world. Four years was a long time. Grant was engaged now with a wedding not far off, and Toby had got himself a job at one of the hotels in Fredericksburg, and would, on any account, think Jake a damn fool for not just having it out with his dad. They sure as heck wouldn't care about Lucinda.

And no one really knew him anymore; no one would understand how he worshipped his father and just couldn't bring himself to hurt him, disappoint him. Even those two boys he'd grown up with didn't really know the man he was now. But after the last conversation with Paige, an only child from a one parent family, he came to feel maybe she would understand.

He tried her phone again and this time left a message.

****

Ray carefully shoved his hat into the overhead bin and slid into the window seat, hoping he wouldn't be next to a chatterer. While people did the slow march up the aisle past him and babies cried, and announcements came incessantly over the speaker system about how to put bags in the bins, wheels down, and to please take your seats so departure could be on time, he peered out the window trying to mentally escape it all, trying to get himself someplace else.

It wasn't that he needed a drink; Carrie had become his new addiction, and it surprised him. Perhaps he hadn't drunk so much for the loss of Robbie and his part in that loss, but for the loneliness, the emptiness of a failed marriage as well as a lost son. Had he ever been in love before, truly in love, the way he loved Carrie? Her vulnerability mixed with control, her aloofness mixed with loving, her wariness mixed with need. He surprised himself, falling in love like this at his age, the intensity of his feelings throwing him and catching him off guard.

While a brief telephone conversation from the car hadn't brought any resolutions as to their relationship, he knew there had to be decisions as to what mattered now. Could he put aside this, that or the other to be with her? Could he be less responsible toward his business, give more responsibility to Jake and the two managers so he could take more time away? And was it worth it?

After living so long on his own—both with and without Leigh Anne—there was no road map as to how to proceed with this new-found happiness and the need and compulsion to be with Carrie.

He punched her number one last time before they put the ban on electronic devices, but she didn't pick up. After the voice mail message finished, he said quietly into the phone, "We're about to take off, but I had to tell you...I love you."

Chapter Nine

Jake gunned down I-35, country music blasting over the cranky sounds of the air conditioning. The heat was up in southern Texas, and Mexico would be unbearable, especially in uniform. His air conditioning barely dealt with the sun burning in through the windscreen, searing the steering wheel and everything else in the front of the car, including himself. Even his sunglasses weren't providing protection, and he snapped down the sun visor and played with it to get the best coverage. Rain would suit his mood better, but there was little enough of that this time of year unless a hurricane hit the coast and moved inland.

He recalled his conversation with his dad, when he told him he was heading down to Brownsville to visit a stud farm down there. The quizzical look on his father's face told him he didn't swallow that. Whatever his dad thought, he was now so caught up in sorting his life with Carrie, nothing much else was going to get a whole lot of attention, and this suited Jake just fine.

What hadn't suited him was the lack of response from Lucinda. All those phone calls to her to no avail. But he'd discovered from her parents that she and her new husband were having a postponed honeymoon in Europe and wouldn't be back for a couple of weeks. Bad luck.

Deep in thoughts of the way his life was going, the

ring of the phone jolted him and made him jump, the sound so sudden in the hermetic world of the car. He shuffled with one hand to grab the phone and tried to surreptitiously put it to his ear. "Hello?" He stole a quick glance at the screen to see who was calling, but glare made it unreadable. Then he heard Paige's voice.

"I see you tried to get me, so I am being unbelievably good-natured today and returning your call. Where the hell are you? You sound as if you're in some laundromat or something."

"I'm driving. Can I call you back in five?"

"For heaven's sake, Jake. Are you the only man in Texas who really cares about driving and talking at the same time?"

"Maybe." He grimaced to himself. "I don't want to get picked up by the cops. Give me five," and he put the phone down.

It was longer than five minutes to the next exit to find a place to stop. Jake parked by the side of the road, long grass and a ditch almost claiming the car. He was sure Paige would be gone by now, wouldn't pick up— knowing her—but she did, first ring.

"What took you so long?" she spat out.

He was taken aback for a moment, then laughed wryly. "Boy, Paige, you're that impatient to talk to me? You hankerin' to hear my Texas drawl or maybe have phone sex or somethin'?" He could picture her in his mind's eye for a moment, probably prancing around in her underwear or a bikini, the usual smirk on her face.

"Didn't you ask me that last time we spoke, Jake? It must be on your mind, not mine. Anyway, I think our sex-of-any-kind days are over. We're too much like brother and sister, now the geriatrics have got so hot and heavy. Why, we've practically committed incest with all the shagging that was going on here last week."

He sat back, trying to think of his father with Carrie. It was a better picture than his father and his mother—more likely. "So, how are you, Paige? What else is happening in the rarefied world of the Hamptons?"

"Not a lot."

He heard a splash and pictured her pacing around a pool.

"You should have joined the party. Why didn't you come, too?"

Jake started up the ignition to put the air conditioning back on. He tried to shake his arms free of his shirt to cool himself as snakes of sweat gathered and soaked through the fabric. "Someone had to mind the place. Dad's so damn enamored of your mother now, it's a wonder he can get anything done." He waited a moment, considering the things he wanted to ask her. "You decide what to do about school? You definitely going back?"

There was the chink of ice in a glass before she said, "Yes. I'm going back. Right after Labor Day. You?"

"Haven't decided. Don't think so. Don't think I can face studies any more, all those books and papers to write, and then the parties. It'll be all kids so much younger than me. Anyway, I'm working here on the ranch and it's fine. I think Dad needs me anyway. But I'm not sure. What you said last time, about maybe needing a business degree sometime in the future, it made me think." Jake sat, feeling a stream of sweat creep down his side like a crawling ant. He fiddled with the air conditioning again before going on. "The other side of this is the money, of course. I don't want to be saddled with more of a loan. We're not wealthy New Yorkers, you know."

Paige didn't answer.

He figured perhaps he'd been rude to make the comparison and grimaced at himself before fiddling again for a moment. "I suppose I could get veteran's…" he went on half to himself. Then he sat forward before slouching back into the seat. "Paige?"

"Still here, Jake. You're worrying me. You're rambling and sound weird. I know that's unusual for me. I'm not usually a worrier."

"Yeah." He took a deep breath, wondering whether he should proceed.

"So?"

"So, you remember I told you 'bout Robbie? Well, I sort of told you about Robbie?"

"He was in trouble of some kind. You told him to join the army to avoid it. Your father doesn't know. That's about what I gathered, as far as we got. So, spill the beans."

Perspiration began to dampen his face despite the air conditioning. There was wet in his hair, on his face, in his groin. He didn't know if it was the heat or his anxiety, but bile rose in his throat. He opened the door and slipped out, leaning back against the car to try to clear his head. The heat of the vehicle forced him away again and he started to pace on the verge.

"Robbie was a drug runner, Paige." He spoke so quietly there might have been possible eavesdroppers nearby. "He was in business with Ty Sheldon for a couple of years. He used to bring the stuff, marijuana mostly, across the border, and Ty would do the dealing, but they'd been partners. When Robbie tried to pull out, Ty threatened him."

"Ummm," she interrupted. "I sort of felt it had something to do with that creep. When I saw you and him at the ranch that day—"

"So, Robbie took my advice and joined the army to get out of it, and Ty found someone else to donkey for him. A year after Robbie's death, I enlisted so I was out of the picture. Until now."

"Until *now*? Oh, Jake, for goodness sake..."

The disbelief in her voice hit him like a gavel.

"Listen. Listen," he repeated. "He threatened to tell my dad. He said if I didn't do the run for him—"

"Jake!"

Paige's tone brought him up short. It was adversarial, dictatorial.

"And there's this girl. Lucinda. Robbie and she—"

"I don't want to hear any more. I don't care about any girl, and I don't care about Robbie. Robbie is dead, Jake. If you want to be a complete idiot, don't tell me about it. You're a fool, Jake, a complete and utter fool." When she went on, her voice was calmer. "What have you done? What have you done so far?"

"I made one run. I'm making a second one right now."

"Going or coming?"

"What?" Suddenly he was fighting the need to heave as he took in air, breathed harder.

"Have you got the shit on you? Have you collected it as yet?"

"No, no. I'm on my way. I—"

"Do you know what kind of an idiot you are? Do

179

you know what trouble you can get into?"

"Of course I know what kind of dang trouble I can get into. I'm not that stupid!"

"Well, it seems you are!" Paige let out a deep breath. "This is to protect Ray? You think Ray is going to care more about a dead son than a live one? You think Ray isn't 'man enough' to hear the truth about Robbie in preference to seeing you in jail? You think Ray wants you mixing with or being threatened into this by that piece of crap, Ty Sheldon? Have you thought at all? Have you thought it through *at all?*"

He could only offer silence for an answer.

Jake stood watching the cars passing on the highway, sunlight glinting off their metal, the whoosh of tires on hot asphalt as they dwindled and wavered in the heat. He sighed at the truth of her words, at his stupidity. He had tried to do the right thing, and it had come out wrong. Or maybe he was just lying to himself.

"This isn't Iraq, Jake, where maybe, just maybe, you sort of had a license to do things not normally permitted by decent men. Oh, decent—I should think that's more important to you than it is to me but, hell, what do I know? Listen to me and listen good. Turn the car around, Jake. Turn the F-ing car around and go tell Ray once and for all. Get the whole thing off your chest and start living normally again. *Turn the car around!*"

****

To Carrie, it was as if someone had let her out of prison, the prison of her aging body, the prison of her demanding career, the prison of always having to be who people wanted her to be.

And the prison of revenge against what she had suffered from her ex, David.

She considered that if a reckoning had been the initial motivation, the other factors had egged her on, taken over, driven her ever onwards. She had been a hostage to her own success. Like a runner without water who would eventually have to stop, she had gone on without love, without a point of reference, without a reason for it all except the revenge, which was now so distant, so vague as to not be there at all. And why? Why had she lived this way? Perhaps she had always been waiting for Ray; perhaps she had known, her body had known something better than all the others, some life better than this one would come along.

She counted her blessings of having this man in her life. He made no demands on her, wanted nothing from her except herself, her love. He cared nothing for what she looked like, loved her for her accomplishments, for what she was—not who she wasn't—didn't give a hoot about anything except her, and didn't care if the whole circus stopped or slowed. He was there for her, one hundred percent. Ray.

And yet, she knew she wouldn't stop the circus that had become her life.

As she thought it through, something was driving her on. Whether it was a sense of responsibility or she actually wanted this life or enjoyed it, she could no longer tell, but she couldn't stop. And she knew it now; she wanted both worlds.

As she listened to his message, that "I love you" over and over again, she felt like a teenager, a young girl in love, and she remembered his touch, his smile, his laugh, his kiss and suddenly nothing else mattered—or seemed to matter—anymore. She could grow old, fail, give up...give up everything, except Ray.

****

Jake came in and threw a bunch of tack needing mending on the kitchen table. The rotund figure of Mabel, clad in her usual black dress with a white apron wrapped around her as it had been for the past eighteen years, stopped wiping the dish she held in her hand. She squinted round, black eyes at him, a face he remembered from his youth, as he sat his gangly frame on the edge of the table.

"What now?" he asked.

"You put that horse stuff on my clean kitchen table? Jake, you know better than that. You get that stuff outta here this minute. This ain't no place for horses, where you all eat. I'm gonna have to scrub that down now."

"It's the best place for mending, Mabel," he answered rather dubiously. "I'll scrub it down when I'm finished."

"*You*'ll scrub it down?" she repeated in a low, doubtful voice. "You get that outta here, Jake. Take it back out to the stable where it belongs. Between the horses and the dogs, I got my life's work cut out for me."

He reluctantly started gathering up the tack again when the house phone rang. He grabbed the extension off the wall in the kitchen.

"Rocking R," he answered.

"What the hell have you done?" came Ty's angry voice.

He kept his back to Mabel who slowly went on emptying the dishwasher. "I haven't done anything. And I'm not going to. I don't want you phoning here, and I don't want you calling round. You get the

182

message?"

"Do I get the message? *Do I get the message?* You listen to me, and you listen good, Jake. You get in your car and you go and do that run or you're going to be one sorry—"

"I can't speak now. And it's no use anyway. I'm going to…clear the matter up." His stomach lurched as he thought of facing his father.

"You don't have to speak. You just have to listen. If you don't—"

Jake hung up. He hit the wall, making Mabel jump before he started to gather the tack. The phone rang again. Slamming his load back on the table to the housekeeper's gasp of frustration, he grabbed the phone off the wall and yelled down it, "Don't you phone here again!"

There was a split second of silence before Carrie's voice caught him as he was about to hang up.

"Jake?"

"Oh, Carrie? Sorry, I thought it was someone else."

"Well, I'm certainly glad to hear that. What with Ray not picking up his phone and that answer from you, I was beginning to think I'd done something awful."

"No. No, not at all. Dad's out with a hunting party, so his cell will be off. How are you?"

"Well. If living off Subway sandwiches and sitting on endless folding chairs in drafty libraries and bookstores is fun, then I'm having a great time. On the other hand…"

"You doin' a book tour?"

"How did you guess?" Her deep breath sounded down the line. "How are things at the ranch?"

"Oh, okay. Fine. Dad misses you." Jake caught

Mabel eyeing him curiously. She put a stack of dishes away, untied her apron and shook it out. "So, if you want the best damn hushpuppies in the state of Texas," he continued in an attempt to appease the housekeeper, "you best come on here."

He could hear the home-help mumble, "That's all we need. A demanding houseguest. I heared about her."

Jake continued into the phone, "Where are you now?"

"Rapid City, South Dakota."

"Well, at least it's west. You could be in Maine."

"No, the tour was planned with some precision. I started two weeks ago in Maine, shortly after the party, and have worked my way here."

"You fixin' to come on after, then? Dad would sure like that." He tried to think what it would be like to have Carrie there, for him, for his father.

"I know." Her voice was subdued. "I'd like it, too, but...I don't know if I can. Maybe at the end of the summer, Jake, when Paige finally goes back to school."

He played with the cord of the phone for a moment before offering, "Paige is a big girl, Carrie. She seems to look after herself real well."

"I know, but—"

"Hang on, I think I hear Dad's truck now."

Mabel grabbed her bag off a hook on the wall and waddled to the door, meeting him and the yapping dogs coming in. "Mr. Ray, you have guests in the house, I want a raise!" Her voice projected over the din of barking.

"What?" There was confusion mixed with a smile on his face as Jake caught his eye. Mabel had been working there long enough for his father to know exactly how to deal with her. "What guests?"

"I'm going now. I got my babies to see to. But you ask Jake. He seems to be invitin' everyone 'round for hushpuppies these days." And with that, she was out the door.

"Hang on, Carrie, Dad's just walked in."

A huge smile spread across the older face.

Jake held out the phone to his father before gathering the tack, then dropped it back down. "Oh, the hell with it," he muttered. The dogs came as one and appealed to him as if they, too, understood they would now be forgotten. He absently gave one a pat and headed for the dog food.

"Carrie, honey?" his father said into the phone. "Where are you, darlin'?"

****

Paige flicked the thermostat down to bring up the air conditioning, then ran her finger along the law books on her shelf. She stood musing on them, then turned to look outside as sun flickered through the trees of Central Park and glinted vehemently on passing cars. The heat forced a slow pace on women who had deferred to sandals while men sauntered, their jackets slung over shoulders.

She'd have to get back to the grind.

She had left the beach for a few days to collect her weighty tomes of advocacy before returning to enjoy the last weeks of summer—on her own. She appreciated her mother had to schedule a book tour according to the necessities of easy travel and promotion, but the solitude this had afforded her was not altogether welcome. Friends came out on weekends, of course, but sitting around the rest of the week with only Carmen with whom to exchange a few words proved outright boring. So, here she was, faced with advanced torts, federal procedure, contract law, civil law, animal law and ethics.

"Animal Law and Ethics?" She remembered Steven laughing at her for opting to take that subject and how the two of them had bandied about the phrase "nonhuman animals" for several days. She recalled trying to get him to discuss whether animals were entitled to rights as property, but he had just gone back to asking her why she had taken the course in the first place. It wasn't *her*, he had said; was she concerned for her former horses?

Paige fanned through the book, almost in pristine condition, and a scrap of paper fell out. Written in Steven's hand it read, *The White Dog at 8pm—appropriate or what?*

Her fingers gripped it, and she slumped into her desk chair, her hand flapping the paper like a pennant in the wind.

Who had she been? Who was she? Had she molded herself to please Steven without even realizing it?

She let the paper slip from her hand, fluttering to her desk like a leaf from a tree, zigzagging in a strong breeze. Then she grasped the note once more and clutched it, crumpled the paper, and threw it in the bin. No use keeping that, she had enough keepsakes, enough memories, enough reminders of what could have been.

****

Ray understood not to plead, beg or make any kind of entreaty. He had come to realize the more he moved forward with Carrie, the more he tried to get hold of her, the more she backed off. While it wasn't a matter of pretending to be disinterested altogether, of not caring what she did, he had to let her set the pace. Going to New York was one thing; it showed her he cared. He had told her he wanted her to be with him; the rest was now up to her. He wasn't going to worry about it; she would come when she was ready.

But Jake was another matter. His son's subdued manner over the last couple of weeks gave him cause for concern. Jake wasn't going out, which was not like him, he played with his food and he appeared listless, lost.

In the soft light of the living room, with the dogs quietly chewing bones or demanding rubs, Ray peered across at his son, beer in hand, head thrown back.

"You want to watch some television? I think Top Shot might be on." His voice cut the night subtly, without alarm.

Jake sat up and took a sip. "No. It's all right." He eyed his father over the top of the can. "Dad?"

"Yeah?" Then quiet. Jake did not go on, so to help, Ray continued. "You know how proud I am of you? Did I ever tell you that? You and Robbie. You two were...are...the best damn sons a man could ask for. I want you to know, okay? I don't know if I ever told Robbie. Sometimes it...it bothers me he maybe didn't know how much I loved him. And you. So, I want you to know. You've made me real proud, Jake. Real proud."

His son downed the beer without saying anything. Then, staring at him, he held the can and crushed it in his hand before getting up and going into the kitchen.

Ray could see him leaning on the table with both hands, head bowed. He shoved a dog away and stood to go in to Jake when his cell phone rang. Carrie's name appeared on the screen.

"Sweetheart, can I call you back?" he started.

But it was too late; Jake walked past him and headed down the hall. The bedroom door clicked shut.

"Well…" Carrie's voice was uncertain.

"Never mind." He paced the room, a sudden feeling of loss washing over him, of being alone. "Where are you?" It was his usual question; the one he trusted would, one day, have a good answer.

"Dallas—"

"Dallas!"

"Changing planes. Or supposedly changing planes. Back to New York."

"I like the 'supposedly.'" He waited for her to continue.

"I don't cook, clean, or do laundry," she recited. "I am and always will be a workaholic," she rushed on. "I get up in the night sometimes when I have an idea, and my mind shuts everything else out at other times, even when you may think you have my full attention."

Ray paced and waited, hoping this was headed his way.

"I don't take much time off, although on occasion I can be persuaded to do so…but even then you may regret it because my mind will always go back to the book. Even making love, well… my attention might be elsewhere."

"I haven't so far found that to be so," he butted in.

"Well. No, I guess not. Long may it continue—"

"You gonna go on like this all night or you gonna tell me where I should pick you up?"

"You're going to pick me up? In Dallas? No.

There's a flight into Austin I can make, and I'll get a rental from there. Stay put and be good."

He put the phone down and sauntered over to Jake's bedroom door, listened for a moment, could see the light underneath and softly knocked.

After a moment, his son's voice came as a croak. "Yeah?"

"Jake? You all right? You wanna tell me what's wrong, son?" When he received no reply he went on. "Carrie's coming. She's on her way now from Dallas."

The door opened and Jake stood, leaning in the doorframe as if for support. His eyes were tired as he took him in.

"Is that all right? About Carrie?"

"'Course it's all right. Why shouldn't it be all right? Anyway," Jake said, turning back into the room, "what the hell would you do if I said 'no,' it wasn't all right?"

Ray studied his son; confusion slid through him as an unwanted guest, tainting his happiness at Carrie's imminent arrival. "I thought you liked her."

"I hardly know her, Dad. But if she makes you happy, then I'm happy for you." He stood playing with something on his dresser, before his gaze traveled back. "It's fine. Really." For a moment, only the crickets could be heard. "Maybe I should go on over to Mom's for a bit. Leave you two together?"

Ray stepped into the room. "I don't think that's necessary. Why would you do that?"

"Oh, you know. To leave you two alone."

"We don't need to be alone, Jake. We just want to be together. Carrie's already made it clear she's gonna be working. I mean, this is your home. I don't want anyone…I don't want you feeling you're being run off."

"Okay." He exhaled with an air of weariness.

For a moment, Ray considered if his son had been crying. "'Sides which," he continued, "Mark says you're doing real well working with the customers wantin' horses."

Jake continued to toy with something on his dresser.

"You gonna tell me what's wrong?" Ray asked at last. "You been moonin' about here for weeks now. And then when I told you before how proud I am of you—"

"I was just overcome," Jake said. "I was just real pleased you'd said all that," he hurried on. "That's all. And I'm real pleased for you Carrie's coming. Really."

Chapter Ten

Ray stood at the door, his gaze raking the blankness of night, waiting. Worry rattled him, and now he had two things to worry about.

He doubted Carrie was used to driving long distance at night on strange roads, and finding the ranch again might not be easy. He assured himself she had a GPS to get her most of the way, and a cell phone in case of trouble.

The worries about his son were a different matter. Jake wasn't settling back to civilian life as easily as he had anticipated, and whether it was something here bothering him or something he carried with him from Iraq, Ray didn't know. But he certainly yearned for his son to be out with it before long.

He had just started back inside when a solitary car passed the entrance, stopped and backed up, its two headlights like moons scoring the ground, drawing the car forward. It came down the turn to the main house and straight for him. He reached inside and flicked on the porch light, attracting a party of moths and other bugs before he let out a sigh of relief as Carrie pulled up in front of the house.

Stepping down, he released the door as she sat, hands still on the steering wheel, motionless, a waxen figure.

"Was it that bad?" he asked by way of greeting.

"Worse. Unimaginable." She reached across at last for her handbag and struggled out, one leg at a time, hardly able to stand.

"I told you I'd come for you." He reached out to stroke her damp face and got a weak smile in return.

"What? Just short of an hour and a half each way to Austin? Are you insane? You may be younger than me, but you're not that much younger."

"Well, I might say I know these roads a helluva damn sight better than you. Been drivin' 'em most of my life."

"Well, I'm here now."

She slumped her head against his chest as he held her, rubbing her back, massaging her shoulders gently. The feel of having her once more in his arms lit a spark within him.

After a moment in which she might have fallen asleep on her feet, Carrie popped her head back and gazed at him, a sleepy smile on her face. "I'm warning you right now—"

"Uh-oh."

"I'm going straight to sleep. And 'sleep' is the operative word here, buster. Got that? Sleep."

Ray smiled, just happy to have her there, but that spark wasn't going to stay a spark for long. A fire was slowly being lit.

"Well. Tomorrow is another day, as they say. And I...*rise* early."

****

Paige placed the last stack of books into her bookcase and let out a satisfied sigh. She had rejected her mother's offer to come back from Texas and help her move into an apartment knowing, as she did, her mother had had only three weeks there so far and sounded settled and happy.

Settled and happy was something Paige doubted she would feel for a while; the aloneness was just too marked. It was still August, and other students would not be back for another ten days or so, but she had decided to brave Philadelphia's summer heat in order to get a head start on studying and getting back to the grind.

The furniture she got out of storage had 'Steven' written all over it—the antique desk his father had given him and insisted Paige keep, the sofa she and Steven had spent a rainy day choosing, and left an umbrella in one shop during a lull in the storm. There were the prints they had agreed were too expensive, but might be a good investment, hanging above the armchair, which in itself had caused repeated arguments.

And finally, there was the bed that had been shared, the bed that had been slept in, ate in, read in and made love in. The year in storage had eradicated Steven's smell; Paige hugged a pillow to her nose, but there was only a slight odor of mildew and the extreme need for cleaning that greeted her.

Steven was gone, Steven was dead; only the memories clung to her, like barnacles, like ticks, like those sea urchins that had to be peed on to be lifted off. That was it—she would have to pee on Steven's memory to destroy it, find the part of her he had made liquid waste and use it to eliminate him. Was that possible? She doubted it; she held no bad memories of him, no 'buts' about their relationship, nothing he had ever hurt or changed or destroyed. She held no weapons with which to fight the gnawing hunger for his being.

So instead, she considered her good fortune in finding this new apartment. How lucky she had been when friends who had graduated, as had all her friends at law school, heard the next tenants for their apartment on Sansom and 41st had withdrawn and the landlord was now anxious for another lessee. She recalled the conversation with the landlord very well: no, she wouldn't go to Philly to inspect it; she knew the area near the Law School well.

And that was it; she was back. And she was alone.

****

Carrie had found space in Ray's closet, no doubt vacated some time ago by 'the wife' and never refilled. Well, what man goes out and buys clothes to fill a space the way a woman might? The bedroom was small and the bathroom impossible, an extension added on to the master bedroom in the fifties, Ray had said, but after all, the ranch house did date from the 1890s. Her cosmetics and toiletries littered the one shelf in the 'outhouse,' as she now called the master bathroom; they paraded along the side of the bath and sat on the top of the toilet.

If she wished to redecorate the house, she recognized the wisdom of keeping her mouth shut. And in a strange sort of way, there was a sense of relief it wasn't expected of her, that the history and the manliness and the outmoded décor were left as a symbol of the differences between life with Ray and her life in New York, her previous other incarnations.

But getting into her stride, finding a routine took time. She didn't like living with so many people in the house, people coming and going; it was proving difficult after so many years on her own, with Paige away at schools and rarely home. Ray had encouraged her to set up out in the enclosed sunroom where she had the view and quiet away from most of the goings on, while he worked in an office at the front of the house.

She dealt with Mabel's resentment of making extra work; she made an uneasy *entente cordiale* with the housekeeper of not invading Mabel's territory but always asking for anything she wanted from the kitchen, and Mabel asking before she cleaned the back sunroom area. No doubt the housekeeper begrudged the new arrangement, but it worked, and she accepted Carrie's occasional request of 'not right now' in a semblance of good nature with a shrug of her shoulders and a feigned ignorance of the back sunroom's mounting dirt for several days more.

But there was also the question of Jake—the feeling he was somehow not comfortable with her presence. He lurked, he skulked and apparently avoided her at times. With his bedroom down the hall from the one she shared with Ray, and no need to share the hall bathroom—converted years ago from a fourth bedroom—she and Jake did not have to see much of each other, except at the occasional meal taken together. She wasn't sure whether he disliked her or was leaving her to get on with her work.

Carrie caught Mabel eyeing her through the glass doors from the main house as she sat considering all this. She felt she had done enough work to warrant a break and get some fresh air, so she closed the lid of her laptop, stepped through the doors to give the housekeeper the 'Okay' sign and headed down to look for Ray at the barns. But it wasn't Ray she found.

Jake stood in the center of one of the corrals with a magnificent chestnut gelding on a lunge, trotting through his paces over carefully positioned poles. Off to the side, the three dogs watched as if they were learning something, too. Carrie leaned her crossed arms on the top bar of the corral fence and observed the training for a few minutes.

"That's quite some animal you've got there," she said at last.

He gave the lunge a small tug with a quiet, "Walk on," before he briefly eyed her. "Yup. He's a beauty."

For several seconds, there was no sound except the beat of the horse's hooves and the click of the poles as he tapped them. A stroke of discomfort hunched Carrie's shoulders and she started to turn away, but instead, put out a hand to attract the dog Alamo. It was Crockett who rose and approached her, a gentle woof emitting as he rubbed against her leg.

"You can push him off you know." Jake gave another gentle yank, bringing the gelding to a stop before he rolled in the lunge and unhooked it. He bent to rearrange the poles in the corral as the horse nickered but stood foursquare.

"It's fine. I like the dogs. I'm not so precious as you seem to think, Jake."

He stood and glanced back at her again, blinking. "I didn't mean...I only thought—"

"Sorry." Crockett licked her hand as she met the young man's steady gaze. "Jake, do you mind my being here? I mean, is it causing you upset or a problem or something because—"

He shook his head. "No. Why would you think that, Carrie? I mean, it's good to see Dad so happy. Fact

196

is, I don't remember him ever being this happy. Why do you ask?"

She had stepped back from a precipice. Yet his behavior didn't seem to gel with his answer. "I just felt...I just wondered because you don't join us much. You seem sort of distant." She leaned once more on the fence, suddenly aware she might have over-stepped her mark. After all, she hardly knew Jake; maybe this was his personality, the way he was. Then she recalled how friendly he had been at the dance hall in Bandera. Could a few drinks have done that?

"Well." He straightened and rehooked the lunge to the head collar. "You're working quite a bit and, you know, I'm out working, or Dad wants to be alone with you. I'm not avoiding you if that's what you think."

"It's just—" A screech like a cat yowling stopped her in her tracks. "What the heck was that?"

Jake laughed. "Surely you've heard that before? It's the kennel door. Admittedly, it's not always that bad. Mabel must've gone in to wash it down as she does sometimes. I'll see if I can't remember to give it some WD40 or something." He let out the lunge, gave it a shake and stood with his eyes back on the Arab.

"Why do you kennel the dogs anyway? Don't you like them inside at night?"

He opened his mouth, then hesitated before going on. "Well, it was my mom who didn't like them inside. She didn't like them licking her in the night and all. You know, they're real smart. They can open the bedroom doors if they've a mind to. Not the kennel door, luckily, but the bedroom doors they find real easy. And if we'da put locks on the doors, they'd have scratched and woke her anyway."

197

Carrie hesitated then plunged, "Where's your mother now? Do you see her?"

"Oh, yeah. She's over in Austin, not too far away, but I think she's set on movin' now. Somewhere north I believe. Wyoming or Montana."

He appeared relaxed about discussing her, so Carrie figured the divorce must be long over. Ray never mentioned the woman, that was certain.

She let Crockett lick her hand for several moments before she slipped it away and studied Jake. He seemed intent on the rhythm of the horse, its balance, but perhaps his mind was on other things.

"Do you hear them barking at night sometimes?" he asked at last.

"No. Do they? I'm a heavy sleeper when my brain isn't going, and Ray's never mentioned any noise. Are there prowlers?" She tried to keep concern from her voice. Who knew what was out here in the middle of nowhere?

He snorted. "No, no prowlers. Or at least none we're aware of. Dad had a bit of trouble a few years back with poachers, but they caught them in the end. And then some years back, we found someone'd been planting pot over in a far corner of the ranch. Dad went ballistic, could've meant losing the ranch had the sheriff's office not been told. Anyway, it's only been deer recently. Deer and other animals set off the dogs sometimes. Nothing to worry about. Well." He tugged on the lunge once more and brought the horse to a halt. "Dad should be back shortly. There was some problem down at the lodge, a leak or something I think."

Carrie stood there, a low sunset trickling color behind the barns. She could see Ray in Jake, his concentration, his care for the animals, the land. "I remember the owner of the stables where I kept my horse doing this lunge work," she said half to herself. "I used to enjoy watching her down in the manege."

Jake barked a laugh as he started to roll up the lunge, and flicked a glance at her over his shoulder. "'Manege.' Wow, that's some fancy word for a corral."

"Well. I guess. But that's what she called it. That or *the school*. Sorry."

The sound of Ray's truck was accompanied by a trail of dust appearing down the lane. As it ground to a halt and the door swung open, the dogs went as one to greet him. Ray tipped his hat back on his head, a huge smile mirroring her own.

"Hey, y'all." There was a note of relief in his voice as he sauntered over to Carrie, his gaze going from Jake to her and back again. "Turned out to be just an overflow from a toilet that was running. I jiggled the handle and fixed it. I'm a genius." He leaned over and kissed her behind the ear, then smiled at his son. "You know you got genius in you?"

Jake's gaze skidded from Carrie to Ray. "I don't know about 'genius,' Dad. I got 'weird' in me is what I got." And he turned back to his gelding, leaving the two of them giggling.

****

Jake waited for Ty to seek his revenge, but the days passed and nothing happened. He figured the wrangler had made empty threats, got someone else to do his dirty work, a partner perhaps, that person he had said would take over from Jake, and he must have figured seeking revenge on him was no longer a high priority, no longer worth the risk.

He finally got through to Lucinda one afternoon and, after tip-toeing around the subject with news, congratulations on her marriage and catching up the last few years, he got up the courage to ask her if her husband was aware of her past with Robbie. He felt immense relief at her somewhat short but slightly puzzled reply that the couple had absolutely no secrets.

Slowly, tentatively, he began to relax, began to get back into his old skin. He went out to mix and didn't worry about bumping into Ty. He even enjoyed seeing his father basking in Carrie's love and adoration, which it was. Jake smirked as the couple came in late from eating out in one of the local haunts, giggling like teenagers who'd done something mischievous. He stood by as his father and Carrie headed out to get some groceries, good-naturedly arguing over who was going to drive the old pickup. There was laughter from their bedroom and there were exchanged glances over breakfast and smiles that stretched, literally, from ear to ear. To his eye, Carrie adored his father, made him happy, and enjoyed being here. And that was all right with him.

Contented, he decided to give Paige a call late one night, even later in Philly, when the muffled sounds from his father's bedroom had silenced into the scratchings of the crickets and cicadas. He lay back on his pillow waiting for her to answer, which she did almost immediately.

"No, you haven't woken me, and yes I am alone."

"How did you know I would ask that, Paige?" He could feel the dent between his brows harden into a crevice.

"Because you're so predictable, Jake. Really. I

hope you're not calling about another drug run?" Her voice was slightly annoyed at this prospect.

"Nope. I took legal advice—yours. I'm a new man." He picked up a pen on his nightstand and twirled it with an air of satisfaction.

"Glad to hear it, cowboy."

Jake guffawed.

"So, is the happy home of three still happy?"

"You know your mother makes the same sigh of ecstasy and relief you do when she comes. They think I can't hear them, but sometimes I do if they're loud enough. It's weird. Them old people making love like that. Don't you think?"

"Jake, really! That is more information than I wish to have about my mother." She sniffed. "Or myself for that matter." There was the scrunch of a pillow being fluffed. "Aside from getting off listening to my mother's orgasm, how are you?"

"Good. I'm good. What's it like being back at school?"

Paige hesitated. "Difficult." She stopped at that.

He wondered how hard it was for her to be there. But then her voice came brighter, more positive.

"Somehow it seems everyone's an idiot. Maybe you were right—they seem so much younger than I am. Even though, in actual fact, at law school, they're really not. But I'll survive. It just takes a bit of getting used to, you know? I'm used to coming back from class to Steven, and he 'ain't' here. It's not good. It's difficult."

"Paige, you'll be okay. I know you will."

"Gee, thanks, pal." She put on a cheerleader voice. "Gee whiz! If you say so!"

"Okay—look, I know you don't think much of me,

don't value my opinion and all. But I know you'll be fine. For what it's worth." Suddenly, he wondered why he'd bothered…but then he knew. He wanted her, he missed her. Carrie was a constant reminder of her, and he wished Paige was here, too.

There was a deep breath let out into the mouthpiece of the phone. "I value your opinion, Jake. I just don't listen to it. Well," she added, "I don't listen to anyone but my gut. *I* know I'll be all right. I'll graduate top of my class as I was meant to do—my new class that is— and I'll kick butt left, right and center. What about you?"

He considered his answer carefully, now the threat of Ty seemed to have passed. "I'll be happy working on the ranch with my dad. That's the way it is out here— that's the way it's always been. And I'm happy with that. I don't see a need for a piece of paper saying I studied what I learned by living here on this ranch all my life. You see the need for that?"

"No, Jake, I don't. You go on and lead the life you want, the life your family knows. It's a good life, I'm sure. And call me again from time to time. I like knowing about my mother's love-making. Really."

****

In the dim bedside light, Carrie lay with her head nesting on Ray's chest, her hand absently playing with the curlicues of hair on his stomach and moving up the dent from his navel. The quiet was almost intimidating, frightening in a way, after life in New York, absent of car horns or ambulances, fire engines or police car sirens heralding accident and emergency in the night.

Her mind wandered from her current book to Ray to the screenplay she'd been re-working to Paige. She worried about her daughter, and then decided she mustn't worry about her, and then fretted some more. In the back of her mind, somewhere deep inside, was that moment when she had seen the pills by her daughter's bedside. But then, Paige had said…what had she said? She wasn't the suicidal type. What type, exactly, was that? Still, it was best to check on her regularly, let her know that just because she was with Ray, she hadn't stopped thinking about her. But now it was far too late to phone; even Paige would be asleep with the time difference.

Carrie shifted slightly, and Ray's voice came in its low notes of semi-conscious rasp, "A penny for them?"

"Lots of thoughts," said Carrie sitting up. "Paige, work…"

His hand gently played down her back before she moved off the bed and grabbed a nightdress, letting it slide down her body like a curtain coming down before her head stretched out of it and her arms found their way.

Ray was watching. "You know, I think that's the first time you've actually got out of bed and dressed right in front of me."

"Is it?" She tilted her head considering this, a small uncertainty rattling her, before she headed for the bathroom. "I must be getting used to you," she called over her shoulder.

"You still frettin' over your body?" His words met her closing the bathroom door.

For a moment, she stayed silent while she washed and got ready for sleep. Then she stepped out. "I shall always fret over my body. You'll be disgusted by it soon. You'll see. Who wants to make love to a withered old hag?"

Ray inhaled, obviously frustrated with having to deal with this again. "You know," he drawled out, "there's two of us aging here. You don't hear me worrying 'bout my old broken down body appearing in front of you with all its flabby bits. I'm not in love with your body, Carrie. I'm in love with you, you dang fool." He reached out a hand and drew her over. "Find something else to worry about, will you?"

He was right; she knew she didn't give a damn what the hell he looked like. To her, he was the best looking damn man on earth. Worry about something else? "I have," she finally answered him. "I should have phoned Paige again today. She sounded too crisp and business-like to me on the phone yesterday." It was going to be a long night. Her mind was turning over too much.

Ray stole a glance at the bedside clock. "She'll be fine," he assured her. "First thing tomorrow, you can call, but I'm sure she'll be fine." He lay back on the pillow. "Anyway, I didn't know Paige had anything but 'crisp and business-like' when speaking. Seems that's the way a lawyer should be...even with her mother," he added quickly. He patted the bed beside him.

Carrie curled herself in again as Ray switched off the low bedside light.

"You think again about how long you can stay? Not that I want you to go—I want to make *that* clear."

"Oh." She gave a quiet giggle. "I guess maybe as long as Mabel lets me." Lying against him, the quake of his laughter quivered against her skin. "Seriously, I don't know. It sort of depends on various things, the book, the screenplay, lots."

"You miss New York? Your friends?"

"Yes. But then, if I were there, I'd be missing you, so which is worse?" She craned her neck to meet his gaze. A sudden feeling of contentment washed over her, and she curled up again, resting her head against him.

For a while, she listened to the broken record song of the cicadas and frogs until that was joined by the soft whistle of Ray's even breathing. But such satisfaction did not send her to sleep; it was a night when her mind would not rest and the restlessness won.

Carrie slipped one leg down and then the other to stand and quietly make her way out the door, drawing it shut behind her. The hallway was pitch black, a night in which clouds blanketed the moon, and, like a criminal, she stole her way to the sunroom. Feeling for the switch, she inundated the room in the white light of the ceiling fan bulb and flipped the computer open, jabbing in her password and sitting, waiting for the home page to appear.

And then the dogs started barking.

Slipping back from the table, she rose to see if she could spot a deer that might have set them off as Jake had mentioned. The void of blackness was menacing, a complete emptiness of life as if she were the last person left on the planet. The glare of the light bulb and her own reflection forced her to lean right up to the cold glass, but nothing greeted her, a vacancy was all there was.

She decided it was nothing more making them bark than a passing animal she couldn't see, and she started to sit down when she became aware of something. Dogs were still barking, but it sounded like there were only two of them barking now, which puzzled her. They were barking more frantically, too, with a sort of whining cry emitted, a terrible yowling of desperation.

And then came the screech of the kennel door.

Hurriedly rising from her chair again, her heart pounding as if it wanted to escape her chest, Carrie rushed to the glass of the sunroom windows, desperately searching the emptiness for a sign of movement. The room's reflections in the glass sketched specters outside, unnerving doppelgangers in an alternate world. Her hand instinctively went to her chest as she searched the void franticly.

And then, two staring, disembodied eyes came floating through this ghostly setting and, catching the light from the room for a second, a knife held out, red stains of blood just dulling its sheen.

Chapter Eleven

The bitter taste of bile still roiled around Jake's mouth as he listened to the two dogs whining and whimpering from the kitchen where he had shut them in, their plaintive cries a testimony to his predicament. He had not as yet been able to deal with the slaughtered Alamo, and he expected his father might do the deed, unpleasant as it was going to be. But his dad was now crouching in front of a shivering and shaking Carrie while the sheriff surveyed the scene, the rotating blue lights of his patrol car reaching through the windows and giving the hall and front room the aura of a deserted fairground.

"Ray, I think you might wanna call Doc Gibbons for Miz Bennett," Dex said between chews of gum. "A little—"

"No!" snapped Carrie. She wrapped the blanket that had been thrown around her tighter to her trembling body. Her gaze fixed on the two rifles, now propped against the wall, that Jake and his father had got out when she screamed. "I don't need a doctor. I don't want a sedative. I'll be fine."

"Sweetheart, you've had a bit of a shock. For all we know, you may well be in shock, medical shock. I really think—"

His father suddenly appeared incredibly old, drained, and no doubt in need of a drink.

"I'll be fine. Really." She patted his bent knee in a gesture of reassurance.

"Maybe you should give her a brandy, Dad." He spoke quietly from his place on the side.

"It's sugary, weak tea for shock as I recall, and I don't want you fussing anymore."

Carrie's gaze sought his father, and Jake had a sense of foreboding as to the turmoil his dad was facing.

"Well, I need a drink." His father stood and glanced around. "I don't know about you all, but I sure as hell need one."

He moved to go, but Carrie reached out and caught his hand.

"Ray, don't. Please don't."

She was probably struggling not to whine, not to make a scene, to not start an argument with his dad here in front of the sheriff.

His father patted her hand as it clung to his before he released himself. "I'll be fine. We all need a drink, Carrie. You, too."

"Well, I'm on duty," put in Dex in a voice a little too upbeat. "Y'all go ahead and have one. I'll start writing this all down if you don't mind my sitting next to you, Miz Bennett?"

"No. Go ahead."

"Tell me again what you saw, what happened?"

Carrie breathed out a begrudging sigh. "I came in here to work as I couldn't sleep—"

"You make a habit of that, ma'am?"

"I don't make a *habit* of it, no. It happens, occasionally, when I need to."

The mounting annoyance in her voice struck Jake

hard, and he sought his father's reaction. His dad stood in the doorway for a moment and handed him a glass of whiskey, then went back to the living room, no doubt for another one for himself. It was obvious to Jake his father would be downing one before re-appearing with a glass, he probably had already indulged, and he would not have just one or two. And Carrie could probably figure that out as well.

"Let me tell you again, Sheriff, one more time. I heard the kennel door *screech*. I knew the sound from previous occasions, so when I heard that, I got up and looked out to see what was happening. The automatic light wasn't on—"

"He must've disconnected it," Jake mumbled. He held his glass between two hands, fearing he might drop it, not having the strength to hold it in one.

Carrie went on. "All I could see were these two eyes coming toward me and the knife. Obviously, the man wore a balaclava or something, and was dressed in all black or I might have seen more. There is no moon tonight with this thick cloud cover—" Her hand went up, pointing into the vacant night. "—as you are no doubt aware. That is what I saw. That is *all* I saw."

His dad came in with a whiskey for himself and handed her a brandy. Her eyes pleaded with him, but Jake knew the attempt was futile.

"And you heard this screech only. You didn't hear anything else?" Dex's gaze moved up from his pad and bore into Carrie with a dubious assessment.

"The dogs were barking," she answered. "But I knew they barked at passing deer or other animals, so it didn't alarm me until—"

"You didn't think at that point to wake either Ray

or Jake?"

"No, no of course not. I knew the dogs often barked, as I've just said. Ray would go berserk if I woke him every time a dog barked out there. For heaven's sake!"

"Dex, is this absolutely necessary tonight, right now? We've all had a real trying time with this, and I think Carrie ought to get to bed now." His father gulped a swallow of whiskey and stared pointedly at the sheriff.

"I'm sorry, Ray, real sorry for all this, but I find if I don't get people to talk right after an event, they forget a load of details. I gotta get this down while it's all fresh in Miz Bennett's mind. Then, if she remembers something else later, she can come on in and see me tomorrow."

"It's all right, I'm fine," Carrie told them both. She sipped at her brandy before continuing. "I was suddenly aware there were only two dogs barking, but barking more frantically, desperately—howling like the hounds of hell I'd say. I got up to look out, and that's when I screamed. I screamed when I saw the eyes and the knife, and then the man disappeared. That's all there is to say, really. That's all that happened."

"What makes you so sure it was a man?" Dex didn't wait for an answer as he turned to question Jake and his father. "Either of you know anyone who would want to do a thing like this?"

Jake's body swam with nausea for a moment, and he had trouble getting the whiskey back up to his mouth. His father's shake of the head didn't seem to satisfy Dex, either.

"Ray, I'm real sorry to ask you this, but what about

Leigh Anne? You know divorces can be messy things. She bear you a grudge? You think she might do something like this?"

"No!" Jake's tone was so vehement, the other three were overtaken with obvious surprise.

Silence resonated in the air like a hammer poised to come down.

"It wasn't a woman, Sheriff," Carrie asserted at last. "Not unless she was over six foot." She took a swallow of the brandy, and shuddered before wrapping the blanket tighter around her shoulders.

"Well, how the heck do you know the person was over six foot, Miz Bennett? You said he was dressed all in black and all you could see were the eyes."

"That's just it," she answered. "From the height of the eyes, I know it was a very tall person. I'm guessing over six feet at least."

Dex tapped his pen on the pad with a shake of his head. "Well," he said, hoisting his belly and moving back in the chair. "Could be a woman in heels. Did you hear a vehicle, a getaway car?"

Jake exchanged inquiring looks with the other two.

It was his dad who said, "Carrie was pretty damn hysterical, screaming her head off. I think we might have missed hearing that, what with the dogs yapping an' all. Sure to be tire tracks out front if your patrol car hasn't mussed them."

"Well." Dex sighed again as he lugged his heft to standing position. "I doubt I'll be able to see anything tonight, but I'll have a look with a flashlight. Any arguments with your clients, Ray? Any disagreements over a bill perhaps, dissatisfaction with a hunt, somethin' like that? Anything at all you can think of?"

His father shot back his whiskey, and shook his head. "Nothing. Nothing like that at all. Most of my clients are either regulars, recommended by regulars, or come here through their firms who have contracts with me. If they were dissatisfied, I'd hear from the firms, but there's been nothing like that, nothin' at all." He banged his glass on the table.

Carrie swayed slightly and his dad gathered her to him as he stooped beside her.

"Really, Dex, I think I better see Carrie to bed. I think this is all just too much for one night now, and we'll all feel better in the mornin'." He grasped her by the shoulders. "I hope."

I won't feel better. Jake leaned back against the wall and swigged his whiskey. *I won't feel better at all.*

****

The odor of Lysol wafted in on a late morning breeze as Carrie sat in front of her blank page on the computer, wondering if she would ever be able to write another word. The page beckoned her accusingly, as if she had made it a promise she didn't keep.

She glanced outside to watch Ray carrying a shrouded Alamo to the grave Jake had dug some distance from the yard. He carefully lowered the canine in before grabbing a second shovel to help put back the top layer of earth. Crockett and Star lay at Carrie's feet, a feeling of desolation so great emanating from the two remaining dogs that, whenever she considered their loss, an upsurge of tears would begin and the dogs would whimper and beat their tails like old women keening and pounding their chests in mourning.

Beyond the glass, she saw Ray dust down his hands and give the earth one last tamping with his boots before heading to a shed to put the shovels away. Jake was filling a bucket from the outside tap, the Lysol bottle nearby, no doubt to wash down the kennel floor for what, to Carrie, was about the millionth time.

No one had had more than coffee for breakfast, and a very subdued Mabel made an unusually quiet circuit of the house.

Carrie reviewed her earlier telephone conversation with Paige, to cry on her shoulder, as her daughter had put it. She'd obviously been the wrong one to seek for sympathy; all business as usual, her daughter had pointed out the loss of a dog was 'hardly, well, you know, he may be man's best friend, but he wasn't a human.' And so, now the funereal air was so ubiquitous, Carrie had a sudden urge to just get out, when the two men entered.

"Had to be someone who knows the place, knows the lay-out," Ray was saying. "I don't understand it at all. He'd been into the shed and tampered with the breaker for the outside lights. Who would do such a thing, Jake? Why would they do such a thing?"

Carrie sensed the younger man was staring at her, trying to read her.

He drew his gaze back to his father. "I have no idea, Dad." He slumped into one of the chairs at the table near Carrie and reached underneath to comfort the dogs.

Ray stood leaning back against the rear wall, his expression drawn into a scowl, no doubt of hatred for the person who did this. He straightened. "We'll keep the dogs inside nights now, if that's all right with you, Carrie?"

"Of course. Of course it is," she replied, tears still

just below the surface.

Ray nodded. "I'd like to speak to Carrie for a moment, Jake, if you don't mind. And I think we have a ranch to run here. Better get back down to business. There's not a lot more can be done today 'less Dex comes by with any news."

Jake towed his long frame from the chair, catching Carrie's eye as he did so. It was as if he were asking her a question, and she had the sudden feeling he had something to say to her, but he only grabbed his hat and left the porch.

Ray waited for the sound of the front door closing.

"You all right now?" He hauled out a chair and sat opposite her.

She slowly put the lid of her laptop down and met his gaze. "You're worried I'm going to leave because of all this, aren't you?"

"Some," he admitted. "I'd like to think we haven't quite scared you off."

"I think I have pretty good protection." She reached across for his hand. "I am worried about one thing, however." She entwined her fingers with his, feeling the callous of his palms against her own soft skin.

"My drinking. I know."

He waited, gulping in air as if he might soon blow away the subject between them, yet she would insist on having it out.

"I had…a few drinks. No one got hurt by it, did they? I didn't drive a car, I didn't puke up, and I didn't beat you—"

"You did snore something awful, and you stank like hell."

Ray grimaced.

"Look," she went on, "it was an awful night, I don't deny that. But how do I know it won't continue? How do I know next time it won't be worse, the next time—"

"Listen—I want to tell you something. After you left back in May and I decided I was gonna try to pursue you, I stopped drinking. But I also went to AA a couple of times. I'm not an alcoholic, Carrie—eh, eh, wait a moment," he said, putting out a hand to stop her from commenting. "I have a habit, not an addiction. There's a difference. I got in the habit of coming in, in the evening, and starting to drink. And, yes, I had to break the habit, but I'm not addicted."

"Some might say you're in denial, Ray. I know you stopped once, though, so…"

"All right." With a sudden movement, he was back on his feet. "I'd rather have you than a drink. I think…"

"You *think* you'd rather have me than a drink?" With a small smile, she raised her brows in question.

"Noooo. I was going to say, I think maybe I should throw it all out. I was keeping it to prove to myself I could resist, but if you'd feel better with it all out of the house…"

Carrie sat for a moment, studying her hands, taking in the prominent veins, the sunken skin. "I think I have to trust you," she said at last. "I think if you tell me you're not going to drink, I have to believe that, *will* believe that. Because otherwise, I'll start wondering what else you've lied about."

****

"I've been expecting your call."

Jake hit his head back against the wall behind his

bed as if he could knock the answer to his problems into himself. "I guess your mom told you, huh?"

"Oh, yes. She had a long session of crying down the phone and a blow by blow description of you retching outside the kennel. Charming. Is she still in shock?"

It was a wonder to him that Paige could manage to sound so disinterested while actually asking questions.

"No. No, I think she's fine. She seemed to be mostly concerned with my dad's drinking." He grimaced a bit. "Maybe not. She was pretty shook up. Said these two eyes came toward her like floating eyeballs or something, and this ghostly knife, like something out of Macbeth. What the hell does that mean?"

She gave a sigh of exasperation. "It's a play, Jake—it's Shakespeare."

"I know it's a dang play, Paige. I *have* been to school." He hit his head again against the wall. "I don't know why the hell I called you. I thought you might be some help."

"Well, Jake. We know whose eyeballs and whose knife they were, don't we? And they didn't belong to Banquo or Duncan."

He snorted.

"You want my advice?"

"Go on, let's have it." *Oh, brother, this is going to be good.*

"Tell Ray everything. From beginning to end—"

"I can't. It'll be even worse now. I have the dog's death on my head now. I can't." He heard himself, heard the note of pleading in his voice as if he were trying to argue with himself, convince himself.

216

"Listen, Jake, you *listen* to me. That maniac is not going to stop at killing a dog. You have to, at the very least, tell the police."

He didn't respond.

Suddenly, she let out, "Jeez, how did you ever survive the army for four years, for goodness sake? You're such a wimp."

He gulped a sharp intake of breath. "You still don't get it, do you Paige? You still don't understand. You and your independence, and your not caring."

"If I didn't care, I wouldn't become a lawyer," she retorted vehemently. "You think I don't care? Do I have to cut my wrists every time something goes wrong?"

"You see everything in black and white, Paige, like lawyers do. But life isn't like that. There are gray areas, too."

"My, but we are philosophical today, aren't we?" she cut in.

"Yeah. Look, we've discussed my problem with telling my father before."

"Tell my mother," Paige railed at him abruptly. "Go tell my mother and see what she says. She must know Ray pretty well by now, aside from in the biblical sense. And Jake?"

"Yeah."

"You are going to have to tell the police. Whatever happens, you must go tell the local police. Tell them your part in it. It's going to be the only way to screw this guy good. Otherwise, he'll bring you down with him."

Putting down the phone, Paige stared for several moments at the textbook in front of her. The desk lamp made an island of light in the darkened room. She tried to imagine Jake now, the violet blue eyes and the strong chin with its dimple, which made him look so much more virile than he acted. Had he been right? Was she uncaring, cold and calculating without feelings for anyone or anything?

No, of course that wasn't true. She dealt with things on her own, as she always had. Yet sometimes, studying at night, she would suddenly be aware of the silence; she would hear it like a scream, as if she stood in some damp, back alley in the early hours of morning, rain glistening on streets reflected in the shuttered eyes of night. Then perhaps a car engine would start up out on the street or there might be footsteps overhead, and she would try to focus again on the book she was holding until the silence disturbed her once more. It was a feeling she didn't like at all, this total solitude.

'No man is an island,' Donne had written, yet Paige saw herself very much like an island. With her mother off with the Ryders and friends now mostly married or in jobs, which gave them little spare time, and she, herself, studying all the hours she could, she sensed an isolation that at times proved unbearable.

She called Jake back.

"Have you ever told your father you loved him?" she asked when he picked up.

There was silence on the end of the phone for a moment. Paige listened to Jake's breath, could almost hear him thinking, ideas floating through his brain and trying to settle.

Then there was a dry laugh. "No. Dad told me a while back how much he loved me or some such nonsense. Said I made him proud. It was weird, and, of course, it only made things worse for me about telling him about Robbie. Shoot, Paige, what the heck brought this on?"

"I don't know how to do it. I think I should—tell my mother that is. But she'll think I'm going to kill myself or something, and that it is my good-bye." Was that what she really wanted? A touchy-feely encounter with her mother?

"Then you'll have to wait 'til you see her. Hey, why don't you fly out? Surprise her. I'll pick you up at the airport an' all—we have a spare room." Although a spare room wasn't where he would want her—*that* was certain.

"I can't, lovely as that would be. I *am* in law school, you know."

"Well. Wait 'til you see her. Throw your arms 'round her or something girls do."

"I'm not touchy-feely, Jake."

"Coulda fooled me."

She let silence be her answer.

"I'm sorry," he said at last. "I shouldn't of said them things about you being uncaring. That's what's brought this all on, isn't it? But, I mean, you do care. You cared about your fiancé an' all, and you've been a big help to me. Even if I don't follow your advice all the time."

Paige smiled to herself. "I have to go. Tell the police, Jake. Remember what I said. You must tell the police."

****

While Dex had no news, he did call round periodically and stop for a coffee and a chat, distracting and rather annoying Carrie. It appeared the crime would go unsolved, unpunished, while the days passed and she and Ray were back in a routine. She sighed at having to spend increasing amounts of time on the phone to New York and Los Angeles to sort out various problems while the ranch got busy in its early autumn hunting season. She sensed Ray feared for the horses but hadn't as yet done more than check them and make sure doors were locked.

"I'm thinking of putting up more security cameras," he told Carrie as he stood, gently massaging her neck as she worked.

She nodded her head in agreement.

"I'm also thinking maybe we can—or rather you can—redecorate Robbie's old room, the guest room, for a study. Gonna get chilly out here in the winter."

She craned backwards and peered up at him. "I appreciate the thought, but I don't know if it's worth it," she began.

"Well, it's worth it to me. Even if you do have to go, it'll be here waitin' for you when you return."

He stood waiting for her to say something, but she only clicked on her mouse and shut the computer down.

He tapped her on the shoulders. "I've been waitin' for the moon to come out—"

"Going to howl at it?" she quipped.

"No. I'm going to take you for a ride and show you something special. Been meaning to take you, but had to wait for a full moon."

"All right. Sounds good to me." Still jangled by what had happened, she accepted his offer with some trepidation. "I hope you're going to bring along a gun." She said it in some jest but wondered about the actual wisdom of going out in the night.

"I don't believe that's necessary. Maybe you want

to go out for dinner again instead? I don't mind. Whatever you want."

"Nope, I'll be safe with you. I guess. And a ride sounds wonderful. Just what I could use—fresh air and a good-looking man to accompany me." She got up and faced him.

"Good looking, huh? Damn handsome son of a gun is what I am." He laughed at her smirk. "Tell you what, you go change into your riding jeans or whathaveyou and I'll go saddle up. Meet me down at the barn. Okay?"

"Okay."

More relaxed having had time to consider this ride, she let him lead her down to the pond with the horses in a slow canter. Ray said the horses weren't run in the dark for fear of not seeing some hole or other obstruction, and Carrie was happy to just get out, get away from the computer and work. She had begun to feel like an old married woman with Ray, the routine the household had settled into a source of comfort rather than one of boredom. Yet, she realized that since the night of the crime, an increasing restlessness, a distance each one had tried to bridge in his or her own way, had permeated the ranch house.

The horses splashed through the creek and started the climb up to the first rise. Carrie remembered there had been a meadow here, a beautiful, spring-flowered meadow, but now there was just the moon lighting a path across to the next rise.

"We'll go slow here," Ray advised, "in case of gopher holes."

The horses picked their way across, straining to have a run and shaking their heads in dismay. Then, at the next ridge, Carrie saw it, understood why Ray had waited for a full moon.

"It's so beautiful," she gasped. "So beautiful."

The moon hung above the still pond, like a grand chandelier above a great polished table, reflected in its tranquil water, immobile. It appeared Carrie could reach out and touch it, the vast orb within her range. For a moment, she saw herself as incredibly small again, a speck in the limitless expanse of universe spreading before her.

"This is where you first kissed me," she said suddenly, the memory surprising her.

"Yep. And you let me, and then told me you were goin' home. Great thing, that. Let a man kiss you and then…" He took in a breath and moved his horse nearer to hers. "I got you in the end, though, didn't I?" He leaned across and brought her face to his, finding her lips waiting.

"You wore me down, Ray Ryder," she said softly. "A girl can take just so much chasing before she succumbs. All those phone calls."

He sat back straight in the saddle. "You gonna give me warning about leavin', aren't you?" There was an unusually serious note in his voice.

"Of course. I'm not even sure when. Things are happening, as you've no doubt gathered from all the calls."

There were pinpoints of light in his dark eyes, boring a tunnel to his soul.

"I'll be back though. You're not rid of me yet."

Chapter Twelve

Jake had once been told by his father he should expect to be shot if he ever interrupted Carrie while she was working. It was a joke, of course, but he was aware there was an amount of truth in it—a large amount of truth. Mabel now avoided the back porch until Carrie took a break for lunch or phone calls. His father recounted he had to sit quietly by Carrie without saying a word, maybe reading or doing a crossword, until she recognized him. "Comes 'round" was how his dad had actually phrased it, as if she went into a trance while writing, as if she had gone to another world like some medium or seer and had to be brought back to the present.

As Jake worked in the office at the front of the house the Friday of the week following his conversation with Paige, he saw his father's newest pickup park in front; Carrie got out and waved his father off down the lane to the lodge. Jake gathered himself and stood waiting as she entered, some shopping bags from Fredericksburg dangling from an arm.

"Your father has the patience of a saint," she affirmed as she spotted Jake. "I just wanted one morning to go round town, and he watched me try on about every pair of cowboy boots in the state of Texas. What a man." A small giggle of joy matched the light in her eyes.

"You don't mind being seen in the pickup, then?" Jake wondered.

"Mind? No, why would I mind? Everyone rides them in Texas and, anyway, this new one is downright luxurious. Don't know what it would look like if someone muddy got in after working, but it's really very comfortable. It's the old one I dislike. I get rattled about in it. I'm sure it has no suspension." She surveyed Jake, his hands in his pockets as he slouched his long frame against a wall, staring at her. "Are you all right? Is something the matter?"

His mouth moved like a fish taking in air. "Can we talk somewhere? I mean, can you spare me a few moments? Please?"

Carrie blinked, wariness and misgiving crossing her face. "I'll just put these away," she said. "You want to meet me in the sunroom?"

He pondered what was going through her mind as she put away her purchases and prepared to meet him, if she thought it was about Paige. Although, he doubted she ever told her mother about their phone conversations. Had Carrie suspected him of some involvement in Alamo's death, been surprised at how severely he had reacted that night?

Jerking out a chair opposite to where she always sat, he stood waiting until she entered. She nodded uncertainly to him as her chair squeaked out on the tile floor and she sat down, placing her computer aside, almost as if it were her symbol he had her undivided attention.

"So." She said the word quietly, more a statement than a question, and waited.

"I don't know where to begin, but I need your

advice. Maybe your help."

Carrie nodded in response.

Jake opened his mouth to speak, but nothing would come out for a moment. His tongue thickened in the desert of his mouth; he needed water.

"Is this to do with your father? Our relationship?"

"No, absolutely not. Well, not really." He finally sat and bowed his head, studying his hands, as if he were praying, biding for a bit more time.

"Are you in some kind of trouble?" she hedged.

"Yeah. You might say that." *Pull yourself together, man.*

"Is this to do with…with Alamo?"

"Yeah." *Go on, go on.*

Carrie stood to open the porch door slightly, letting in the perfume of the warm autumn day before she sat back in her chair, staring at Jake, her hands folded together on the table. "I wondered, you know, when it happened, why, who would do this? When I told Paige, there was something in her voice as if she knew something, something she wasn't telling me. And then I thought of the way you looked at me that night, as if you were asking something, needing to talk to me then. I guess as a writer you make studies of people. I just had a hunch. You're generally such a calm person, Jake…well, generally." She gave him a little smile. "Of course, you would be badly affected by that…that slaughter of your dog. But it just seemed, for someone who had seen what you've no doubt seen, it seemed so…" She stopped, no doubt realizing he was waiting and she was prattling on. "Go on, please. I'm sorry. Go on."

So, this was what was called 'biting the bullet.'

Jake sucked in air. "Dad doesn't know this. He doesn't know any of what I'm going to tell you. And that's part of my problem."

Carrie gave a small nod of her head to say she understood.

"You remember Ty Sheldon?"

"Of course. At the Lone Star. There was something…unpleasant about him. I could never put my finger on it."

"Well, I could. He's into drugs—in a big way. He has them run up from Mexican border towns and sells them in Austin and San Antonio and other places." He took a deep breath and gazed straight into her eyes. "Robbie was his partner."

Her lips parted with a small gasp, and she leaned forward.

"For a time…" He breathed out slowly, finding the will to go on. "A girl he'd been seeing a while, Lucinda her name was, she got in trouble, pregnant. Robbie didn't have enough money for an abortion, not a decent one anyway, and he knew Dad would go ballistic if he told him, force him to marry the girl. So he tied up with Ty, became his partner. He brought the drugs up from Mexico, and Ty sold them, that was the deal. He made enough money after one run to have Lucinda fixed. After that, it was, like, this is good money, so he made another couple of runs. Then one day, someone Ty had sold to crashed his car while high. It was in all the local papers—this kid was high on marijuana when he died." Jake stopped a moment, as Carrie shook her head in consternation. "Robbie decided he wanted out, said he didn't need the money anyway and Dad might eventually get suspicious. Like me, he didn't want to hurt Dad. It was just…something that happened."

"Was he…was he earning money outside of that at the time?"

The question hung in the air. Carrie must have known Robbie was only working at the ranch. "Dad paid him for work on the ranch if that's what you want to know. We're not prisoners here." He shuffled a bit on his chair. "Dad's always been fair with us—strict, but fair. Mom never had much to do with us once we grew past babies. It was always Dad we turned to, Dad who had the last word. When Robbie wanted to breed them Arabs, Dad gave him the go-ahead, encouraged him, and paid him pretty well for setting it all up and overseeing the whole operation. But Robbie liked to take Lucinda out, treat her well, and buy her stuff. Expensive stuff." He shrugged, trying to recall all the ins and outs of what had happened, keep the story to the facts. "So, Robbie wanted out, but Ty threatened him. I think he threatened to tell Dad, in fact. That's always been Ty's game—he was always jealous of us and Dad when he and Robbie were hangin' 'round together because his own Dad split when he was little." He sat with his hand across his mouth for a moment considering this. "Well," he continued, "at the same time, Dad was beginning to get on to Robbie about enlisting, 'cause of course every other man in this family has served since the beginning of time." He snorted and sat back, grimacing a bit, before he blurted, "I encouraged Robbie to join to get the hell away from Ty."

"Your father thinks…your father blames himself for Robbie joining, Jake. Why didn't you ever tell him? He drank because of this. It eats him up when he thinks of it. Why would you let him go on like that?"

"How could I not? Dad would never believe Robbie would listen to me, take my advice, over his. 'No, Dad, it was me who encouraged him to enlist'— just like that? Plain and simple? No. To tell him it was me who had encouraged Robbie to join meant I would have had to tell him the whole story, everything I just told you: the pregnancy, the drugs, the lot. Isn't it better for him to think he encouraged a good son to join— which, as I say, every man in this family has done— rather than tell him all that crap about Robbie, how he wasn't the son Dad believes him to be? I couldn't do it, Carrie. I just never could do it. Much as he drank, much as he blamed himself, I just couldn't do that. Think of this: every single man in this family has, as you know now, served in the army. All Dad did was encourage Robbie to follow suit. If I then told him, after Robbie's death, why he had actually joined, it wouldn't be just those things Robbie had done *prior to joining* that upset him, but the mere fact his son hadn't really given a damn about the family tradition at all. I saw the whole thing as throwing him further over the edge, not helping at all."

Carrie pushed herself away from the table and stood.

Out the window, the changing colors of the leaves, the changing scene spoke of chill nights to come and mists that would settle and claim the colors off the land.

"So why, after all this time, did Ty come—because I assume now it was Ty, that is what you're getting to, isn't it? Why did he kill Alamo after all this time?"

Jake sucked in a breath as his body flinched from the truth. "He threatened me with telling Dad about

Robbie if…if I didn't do a run for him. He said it was only one run, and I was stupid enough to believe him."

Carrie sank back into her chair.

"When he wanted me to do a second run, I started out but…well, I spoke to Paige. She called while I was driving there and told me to turn back. I mean, I needed someone like that to yell at me, to make me realize I was just getting into the same situation Robbie had got into. Getting myself into really deep water." He tapped the fingers of his two hands together, impatient with his own stupidity. "Gonna make a damned good lawyer, your daughter," he jested. Then, leaning forward again, he went on, "So, obviously, killing Alamo was Ty's revenge for me not going through with it, letting him down. But I don't know if he has anything else in store. There's no way of knowing what that bastard will do. Another dog? A horse next perhaps? One of us? I just don't know what to do. And even if I now tell Dad the whole story, will Ty stop?"

Carrie stood suddenly as if she were about to swing into action. "You must tell that sheriff, Jake. You must. And you must tell your father the whole story, beginning to end, just as you've told me. You can't let this spiral on like this."

"Is it 'o what a tangled web we weave…'?"

Carrie stared at him. She hadn't smiled when he mentioned Paige, and she wasn't smiling now. Her mouth puckered and Jake had the feeling she would tear him limb from limb if she could.

"That's exactly what it is, only you haven't actually deceived, you've just neglected to tell him things. Or maybe you have deceived him, by letting him believe he sent his son to his death. The whole thing is crazy, Jake. Neither of you were responsible for Robbie's death. He made his own choices, his own decisions, some good, some bad, and he took the consequences. In any case, if every man in this family has served in the army, don't you think Robbie would have eventually gone anyway? Just like you did. Listen to me, Jake. Ray will understand. He'll understand why you held all this back, and I think, I believe, he'll really respect you for telling him." She slumped back onto her chair, her gaze still boring into him.

Jake shook his head. "I can't hurt him like that, Carrie. He thinks the world of Robbie. And last time I tried telling him, he started this whole saga about how we'd made him proud, that he was so proud of us both, and how much he loved us."

"He does love you! You think he's going to love you less for this?" She smacked the table. "Jake, please. I can't do this for you, if that was what you were hoping. I can't! Ray and I are just so open with each other—we have no secrets from each other, nothing. And now you've told me this. Please, please tell him. I can't."

It suddenly hit Jake he wasn't sure, in truth, what Carrie could do. He had followed Paige's advice to discuss it with her mother, but what could come of this? He shook his head more from sorrow than agreement. "I know," he said. "I just wanted your advice I guess."

"Well, that's my advice, Jake. That, and I think you had better tell the sheriff. Everything. They'll let you off if you go to them now. I know they will. And you'll end this hold Ty has over this family, put him away, stop him from doing anything further. Think of the lives he is ruining."

The front door opened and Jake pivoted in his seat to catch his father walking in, a spring in his step as he hung his hat on the hall hook and peeped through the glass at them. Carrie managed a wave and a smile while he reluctantly nodded in greeting to his father.

"What am I missing?" A questioning gaze slid from Jake to Carrie. "If ever there were a couple of folks up to no-good, I tell you…"

She got up and went to him, putting her arms around him as he kissed the top of her head. "I think I might manage to cook you dinner tonight," she said with a smug expression on her face.

"Really? That'll be a first. Jake, you gonna risk being poisoned?"

****

Carrie was relieved Ray had not asked her what her pow-wow with Jake had been about. In the quiet of the bedroom when he went over the day's events, she braced herself for the question. But he was not pushy, he never dug for information. His patience for letting things unfold was extraordinary. And in this case, for that, she was thankful.

The question of how Jake had let this go on for so long, how he had succumbed to Ty's Machiavellian dealings, ran through her mind. Ray would be hurt; he would hurt badly from the story his son would tell him, and she wanted to be there to ease his pain—and stop him from resorting to the bottle. But as a week passed, and Jake didn't make a move, Carrie decided she couldn't egg him on; this had to be his decision.

And then Paige called.

"I imagine you know about Jake. Or at least I'm hoping you know…"

"He told me. Everything I think. But he hasn't told Ray yet."

"Shit." There was silence on the phone and Carrie could tell her daughter was pacing. "Maybe I should call him."

"I don't think so, Paige. I think this now has to be Jake's decision. We've both told him what we think. We've both told him to tell Ray and tell the police, haven't we? It's now up to him." She took a breath but when her daughter made no reply, she continued, "He's probably just waiting for the right moment, and it isn't easy. He has to get Ray at—" She stopped. She'd been prattling on with no response from her generally opinionated daughter. It struck her as odd. "Paige?"

"I'm here."

"You're unusually quiet. What's the matter?"

"I have a new roommate, Mom." Paige almost blurted it out, knowing as she did her mother would be nothing short of stunned.

"A roommate? That's wonderful! Who? Why? When?"

"About a week ago. I mean, you're forking out for this two bedroom apartment because it was the only thing I could get so close to school starting, and I just thought, well, it's ridiculous for me to be rolling around here on my own. I mean, it's nice at times, but at other times not so nice." Paige thought again of that silence, that quiet that had spooked her in the night, and shivered.

"Well, who is it? Tell me everything."

Her mother would hope it was a man, but she let it pass.

"Her name is Deirdre Everton. She was living way

232

out of town with family friends and commuting in, which was ridiculous of course, so she's absolutely ecstatic she saw my ad and is now so close to campus."

"I bet she is."

"I'll send you the rent. I mean…"

"Oh, Paige, for heaven's sake. That's the last thing I'm worried about."

"I know, but… Look, I'll take over the utilities and the other bills then, it's the least I can do. Okay?"

"Fine."

She envisaged her mother rolling her eyes.

"So, what is she like?"

"Outgoing, a bit too chatty at times, but if I tell her I'm working, she does shut up and seems to know now when to leave me alone. She's a good cook. And she's about a gazillion feet tall and blond and from Austin."

Her mom burst out laughing. "Oh, Paige. You didn't choose her as a possible match for Jake, did you?"

"Absolutely. Absolutely, they're a perfect match. Nothing in common I know of, of course, except maybe Texas. But they're a perfect match."

****

What Jake and Carrie might possibly have been discussing so seriously ran through Ray's mind with various permutations, but he didn't dwell on it. For all he knew, his son was still considering going back to school and was sounding out Carrie on her feelings on the matter. Sooner or later, birds came home to roost, and if he was meant to know, it would come out.

Yet, Jake's listlessness had reached epic proportions. Although he knew from experience his son's temper could be sparked with flint-like immediacy, the boy had actually always been a gentle child, a worrier, the softer of the two brothers, thinking things through and analyzing them until he would take action. Then there was the day Jake had announced he was going into the army, a decision that had surprised Ray and, after Robbie's death, frightened him. Yet, what could he have done? His son had been adamant. Every man in his family had served, and Jake had said he had to follow. It had stunned him; having used those very same words to get Robbie to enlist, when Jake had told him of his own decision, it had been a terrific blow. But he was home now—home safe, sound…and unhappy.

He stood watching Jake come toward him at the barn, his son's loping walk a mimic of his own saunter.

"What's up?" He kept an eye on one of the new stable boys currying a horse.

"I'm worried 'bout the horses." Jake's voice was flat, but then, no explanation was really needed.

Ray took a hoof pick to show the stable boy how to use it. He put a hand to his back as he bent over.

"Where the heck is Stacey and the other stable girls?" Jake asked, making a grab for the pick. "Here, let me do that, Dad."

"I'm not that old yet!" He straightened and gave his son a stern face before bending and sliding his hand down the horse's cannon to lift its hoof. "Stacey's off sick, and the others are busy. So, what's brought on this worry 'bout the horses all of a sudden? It's been a time since Alamo was killed. You think this person is gonna strike again? You got some ideas on this?"

As he glanced back at his son, there was no doubting the worry on Jake's drawn face.

"I think we ought to keep the horses stabled at night and have more security lights put up."

"I've ordered that already," Ray answered. The pick threw out small clumps of dirt. "Man's coming Monday to put them up, wire them in. What else?"

"I…" His voice trailed off.

Ray straightened again.

"I guess that's it. Seems you have everything under control then."

"Well, Jake, if you've got some ideas or want to say something 'bout this, I'm all ears. I'm open to suggestions. Let's hear it, son." He took in the solemn face and knew something was wrong.

"No. Nope, it's fine. That was all. I worried 'bout the horses, the paddock and barn being away from the house and all, we might not hear anything. I mean, if someone has it in for us, they may well come back."

"You think a camera or two might be a good idea down here? Cost a bit, of course, and means we have to check the tape or whatever the hell it is every so often and all. 'Less, of course, we get it hitched up to a computer in the house or some such system. Rather fancy bit of tech stuff if you ask me, and more likely than not, if anyone strikes, it'll be while we're sleeping."

"Well, it's up to you, Dad. I think we can manage with a computer system, but then, I also think something that sets off alarms might do as well. Makes more sense, don't you think? If we wait to watch a screen, it may be too late. You might consider a driveway alarm, I think they call them."

"Well, a driveway alarm might drive me nuts with so many people coming and going. You got guests goin' on out for dinner and comin' back late. But the cameras—I'll get it done with the lights. Larry actually told me the Double Bar M got themselves some fancy system that sends alarms to their cell phones, but it's a pain in the butt since animals set it off every so often. I don't think we need that." Ray held out the hoof pick to the boy. "Here, you try that now on the next one, okay?"

His son still stood there, watching, waiting.

"Was there anything else, Jake?"

"No…nothing at all."

****

Carrie finished the final read-through of her manuscript and sat back with a sense of deep satisfaction. She clicked it into an attachment to her agent and tapped in a brief note before taking a breath and pondering whether to take a few days off to do some more riding and hunting with Ray if he had time. Her love of living on the ranch was beginning to make her find more and more excuses why she didn't have to return to New York.

Getting up and stretching, she stood watching birds fly across the dappled horizon, a flapping V like some Busby Berkeley formation. The mackerel sky was sliding into evening. Texas was still very warm for October, and she opened the sunroom doors a bit, before turning to open the doors into the house.

And then she saw her. A thin, blonde woman about the same age as herself stood in the front hall staring at her.

Suddenly, Mabel toddled into the picture. "Mr. Ray is down at the hunt office now. You go on down there, you wanna speak to him." The housekeeper's no-

nonsense tone was at one of its more intimidating pitches.

For a moment, Carrie wondered if this was some troublesome customer who had been here before, whom Mabel knew. But something told her it wasn't; something told her exactly who this was. She started down the hallway.

The woman's gaze ran over Carrie, an obvious momentary assessment, making no disguise of the fact as the blonde's face screwed up into a rictus of disgust. Carrie noted the dark roots long overdue to match the remains of her uncombed hair, the casual clothes crumpled and hanging on her thin frame.

"Who the hell are you?" this unwanted guest asked while continuing to stare her down. She fished in a pocket of her jacket, pulled out a pack of cigarettes and proceeded to tap one out.

"I'm Ray's friend." Carrie kept her voice unemotional, inoffensive. "Can I help you?" She saw Mabel's eyes grow big with apprehension as the generally authoritarian housekeeper almost tripped a step back.

The other woman flipped open her lighter as if she expected to be dared not to. "Ray's *friend*. Wow, he didn't waste any time, did he?" she said, blowing a long cloud of smoke that just missed Carrie. "Who the hell are you? What's your name?"

"My name? Carrie Bennett." She forced herself to stay patient, to not lose her temper. "May I ask who you are?"

"I'm his wife."

Carrie put her hands on her hips, her temper slowly oozing out like a running sore. "You mean, his *ex-*

wife."

"Noooo." The woman stretched out the word, blowing another funnel of smoke into the sultry air. "I mean, his *wife*."

Chapter Thirteen

Carrie stood staring at the last person she wished to ever meet. "You mean, his ex-wife," she repeated so there could be no mistake.

Leigh Anne Ryder blew more smoke directly at her in a short puff of hatred. "I know what I mean Miss Carrie Bennett. He tell you we were divorced?" When she received no reply, the woman continued. "That's typical. A little stretching of the truth, huh? Nothing's settled. I just might want to come back."

Mabel threw up her hands and headed back to the safety of the kitchen.

"You think Ray will want you back?" Carrie tried to keep malice out of her voice, but it proved exceedingly difficult.

"I don't give a shit what he wants. We're still married. This is my home. I can do what I damn well please. He can't throw me out." Her gaze ran over Carrie as if memorizing details once more. "Beats me what a woman like you sees in a broken down old drunk like Ray Ryder."

"He doesn't drink anymore." She took a sharp intake of breath as she recalled Ray's recent evening after Alamo's murder, but she didn't bother to elaborate. "He stopped months ago."

"Well," said Leigh Anne coming farther into the room and dropping her cheap handbag on a sofa as if to challenge her rights here. "He's stopped before, sweetheart, and he *always* starts again. Can't help himself." She searched around for an ashtray, but they were gone. The length of ash on her cigarette dropped to the floor. "Mabel," she called, "You best be getting me an ashtray if you don't want to be cleaning up after me."

The housekeeper stomped in and plunked one down on a side table by Leigh Anne. She stood staring at her former mistress with hands on hips before turning on her heel and heading out.

"I've known the man for thirty odd years—odd being the word here, mind you—and he's *always* been a drinker. He's not gonna stop now just for some fancy woman he's tied up with, believe me."

For a moment, Carrie wondered if Leigh Anne meant "fancy woman" as a euphemism for whore or mistress. "Well, he's stopped now," she said quietly.

Ray's wife sat herself down in the armchair next to her ashtray and leaned back, squinting up at her. There was a self-satisfied smile on her worn face, a face that dared Carrie to ask her to leave.

That did it. She'd had enough.

Carrie marched down the hallway to the bedroom she shared with Ray—which he had once shared with Leigh Anne—and slammed the door shut, hearing the woman's throaty laughter taunting her.

Several phone calls later, and with a quick shove into suitcases of everything she possessed in that room, she marched back out to retrieve her laptop from the sunroom and headed to the door.

Leigh Anne was gone, but Mabel rushed out to stop Carrie.

"She's gone now, Miz Carrie. What you going off for like that? She ain't never been no good. I worked for this fam'ly for more years than I can remember, and the things I seen that woman done don't bear thinking about. You gonna up and leave Mr. Ray now?"

"I have to, Mabel. I'm sorry." She made a grab for the door.

"You were the best thing that ever happened to that man."

Carrie stood for a moment, her gaze running over the living room in this house where she had spent so many happy hours. She was sickened by the betrayal she now faced, the loss of all she had set her heart on, the future she had thought was hers.

"I'm sorry, Mabel. I have to go." She started to tug the door open.

"But why, Miz Carrie?"

Carrie stopped in her tracks, wondering why this housekeeper was suddenly all friendly after several weeks of a sullen, though tentatively softening, approach.

She put down the bags for a moment and gave her a quick, hug-like grasp. "He lied to me, Mabel. That's why. He *lied*."

Outside, her hands trembled as she shoved the key in the ignition and set off.

The scene with Leigh Anne replayed in her mind, the times Ray could have admitted the true situation, the times he could have said *something*. But no, nothing had been said. Ever. He had let the weeks pass never ever mentioning that he was still a married man, that the divorce had never gone through—that there was the possibility Leigh Anne might march back in.

Carrie gripped the wheel as the angry red glare of a low, mid-October sun confronted her, forcing her to snap down the sun visor. Her mind wasn't on her driving; her mind was running over, again and again, the exchange with Leigh Anne, fury driving her on so she almost missed her turn for the Austin airport through the rage that blinded her.

****

Ray faced his wife across the expanse of his desk in the hunt office; the tension of confrontation mixed with his dislike of her being on his turf. There was a second's pause before she snatched up a piece of paper from his desk and scribbled a figure on it.

"That's what I want in final settlement. It's fair, it's a compromise, and I'm out of your life for good. And you can marry your fancy woman." Leigh Anne went and slammed the door on Larry Gruhl tidying up papers in the main outer office.

"Was that necessary?" Ray asked calmly as she turned back to him. He glanced at the figure on the paper. "I have to think about this. It's more than I've got, Leigh Anne, as I'm sure you're aware."

"I'm aware of nothing, Ray. I have no idea what your bank balance is. Never have. Maybe that fancy woman of yours will help you out. She looked like she might have a few dollars to spare."

Aware his wife was baiting him, he chose to ignore the remark. Then it struck him. "How did you know about Carrie?"

She didn't answer, but rather asked, "She the Carrie Bennett who writes the romances?"

"I said," his voice rising a notch, "how did you know about Carrie? Jake tell you?"

Leigh Anne scrabbled in her pocket again for a cigarette.

Ray covered his mouth to stop himself from breathing the smoky air. Or prevent angry words from escaping. He managed to maintain a semblance of patience as she got out her lighter, flipped out a flame and inhaled deeply.

"Where is Jake, by the way? I'd like to see him."

That wasn't an answer to his question. Ray felt his patience waning and giving way to anger, but he managed to hold on as fear sent his heart racing. "I sent him over to Bandera and then on to Austin on business. He's probably hoping to visit you there."

Leigh Anne shook her head at this bit of news. "Well. When you gonna decide, Ray?" she asked at last. "I can't hang on forever. This goes to court, it'll cost us both."

"You have the money for that, Leigh Anne? You ought to think on that some. The longer this goes on, the more it costs. The only winners will be the damn lawyers. You think on that, and I'll think on this." He held out the paper with the sum on it.

She adjusted her handbag on her shoulder and put a hand on the door. "Miz Carrie Bennett was none too pleased to find out we were still married," she threw at him as she jerked open the door. "I think you might find you'll be sleeping alone tonight."

As soon as he heard the retreating sound of Leigh Anne's pickup, Ray grabbed his jacket and hat off a hook and, with a nod at Larry, dashed for his own vehicle. It screeched to a halt in front of the house, and he ran inside.

Mabel immediately slammed down her dustcloth

and went to him. "Oh, Mr. Ray, I tried to tell her. I tried to get her to stay, but she's gone now. Cleared out. Jus' got in her car and went."

Ray gasped at her in disbelief. "Where did she go? You know?"

"No, sir." She shook her head. "She jus' said she had to go, that you'd *lied* to her, and she was off."

Panic slid through him pulling loss with it. His stomach churned with uncertainty. "You know anything, Mabel? Where she went? Which airport? Which hotel?"

"No, Mr. Ray. She didn't tell me nothin'. Not a word. Jus' packed her bags and hit out like the wind was blowing her. She spoke with Miz Ryder for a while, and then headed on in to your room, made a few phone calls and packed up."

Ray strode into the bedroom, the bedroom he considered *theirs*, and explored around. Not a single item of Carrie's was left, not a thing in the closet, not an item on the shelf of the bathroom. No note. Nothing. Nada.

He lifted the house phone and punched in her cell number without much hope. She didn't answer. Of course not; it would display his number, and she wasn't talking to him.

Come on, Carrie. Come on.

He sent a text from his cell phone: *Please answer. I need to talk to you. Let me explain.* Again, no response.

And then, written on the telephone pad, he spotted two numbers in Carrie's scrawl. One-eight-hundred numbers. If one was the airline, he might be able to figure which flight she was on and from where she was flying—Austin or San Antonio. He could search the internet to check the flights, and he just might be able to beat her there. They sure as heck wouldn't tell him her flight. *Pick up, pick up, pick up*, kept going through his mind.

"Hilton Austin Airport, how may I direct your call?"

Ray tried to get the tension out of his voice. "Sorry, which Hilton is this?"

The girl hesitated, obviously confused by the question, suspicious. "It's...the Austin airport location, sir. How may I help you?"

"You have a Carrie Bennett there at the moment? Can you put me through to her room please?"

"One moment, sir." After a few minutes she said, "I'm sorry, sir. Miss Bennett has not checked in as yet. May I take a message?"

He put down the phone and grabbed his keys.

****

The smell of plastic and stale air hit Carrie as she sat for a moment on the edge of her motel room bed, still dressed in her jeans, the cheap bedspread rustling slightly as she lay back to stare blankly at the ceiling. Somewhere inside her, love tried to free itself like a perfumed scent from a sealed bottle. In this moment's peace among the debris of her overnight things, scattered like rejected toys, she was jolted by the sudden bell of her room phone.

"Good afternoon, Miss Bennett." The young woman's voice came over in saccharin efficiency. "There's a Jake Ryder here to see you. May I send him up?"

Carrie gulped in air with the surprise. In her present state of upset, she didn't think through how

Jake would know where she was, yet it made sense to her since he was supposedly already in Austin. She owed him a good-bye if nothing else.

A hesitant, "Yes, of course," went barely audibly down the phone before she placed the handset back on the cradle.

At the knock, Carrie proceeded to open the door in a numb state of confusion, not looking through the peephole. She stood there dazed, her mixed emotions slowing her reaction as she tried to slam the door shut, but Ray was too fast. He managed to get his booted foot in and get through, backing her into the room.

He put up his hand to ward off any words, any vitriol she might spew.

"Listen to me, just listen to me," he started.

"You must be joking! Why should I ever listen to you again? You lied! You blatantly lied to me—you said you were divorced." The pain scratched at her heart. Seeing him there, wanting him still, yet knowing they were finished, bruised her insides.

Ray paced the narrow room, stopping to stare out at the grim concrete gray of the airport environment. In the distance, a plane lifted and tilted into the foam of cloud. When he spoke again, his voice was modulated to a less threatening, more reasonable tone. "No, Carrie—I never said right out I was divorced. Or maybe I did, but it was that first night—that night at the dancehall. And I never in a million years could've foreseen you and I would have any kind of relationship."

"Oh! So lying to a perfect stranger is fine, but to someone with whom you have a relationship—" Her voice pitched uncontrollably.

"Oh, be reasonable. I was half-cut and wasn't thinking one way or the other. It was an explanation as I recall. You'd asked me why I used the word, 'was' about Leigh Anne, and I explained it away. Carrie, what the hell difference does it make?"

His exasperation rose a notch as she quaked with her anger.

"What difference? What *difference*? It makes a world of difference. I had to stand there while that woman told me she might 'come back,' while she taunted me with smoking to let me know I had no rights in that house to ask her to stop, to ask her to leave. Do you know what that was like?" Her balled fists shook at him.

"Of course you have rights. It's the way she is..."

"If you lied about that, what else did you lie about, Ray? When you said—"

"I didn't lie about anything else. I didn't lie about that. If anything, maybe a white lie. It was a conversation we were having, for goodness sake. You don't go into your whole marital history with someone you just met." He paced again, as if trying to recall the evening calmly. A growing sense of the futility of arguing with her, a premonition of an impasse, began to feed his ire. "You were angry with me for overhearing your phone conversation, the kids were inside dancing, and I was drunk. You think I was going to go into a whole explanation of Leigh Anne and I separating, and how I was trying to get her off my back?"

"How many times could you have corrected it?"

"Oh, for heaven's sake, Carrie," he shouted back at her. "You don't go complaining about an ex-wife, or, pardon me, *soon* to be ex-wife, to a woman you've just met. You—"

"You act as if the chance never presented itself after that, as if it were never mentioned. It was mentioned plenty, Ray. You could have said—somewhere along the line, you could have corrected it. But no, you left it. You let me believe you were free and clear." Her voice receded into a hoarse rasp as she scrabbled in her handbag to bring out a tissue. She was stunned he didn't understand what it had cost her just to form a relationship with him, and to now discover that relationship had been a total fraud, that she was suddenly 'the other woman.'

"Well, what possible difference does it make?" He waited for a reply. "Come back, Carrie. Let's discuss this and sort it out at home."

"It's your home, Ray, not mine. It's yours and Leigh Anne's. Please go." She dabbed at her face as their gaze met briefly before she turned away. Love gnawed at her insides as it fought with her distrust.

"I'm not going, Carrie. I love you." He paced the room again, slaloming around the maze of furniture as he ran a hand through his hair before he stopped in front of her. "You know that, and I wouldn't do anything to harm you. And I think you love me."

The words lay there between them with a heat that would scorch if touched. She said nothing as the television in the next room sounded through the wall, grabbing his attention for a moment.

"Please come back."

"No!"

He stood in front of her finally, pleading with his eyes, exasperated, defeated. "You know what your problem is, Carrie?"

"No," she said, hands on hips. "But I'm sure you're going to tell me."

"You write all that romance, you create *all* those perfect worlds for yourself, all those happy endings. The heroes who are all so perfect—"

"How would you know anything about my books? Did you ever read one?"

"'Course I did. I spent all those hours flying from Texas and traveling to the almighty Hamptons to see you, reading your damn books. Stewardess or flight attendant or whatever the hell you call them nowadays thought I was a pansy." He paced some more and ran his hand over his face before turning back to her. "You create all those beautiful, perfect people. You escape to those perfect worlds you create and you can't cope with the real world. You can't cope with your own aging, for goodness sake, because you think your body isn't desirable any longer. You can't cope with your daughter's mourning because death and loss aren't in your world. And you can't relax, you're a workaholic because the world you create in your books is so much better than the world you see around you. I feel sorry for you." He went on pacing. "I do. Because no one and nothing is ever going to live up to your expectations, to your fictional world. That's why you run from every relationship you have. That's why, after twenty-four years, you're still alone, Carrie. We had a chance for happiness here and you just had to find some way, whatever way you could, to destroy it."

"And you, Ray, how do you cope?" His words had seared her. Tears of frustration tracked down her cheeks, but the tissue was useless now, worn thin in the friction of her palm. "You go running for the Jack

Daniels at the first sign of trouble, anything you can't face, anything you can't deal with, you go straight to the drink," she tallied him, the tears washing her face. "What's your excuse? And you stayed married to a woman you say you never loved for—what?—nearly thirty years. If you're so brilliant, if you have so many answers, what's your answer for that?"

He took in a deep breath, meeting her piercing gaze. "You know damn well what my answer is. Like most people, I had kids first, and I didn't want them hurting. I had a sense of duty, of doing the right thing by staying by Leigh Anne—"

"Oh, that is such a good excuse!"

Ray ignored her. "And you sleepwalk. You sleepwalk through bad times. You go through the motions, day in, day out. You find a routine. You manage. You get involved with one thing and another that distracts you from the fact you're so damn miserable. And then one day something happens, a crisis, and you might get your wake-up call."

He waited, and she knew he was hoping to somehow get through to her, somehow make her understand, but she shuffled once more in her bag to escape the truth of his words. It would be so easy to say, yes, she'd been wrong, what did it matter, yet deep inside, as much as she yearned for him, hungered for his touch, the betrayal had been too great.

"But you, Carrie, in your perfect world, you'll never get that call, will you? You'll just write it out, won't you?"

"Is that it? Are you finished? Because I really would like to be alone now." A sense of loss snaked through her body, an emptiness, a knowledge this love she had found was over.

She held the sight of him for a moment, the creases and lines of his face, the black velvet eyes, the way his hair fell over his brow. She tucked it in the pocket of her memory for some future time she might be able to review it, to think of him.

"No. I want to ask you one other thing, and I'd like you to think on this real hard. When you saw Leigh Anne, when you saw what kind of a woman she was, did you wonder, did you ask yourself how the two of you could have a relationship with the same man? Did you feel so damn superior to her, the mere thought she had been my wife just disgusted you? Is that not the real reason you fled? I mean, if she had been some upper class beauty, you wouldn't have minded that little white lie, would you? But it really bothered you to see some worn out, rough looking gal—"

"Oh, you are such a frigging psychologist, aren't you, Ray? You have a frigging answer for everything." She threw her tissue into a bin as the anger came out like an abscess releasing its pus. "You're such a great psychiatrist and mind-reader—oh, and father—you don't even see what's going on in front of your own eyes."

Confusion crossed his face. "What's going on in front of my eyes? What's that supposed to mean? What are you talking about?"

"I'm talking about Jake, and I'm talking about Robbie, Ray. Jake came to me because he couldn't go to you, couldn't hurt you with what he had to say, what he wanted to get off his chest for so long. He wanted to be able to tell you it wasn't because of *you* Robbie joined the army, it was because of *him*...only he couldn't tell you the truth behind it because he knew it would hurt you so."

"What truth? What are you talking about?"

Carrie hesitated, knowing the pain it would cause him, even now reluctant to let him hurt like that. Indecision twisted her insides, yet Jake's secret could no longer be kept—for all their sakes. She lowered her voice. "Robbie was in trouble, Ray. He'd been running drugs up from Mexico—"

"You're lying!" he shouted.

"You think so? Well," she said backing away from him, escaping the anger and pain etched on his face. "Ask Jake. You think you have two perfect sons, don't you? You think serving in the army makes every man absolutely honest and true. Well, Jake's been protecting you from knowing this for...what? Five years now? Jake loves you so much, Ray. To protect you from knowing about Robbie, he's got himself into trouble with that Ty. But, oh, yes," she said gathering a cutting edge to her voice, "what do I know? I only create perfect worlds. I can only deal with those." She waited as he stared at her, stared uncomprehending, not wanting to believe anything she said. "Are you going to leave now or shall I call security?"

Ray opened the door and stood with his hand still on the handle. His gaze met hers before he glanced around the hotel room, suddenly aware of the contrast between Carrie's expensive luggage standing on the cheap carpet, her cashmere sweater flung over the regulation hotel chair, her expensive cosmetics strewn over the nylon bedspread.

"What was it, Carrie, that possessed you to stay here for a night?" The sense of loss that had been evident had given in to spite. "Airlines didn't have any first class tickets left? Only economy until tomorrow?"

"Get out!"

****

Arriving home in the late evening from Austin, Jake thought nothing of the fact the house was dark. His father and Carrie occasionally went out to eat, or for an evening ride, leaving him to eat whatever Mabel had left for them. But there was something eerie this time about the quiet, something almost too black about the dark. He strolled down to the stables to just check the horses.

Creaking open the stable door, his gaze traveled down the row of stalls and found all the horses accounted for, but he couldn't shake himself of the feeling something was wrong.

He sauntered back to the house, wondering whether his dad was going to be sitting there in the dark again, Carrie asleep, but there was no Dad, no Carrie. The pickup wasn't out front. A good sign. But then neither was Carrie's rental car. He flicked on the lights, headed into the kitchen to start getting the grub together, but was hit by the odor of cigarette smoke hanging in the air like an uninvited guest. A washed ashtray sat there on the drying rack. Jake stared at it several seconds while his brain churned around and he tried to make sense of it. Could be a number of people who come to the house. But most wouldn't smoke inside. He lifted it, turning it around in his hands as if there might be evidence of the user of this object, then placed it back down and strode down the hall.

The lights in his father's bedroom made a showcase of the emptiness of it, as if a tide had rolled in taking out debris scattered along a shore. A quick glance in the bathroom confirmed what he feared.

And then his phone rang.

"Jake?" came the voice. "It's Mike Mulligan. I think you better come and collect your dad. He's flat out on the floor and there's no way I want him driving home."

Chapter Fourteen

Jake's night had been torturous, and he awoke feeling as if he'd been the one on a binge. He'd managed to get his father home with the help of Mike Mulligan, dragged him down the hall and left him to sleep off his bender. Now, fearing he would never be able to tell the truth about Robbie, the slain Alamo and his own questionable involvements, he made his way wearily down the hall to face his dad.

"You wanna tell me what happened?" he asked his father as he placed a cup of coffee on the bedside table at seven a.m.

Getting up on one elbow, his father stared at him, bloodshot eyes straining at Jake as his dry mouth opened and shut before he could speak. "Why didn't you tell me, Jake? Why didn't you tell me 'bout Robbie? And you now…why?"

Jake collapsed onto a chair in a corner facing the bed and grabbed a swallow of his own coffee. A finger of chill ran down his spine despite the hot liquid; numbness paralyzed him. It was out. Out at last. "So, she told you. All right, but tell me first what happened with Carrie. Was Mom here?"

His dad shuffled like a cripple into a sitting position and grated the stubble on his face. "Yeah, Leigh Anne was here. She told Carrie we weren't divorced and she might want to come back—"

"Would Carrie believe that, that Mom might come back, or that you'd take her back?"

"Carrie thought we were already divorced." His father reached across for his cup, but his hand was shaking and he dragged it back. "Damn it," he said. "I said such terrible things to that poor woman, such terrible things."

He ignored the last remark. "Carrie thought you were already divorced? All this time she thought you were divorced?"

Jake's tone held his disbelief as his dad slowly nodded in confirmation.

"I told her the first night we met I was divorced—it was just a passing remark to someone I hardly knew. I just never got round to correcting it. What difference could it make? We hadn't discussed marriage, so it didn't seem important. It was a matter of time. I'd told her I loved her, Jake. She knew there was no way I was going back to Leigh Anne or was gonna let Leigh Anne come back. I'm sorry to say that to you, 'bout your mama, but there just wasn't." He threw his legs over the side and moaned into a full sitting position before reaching again for the coffee, taking it in both hands with a shudder and getting it to his mouth. When he'd managed to put it down, he drove himself to stand and stumbled around the bed to the bathroom.

Jake waited for the flush before he called out, "You know, I really liked Carrie. I just never understood what you two had in common, how that all worked out."

His father came back out and stood a second, regaining his balance before making his way back to his cup of coffee. "She's not who you think she is, Jake. She doesn't want anything, Carrie. She has all this money and success and it really means nothing to her. I think all she ever wanted was to be loved. I think that was the shock of her husband leaving her. All she wanted was someone to love her for herself. And then she had all this success and everyone just wanted to know Carrie Bennett, the author. Except me. I just wanted Carrie Bennett. And she was so damn easy, you know. She wanted nothing—"

"She wanted nothing because she already had it, Dad."

"No. She really didn't want anything. Oh, she loved her house and she loved some things she had, I guess, but she was so easy. Little things pleased her. Not like your mama. Nothing was ever good enough for Leigh Anne. Nothing I ever did, no matter how hard I tried, could ever please that woman. But Carrie...it was the difference between night and day." He grimaced again. "Why was that white lie so important? It was only a matter of time."

"So, why don't you go after her?"

His father shook his head as a flash of pain creased his face. "I did go after her—I followed her to the airport hotel where she was staying. That's when she told me 'bout you and Robbie. And—oh, Lord. I said such awful things, Jake. We both did. I think we need to give it time to heal. Such terrible things were said. And I need to clear things up here. With you. We need to get this out now, Jake. Once and for all. What you've been carrying around with you like...like some poison eating you up, slowly running through your system. You think I didn't notice? I don't know what I ever did to you to make me seem so unapproachable, but I'm sorry as hell for it."

Jake sat staring into the pool of his coffee cup for several moments. "I don't know either, Dad. Really I don't. It wasn't ever anything you did, that's for sure. I just didn't want to disappoint you, I guess. And I didn't want you to think you had failed us somehow, that Robbie doing what he did somehow reflected on you. It didn't. I just didn't want you drinking again either." He listened to his father's snort at this. "Can you promise me this is the end, now? You want Carrie back, but you can be sure as hell she won't walk on back through that door if she has an inkling you're drinking. You stopped once. You can do it again."

His dad lifted his coffee to his lips and peered at Jake before he stared into the cup as if it could tell his future. "It's a deal. I'll go back to AA," he said as he took a sip and put it back down. "Now, tell me the whole damn story."

****

Carrie threw the suitcase on the bed and collapsed beside it. For the entire flight and taxi ride to her apartment, she had sat, zombie-like, an empty shell, a tree stripped of its leaves. There was such a vacancy, such hollowness, a vacuum inside, it was impossible to think. Talk, at check-in, with the flight attendant, with the taxi driver, and the doormen at her building, who cheerily greeted her, had been so sparse and monosyllabic, they probably thought her unconscionably rude. She went through the journey on automatic pilot, more than bereft, more than empty. She had aged one hundred years in less than a day. In short, she might as well have been dead.

If loneliness were the problem, she could call any one of several friends, starting with Diana Shawcross, and they would come running to her side within the hour. But she didn't wish to see anyone, didn't want to talk. Her feeling of betrayal, of abandonment, was so complete, all she now wanted was sleep. Sleep, and to hide herself away, hibernate for a very long time, because that would stop her brain going, would stop her rewinding the scene in the hotel room.

Had she and Ray really said such horrible things to each other? Ray, who was always so laidback and even-tempered, who always saw the funny side of a situation, who had been so affectionate and caring, had shouted at her, had criticized her and, worst of all, had lied.

And she had hurt him in return, and for what? Why? Had one white lie been so truly terrible? Was there really such a huge difference between the Ryders being separated, on the verge of divorce while obviously living apart, to being *actually* divorced?

"I don't think that was it," later ventured Paige, who patiently listened to the whole sorry tale while Carrie sobbed to her over the phone. "I don't think that was it at all."

"Then what was it?"

"It was because you felt you belonged there, Ray was yours, life there was yours, and suddenly that stupid woman came along and told you otherwise, so you felt threatened. And I guess you then blamed Ray for having put you in that position, for having not protected you."

She could hear some music in the background and Paige speaking to someone else in a lower voice.

"What are you doing?" Her tone was suddenly alert.

"I'm learning how to make Welsh Rarebit. Or

maybe it's Welsh Rabbit. I'm not sure." There was a load of giggles to follow.

"Oh. I'm sorry. I didn't know you were having guests or whatever."

"Oh, for heaven's sake, Mother. Deirdre and I are just grabbing a quick dinner before heading back to the books. It's only cheese sauce on toast really."

"I know what Welsh Rarebit is, Paige."

It suddenly struck Carrie she was alone on this one, no one had the answer, the answer had to come from her or Ray.

"Look, I better let you get on. I'm sorry. I think I might go out to the beach tomorrow."

"You'll be cold and miserable. And there's no one there." There was a second's silence. "I know you like it there out of season, but I really think it's better for you to be in the city with friends at the moment."

"I don't want to see friends, Paige. I'm going to have to make some revisions on the book soon. They're trying to rush this one through. I might as well be out there in the peace and quiet."

"Have it your way," her daughter said with some resignation, if not disinterest. "But remember, you're going someplace where Ray has been. He'll haunt you."

"He'll haunt me wherever I go. He's in my head."

"Well, I really feel you ought to phone Ray and talk to him. Try to sort things out. You love the man, and he loves you. This is just…really stupid."

"No, Paige. No, it isn't. It's sad is what it is. Sad it's happened, and sad it can't be fixed. You can't take back a lie, and you can't take back all those horrible things we said. It's not as if they are floating around and can somehow be swallowed again, and the memories aren't going to go away. It's over."

****

When Jake had finished telling his father about Robbie, Lucinda, Ty and himself, just the way he had told Carrie a couple of weeks before, his dad said the same thing she had said, came to the same conclusion to go to the sheriff.

"Well, this puts me in one helluva position, Jake." Dex played with a pencil while listening to his story, tapping the eraser on some papers every so often and then doing baton twirls around his fingers. He tapped it down several times now, eyeing Jake with a thoughtful squint across the expanse of the cheap metal desk in his office. The caterpillars above his eyes danced as he peered at him. "See, it's like this now. You've admitted to a crime. You speculate Ty Sheldon has killed your dog in retribution for not continuing to commit this crime—a felony—but, as you know, we have no proof of this, nor do I have proof Ty has them drugs or is dealing them. See what I mean? All I know for sure from this conversation is what you've admitted to doing yourself."

"You know damn well, Dex, Ty has dealt drugs," interrupted his dad. He shifted uncomfortably on his folding chair from the corner.

With the odor of stale coffee and musty air, his father's gut would be churning, but then, so was Jake's—but for different reasons.

"He's been charged before and he's out on parole now," his father continued.

"I know," countered Dex. "But we have no proof he's done it again. See, it's Jake's word here against Ty's, *if* I ignore the fact of his confession. It's just Jake saying he thinks Ty has drugs. What good is that? I can get a search warrant, but you know sure as hell, Ray, there ain't gonna be no drugs in his place. He's too damn smart for that. And now, if Jake here is confessing to bringing in drugs across the border, he's gonna be in a mess of trouble, so what do you want me to do? What the hell am I supposed to do with this bit of news?"

The silence was punctuated by the drone of a fly. Dex got to his feet, grabbed a spiral-bound notebook from his desk, and took a wild swat at the insect, leaving a bloody mark on the institutional green wall.

"Anyway," he went on as he lowered himself back into his rickety desk chair, "I'm not even sure I can get a search warrant. 'On what grounds' is what the judge would ask me. So, all I could do is tell him on the basis of Jake's confession. I cain't lie. Is that what you want? We're opening a whole dang can of worms here." He tapped his pencil several times, eyeing Jake once more. "You should of brought a lawyer with you, Ray, you know that."

"I been dealing with enough dang lawyers over the past few months. We don't need another one."

Dex turned back to Jake. "How much marijuana did you say you brought in?"

He shrugged. "'Bout a five pound loaf I'd think. I fit it in my satchel, so it couldn't have been much."

"Well." The sheriff grunted and leaned forward a bit. "It could mean two years in jail and a ten thousand dollar fine. So, that 'not much' could cost you some. It's a felony, Jake." The chair creaked as he sat back again. "'Course, the fact you came on in here to admit it of your own free will when you could've gone and got away with it, and the fact you're a Vet and served your country would weigh pretty heavy in your favor, I'd say. But I can't swear to that. Nothing is certain. Depends on what judge you get and what mood he—or she—is in that day. Man wakes up and has an argument with his wife, it sorta puts a whole different shine on the day. You see what I mean? You committed a felony and that, as they say, is that." His gaze danced from one to the other. "So, what do y'all want to do?"

Jake considered his father who sat forward, his chin resting in his hands, his elbows balancing on his thighs. He exchanged a questioning look with him.

"Jake said before we came here he was willing to pay his debt. My thinking is he's paid enough."

"And, as I said, I think the judge will think that as well. But I can't make the guarantee. I can give him a character reference, of course—"

"Can I say something? Seein' as how this is me y'all are discussin'?" Jake breathed hard as he took in the two of them. "I remember that kid, the one who died in the car crash while he was high on drugs. I remember how Robbie felt after hearing that. I don't want to feel that way. I want to get Ty and get him once and for all. And if the only way the judge or the court or whoever is going to listen to me is by me confessing now, then that's what I'm gonna do." He raised his gaze to Dex. "You want to take down my confession?"

"You sure you don't want to call a lawyer here now? Maybe let's reconvene in a day or two when you've had some time to think this over?"

There was the squeal of a chair as Jake's father sat up and held his head for a moment. He reached in his back pocket for his cell phone. "Guess I'll call my guy,

Jake. There's sure as hell bound to be someone in that damn firm who handles this kind of mess."

****

The streets of Philadelphia shone in the evening dusk, aureoles of white on the pavement from streetlights overhead, scattered leaves and chestnuts covering the walk. Students were bundled against the cold, their woolen scarves flapping out behind them or wound round their necks for protection. Paige wrapped her coat close and fell into step beside Deirdre whose stride was so much longer and quicker than her own.

"Hang on. I want to stop at Wawa and pick up a donut or something. I'm starved."

"You're always starved, Paige," commented Deirdre, following her into the brightness of the shop. "For such a little gal, I wonder where you put it all."

The girls snaked through the aisles to the pastry section. Paige picked up the tongs and lifted the lid of the donut container. She grabbed a wax paper square and dropped a chocolate donut into it, offering it to Deirdre.

"No, thanks. I'm hoping they have some sort of food at this party."

"Don't count on it." Paige got in line and waited to pay, already nibbling at the sweet confection and licking off the icing. By the time she was at the head of the line there was only a sorry morsel left to show the girl on the cash register.

"Well, that was good," she commented as she followed her roommate outside into the chill of the night. Waves of frosted breath fogged the air as she dusted down her hands and breathed deeply. "Anything round my mouth?"

Deirdre shook her head.

"Well, let's go."

This was the first party in nearly four years, other than one of her mother's, Paige had been to without Steven. She and Steven had never done things separately while at school together. Yet, he had never suffocated her, or maybe she had never comprehended she was being suffocated, subsumed under Steven's bigger personality, his commanding being. She had never considered herself anything but independent, a free agent, a free will. But here was what she now recognized: she had been half of a whole, a one of two, and what she had taken for independence had really only been the freedom to stay with Steven, the ability to join in a consensus of opinion as to what activities to pursue, or even what decisions might be reached.

This new vacuum presented a conundrum, and Paige suddenly found herself wondering, there—right there as she walked to a party she would have previously attended with Steven—if law school was what she really wanted. Had she been hauled along by Steven, thrust along by her family history? Had she ever thought of, considered, the alternatives?

The apartment was sultry with the press of bodies and the blue haze of cigarette smoke and the aroma of drink. A single spilt beer, not properly mopped up, gave off a sickening sweet smell intensified by the humidity of the room. Some unidentifiable music blared in the background as Paige and Deirdre inched their way farther into the crowd, nods of recognition and excuse me's serving as passports to the kitchen. Opened bottles of wine and paper cups and salad bowls of chips were laid out haphazardly on a table and the worktops while fellow guests conversed in the crowded space. Deirdre gave a wave to someone stuffed into a far corner and made her way over to them while Paige swerved back into the main room, her coat still hanging loose about her.

She hid against the wall behind a couple in heated discussion, and put her drink down on a table to peel off the coat.

"Here, let me help you with that." A man dragged the article free and handed it back. "John James," he said, offering his hand.

"I beg your pardon?" Paige's brow knit in misunderstanding.

"It's my name. John James. And you're Paige Bennett."

"I know who I am," she replied with some annoyance, the merest hint of a smile just turning her lips.

John James stared at her, trying to catch her eye, but Paige sought someone more interesting, less fawning. She sipped at her drink and glanced around the room to see whom she knew.

"I heard you can be rather prickly," her unwanted admirer continued.

"Have you? Well then, why bother?"

"I also heard you are rather brilliant."

"Oh, garbage." Pinned to the wall, for a moment she wanted to dash outside. She moved away a slight bit, but this new stalker moved with her.

"I have Advanced Tort tomorrow," he went on, "you know—"

Paige slammed down her drink on a nearby table. "Excuse me, my phone is ringing." She fished inside her coat pocket and brought it out, just able to see Jake's name flashing on the screen face. Moving swiftly toward the door, she leaned into the corner there and flipped the phone to her ear. "Jake," she yelled, "I won't be able to hear you well. I'm at a party. Hang on a minute while I get outside." She shuffled back into her coat and got out of the apartment, down the steps to the front door of the building and into the freshness of night air.

"I thought maybe we would no longer be speaking, Jake. Your father really screwed up my mother." Annoyed at having gone to this party, confused and upset about being in law school, and now being forced to think of her unhappy mother, Paige was going to make sure Jake was the recipient of her ire.

He hesitated. "Well, my dad went to pieces when Carrie left. Look," he went on after a deep breath, "let's leave them out of this. That's not why I called."

"Oh, so to what do I owe the pleasure?" And then that awful John James…

"Thought you'd like to know I went to the sheriff and confessed."

That caught her. The silence stretched so long Jake's voice finally came back with another, "Hello?"

"I'm here. So, what happened?"

"Not a lot. Well, nothing as yet. I mean, I haven't handed in a written confession as yet. We're waiting for my new lawyer to decide how to handle this. He wants to make sure it's word perfect or something. I have to go see him next week and then maybe on to the sheriff's office again."

"You know you can go to jail."

"Yeah, but everyone says they doubt it. Suspended

sentence is what they think, seeing as how I'm handing myself—and hopefully Ty Sheldon—in on a platter."

"Good. Well." Paige sat down on the cold stoop, immediately wishing she hadn't as the damp seeped through her pants.

A couple shoved by in single file, the man glancing down with a scowl while following his girlfriend up to the front door.

Paige stood again, arranging the coat so it hit the step first and protected her. "I'm thinking of leaving law school," she blurted out.

"No, you're not." Jake snickered at the idea.

"Oh, yes, I am."

"When did you decide that?" His disbelief was audible.

"Just now," she replied with some nonchalance. "I'm not sure this is what I want any more."

"Well…don't make any hasty decisions, Paige. You can do an awful lot with a law degree, or so I've been told." There was still a note of surprise in his voice.

"Oh, look who's the authority on this now. Maybe you should go to law school?"

"Right. Almost. I hated studying the first time round. Hate offices, too. Best thing about being in the army was being outside most of the time."

"Even if you were being shot at?" She voiced a hint of humor in her tone.

Jake laughed. "Yeah. Being shot at outside beats studying and working in an office in my book." He chuckled again. "Listen, don't leave Philly just yet, okay? I might be up there sometime soon. Soon as I clear up this mess, I need to go see some horses at a farm in Pennsylvania."

"Near Philly?"

"Noooo. Not near Philly, but I need to fly in somewhere. Anyway, it's close enough. Text me your address, will you?"

Paige surveyed the night sky, pinpoints of stars just showing through the leaf canopy thinning with autumn. She liked the thought of seeing Jake again. If honest with herself, she looked forward to it.

"What are the stars like in Texas tonight?" She smiled to herself, knowing immediately what his answer would be.

"'Big and bright.'" He laughed. "I don't know. I'm inside at the moment. Why?"

"Maybe I'll go practice law in Texas," she mused out loud. "Maybe that's what I'll do. Immigrant law or animal law or some such thing. Go into practice with Deirdre."

"Who the hell is Deirdre, for goodness sake?"

"Oh! Didn't I tell you? She's your wife."

****

When Jake could stop laughing about Paige's idea he was going to marry some leggy, blonde lady lawyer from Texas, and had hopefully convinced her this notion was going nowhere, he hung up and laid back on his bed for a moment, absently petting Crockett's head. Star was curled at his feet and gave a whine of complaint as Jake first stretched and then swung off the bed, planning to have a look at the computer screen relay from the new stable cameras. The light was now out under his father's door. His dad had been turning in early, reading in bed most nights since Carrie's departure, no doubt an attempt to keep her absence—

and drink—off his mind.

Glancing out the front windows as he passed through the living room, everything outside remained still. The cricket and cicada songs were like fiddles without strings, no doubt playing a country song. But that was the only sound he could hear as he switched on the office lights and moved the computer mouse so the picture came into view. He clicked into the camera icon and waited while it opened.

No movement. The camera gave a perfect view right down the line of stalls and accounted for every horse. Jake sat back in the desk chair, which creaked as he tipped it back, cracking his knuckles with mild satisfaction. He yanked the blinds closed on the blackness of night and stared at the screen for a last survey. All good.

And then, just as he reached across to click the mouse to close, he saw the barn door slowly open.

Chapter Fifteen

Frantic, Jake started to scrabble through the desk drawer for the key to the gun vault, but it was useless as he couldn't remember the combination.

"Dad," he shouted, panic rising. "Get up and bring your gun to the barn. He's here." He dashed for the front door, not knowing whether or not he had woken his father, or whether his father had made sense of what he had yelled.

Flying down the front steps, he hit the lane leading to the barns and stable at a run; gravel pierced through his socks to remind him he hadn't put on boots. The whine of insects met him as an owl suddenly rose out of a tree. And then there were the horses whinnying. Up ahead, there was no car or other vehicle to be seen, but he was sure Ty was in there, sensed it in his bones, knew it as a fact.

And then, in front of him, was the hint of light coming from under the stable door.

"Stop!"

Jake flung open the door and faced Ty who had a hurricane lamp at his feet and his hunting knife in one hand. He was about to lead a horse from its stall.

"Stop, Ty. It's enough. Stop." He strode toward his enemy, facing him down. His shadow loomed in the orange glow from the hurricane lamp, making it feel more like a romantic tryst than a hostile confrontation.

"Well, look who's here. Just in time to join the party." Ty sneered. "Which one shall I take, do you think? This one looks pretty good to me. How much horsemeat is that? How much is he worth? Couple of thousand? Ten thousand? What? You know, I have no idea about these things."

He put out his hand. "Give me the knife, Ty. You're not going to do anything."

Face to face, he didn't predict the sudden change, the sudden movement of Ty's arm to bring the knife down on his own. Jake yanked back too late, the cut catching the side of his hand, blood rising and beading along the line of the incision.

His opponent took a slow step toward him. "What are you going to do now, Jakie? Huh? Tell me. What are you going to do now? You want to be a hero like your brother? You ridin' in to save the day? I tell you what. I'll put down the knife and we can have it out. Man to man. How's that?" There was a mocking laugh as his face twisted into scorn, the scar down his left cheek pinching the skin into two ripe drupes.

Jake's right hand throbbed. He glanced at it and sucked at the blood that was flowing, but from experience, he didn't panic, bleeding always appeared worse than it was. "You think there's any point, Ty? I've got you now. You'd have to kill me to get away. I've caught you. It's finished. My dad'll be in here any minute now."

"Your dad? That old drunk? You expect me to believe that, Jake? Why he's prob'ly out cold. You haven't got me, not if you can't speak, Jake." Knife still in his hand, Ty darted another step toward him.

Jake backed against a stall door.

His adversary gave a quick look over his shoulder toward the side door into the tack room and connecting door to the yard. "You know, your brother," he went on taunting, "he used to bring girls round here and have them, out there in the tack room. Him and me. Then one night, he brought Lucinda. I know you remember Lucinda, how she was back then, Jakie. All that long blonde hair, big blue eyes, real mean on a horse, rode the barrel races for a time like your mom."

Jake inched sideways. He should be holding his arm above his head to stop the bleeding, but hesitated doing anything that might alarm this maniac. "I remember," he said quietly.

"You know, I was in love with that girl. I was so crazy 'bout her I would have done just about anything to have that girl. 'Course, Robbie knew. You looked up to your brother, didn't you, Jake? 'Course you did. And your dad, well, your dad thought the sun shone out of Rob's backside, didn't he? Thinks that of you, too." Ty's face pinched in on itself, his eyes narrowing with the harsh memories that made his face pucker like he'd swallowed a bitter pill. "You know how I got this scar?" His dirty finger skipped down the rucks of his weal as if he were making sure it was still there.

"You fought with Rob." Jake let out a slow breath as he tried to move farther away. "You fell and hit your head on the end of the pitchfork…"

His opponent ignored him. "He didn't have to do that, did he? Rob. He didn't have to take my gal. He could've had just about any girl he wanted, could Rob. They adored him. The dark eyes like his daddy. What is that? Some Injun blood? You got Injun blood in you, Jake? Comanche? Apache?"

273

Keep him talking, keep him talking. "Something like that," he replied in a whisper.

"Yeah, Rob was real sneaky. Just like the Injuns. Tell you what," he said, his voice getting low now, "maybe I got some Injun blood in me, too." He made a sudden turn toward a horse, the knife glinting with the low light of the lantern as the animal reared up, whickering in panic.

He lunged for Ty, grabbing him with his bleeding hand, while the other man found his footing and twisted, sinking the knife into Jake's shoulder, drawing back and going for another stab. Jake moaned through gritted teeth as pain shot through him, electricity traveling the nerves of his body. He crumpled as his legs gave out, and he skimmed down the stall door.

Rolling to his side to avoid another thrust, he kicked Ty's foot out from under him, causing the wrangler to trip. As Ty fell, shadows played on the walls, the horses panicked and were nickering in their stalls, and there was the smell of the hay scattered about the floor. Jake's shoulder pounded now, and for a moment, he wondered if those sights and sounds would be his last, but Ty was scrambling for the knife he had dropped. Jake reached out, aching, shoulder throbbing, but the handle wasn't within reach, and he just managed to get his fingers near the blade. Ty hastily shuffled to his knees, spotting his stretch and, standing, brought his foot down on Jake's cut hand, pounding his fingers onto the flat edge of the knife blade.

The pain was too much.

Jake yanked his hand away, rolling on his back, fighting his body's desire for oblivion, to pass out, for the pain to stop.

Ty stood over him now, loathing etched across his face, his old scar whitening with the intensity of his hatred. "You're an idiot, Jake," he spat. "You could've made good money. We could've been in business together, expanded, and got more in. It was working well. But you, like Rob, had to quit. You got morals?" He reached into his pocket now, lifting out a box of matches. He tossed them into the air, playing with them several times before opening the box and selecting one. "I'll show you what morals *I* got." He struck the match and held it up, showing the bright yellow flame before he let it fall.

Jake twitched his face to avoid the match, then reached in agony to smash out the flame with his hand.

Ty laughed. He lit another one, dropping it carefully onto Jake's scalp.

Jake threw his head about then tried to see where the match was. He assumed it had gone out with his twitching. "Ty…" he started.

"Ty…" his enemy mimicked in a whine. He lit yet another match and held it high above Jake. "How 'bout this? You think you can stomp out this one?"

The match flickered out so he lit one more, and then, before Jake could fight the pain arcing through him and move, Ty threw it into a stall.

Jake winced on to his side only to receive a kick in his gut.

"Good luck," said Ty, glaring down at him. "Have a nice life," he continued as he lifted the lantern to head to the back door.

Jake scrambled to his knees, doubled over with the pain in his gut, his shoulder and hand both pounding. He could feel the wet of his own blood soaking through his shirt now, took in the smears of blood on the panel of the stall. The horses were whickering in panic, bucking against their stalls as smoke started to spiral up and the straw caught alight. He tried to grab the stall release as he shuffled to his legs, but his limbs wouldn't hold him.

He glanced back at the scarred and evil face of Ty, his eerie laugh mocking him.

Wind blew in from the stable door, fanning the flames for a moment. The overhead lights snapped on, and there stood his father, rifle pointed down to the other end of the alley between the stalls as the flags of smoke waved up.

"Freeze, Ty. That's it. Stay right where you are."

More straw flared up, and the horse there kicked out with fear.

"You wouldn't shoot me," jeered Ty, turning to face Jake's father. "You haven't got the guts, you old drunk."

"I think he would," said a voice behind him. "But in any case, I certainly would." Dex stood there, gun pointed at Ty's chest, the most sour look on his face anyone in Gillespie County would ever see.

Jake was on his feet at last and opened the stall where flames danced and licked at the walls of the stable. He swayed somewhat, but was able to lead the panicking horse out as his father grabbed the fire extinguisher off the wall and came running to reach him.

Ty snarled at him, disgust and jealousy written on every muscle of his face. "Good luck, Jake. You'll need it. You're just like your brother. You just don't know when to quit, do you? You just have to go on and save the world."

And that was the very last Jake heard for a while. Suddenly everything was too much, too much pain, too much longing for the oblivion sleep would finally bring. The shadows flickered above him as the voices grew dim and faded out.

****

Ray peered over the top of his reading glasses as Leigh Anne came in to the hospital room. She flung her bag on the chair in the corner before she sat down on Jake's bed. The heart monitor attached to their son blipped its song without hesitation as if it were a metronome for the low conversation emanating from the next curtained cubicle.

"Well, how'd you do this, Jake?" she started. "You come back from Iraq in one piece, and within the year, you go and get yourself busted up and in hospital. I hope to hell you got yourself medical insurance or veteran's or something."

His son exchanged a look with him.

"It's fine, it's all taken care of, Leigh Anne." Ray took off his glasses and lifted the case from the inside pocket of his jacket. "You weren't going to be paying anyway, so what are you worried about?"

"Well, I'm worried 'bout my boy here, Ray." She stood to face him. Then, with a sly smile on her face, she went on, "And I don't want to see you losing any money. I got my old age to consider."

He folded the glasses away and stuffed the case back in his pocket, as if he were keeping them from Leigh Anne, along with his cash. "Well, I got your 'last offer' from your lawyer, and I'm going to be dealing with that, so let's just say your "old age" is taken care of." He nodded across at Jake.

"How are you, Mom?" His son's voice came out croaky with sedative. "You headed north then?" He shifted slightly, wincing with obvious pain.

"Yeah, tomorrow." She sat back down on the edge of his bed. "Just come to say good-bye." She gave a glance to his bandaged hand and shoulder before her gaze followed the drip tubes. "Doctor said that bastard just missed your heart by a couple of inches."

"Doctor said he'll be right as rain in a few days," Ray corrected. "They're just keeping him in on an antibiotic drip to make sure there's no infection." He stood and stretched, studying the prone figure of his son, wishing he could have replaced Jake in the bed. Having been up most of the night dashing between the Hill Country Memorial Hospital in Fredericksburg and back to the ranch to help Mark Shandler calm the horses and dogs and see to them, and then back to the hospital again, exhaustion now creased his face and dulled his eyes. He rubbed at a day's worth of gray growth stubbling his face, making him feel older and worn. "Jake's gonna be fine, absolutely fine."

"Well, 'course he is," said Leigh Anne, taking the bandaged hand for a moment before she let it drop. She stood again and faced him. "Well. You gonna marry that Bennett woman?"

Ray guffawed and arched a brow in answer.

"Well, whatever," she continued. "I guess it's up to the lawyers now." She gathered her bag from the corner, hesitated, then bent to kiss her son on his forehead.

From inside his bedside cabinet, Jake's cell phone started ringing.

"Want me to get that for you?" Leigh Anne made a move toward the cabinet.

"No, it'll be fine."

His son's gaze slid to him as he came around the bed to open the cabinet and pluck out the ringing phone.

"You're not supposed to have these on in hospital, Jake. Don't they interfere with the machines or something?" He held out the phone, got a slight shake of his head from Jake, and answered it himself. "Hello?"

"Well, I'm off." Leigh Anne stood uncertainly for a moment, staring at him as he listened to the voice on the other end. "Have a nice life, Ray. I hope you sort yourself out sometime."

"Hang on, just a minute," Ray said into the phone. He held it down and took in his wife. "You, too, Leigh Anne. I hope somewhere down the road you find what you've been lookin' for."

She nodded her answer and turned to go, stopping in the doorway for a last look at her son. Then she gave a little wave and was gone.

Ray put the phone back to his ear. "Sorry, who is this?" he growled.

There was a split second pause. "Is that Ray?"

A small smile of recognition found its way around Ray's mouth. "Well, that sounds to me like Paige Bennett. How you doin'?" For a moment, he wondered if this was as close as he'd ever get to Carrie once more.

"Oh, my gosh. What's happened to Jake?"

"Well, don't panic now. He'll be fine. He's just playing possum for a while." He caught his son's gaze and exchanged a smile.

"Playing possum?" Paige repeated. "Isn't that, like, playing dead?"

"Yeah, well…remember, I did say 'playing.'" *So this is interesting, Paige concerned about Jake.*

"What happened? Can I speak to him?"

Ray raised an inquisitive brow at his son whose left hand came out for the phone. "Yeah, sure." There was a momentary hesitation before he ventured, "How's Carrie, Paige? She well?"

"Uh…as well as can be expected."

"Well, what the heck is that supposed to mean?" A jab of concern hit him as he plunked down in the vacated corner armchair, a longing swimming through him.

"Well, you know. She's not happy, Ray, but she's keeping busy. She's out at the beach at the moment, working and trying to keep her mind off things."

"What sort of things?" Was this a game they were playing?

Her exasperation with the two simmered over in a long, deep breath. "Look, for heaven's sake, why don't the two of you just grow up and speak to each other? Can't you phone her or something and ask her yourself?"

Ray sat there thinking as if he had forgotten he'd been on the phone. It was Paige's "Hello?" which brought him back to the present.

"I'll hand you over to Jake now, Paige. Tell your mama I'm sorry, will you? Or tell her I said hello. Here's Jake."

He collapsed back against the bedside chair and listened with half an ear as Jake tried to recount the story of his encounter with Ty Sheldon. His son's voice was groggy and it was taking great effort to keep talking, but the drone had a somnolent effect on Ray, who let his mind wander to Carrie. He had buried thoughts of her under the weight of worry about Jake and the ranch, blocked her out as best he could, but now, she had come back to haunt him.

He missed her; he missed her tremendously. But the reality was, if he was truthful with himself, she had never really left. She had been sitting there in the wings all along, always ready to get into his consciousness and ask him why he hadn't phoned, why he hadn't tried harder to get her back.

Tonight, he would go home when he left the hospital and face the excruciating quandary of there being plenty of booze on the premises at a time when he needed it most. That little voice in his ear would scream at him, and lord only knew what the answer would be. Hopefully, exertion would win out and he could just go to bed without a drink. And he wouldn't have to go over why he hadn't phoned her, why he had let her go so easily. The answer he kept getting when he waited for it, possibly a lie to himself, was he and Carrie both needed more time.

Time.

It could make or break the situation, and he really didn't know which, but for now, that's what he assumed. Time.

Jake handed the phone across to Ray and lay back, no doubt exhausted with the effort.

"She's crazy," he mumbled.

"Well. I guess I might know where she gets that." Ray rested his head back against the chair once more.

"She wanted to come down for Thanksgiving. She's trying to fix me up with her roommate who, apparently, is from San Antonio."

His father shook his head in disbelief, a small smile escaping.

"I told her she best be spending the holiday with her mother, and I'd be up in Philly in a couple of weeks."

He sat up, alert. "You still fixin' to go up north? You know that can wait. Really. There's nothing so urgent about that stallion. I don't think it's goin' anywhere. Or I can send Mark. After all, he manages the horses. Which reminds me, I better phone him and see what's happening."

"No, I want to go. I think I need to see Paige, if nothing else. We been speaking regularly on the phone and all." He drew in a deep breath. "Yeah, I gotta do that. Anyway, I think I convinced her to make it up with her mother, since they had argued about the Thanksgiving holiday, and I've talked her out of coming down now."

Ray rubbed the stubble of his chin and reached into his back pocket for his own phone. "She was going to let Carrie have Thanksgiving on her own?"

"Something like that. But she says Carrie has plenty of friends she entertains over the holidays, so she wouldn't be alone anyway."

"No," said Ray, punching in Mark Shandler's office number. "I guess she'll never be alone."

****

Carrie curled her toes to scrunch the damp cold sand before releasing them again. The November chill coursed through her, and she draped her jacket tighter around her. Waves rolled in, pounding the shore, hammering the tide line before heaving back to reveal a cornucopia of detritus, shells, seaweed, sea glass and pebbles. Tiny air holes opened in the wet sand. What had Ray joked? That it was so monotonous, all that water just going in and out. She tossed her head with the memory, her gaze following down the line of the beach studded with the row of now-vacated houses, standing blindly, waiting for the winter storms. Windows were shuttered, shrubberies covered, patio furniture stored away against the corrosive invasion of salt air. Carrie could feel it in her lungs, the briny damp that made her feel as if she had a sore throat.

Absentmindedly, she drew a huge heart in the sand with her pedicured toe, then scratched it out furtively, as if the windows of her own house were watching eyes. Down the beach, another solitary figure walked a dog, which ran and played, enjoying at last the freedom of the empty shore.

She ran a hand through dank hair knotted by the wind and tucked some strands behind her ear. What was he doing now? Where was Ray? Those days sitting out back in the enclosed sunroom were another lifetime, and yet, that place and those people still existed, were going about their business, getting on with their lives without her. It wasn't something she had conjured up, something she had imagined, something she had written.

She headed back to the warmth and security of her kitchen. Carmen would have lunch waiting now, soup and toasted cheese, and after, she would sit and go over the final galleys. They had certainly rushed this one through, to take advantage of the holiday book-buying season. She brushed the sand off her frozen feet in the mud room. Ray had been right about one thing: she wanted a happy ending.

And this time, she couldn't write it.

Chapter Sixteen

Ray stood staring at the bottle of Jack, his mind blank, his sense of time lost. With the thump of Mabel's vacuum being dragged down the hall, he glanced over his shoulder, then gave the bottle one more look. He hefted it in his hand for a second before he slowly tipped it over the sink to watch the dark golden liquid disappear down the drain before he pedaled the kitchen bin open and dropped the bottle in.

He sauntered down the hall, peering once into Jake's room, where Mabel now dusted, and then stopped briefly at Robbie's. Print-outs of his late son's emails were spread out on the table in the back sunroom where he had left them, the table where Carrie had so completely gone into her world, become so focused each and every day on her work. But it wasn't Carrie he wanted to think about now—it was Robbie. He slumped into the chair, fingering those old letters. Had he ever really known his son, had he ever understood him? Lord knows he had tried; he had certainly been under the impression he knew both boys. So, here were Robbie's emails from overseas, his letters while he did his tour of duty. He had read them when they'd arrived, printed out each and every one and read them again after the soldiers had come with the news, read them yet again after the service. They were stories about his days, stories about the men with whom he served, stories…but no pointers. And the pictures that lined the living room, those captured moments in time—they, too, told nothing more, gave away no secrets, no hidden messages, unraveled no mysteries as to the man his son had been. Robbie winning prizes, Robbie in action as an athlete, in football or army uniform—those photos, too, told a story, encapsulated a life. But as to the man behind the smile, nothing.

Mabel's vacuum screamed from the bedroom as the front door slammed and Jake walked in. His son stood there by the door for a long moment, staring at Ray down the hallway before he put his hat on a peg and struggled out of his jacket, his arm still stiff and his hand still bandaged.

"You're supposed to be taking care of that, Jake, not doing too much, the doc said," Ray called down the hall. He adjusted his reading glasses on his nose and peered at his son over the top.

"I'm being careful." Jake came and slouched in the doorway, his legs crossed at the ankles as he leaned against the frame. "Rob's emails?"

There was no note of surprise in his son's voice, no real question.

"Uh-huh." Ray jabbed the glasses back and took up one print-out, before setting it down again with a sigh.

His son carted out the chair opposite him and folded himself onto it before resting his chin in his good hand. He scowled. "What do you want to know, Dad? What is it you want to know?"

"I guess…" He breathed out as if the troubles of the world were pressing the very air from his lungs. "I guess I want to know who he was, why he did the things he did. Everyone has a secret life, Jake.

Everyone has hopes and dreams and fears and, well, secrets. But you bring up a child, you live with them more or less their entire life and you think you know who they are—were. Then one day, you find out you didn't know them at all. You find, instead of the young man who begged you to take on the horse breeding, the young man who'd been so dang popular in high school, football team and I don't know—goodness knows what else—you suddenly find you had a son who shirked his responsibilities, who—"

"He didn't shirk his responsibilities, Dad! What responsibilities, for chrissake?"

"Lucinda for a start."

"No, Dad—that's it. That's just it. Your reaction, that's what Robbie feared." Jake leaned back and tapped the table.

Outside, leaves fluttered like pennants and flew off in the wind.

"Maybe your generation felt they had to do that, maybe it was right for you. Robbie could see what he had done, what his birth had done to you. To Mama. He didn't want the birth of some unwanted child doing it to him and Lucinda. He wanted to live, grow, and mature until he was ready for a wife and family. Lucinda was still in school, still doing her barrel racing and all the rest of it. They didn't feel they had to pay the rest of their lives for one mistake."

Ray thumped the table. "If I had it all to do again, I'd have done it just the way it was…at least from the decision to marry your mother. I never regretted that, you know. We may not have seen eye to eye, we may have grown apart, your mama and me, but when it came to having you boys, I never regretted it for one second."

"I know you didn't, Dad." Jake tipped his chair back for a moment. "We never felt anything but love from you, Dad. And that's a fact. You were always fair, firm but fair. But you've made *your* mistakes, and no matter what you said or what you did for us, we were always going to make our own. That's all it was—Robbie made some mistakes. He paid for them."

"He paid the highest price, Jake!" Ray's fist crashed down like a gavel among the letters.

Jake leaned into the table once again, his head back in his good hand as his icy gaze bore into his father. "That was no mistake, Dad. Robbie knew exactly what he was doing that day in Afghanistan. He took a calculated risk in which the odds were totally against him and he lost outright. But he knew *exactly* what he was doing."

Silence settled between them then. It fell like a silken scarf picked up on the wind that drifts to earth with the calming breeze.

"Let me tell you something," Jake continued as the late afternoon sun found its way through the trees. "I don't know what it was like when you did your tour of duty. I don't know what sort of fear you faced, what sort of courage you had, what stupid acts of bravery you performed. But Iraq these days can't be much different from serving in Afghanistan…and you're numb there. You run on a sort of auto-pilot. You make sure all that training you had pays off, that you just know damn well what you're doing out there. You try to shut out fear, you count on your buddies to cover your back and you cover theirs, you look forward to the next bit of news from home, and you get on with your life and take each day as it comes. And when *that* split-second happens, that...that incident in which you have no time to think, that's when your real character comes out, that's when everything you are is laid bare on the slab. So, if you want to know who Robbie was, that's who he was, Dad. Everything he was, every last bit of Robert Andrew Ryder, was distilled down to that moment. That one moment said everything about Robbie you'd ever need to know."

Ray stood immobile and, not for the first time, his eyes burned with unshed tears for his lost son. The merest shake of his head was all the acknowledgement he could give Jake, but he knew his son would comprehend his acceptance of those words. He could see the truth of what Jake had said.

His son slid back from the table as Mabel clumped out of his room with the silenced vacuum and grumbled down the hall at them. "Mr. Ray? You gonna get outta there or you still taking a trip down mem'ry lane?"

His gaze met Jake's as he, too, rose to his feet and shuffled the letters back into a pile. "You can come on in now, Mabel. I think I'm done in here for now, thanks." He removed his glasses and tapped them into his shirt pocket. "If there's anything you ever want to tell me, Jake..." He let his statement hang there.

Jake's mouth spread into a sly smile as he scratched his head in a semblance of thinking. "You know, Dad." He met his father's glance. "I may be livin' at home now and working here, but outside of that, I sorta feel the rest of my life might be headin' into the category of 'none of your dang business.'"

Ray shook his head in compliance. Then his own mischievous smile curved his lips. "Paige?"

"Like I said, none of your dang business."

****

Some of the photos in the older albums curled at the edges, their glue or corners gone, nothing much to hold them, while their occupants stared up at Carrie accusingly. *You haven't cared for us*, they shouted. *You left us here unseen, untended.* Those Kodak moments were fading fast, both from her memory as well as the physical page, yet they still made a storyboard for her life and that of Paige.

Her daughter's baby pictures, the smiling, joyous parents, snapshots displaying the typical young American family, these were what took up the first album. Had she ever been that young? That happy? She remembered how David had proposed to her, during a moonlit walk on the beach near his parents' Southampton home, when, in the stillness of a late evening, he had suddenly got on bended knee and produced the ring. Had there ever been any doubt in her mind? Had she ever had second thoughts prior to the 'Big Day?' And what was it she had missed, obscured about him, about his character, in her rush to tie the knot? Aged just twenty-three, had she known what she was doing? Had she known *anything*? It must have been there, the fault line; he could not have changed so in just three years.

She closed the album carefully, so the loose photos would not fall out, and shoved it back on her shelf. The next one was their last year. Somewhere along the line, somehow, the photos showed a subtle change. Still young, Paige still happy, she and David began to look like separate beings, people thrown together for a momentary shot. She could see it in the body language, the way she and David drew away from each other, the way he no longer leaned in, the way her smile was more tentative as if it would fade in the very next instant. Nowhere did she look at him or David at her. And toward the end of the album, poor Paige appeared to understand what was happening in her life, as if she had made a conscious decision to 'go it alone.' Aged just three, she stood as if she were ready to take on the world, a scowl on her face and her little hands in fists.

For a moment, outside her window, shadows played against the deceptive sunshine in Central Park. Below, in the distance, people rushed against the cold, hats yanked down and gloves protecting against the late-November frost. She lifted another album down, one from Paige's boarding school days, and gasped at the changes she saw. It wasn't simply the styles and fashions so radically altered from those horrid '80s trends, it was how *she* had altered. She had aged. While her daughter had blossomed into a young woman, had grown up, she had worn out. Her face had become lean, her body thinner—maybe more fashionably so but, still—her workaholic life had become evident in every line of her face. How had time passed so quickly? How had she let it slip away so fast? When did she stop paying attention to the passing days, months, years? How had she let herself get from that proposal on the beach, standing there in her red chiffon dress with that diamond on her hand and David looking for all the world as if he had just conquered the universe, to this moment, alone in an apartment, no man in her life and nothing more to look forward to each day than the next white page?

When the phone rang, it was like a shot, a moment in which Carrie's life passed before her like a speeded up reel until the call's persistence got her to move and grab the phone.

"What took you so long?" Paige's voice—pissed off, in the vernacular—came at her.

Carrie let out a reluctant sigh of her own impatience. "I was busy, Paige. I had to finish something." She lied for no particular reason except to avoid her daughter's mocking of her reviewing photos and taking stock of her life.

"Well, you wanted me to call and let you know we'd got in all right so here I am. We've arrived and everything is okay."

"What's the weather like?"

"Cool. Fine. Dry." She stopped. "Mother, if you want a weather forecast go online. I—"

"Sorry to waste your time, Paige." There was a sullen stop. She hesitated. "You going to see Jake?" she asked at last.

Her daughter's voice came more upbeat. "I hope. Though, he doesn't know I'm here as yet. He thinks he talked me out of leaving you alone." The statement with all its implications was left to hang there. "You'll be all right, you know. You'll have a wonderful time up in the Berkshires."

"I'm not sure yet if I'm going to Diana's. She's planning a whole shindig, a party on the Saturday. I'm not sure I'm in the mood for such a thing."

"Please go," insisted Paige. "Go or phone Ray. One or the other. But stop moping around as if the greatest wrong in the world has been committed against you and you'll never live again. Really. It was your decision to leave Texas, and it can be your decision to pick up the phone."

****

Jake whistled as he shouldered open the door to the OST café and searched around for Paige. Of course, she would be sitting in the next room, hidden away on her own. As he sauntered toward her, she glanced up from her book and a smile that threatened to become a laugh opened up her face into a glow he didn't remember. She looked even more beautiful, if that were possible—healthier, happier—and he guessed that made two of them.

He stood over her for a moment without saying a thing before he bent to kiss her cheek. An expensive perfume, like summer wildflowers, just managed to briefly blanket the fries and burger odor of the restaurant. And suddenly he was happy, just so happy—relieved might have been a better word—he couldn't stop smiling as he creased himself into the chair opposite, gripping the table with his left hand.

"You're smiling like an idiot." Paige closed the book and a small dent appeared between her brows. "That's pretty amazing. And there's not even a vague possibility of sex, Jake. What gives?"

"Oh, I'm just real pleased to see you, Paige. Guess I never thought you'd ever be back in Texas again." He played with the corner of the greasy menu while his bandaged hand tapped his hat with a small adjustment.

"You didn't want me to come."

"That's not true. That's not true at all. I just thought you shouldn't be leaving your mama and all." It was so good to see her, to just look at her. Even if she was her usual snappy self.

"Are you going to take off that hat?" she queried suddenly, her head tilting with the question.

Jake leaned forward and rested his chin in his good hand, smiling steadily as his gaze continued to devour her. "Texans don't remove their Stetsons for a mere lunch, Paige." He kept back a laugh. Whatever the truth, he wasn't going to be bullied by her.

She flipped open her menu, her gaze meeting his over the top before she closed it again and a stream of giggles issued forth like bubbles from a child's blower. "It's good to see you, Jake. How've you been?"

"You know how I've been, Paige. You call me 'bout every other day."

"I do? Well. I mean, my goodness, you almost got killed by that bastard—the evil Ty as my mother and I called him."

"'The evil Ty,' huh? That's a pretty good name for that shit."

"Has he been sentenced yet?"

"No. We haven't got to court yet. I have to testify, which will be no fun, and my lawyer's still working on a deal."

"But you're a free man."

"I'm a free man," he repeated. "Freer than I've been for a long time."

Paige nodded in agreement as the waitress came over to take their order.

He played with his napkin as if he would make an origami figure of it while the girl gathered up the menus and left. "Thought you wanted me to meet your friend. Thought you had me married off to this gal."

"I did. I do. But she was busy with family visiting, and after the Thanksgiving meal yesterday, I'd had enough of backslapping and "glad to meet y'alls," not to mention endless questions about my mother. Texans are such an outgoing bunch. We're a bit more reserved up north."

Jake snorted his agreement. "And is that a good thing or a bad, do you think?"

In answer, she gave him a mysterious smile, a smile he couldn't read. He wished something inside her had melted, that she could feel it go, could feel the core of white hot anger she'd carried around since Steven's death dissolve and slip away like water down a drain. But it was probably wishful thinking on his part. For a moment, she didn't speak as his gaze continued to question her, continued to take her in, devour her.

And then, with a breath, as if she had been a doll that had been wound up, she assured him, "Neither. Just different. But I guess I'm used to the more reserved."

The meal came, and as he slathered his burger in hot sauce and salt and she picked at her salad and stole an occasional fry from his plate, he also stole glances at her. He could tell she was receding into her own separate thoughts before venturing out to rake him over as he memorized her features, her face, for a later date. It was like reeling in a fish—letting out the line, then winding it in slowly.

"We can go riding after lunch," he offered. "I have friends with a ranch nearby."

"No. It's fine. I have to get back. It's a bit of a drive, and I said I'd be back for dinner. Maybe a walk round town. It's an interesting place, Bandera. I saw this saloon with bras hanging on the doors…"

"The 11th Street Cowboy Bar."

"Is that it? Very un-PC. Do girls actually go there?"

His gaze met hers once more, and he wanted her.

He wanted her so badly the room swam around them for a moment. "Girls actually go there," he said quietly. His hand held the next bite poised above the plate, his gaze fixed on her. If he leaned across to kiss her, her mouth would be there waiting for him, would be sweet to his taste, her tongue would find its way in, she would respond and her hand would touch his face with a gentleness he needed. But instead, he slowly put the food back on his plate and reached across for her, found her hand and played with it like an unknown, as if he were blindfolded and had to figure out exactly what it was he held.

"Jake…" She slipped her hand out of his.

"I know—you're still in love with Steven. And I'm just a good ol' boy from Texas and not your style anyway."

"That isn't it. That isn't it at all. But Steven is…was…" She played with her food for a moment as a bit of salad leaf fell from her fork. "I'm so glad you're rid of that burden now, Jake. All that misery you were carrying around with you, about your father not knowing about Robbie and all, and about the stupid things you did to keep him from knowing, and about the drugs. Just everything. You must feel great relief—"

"Great relief," he repeated.

She hesitated as she swallowed a mouthful of salad and took a sip of her diet Coke. "But it doesn't mean I'm about to—"

"I know what it doesn't mean, Paige. I know you're not going to fall in love with me jus' 'cause everything else in my life seems to be sorting itself out. I know all that." He took a bite out of his burger. He chewed for a while and, after he had swallowed, said,

"All it means is, I'm looking forward now, I'm not looking back. I'm not looking to Robbie or to run my life in trying to cover up things or please my dad or anything else like that. I know all that. Iraq is behind me. I've done my service and pleased my dad. I'm my own man now. And forever." He took another bite and picked at some fries. "We prob'ly have nothing in common, you know. I know that as well as you. We hardly know each other, truth be told. But I think...there's something there. I can't put my finger on it. And maybe it's my imagination—just because I like to look at you. Just because you are so different. And smart. And sassy. Unpredictable like. Or maybe it's the same thing my dad sees in your mom. Have. No. Idea. But there's something between us that's real. And good. Real good." He smiled at her as he took another bite of his burger, a splotch of sauce oozing out just below his lips.

Paige reached across and wiped it away with a finger. And smiled.

****

Carrie rather liked the way the Shawcrosses called their home 'a farm,' although it was hardly a farm in the true sense of the word. Yes, there was a barn and, yes, they had horses, but that was about as far as the similarities went. She liked being there; it was quiet country—rolling hills and babbling streams with beautiful prospects from every window—and it reminded her of Hill Country, Texas.

The people invited over tonight, however, were anything but Hill Country folk. Diana's local friends were other displaced New Yorkers, and these were supplemented by those who drove up from the city or such outposts as Greenwich, plus houseguests like herself who filled the spare rooms. The hum of conversation and the chink of glasses found its way into her awareness as she leaned over her dressing table for a slight adjustment of her necklace. She flipped open her laptop for a quick catch-up on emails before heading downstairs. And that is when she saw the note.

Dear Carrie,

I guess that sounds kind of formal but then if I just put 'Carrie' it would sound like I was mad at you or something and I'm not. Then again, if I put 'Carrie dear' you might take offense, probably being still mad at me, so... What the heck. Look. I'm writing to let you know how things are at the moment because I thought you should know, would want to know. I'm not trying to inch my way back into your life. Don't think I could, though the good Lord knows I want to. But more on that later.

So. I'm writing to let you know I got the whole story from Jake in the end and it's thanks to you. And I mean that. Thank you. Don't know why my own son felt he couldn't tell me himself, but he didn't feel he could tell me all that business about Robbie and Ty and the rest of it so, as painful as it was at the time to hear those things from you, I appreciate knowing and appreciate the fact it led to a burden being lifted from Jake he needn't have carried. Of course, he's in a right mess now with the police but we're sorting that out and, hopefully, it'll all come right in the end. I doubt he'll have to go to prison. Seems more like a fine and suspended sentence. So, thank you for telling me. And I do mean that. Even though I sort of guess your intentions weren't particularly friendly at the time.

As for what I said to you, well, I had no right and I didn't mean the half of it. Actually, I didn't mean any of it. Fact is, I get angry and any old thing can come out of my mouth. I just didn't see—at the time—how one white lie about the divorce could've done so much damage. Maybe I was wrong to think that and, then again, maybe I wasn't. Depends really. But the divorce is now going through and Leigh Anne is gone up to Wyoming with her boyfriend and so that, too, is finished.

Listen, I could rush up north there again and try to whip you off your feet or something, I could try phoning you, I could try a dozen different things to win you back. Which, of course, is what I'd like to do. But I don't really think I'm the problem, Carrie. I think you have to decide what you want. And how much you want it.

And if I'm 'IT' then, well, then I'm here for you. As I always will be.

Ray

Carrie finished reading, then slipped on to the stool in front of the dressing table and read it again. She drew a tissue from the mother-of-pearl box and dabbed at her eyes before reading it one last time.

He was right—she had to make up her mind what she wanted, and how to go about getting it, but that wasn't going to happen overnight. Nor was she going to be swayed by one email. He had hurt her, hurt her badly, lied to her, and that, for now, was still in her thoughts. She took one last perusal in the mirror, fixed her make-up with another dab and finally headed to the stairs.

As she stood at the top of the landing, the gaiety of the gathering didn't match her mood, and she hesitated before descending. Then, one step at a time, she was sucked into the party, forced into the holiday season atmosphere. She certainly needed a drink.

As she meandered over to the mixologist at the impromptu bar, Carrie caught Diana's gaze—which slid to a corner where Charles Langtry stood. Carrie let herself give Charles a peremptory glance before she followed that with a smile to the bartender. "Jim and Ginger please."

"Sorry?" he queried.

"Jim Beam rye and ginger ale please. On the rocks."

The bartender nodded his understanding before turning to do the mix just as Tom Shawcross sidled over to her.

"You've been a bit down, we've noticed. Going to try to enjoy yourself tonight?"

"Going to try," she confirmed.

"Charles is here. With a friend." His head tilted in the direction in which her ex-boyfriend was located. "Will it upset you?"

She studied Tom for a moment. His look was benevolent, meaning well. But then, Charles was here in the room and Tom, or Diana, had invited him, so what could be done now?

"He won't bother me, Tom. He never has. It was

me who broke up with him, remember?"

"Ah, yes." Her friend handed his glass to the mixologist for a refill as the other man slid Carrie her drink across the bar. "Well," he went on. "No punch ups tonight then. He's with a new girl."

"So I see. And by the way, I was never a 'girl,' Tom. Maybe that was the problem." She gave her host a small smile, leaning back against the bar to take a slow sip of the drink as ice tried to force its way into her mouth. She gulped. As her gaze met Charles' she took in his companion. About Paige's age, maybe a spit older. Legs as long as a racehorse, and hair as golden as a summer day. And dressed in the shortest pink baby doll dress Carrie had ever seen. A Barbie doll. A flamingo. A perfect flamingo, right here in the Berkshires.

And then she laughed.

Chapter Seventeen

Jake leaned forward to count out some bills to the taxi driver before opening the door into a buffeting wind. Leaves flew by as if they were late for appointments. He flipped up the collar of his new coat and tucked in his muffler as some extra protection against the blast. Glancing up at the building, he hoisted his overnight bag onto his shoulder, and checked the address before proceeding up the steps into the shelter of the foyer. A smell of disinfectant and damp greeted him as he took in the battery of brass mailboxes, some hanging invitingly open, and found the one for Bennett. He jabbed the button beneath it several times until a cranky voice came over the intercom.

"You only have to ring once, Jake!"

He smiled to himself. Paige had no doubt spied his arrival from an upstairs window and knew it was him. As the door buzzed its release, he shouldered it open to a flight of steps and skipped them two at a time before coming to the first floor and apartment one-ten. The door opened as if by magic, but it wasn't Paige standing there.

A leggy blonde extended her hand with a "Hey, how you doin'?" that made him feel, literally, as if he were home. After shaking his hand, she showed him in to their small sitting room.

"Let me take your coat, dang northern weather.

And just leave your bag there. Paige is having a late day. She's just dressing. Can I get you something? Coffee perhaps? I'm Deirdre, by the way, Paige's roommate."

"Oh. Jake Ryder." He plopped his bag down and started to extend his hand again, then remembered he and Deirdre had already shook and let it drop. He slipped off his coat and muffler and handed them to her to hang in the closet by the door.

Paige had been right, though—Deirdre was a good-looking woman. Her soft cashmere top caressed neat little breasts and came down to a pair of jeans showing off the rest of her figure. A little, turned-up nose gave her a mischievous air combined with the sky blue eyes, and her long, blonde hair was tied back loosely with a ribbon. Her whole demeanor spoke of southern hospitality, a big Texas welcome. It almost made Jake laugh, and he wondered what Paige had told Deirdre about him, whether she had told this woman he was meant to be her future husband. Somehow, he guessed not; he figured that joke was kept for him.

"So, would you like coffee?" Her soft drawl brought him back to the present.

"Uh. No, not right now. But thanks."

"Jeez, you look fantastic." Paige's voice burst into the room. "Your hair's grown in!"

Jake, just about to sit down, jumped back to his feet, and stood there somewhat awkwardly. He gazed at Paige standing in the door to her bedroom and ran a hand through his hair. "Yeah, guess it has. Well, you mustn't have noticed it last time. It's almost three weeks since you saw me, Paige," he pointed out.

"So it is. And you were wearing your Stetson."

She came forward, arms extended to embrace him, as if to claim him, and he dipped down to her for a peremptory exchange of kisses, though she did not let go. She stood smiling up at him.

"Gosh, fancy you being in Philly, Jake. You look so out of place."

At this, Deirdre laughed. "Well, you can take the man out of Texas, but, you know… Anyway, I best be heading off to the library, got a mess of studying to do." She grabbed a coat from one of the hooks by the door and shoved it on, throwing a scarf about her neck and collecting a satchel of books. "Nice to meet ya, Jake. See you down home sometime, hey?"

"Yeah. Sure. Nice to meet ya." He stood quietly while she went out, and then grimaced at Paige. "So, that's who you'd have me married off to, huh? Somehow, I don't think so."

Paige didn't reply, trying to hide a smile. "How did the horse buying go? Lancaster, did you say?"

"Yeah. Stallion wasn't quite what I wanted. Funny place, though. Interesting, those Amish. All them folks drivin' around in buggies. It's sort of like some giant movie set. Or steppin' back to another time. Have you been?"

"Not for years. But we see them sometimes in town here, selling vegetables and stuff. They strut around talking on their cell phones, which seems somewhat incongruous. Anyway, I think Mother set a book there once or something and dragged me along. As she does."

"How is Carrie?" He wondered for a moment if he should ask, but Paige looked so relaxed, so…what was it? Different somehow. More at peace with herself.

She strolled back toward a small kitchen area off

the main room, and Jake took this as his cue to sink into one of the sofas. The room was a typical student apartment. It could have been almost anywhere, although this one had been better furnished than most. Actual paintings were hung on the wall rather than posters, and the comfort of the sofa told him it hadn't been a hand-me-down, but rather purchased new.

Paige fussed with two mugs and came back with coffee.

"Did you find us all right?" she asked, handing him his mug, obviously avoiding the subject of her mother.

"Yeah, I did what you told me to do. Made sense to hand the car back in at Philly airport and come by taxi. Especially as I'm flying out of Newark tomorrow night. Easier to catch the train up really."

"Why Newark?" Plopping herself down into an armchair catty-cornered to him, Paige blew over the top of her mug before taking a tentative sip and, apparently deciding it was too hot, lowered it between her hands for warmth.

"Cheap flight. And since Dad is looking for ways to save money while paying off my mother—"

"They finally divorced?" She picked some fluff off her sweater and flicked it aside.

Jake stared at her until she raised her gaze to him. "You want to discuss that?" he offered.

"Not right now. Maybe later."

He ran his gaze over her, remembering how very beautiful she was, remembering the moment he got into that car so many months ago. Her rich brown hair was slightly disheveled from sleep now, but her face had a glow, the cupid's bow lips suppressing a smile beneath her huge eyes. His heart fluttered.

"In Bandera… I tried to get you to talk back in Bandera, but it was so rushed, that day, and…" He put the coffee mug down on the floor. "Did you ever realize it's often *you* who phones *me*, Paige?" He probed her with an inquisitive nod. "I just wondered, why? I mean, it had nothing to do really with Carrie and Dad, did it? And I don't think you were really that concerned for my health after the fire an' all. Were you?"

Paige continued to hold her coffee as if it were utterly important she not let it go.

He grimaced. "Most gals would've had a one night stand, or a vacation romance, whatever the hell you want to call what went on back in April, and then they'd've gone on back home and forgotten about it. Maybe said the occasional 'hi' on Facebook, sent a text now and then, whatever. But you, you actually phoned me, you kept it going. I mean, I understand I did a lot of the calling, but recently, you know, it's been you. I just wanted to know why?"

"You *began* phoning me as I recall. Maybe I just wanted to talk to someone who wasn't…here." There was a note of petulance in her voice. "Anyway, did you come all this way for that?" Her voice took on the edge he remembered so well, the defensiveness, the wariness.

He ran his hand over his face and studied her for another moment. "I don't know whether I would've come all this way if I hadn't of had to go to Lancaster. I can't answer that to be truthful. Probably not, after seeing you in Bandera." When she said nothing he continued, "But I would've asked you the same question sooner or later. On the phone if not in person. Long distance relationships—whatever their nature—

friendship, lovers, whathaveyou—they don't usually work. And, you know, there's Steven. I understand about Steven, that you're probably not ready for another relationship. I got all that. And I understand, well, I understand there's a difference between a woman in grad school and a rancher's son from—"

"Oh, for heaven's sake! Don't give me that bit of crap, please. My mother, bless her, is in love with your father. She doesn't see the difference, as much and as often as I've pointed it out to her…"

"So, you did point it out. You do see the difference," he pressed.

"I see *a* difference, but it doesn't mean I attach any significance to it. Ray was just so different from anyone my mother had dated in the previous twenty odd years. That's all." Paige took a gulp of coffee. "This is ridiculous. Are you asking me what my intentions are? Is that what you want to know? Were you expecting me to say, 'you had me from hello?'"

Jake threw his head back and laughed. He ran a hand over his face as he gazed at her.

Paige's mouth puckered in contemplation. "We can't be just friends then?"

"That's usually the guy's line, isn't it? Friends with benefits?"

"Oh, Lord. How are you, anyway? I didn't even ask. What happened about your confession? What happened about your stab wound? I see no bandage, which is good. You haven't told me anything."

"Well, obviously I'm fine, otherwise I wouldn't be sittin' here. As for the drug charges, my lawyer got a plea bargain or whatever it's called for turning state's evidence. I'll have a suspended sentence and a fine.

Ty'll be arraigned on several counts, including attempted arson. That's it." He didn't let his gaze leave her, wouldn't be sidetracked from his mission. "You gonna finish the other conversation or we gonna dance 'round that all night?"

"'All night?'"

He tried unsuccessfully to stop himself from smiling. "Well, I thought I could crash on the floor or something."

"'Or something?'" She slammed her cup onto the small table by her side. "You're incredibly good-looking. Has anyone ever told you that?"

"Why is it I hear a 'but' coming?" He stood suddenly and moved to the window overlooking the street. Down below, dry leaves were whipping around in mini twisters as bundled students hurried to warm places in the December cold. "Boy, when I got in that car that day and saw you, I thought I'd got in some vehicle bound for heaven."

"Oh, what crap, Jake, for heaven's sake. Stop being so poetic and silly. Grow up." She picked absently at a hang nail. "You thought no such thing. If anything, you wondered why we picked you up, two women alone. And you were headed home from Iraq, so I would think your mind was on anything—maybe not," she cut herself off. "I suppose you were thinking about sex after all those months. Maybe that's it, Jake. After so long away from women, you just fell for the first half-decent looking woman you met."

"You're more than half-way good-lookin' Paige, and you damn well know it. And there's more to it than that. Maybe when they say opposites attract it's true." He flicked the curtain, leaving his hand in a fist. "I may have been an imbecile 'bout some things, certainly 'bout the whole Robbie matter, and you may well think me poetic and silly, but I know my own dang feelings. What I don't know are yours." He remained by the window, the diffused light coming through the sheer curtains. "So, you gonna answer my question then?"

"You want to know if I'm really in love with you, is that it?"

"Yeah, I guess."

"Are you going to ask me to stop phoning you if I say no?"

"Not sure."

"Well, that's my answer, too. 'Not sure.'" She waited, looking across at him. "Right now, I could fall into bed with you, but it would be like incest I think. I don't know. I know it *isn't* incest, but it would feel like it. Don't you think?"

"No."

"Okay. I see you as that friend with benefits, then. I don't know what my feelings are beyond that. I'm numb. It's probably still too soon for me to think of having another relationship. I don't want to hurt you, so if you think you're headed that way please let me know and I'll never darken your door again. Or whatever. I don't know—as I told you—what I want to do with the law degree—I thought of ditching it as you know, but have decided it's probably worth having for the moment. Beyond that, I have no idea where I want to be or who with. I told you all that, more or less, in Bandera. As for Steven, I look back on him now—on us—and I'm confused. I know I loved him, and I know he loved me, and I know if he lived we would've married, and I'd never have had second thoughts about it. Maybe the mind has a way of compensating for loss I haven't quite figured out as yet. But whatever I felt for him and whatever I feel for you, they're so different... They may both be 'love' but, really, I just don't know." She stopped and her gaze slid to him askance. "I mean, do you really want a relationship with a New York lady lawyer?"

"Would you ever want a relationship with a...an uneducated rancher's son?" he countered.

"First off, you're not uneducated. Unschooled perhaps, but not uneducated. Second...I don't know what second is. If you're asking me what I see in you, I see someone who is completely honest, someone who is so unlike Steven I know for sure I'm not trying to replace him, someone who is unlike *any* other man I've ever met because you're...you're...I don't know quite how to describe it. You're basic. You're an innocent. You're 'what you see is what you get.' It's probably the same damn things my mother sees in Ray. I like talking to you—it gets me away from life here, it makes a change. And, strange as it may seem to you, I did enjoy your company. Well, of course I did. Most of the time we were together, we were having sex—and it was pretty damn good."

Jake stood there, their gazes locked on each other, a quiet stretching punctuated only by car horns and laughter from the street below. "Well, I guess it's gonna have to be 'wait and see' and I leave here none the wiser, huh, Paige?"

"I wouldn't say that. You're a little bit wiser, even if you haven't got a clear answer. Look..." She sighed, getting to her feet, a weary note now evident. "I have to get back to the books. Stay by all means. I'll cook you dinner later, and you can spend the night, but I'd like you to do me one favor."

"Oh? What's that?" His brow crinkled with suspicion.

"If you're flying from Newark in the evening, I'd like you to get up and go see my mother in New York tomorrow morning. I'll be happy to pay for the train ticket if you're short but... Try to talk some sense into her, will you?"

****

Jake got out of the subway at the Museum of Natural History, a cold blast of frosted air burning his face. As Paige had directed, he faced Central Park, trees shaking their dismay at the wintry weather. *"If you face the park,"* she had said, *"then to your left is north and to your right, south."*

He headed north and found the building, just as she had described, an impressive portico jutting out into the street, giving pedestrians temporary relief from the elements. A white-gloved, uniformed doorman swung open a heavy bronze inlaid door before Jake was faced with another attendant.

"I'm here to see Ms. Carrie Bennett, please."

"Yes, sir, go right on up." The man pointed toward two impressive elevators, all etched glass and brass.

Relieved of his overnight bag in a locker in Penn Station, Jake probably *did* look like he belonged here. Yet something wasn't right. He stopped in confusion, wondering if Paige had changed her mind and phoned her mother ahead to warn her of his visit. She had told him the doorman would call upstairs to ask Carrie if it was all right to send him up, and he would certainly know then whether he was welcome or not. But now, sent straight up, he was puzzled by the whole procedure.

The elevator opened, a hint of pine greeting him from the Christmas wreath within, and he pushed the button for fourteen and waited, nerves jangling.

The door opened into a vestibule for two apartments, a filled coat rack outside one. The holiday décor did nothing to make him jovial as a maid came out and confirmed this was Ms. Bennett's residence. She offered to take Jake's coat, which he handed to her before she led him inside and directed him to the living room. Now he understood: Carrie was having a party, and everyone had thought he was a guest.

He stood there in the marbled entryway, an elegantly decorated tree in the corner another sign the Christmas season was here. Uncertain what to do now, he wanted to tell the maid he would return another time, but she had already gone. He stood there feeling foolish and out of place.

Just as he started back to the door, he heard Carrie call his name.

Puzzled surprise mixed with worry flitted across her face as she advanced, a glass of champagne in her hand. She carefully drew the living room door partially closed, shutting off the murmur of voices and laughter. "How…What are you doing here? What a pleasant surprise. How are you?"

"I'm fine." He stood solemnly staring at her, taking in the elegant appearance so different from what she had worn at the ranch, and not knowing where to begin.

"Is your father all right?" The words tumbled out like a child's blocks falling.

"My father," Jake repeated as if trying the word out

for size. The question seemed so formal, such a strange way for Carrie to be asking about a man she had lived with for a time, slept with, supposedly loved. "Yeah."

And then it hit him, either he must do what he had come to do or leave it, and there was no point in turning back now. He had nothing to lose. He was face to face with her, and she was waiting for some word, some reason for his being there.

"I'm sorry—I didn't know you had a party on. I...I saw Paige in Philadelphia, and she suggested I come before heading back. She didn't say you had a party on today."

"She probably forgot. She has so much to deal with these days." There was a moment's hesitation. "Well, I'm so glad you did come," Carrie began, going into hostess mode. "Can I get you a drink, something to eat? Please join us. It's just a little luncheon party for the launch of my new book."

"I guess you're busy then." He screwed up his face. "Maybe I shouldn't have come. I thought we could talk for a minute."

And then he could see the light going on, the realization washing over her. "Of course we can talk. Come with me."

He followed her down a hallway to what appeared to be her study. Overlooking the park and all in white, it had a calming effect on him as it no doubt did on her when she worked.

When she waved at a chair for him to sit, Jake declined with a shake of his head. "I won't be long. I don't want to keep you from your guests," he said, spotting a stack of books on her desk. *Dances of the Heart* the cover read, by Carrie Bennett.

"Is your father all right?" she asked again, distinct concern in her voice now. "Did he send you?"

"No. No, he didn't send me. Fact is, he doesn't even know I'm here. I came up to check out some stallions at a farm in Pennsylvania and went on to Philly to see Paige while I was there. It was really her idea I come—though I have to say I thought it was a good idea, until I got here." His mouth curved into a small smile. "Dad would probably shoot me if he knew. Well, maybe not but, you know, he won't like me meddling in his love life."

Carrie put down the glass of champagne she'd been holding and took a breath. "His love life," she repeated softly. Her gaze fled to the window as it rattled slightly in a gust of wind. "Did you...I mean, I know you cleared up everything with him in the end. You told him about Robbie and what you had done and all...all of that. He wrote—"

"He did? He didn't tell me." Jake sucked in air. "Did you reply?"

"No. No, I didn't."

"Did you know what Ty had done—after you left, I mean. After Alamo?"

"Paige told me. She kept me posted you were recovering, were well. And then I knew you had seen her in Bandera." Carrie rested a hand on the desk as if for support, a look of regret crowding her features. "Listen, Jake, I'm sorry I butted in. I mean, I know you asked me to help that night at the ranch, but it wasn't my business to do so, and I apologize for that. But things were said—by Ray and me, both of us—and it just came out. I truly am sorry for that."

He decided to let it all be; this wasn't about him, it

was about Carrie and his father. "Well, you paved the way for me, didn't you? I mean, there was no turning back." As she started to protest and apologize again, he put up a hand. "Don't get me wrong, Carrie, I was grateful. Paige kept telling me I had to tell Dad the whole story, but it just kept going on until you stopped it. It was getting worse if anything, what with Alamo being killed. I was just a coward, I guess. I couldn't face hurting him, not the way he felt about Robbie, not when he told me, as he had, how I had made him proud. He wasn't pleased I'd done what I'd done, that I'd let that bastard Ty threaten me into things. That sure as hell didn't make him proud. But I think we understand each other better now, and I think he respects me for finally telling him everything. Well, sort of respects me. He did say if I ever did anything like that again he'd run me off the property for good, but it won't happen anyway." He gave Carrie a sheepish smile.

"Well, I'm glad to hear all that, Jake." She glanced at the pile of books on her desk. "Is…is he well—Ray? How is he?"

"Misses you like anything. But he's not drinking if that's what you want to know. He had one great binge when you left, smashed a few things and then sobered up."

"Well, then, he worked me out of his system," Carrie said.

"No, no he hasn't worked you out of his system. I can see it in his face. He's been real busy this past autumn, but I can see how he misses you. It's like a part of him is gone. I told him if he drank, you sure as hell wouldn't come back and he had better be sober the day you walked on in the door."

There were tears sneaking down Carrie's face. Jake pulled a clean handkerchief from his pocket and offered it to her but she reached for a tissue from a box on her desk, plucking out one to dab at her cheek.

"Perhaps you should know we said some awful things to each other, terrible things. Maybe, in the end, we were too honest with one another."

"Well, at least you got everything off your chest. A lot of couples go for years letting things stew, letting things fester. Then they get divorced because of it, because they never cleared the air." He tried to keep the note of pleading out of his voice now, but he was exasperated with the two elders. "They're divorced now, you know," he went on. "It's final at last. Mom took his last offer and moved up to Wyoming with this guy. I don't know why she thinks it'll be better there, or she'll be happier there, but I hope she is."

Carrie reached out as if to comfort him, then drew her hand back.

There was a knock on the door, and a man, about Carrie's age and well-dressed, smart silk tie gleaming from an expensive shirt and suit, took a step inside the door. "Carrie? Everyone's waiting. You coming back soon?"

"I'll be back in a moment," she replied. "Do you want to join us?" she asked Jake, as the man left. "Come have a drink. Have you had lunch?"

He shook his head. "You seeing someone else now then?" His voice was almost truculent, disappointed.

Carrie smiled. "No. He's my agent, Jake." She nodded to the stack of books and picked one up. "Will you give this to Ray for me?"

She handed it to him and he flipped through,

suddenly stopping near the front. "'To Ray Ryder. No one does the Texas Two Step like you,'" he read. He looked up at her, perplexed and uncertain now. "You dedicated it to Dad. Is it about the two of you then?"

"No. Though I'm sure he may recognize a few scenes." She guided him back to the front lobby and motioned to the maid for his coat. "Tell him…tell him I'd like to know he's well from time to time. Tell him I'm sorry. For any pain I caused. I'm sorry."

Jake struggled into his coat, slipping the book into a pocket. "I'm sure he's sorry too, Carrie. Real sure."

****

Ray sat with the book in his lap, his reading glasses hanging by one arm out of his shirt pocket, his phone in his hand. This was going to be the only way, a start perhaps—or an ending, he wasn't sure which. If he phoned her, if he Skyped, it was far too invasive at this stage, after so many weeks. Another email was at the other end of the scale; she hadn't answered the first, so why would she answer the second? It had to be this or nothing, a text, short and sweet, that would appear on her screen, that she could delete or answer as she chose.

No, she wouldn't answer. That was a fact. He would have to make the chase.

He could beg her to come back, ask to see her, ask if he could go to New York to discuss things, but none of that made sense now. No, it had to be something basic, a beginning, something he could perhaps build on the way he had with the phone calls when she and Paige had first left Texas.

In some ways, Carrie had made the first step by dedicating the book to him and asking after him. On the other hand, if Jake hadn't gone to see her, would she have sent him a copy?

Ray reflected on this; did Carrie leave those words in print for him to discover, thinking he might just buy the book at some stage? Or would she have sent it? With a note? Without a note? He could ruminate on that for hours but it would get him nowhere.

The early winter light was filtering in, the evenings long past drawing in, days shortened now to the briefest of warm hours. A pervasive chill combined with just sitting for a while made Ray consider getting up and turning on the heat. The temperature had struggled up to sixty earlier today, but he figured a cold night was ahead. The rumble of Jake's Chevy coming down the lane signaled he had to finally make up his mind.

He slowly tapped in the brief message:

Thanks so much for the dedication. It meant a lot. I hope you and Paige have a merry Xmas. Miss you, Ray.

Chapter Eighteen

"Mother! For goodness sake, I have a final tomorrow. I can't tell you what to do. You have to decide for yourself." Paige blew out a breath into the phone and tipped back in her desk chair, the circle of light from her lamp highlighting the unread page. The loneliness of silence enveloped her, along with the knowledge Deirdre had already finished her finals and headed back to the comparative warmth of Texas, her term finished.

"This is the second time he's written to me, Paige."

She smiled to herself at the small note of happiness in her mother's voice. Still, she had to see both sides of the question. "Or, then again, it might have been incredibly rude not to write and thank you," she teased.

"He says, 'miss you.' I'm so damn indecisive when it comes to Ray. He makes my head spin."

Now it was exasperation, Paige noted.

"Okay. Here's what I think, for what it's worth. He's emailed you, he's texted you. Now *you* have to decide what to do. I cannot, nor will I, decide for you. What I will do...no, never mind. I won't."

"Won't what?"

Paige could envisage her mother's creased face. "I have to go. See you in a couple of days, Mom. Bye."

She tapped the 'end call' button, found Jake in her contacts list, hesitated, then put the phone down. It was ridiculous to phone him when she had no time to talk, unfair. She wrapped herself tighter in her baggy sweater and, thinking what the heck, stabbed at his name to dial his number.

"I have to go," were her first words.

"What?"

Jake laughed, and Paige conjured him, the now-long, dark hair hanging over those violet-blue eyes.

"I have a final tomorrow and have to go, but I rang to say one thing—my mother is pleased to have heard from Ray."

"She heard from him? First I'm hearing of it." There was bewilderment in his voice.

"Ah-hah! Your father is playing his cards close to his chest. He texted my mother his thanks for the book with a 'miss you' at the end. Seems to me we got the ball rolling, cowboy."

Jake snorted. "So, is she going to reply?"

"I doubt it. Not right away, anyway. Try to get him to keep texting. Wear her down. Wear her out. She'll succumb. Gotta go. Bye."

Jake wondered if he should try the same method on Paige. He sauntered down to the office at the front of the house where his father was doing some late work, the dogs at his feet. He stood in the doorway, peering at his dad who was deep in concentration, just finishing adding up a column by the look of the taps of his pencil.

His father peered over the top of his glasses. "Is there something wrong?"

"I got a message for you from Paige," he offered with a little smirk.

"Paige?" His dad shuffled some papers aside and

sat back, his shadow elongated along the wall. He removed his glasses and swung them in his hand for a moment, a guilty smile on his face.

"Yeah, Paige. You remember Paige Bennett, don't you?" Jake couldn't stop his grin from widening.

"I remember Paige Bennett. She's that little beauty you keep speaking to on the phone and went up to see under the guise of checking horses in Pennsylvania, as I recall. That the one?"

Jake shuffled at his own guilt, drawing an imaginary line with his toe on the wooden floor. "Yeah, I guess that's the one." He scratched his neck for a moment, waiting.

"So, what does Paige say? Her mama thanks me for the text but asks I not write again?"

"Nope." Jake tapped an imaginary tune on the wall and grinned. "Says Carrie was positively over the moon to hear from you, but—"

His dad burst out laughing, throwing his head back and playing with the glasses still in his hand. "You two, I tell you. That is such a lie." He settled down. "Come on now, what did Paige actually say?"

A bit sheepishly, Jake explained, "She says Carrie probably won't reply…just yet…but you should wear her down."

He put his glasses back on, bending over the papers once again. "Wear her down, huh? Dang woman has me worn out, and now I gotta wear her down." He glanced up briefly. "We'll see."

Ray waited for his son to beat his retreat back into the living room before he got up and closed the office door. He dragged his phone from his back pocket and studied it as if it would magically come up with the answer of what should be next. A joke? A plea? No, he and Carrie wouldn't be able to go on unless the air was cleared once and for all. He tapped out:

We both said things we didn't mean. You
know that. Ray

****

Carrie read the words for about the fiftieth time the next day. No, they *had* meant them, that was the thing; those words had been true, just about everything they said to each other was true. Where did that put them? Was Jake right that day he had visited, when he said they had at least cleared the air?

Sitting at her desk, the staccato beeps of another message came through.

I have no two-step partner now. My feet
will forget the moves. Ray

Oh, no … He was doing the same thing he had done with all the phone calls.

She clicked the phone off, figuring anyone who didn't get her on her cell would know the apartment number anyway. But concentration on work wasn't easy. At five p.m., she had a reading and book signing at the local Barnes and Noble for which she had to prepare. She still hadn't chosen which segment to read, and she had to change her clothes. At least the reading should prove a temporary distraction.

****

Ray got in the passenger side of Jake's car and slammed the door. "So, you really think Crockett and Star are gonna welcome a new little friend, do you? You really think a third dog'll fit in?"

His son started up the engine as he glared across at him and back to the front. "'Course another dog'll fit.

322

Doesn't seem right without three."

"You choose one already?" He yanked down the seat belt and clicked it into position.

"Yeah, I sort of thought this one bitch had a nose on her. See what you think."

"You gonna take on the training, Jake? I got my hands full."

His son gave him another sideways glance as he drove down the ranch road and turned left. "Well, it's a good thing Carrie isn't here, then. You'd have no time for her, would you?"

Ray noted the puckered smile on Jake's face and glanced out the window. "I don't think I need worry 'bout that none," he replied quietly.

"No word as yet? Even Christmas wishes?" Jake's gaze remained on the road. There was only silence in answer.

Carrie never replied, but that was better—much better—than a curt response asking him to stop. Through Christmas and New Year, Ray lived with the hope he would one day make her laugh, or she would succumb, or just plain come to her senses. He just couldn't gauge her reaction. There was no further word from Paige either, so he had no idea where he stood.

He adjusted his hat and looked back to Jake.

"You gonna do all that paper bag banging and shooting blanks and stuff?"

"I reckon. Anyway, if the dog's any good, she'll just follow along with Crockett and Star and learn real quick. You know it's always easier when there's a trained dog for them to follow."

Ray mulled this over a second. "Too bad we can't train women like that," he mumbled.

His son smirked and laughed. "Oh, Dad, you got it bad."

He took stock of the scenery, trying to suppress thoughts of Carrie, but it wasn't working.

"What do you want to call her, Dad? We got a good Texas tradition to uphold here. I think we might be running out of names. Yellow Rose? Rose for short?"

****

We have a new puppy. I'm calling her Two Step. Ray.

Carrie put the phone down. The messages would continue; she had no doubt now. They would continue until either he got tired of it, met someone else, or she put a stop to it. Yet, she couldn't do that, couldn't end it once and for all.

And then she decided he hadn't signed off with 'love' as yet and wanted to wait to see... Yes, she reflected, that's a good excuse for letting it continue and waiting to see if it will happen, if he would ever dare.

But as a few weeks went by and the messages continued, she realized that slowly, subtly, she began to look forward to them, she began to check for them, to expect them, to be disappointed when there weren't any, or when they were from someone else.

Mabel is complaining I let you go. Come back and make us both happy. Ray.

Crockett wants to slobber over you. Can I say, me too? Ray

Carrie had to laugh; it was his sense of humor, but she preferred the one that said, *Texas is incredibly big without you.*

"What are you doing?" asked Paige, coming into the kitchen one day late in January, home for a weekend. "Diana and I are waiting for you. I thought you were making hot chocolate and we were going up to the roof?"

Carrie slipped the phone away onto the worktop and pursed her lips, trying to hide the guilt from her face. "Milk's just boiling," she said, attempting to distract her daughter unsuccessfully.

"You got another one?"

Paige sidled over to the counter and reached for the cell phone, beating Carrie to it and holding it aloft.

"Hey, give me that!" She was torn between the milk about to boil over and the incriminating phone. The milk won.

"Ooooh," drawled out Paige. "Is this a new one? I didn't hear it beep."

"Give me that! It doesn't beep if it's already on the message page." Carrie made a grab for the phone, but again, her daughter whisked it out of reach.

"'*Surely that bed is too big for you. I know mine is. Ray.*' Wowie, things must be heating up. I don't get texts like that from Jake."

Carrie carefully poured the hot milk into waiting, chocolate-filled mugs. "I didn't know you had any reason to *expect* texts like that from Jake." She raised her eyebrows inquisitively.

"Wait a minute! You had it on the message page then. You keep checking or re-reading or what? What, Mother?" Paige waved the phone in Carrie's face.

"Oh, shut up," she advised playfully. "Give me my phone and help me carry this lot out to the roof." She snatched the phone and tapped out of her messages, then stuck it in her pocket.

Her daughter grinned and bent to get a tray out of the hutch. She placed the mugs on it before turning. "Why don't you go back? Why don't you just go back?"

Carrie tilted her head in consideration of her beautiful offspring. "Come on," she said, "Diana is upstairs freezing."

Outside on the roof, a watery sun made little attempt to have any calefacient effect, but for late January, it was certainly warm enough to bundle up and enjoy being in the fresh air for a short while. Diana lay on one of the chaises that braved the weather all year on Carrie's roof terrace, a broad space overlooking Central Park with privacy from onlookers below thanks to its height, and shielded by its potted trees and plants. Suitably cocooned in woolens and cashmere, her friend snuggled under a tartan blanket.

Carrie scraped a chair out from the ornate caste iron table she had there as her daughter set the tray down and went to hand her mother's old friend her mug. A heavily be-ringed hand snuck out from under the protection of the blanket, and Diana shuffled carefully to try to sit up.

"Here, I'll prop you up, old lady," Carrie teased as she came round to fix the chaise into a sitting position.

"Listen," her friend threw back as she bent forward for Carrie's adjustment, "if I'm old, what the hell are you?"

As if in reply, the phone snapped out its telegraphic response. Carrie instantly yanked it out, read the message and laughed.

"Come on now—share. Be good, tell Diana." She

exchanged a look with Paige who scraped another chair from the table, held her coat close to her bottom, and sat down, arms crossed with a demanding raised brow.

"What is that? The third today? He must be getting desperate, Mom."

Diana giggled. "It must be his New Year's resolution to win you back."

"Oh, shush, the two of you." Carrie had to press her lips from smiling as she finally sank onto the waiting chair. She glanced from one to the other. "It says, '*I want to grow old with you and watch every single one of your wrinkles appear. Ray.*'" She put a hand to her stomach to calm the butterflies there and gulped in the cold air.

"Gosh, is he a mind reader?" Diana sipped her cocoa. "We just finished saying we were getting old and that comes through. That's positively weird. He's not outside, is he? Downstairs?"

Carrie panicked and actually peered over the roof's edge.

"Oh, Mother, for heaven's sake." Paige shook her head.

"I liked Ray." Diana settled back to her pronouncements. "I know what you saw in him. He was so upfront. He had no guile and was so honest."

Carrie flinched slightly. "Honest" was not the first word that came to mind when she thought of Ray now.

"Oh, come on, Car—did you really think he was going to get back together with that woman? The way you described her? No way."

"He married her, didn't he?" Carrie took a petulant sip from her mug while her gaze shot arrows at her friend over the top of it.

"At first I thought, 'cowboy,'" Diana continued. "I thought you'd lost your mind. Really. But then when I spoke to him, he was so honest—and intelligent. There was no hidden agenda, no deviousness or sense of alternative motives I thought. He certainly wasn't after your money. He wasn't impressed by any of it, any of us. He was just really easy to get along with. He didn't mind speaking his mind, yet he was so damn likeable. Even Tom liked him—and, believe me, that's saying a lot."

"Well," she countered, "he wasn't quite honest enough. He said he was divorced."

"Oh, for heaven's sake, Carrie, come on," Diana growled in response. "So what? You made a mountain out of a molehill. You saw the ex-wife and you panicked, left before he could leave you. Why?"

Carrie took in another deep breath of the chilled winter air. She played with the phone in her hand for a moment, then tapped it on and read the message once more. There suddenly came to her a sense of belonging, this man was actually hers, there waiting for her. Free and clear. She knew she could go—no, she *yearned* to go to him, have him, be with him. Her gaze went to Paige.

"Go grow old with him, Mother. Get shagged to death, or at least kissed 'til your lips hurt. You can work out the distances, the places. Go on and tell him you're coming. Or don't as the case may be." Paige wiggled her eyebrows.

"And what about you, darling? What will you do?" She looked tenderly at her only child. A line of worry pulled between her brows as she bit her lip.

"Me? At some stage, I'll get a kind, sweet step-brother in Jake, no doubt, who'll drive me crazy but I'll put up with at Thanksgiving and Christmas. And probably, eventually, marry off to a friend."

"I thought…"

"Who knows?" Paige smiled. "But it is a bit weird, don't you think? For me to be in love with Jake and for you to be in love with his father?"

Carrie's eyes went wide. There, her daughter had said it at last. It was out. *Deal with it. Deal with it, Paige.*

"You're talking in riddles, the two of you," pestered Diana. "Make sense."

But Carrie's phone beat out its announcement. She picked it up, gazing at it for a long time.

I want my own happy ending. I love you. Ray.

Her smile slowly spread out like the sun on the late afternoon horizon.

****

Slants of light fell through the blinds, laying a linear design on the papers as Ray went over his figures once again, trying to concentrate and think about anything except Carrie, anything except her. The smooth hum of a motor approached and, grateful for the diversion, he lifted the slats apart to see a car he didn't recognize come to a halt out front. He figured it might be a potential client who didn't see the road sign pointing to the main office. He momentarily straightened his desk, pushed a hand through his hair and grabbed his hat.

The screen door slammed behind him at the same moment Carrie shoved the car door closed and turned, surprise written on her face at finding him there in front of her. For a moment, they stared at each other across the expanse of Texas earth. He tried to suppress his own smile slowly sneaking out while her smile widened, as if invisible hands were simultaneously painting them both on.

Ray leaned back against the porch door in the same easy way she had found him at East Hampton station that day, hands across his chest, hat slouched slightly forward.

"Can I help you, ma'am? Are you lost?" His humor and his pleasure at seeing her there were barely suppressed, but he was playing for time to give himself a moment to adjust to her return, to this best of all possible events in his day.

"I'm here to do research, mister," she explained, her own happiness sparkling in her eyes.

"Research, huh? Research?" He scratched his head with a small intake of breath. "Just what kinda research would that be, ma'am?"

"Research for a book I'm writing." She took a hesitant few steps toward him, tilting her head in an enquiring manner.

"Now, just what kinda book would that be? One about…hunting? Horses? Texas? One of those?"

"Nope. 'Fraid not." She put on a fake drawl, "It's a love story…"

"A love story!"

"…'Bout an older woman who falls in love with a cowboy here in Texas."

"Is that so?" Ray scratched his head again, a bubble of anticipation, joy at seeing her, making him catch his breath. He came down the porch steps before stopping and looking across at this woman he hadn't been able to get off his mind, this woman who drove him to distraction, this woman he loved so much. "See now," he went on, "I'd really prefer it if you were to say 'rancher' instead of 'cowboy.' Even better, I'd prefer it if you were to say 'falls *madly* in love.'" His hands rested lightly on his hips now to keep them from grabbing her and crushing her with his desire.

Carrie crossed her arms. "All right then, *madly* in love."

"And I would like it even more—much more in fact—if you were to say she fell madly in love with the 'best-looking damned rancher in the entire state of Texas.'"

Carrie giggled. "Okay. There's no doubt about it. To her eyes, he certainly *is* the best-looking damned *rancher* in the entire state of Texas."

"Is that so?" Ray rubbed his chin for a moment, contemplating the answer. "Now, this here research you're doing? Just what kinda research would that be again, ma'am?"

At this, her giggles evolved into an outright laugh. "Intensive research," she replied. "Thorough and exhaustive."

"Thorough and exhaustive, huh?" he repeated quietly. "Well, you better get on over here, darlin', and start that research right away."

Carrie's smile stretched wider as she came up to him, but he put his hand out and stopped her. "Hang on, hang on."

"Now what?" she asked. Her gaze met his with the same impatience he'd not been able to overcome.

"This here book, does it have a happy ending?"

"Oh, you bet, mister. *You bet!*"

A word about the author...

Andrea Downing likes to say that when she decided to do a Masters Degree, she made the mistake of turning left out of New York instead of right to the west, and ended up in the UK.

She eventually married there, raising a beautiful daughter and staying for longer than she cares to admit.

Teaching, editing a poetry magazine, writing travel articles, and a short stint in Nigeria filled those years until in 2008 she returned to NYC.

She now divides her time between the city and the shore and often trades the canyons of New York for the wide open spaces of Wyoming.

Loveland, her first book, was a finalist for Best American Historical at the 2013 RONE Awards. *Lawless Love*, a short story, part of The Wild Rose Press 'Lawmen and Outlaws' series, was a finalist for the 2014 RONE Best Historical Novella award.

Dances of the Heart is her first contemporary novel.

Thank you for purchasing
this publication of The Wild Rose Press, Inc.

If you enjoyed the story, we would appreciate your
letting others know by leaving a review.

For other wonderful stories,
please visit our on-line bookstore at
www.thewildrosepress.com.

For questions or more information
contact us at
info@thewildrosepress.com.

The Wild Rose Press, Inc.
www.thewildrosepress.com

Stay current with The Wild Rose Press, Inc.

Like us on Facebook

https://www.facebook.com/TheWildRosePress

And Follow us on Twitter
https://twitter.com/WildRosePress

www.ingramcontent.com/pod-product-compliance
Lightning Source LLC
Chambersburg PA
CBHW071523260626
47170CB00002B/482